"Nobody does it better."

—Meredith Duran, New Y̶... or

"Utterly timeless charm... Tl... with wit... And beneath that period speech, the ring of truth, the human flaws and virtues, speaks just as perfectly to today's reader."

—Nora Roberts, #1 *New York Times* bestselling author

"Georgette Heyer was **a masterful writer**: the impeccable research, the bone-dry wit, the twists and turns of plot—as complex and neatly balanced as a Regency country dance."

—Loretta Chase, *New York Times* bestselling author

"If I had to choose just one word with which to describe Georgette Heyer's books, I would say that they *sparkle*."

—Mary Balogh, *New York Times* bestselling author

"If you want **a great story**, if you want to laugh until your sides ache, if you want to know characters so well you will scratch when they itch, then Georgette Heyer is the novelist for you."

—Catherine Coulter, *New York Times* bestselling author

"Every delightful quality of Regencies—humor, charm, elegance, derring-do—was written first and brilliantly by Georgette Heyer. She is the giant upon whose shoulders the entire romance genre stands— **the first, best, and brightest** of historical romance."

—Grace Burrowes, *New York Times* bestselling author

"Georgette Heyer's Regency romances are **delightful**."

—Philippa Gregory, *New York Times* bestselling author

"Heyer's women were **spunky, daring, and outrageous**...her heroes the stuff of dreams."

—Diana Palmer, *New York Times* bestselling author

"One never forgets one's first Heyer."

—Mary Jo Putney, *New York Times* bestselling author

"Romance, adventure, **side-splitting humor**—no one writes like Georgette Heyer!"

—Lauren Willig, *New York Times* bestselling author

"Georgette's characters are **vivid and unforgettable**... [She] transports her readers to a world where passion and manners collide."

—Teresa Medeiros, *New York Times* bestselling author

"Whenever I wish I could just chuck it all and live in a world of **quick-witted characters**, handsome gentlemen, and elegant drawing rooms, I curl up with a cup of tea and Georgette Heyer."

—Laura Kinsale, *New York Times* bestselling author

"Georgette Heyer has made me laugh, lose myself in the **poignancy** of the characters, and dance around the room in anticipation for what will happen next—often, all at once."

—Cathy Maxwell, *New York Times* bestselling author

"Nobody catches the flavor and fun and pure **delicious** nonsense of the English Regency better than Georgette Heyer."

—Kasey Michaels, *New York Times* bestselling author

"On a rainy afternoon, when your heart is breaking, there's no greater gift than to re-immerse yourself in the delightful world Georgette Heyer created. It is delicious comfort of the most basic kind—La Grand Georgette's work is a **treasure beyond price**."

—Anne Stuart, *New York Times* bestselling author

"For me, Georgette Heyer opened all kinds of worlds of fun and fantasy, and yet also lets me feel the **incredible, living reality** of her characters... Times change, but human nature does not."

—Heather Graham, *New York Times* bestselling author

"**Warmth and humor**, intelligent characters and witty conversations, glamorous clothes and places, all written with a faultless sense of pacing."

—Karen Hawkins, *New York Times* bestselling author

"Georgette Heyer was **a master with words**. With a short phrase, a simple description of a telling gesture, she could wring your heart, tickle your fancy, and suck you right down into the story."

—Linda Howard, *New York Times* bestselling author

"The **joy** of Georgette Heyer is reading her books over and over."

—Elizabeth Doyle, *New York Times* bestselling author

Also by Georgette Heyer

Mystery

the Grand Sophy

Georgette Heyer

SIGNATURE COLLECTION

Includes Glossary of Regency Slang and Afterword by
Jennifer Kloester, Georgette Heyer's official biographer

sourcebooks
casablanca

Published by Sourcebooks Casablanca, an imprint of Sourcebooks, Inc.
P.O. Box 4410, Naperville, Illinois 60567-4410
(630) 961-3900
Fax: (630) 961-2168
sourcebooks.com

Originally published in 1950 in Great Britain by Heinemann, London.
This edition issued based on the paperback edition published in 2009 in
the United States by Sourcebooks Casablanca, an imprint of Sourcebooks,
Inc.

Printed and bound in Canada.
MBP 10 9 8 7 6 5 4 3 2 1

One

THE BUTLER, RECOGNIZING HER LADYSHIP'S ONLY SURVIVING brother at a glance, as he afterwards informed his less percipient subordinates, favoured Sir Horace with a low bow, and took it upon himself to say that my lady, although not at home to less nearly-connected persons, would be happy to see him. Sir Horace, unimpressed by this condescension, handed his caped greatcoat to one footman, his hat and cane to the other, tossed his gloves on to the marble-topped table, and said that he had no doubt of that, and how was Dassett keeping these days? The butler, torn between gratification at having his name remembered and disapproval of Sir Horace's free and easy ways, said that he was as well as could be expected, and happy (if he might venture to say so) to see Sir Horace looking not a day older than when he had last had the pleasure of announcing him to her ladyship. He then led the way, in a very stately manner, up the imposing stairway to the Blue Saloon, where Lady Ombersley was dozing gently on a sofa by the fire, a Paisley shawl spread over her feet, and her cap decidedly askew. Mr Dassett, observing these details, coughed, and made his announcement in commanding accents: 'Sir Horace Stanton-Lacy, my lady!'

Lady Ombersley awoke with a start, stared for an uncomprehending moment, made an ineffective clutch at her cap, and uttered a faint shriek. 'Horace!'

'Hallo, Lizzie, how are you?' said Sir Horace, walking across the room, and bestowing an invigorating buffet upon her shoulder.

'Good heavens, what a fright you gave me!' exclaimed her ladyship, uncorking the vinaigrette which was never out of her reach.

The butler, having tolerantly observed these transports, closed the door upon the reunited brother and sister, and went away to disclose to his underlings that Sir Horace was a gentleman as lived much abroad, being, as he was informed, employed by the Government on Diplomatic Business too delicate for their understanding.

The diplomatist, meanwhile, warming his coat-tails by the fire, refreshed himself with a pinch of snuff and told his sister that she was putting on weight. 'Not growing any younger, either of us,' he added handsomely. 'Not but what I can give you five years, Lizzie, unless my memory's at fault, which I don't think it is.'

There was a large gilded mirror on the wall opposite to the fireplace, and as he spoke Sir Horace allowed his gaze to rest upon his own image, not in a conceited spirit, but with critical approval. His forty-five years had treated him kindly. If his outline had thickened a little, his height, which was well above six foot, made a slight portliness negligible. He was a very fine figure of a man, and had, besides a large and well-proportioned frame, a handsome countenance, topped by luxuriant brown locks as yet unmarred by silver streaks. He was always dressed with elegance, but was by far too wise a man to adopt such extravagances of fashion as could only show up the imperfections of a middle-aged figure. 'Take a look at poor Prinny!' said Sir Horace to less discriminating cronies. 'He's a lesson to us all!'

His sister accepted the implied criticism unresentfully. Twenty-seven years of wedlock had left their mark upon her; and the dutiful presentation to her erratic and far from grateful spouse of eight pledges of her affection had long since destroyed any pretensions to beauty in her. Her health was indifferent, her disposition compliant, and she was fond of saying that when one was a grandmother it was time to be done with thinking of one's appearance.

'How's Ombersley?' asked Sir Horace, with more civility than interest.

'He feels his gout a little, but considering everything he is remarkably well,' she responded.

Sir Horace took a mere figure of speech in an undesirably literal spirit, saying with a nod: 'Always did drink too much. Still, he must be going on for sixty now, and I don't suppose you have so much of the other trouble, do you?'

'No, no!' said his sister hastily. Lord Ombersley's infidelities, though mortifying when conducted, as they too often were, in the full glare of publicity, had never greatly troubled her, but she had no desire to discuss them with her outspoken relative, and gave the conversation an abrupt turn by asking where he had come from.

'Lisbon,' he replied, taking another pinch of snuff.

Lady Ombersley was vaguely surprised. It was now two years since the close of the long Peninsular War, and she rather thought that, when last heard of, Sir Horace had been in Vienna, no doubt taking mysterious part in the Congress, which had been so rudely interrupted by the escape of that dreadful Monster from Elba. 'Oh!' she said, a little blankly. 'Of course, you have a house there! I was forgetting! And how is dear Sophia?'

'As a matter of fact,' said Sir Horace, shutting his snuff-box, and restoring it to his pocket, 'it's about Sophy that I've come to see you.'

Sir Horace had been a widower for fifteen years, during which period he had neither requested his sister's help in rearing his daughter nor paid the least heed to her unsolicited advice, but at these words an uneasy feeling stole over her. She said: 'Yes, Horace? Dear little Sophia! It must be four years or more since I saw her. How old is she now? I suppose she must be almost out?'

'Been out for years,' responded Sir Horace. 'Never anything else really. She's twenty.'

'Twenty!' exclaimed Lady Ombersley. She applied her mind to arithmetic, and said: 'Yes, she must be, for my own Cecilia is just turned nineteen, and I remember that your Sophia was born almost a year before. Dear me, yes! Poor Marianne! What a lovely creature she was, to be sure!'

With a slight effort Sir Horace conjured up the vision of his dead wife. 'Yes, so she was,' he agreed. 'One forgets, you know. Sophy's not much like her: favours me!'

'I know what a comfort she must have been to you,' sighed Lady Ombersley. 'And I'm sure, dear Horace, that nothing could be more affecting than your devotion to the child!'

'I wasn't in the least devoted,' interrupted Sir Horace. 'I shouldn't have kept her with me if she'd been troublesome. Never was: good little thing, Sophy!'

'Yes, my dear, no doubt, but to be dragging a little girl all over Spain and Portugal, when she would have been far better in a select school —'

'Not she! She'd have learnt to be missish,' said Sir Horace cynically. 'Besides, no use to prose to me now on that head: it's too late! The thing is, Lizzie, I'm in something of a fix. I want you to take care of Sophy while I'm in South America.'

'South America?' gasped Lady Ombersley.

'Brazil. I don't expect to be away very long, but I can't take my little Sophy, and I can't leave her with Tilly, because Tilly's dead. Died in Vienna, couple of years ago. A devilish inconvenient thing to do, but I daresay she didn't mean it.'

'Tilly?' said Lady Ombersley, all at sea.

'Lord, Elizabeth, don't keep on repeating everything I say! Shocking bad habit! Miss Tillingham, Sophy's governess!'

'Good heavens! Do you mean to tell me that the child has no governess now?'

'Of course she has not! She don't need a governess. I always found plenty of chaperons for her when we were in Paris, and in Lisbon it don't signify. But I can't leave her alone in England.'

'Indeed, I should think not! But, my dearest Horace, though I would do anything to oblige you, I am not quite sure –'

'Nonsense!' said Sir Horace bracingly. 'She'll be a nice companion for your girl – what's her name? Cecilia? Dear little soul, you know: not an ounce of vice in her!'

This fatherly tribute made his sister blink, and utter a faint protest. Sir Horace paid no heed to it. 'What's more, she won't cause you any trouble,' he said. 'She has her head well on her shoulders, my Sophy. I never worry about her.'

An intimate knowledge of her brother's character made it perfectly possible for Lady Ombersley to believe this, but since she herself was blessed with much the same easy-going temperament, no acid comment even rose to her lips. 'I am sure she must be a dear girl,' she said. 'But, you see, Horace –'

'And another thing is that it's time we were thinking of a husband for her,' pursued Sir Horace, seating himself in a chair on the opposite side of the fireplace. 'I knew I could depend on you. Dash it, you're her aunt! My only sister, too.'

'I should be only too happy to bring her out,' said Lady Ombersley wistfully. 'But the thing is I don't think – I am rather afraid – You see, what with the really dreadful expense of presenting Cecilia last year, and dearest Maria's wedding only a little time before that, and Hubert's going up to Oxford, not to mention the fees at Eton for poor Theodore –'

'If it's expense that bothers you, Lizzie, you needn't give it a thought, for I'll stand the nonsense. You won't have to present her at Court: I'll attend to all that when I come home, and if you don't want to be put to the trouble of it then I can find some other lady to do it. What I want at this present is for her to go about with her cousins, meet the right set of people – you know the style of thing!'

'Of course I know, and as for *trouble* it would be no such thing! But I can't help feeling that perhaps – perhaps it would not do! We do not entertain very much.'

'Well, with a pack of girls on your hands you ought to,' said Sir Horace bluntly.

'But, Horace, I have not got a pack of girls on my hands!' protested Lady Ombersley. 'Selina is only sixteen, and Gertrude and Amabel are barely out of the nursery!'

'I see what it is,' said Sir Horace indulgently. 'You're afraid she may take the shine out of Cecilia. No, no, my dear! My little Sophy's no beauty. She's well enough – in fact, I daresay you'll think she's a very pretty girl – but Cecilia's something quite out of the common way. Remember thinking so when I saw her last year. I was surprised, for you were never above the average yourself, Lizzie, while I always thought Ombersley a plain-looking fellow.'

His sister accepted these strictures meekly, but was quite distressed that he should suppose her capable of harbouring such unhandsome thoughts about her niece. 'And even if I was so odious, there is no longer the least need for such notions,' she added. 'Nothing has as yet been announced, Horace, but I don't scruple to tell you that Cecilia is about to contract a very eligible alliance.'

'That's good,' said Sir Horace. 'You'll have leisure to look about you for a husband for Sophy. You won't have any difficulty: she's a taking little thing, and she'll have a snug fortune one of these days, besides what her mother left her. No need to be afraid of her marrying to disoblige us, either: she's a sensible girl, and she's been about the world enough to be well up to snuff. Whom have you got for Cecilia?'

'Lord Charlbury has asked Ombersley's permission to address her,' said his sister, swelling a little with pride.

'Charlbury, eh,' said Sir Horace. 'Very well indeed, Elizabeth! I must say, I didn't think you'd catch much of a prize, because looks aren't everything, and from the way Ombersley was running through his fortune when I last saw him –'

'Lord Charlbury,' said Lady Ombersley a little stiffly, 'is an extremely wealthy man, and, I know, has no such vulgar consideration in mind. Indeed, he told me himself that it was a case of love at first sight with him!'

'Capital!' said Sir Horace. 'I should suppose him to have been hanging out for a wife for some time – thirty at least, ain't he? – but if he has a veritable *tendre* for the girl, so much the better! It should fix his interest with her.'

'Yes,' agreed Lady Ombersley. 'And I am persuaded they will suit very well. He is everything that is amiable and obliging, his manners most gentleman-like, his understanding decidedly superior, and his person such as must please.'

Sir Horace, who was not much interested in his niece's affairs, said: 'Well, well, he is plainly a paragon, and we must allow Cecilia to think herself fortunate to be forming such a connection! I hope you may manage as prettily for Sophy!'

'Indeed, I wish I might!' she responded, sighing. 'Only it is an awkward moment, because – The thing is, you see, that I am afraid Charles may not quite like it!'

Sir Horace frowned in an effort of memory. 'I thought his name was Bernard. Why shouldn't he like it?'

'I am not speaking of Ombersley, Horace. You must remember Charles!'

'If you're talking about the eldest boy of yours, of course I
remember him! But why has he to say anything, and why the devil
should he object to my Sophy!'

'Oh, no, not to her! I am sure he could not do so! But I fear
he may not like it if we are to be plunged into gaiety just now!
I daresay you may not have seen the announcement of his own
approaching marriage, but I should tell you that he has contracted
an engagement to Miss Wraxton.'

'What, not old Brinklow's daughter? Upon my word, Lizzie,
you have been busy to some purpose! Never knew you had so
much sense! Eligible, indeed! You are to be congratulated!'

'Yes,' said Lady Ombersley. 'Oh, yes! Miss Wraxton is a most
superior girl. I am sure she has a thousand excellent qualities. A
most well-informed mind, and principles such as must command
respect.'

'She sounds to me like a dead bore,' said Sir Horace frankly.

'Charles,' said Lady Ombersley, staring mournfully into the fire,
'does not care for very lively girls, or – or for any extravagant folly.
I own, I could wish Miss Wraxton had rather more *vivacity* – but
you are not to regard that, Horace, for I had never the least inclination towards being a blue-stocking myself, and in these days,
when so many young females are wild to a fault, it is gratifying to
find one who – Charles thinks Miss Wraxton's air of grave reflection very becoming!' she ended, in rather a hurry.

'You know, Lizzie, it's a queer thing that any son of yours and
Ombersley's should have grown into such a dull stick,' remarked
Sir Horace dispassionately. 'I suppose you didn't play Ombersley
false, did you?'

'Horace!'

'No, I know you didn't! No need to fly into a pucker! Not
with your eldest: you know better than that! Still, it is an odd
circumstance: often thought so! He can marry his blue-stocking,

and welcome, for anything I care, but none of this explains why you should be caring a fig for what he likes or don't like!'

Lady Ombersley transferred her gaze from the glowing coals to his face. 'You do not perfectly understand, Horace.'

'That's what I said!' he retorted.

'Yes, but – Horace, Matthew Rivenhall left his whole fortune to Charles!'

Sir Horace was generally accounted an astute man, but he appeared to find it difficult correctly to assimilate this information. He stared fixedly at his sister for a moment or two, and then said: 'You don't mean that old uncle of Ombersley's?'

'Yes, I do.'

'The Nabob?'

Lady Ombersley nodded, but her brother was still not satisfied. 'Fellow who made a fortune in India?'

'Yes, and we always thought – but he said Charles was the only Rivenhall other than himself who had the least grain of sense, and he left him everything, Horace! *Everything!*'

'Good God!'

This ejaculation seemed to appear to Lady Ombersley as fitting, for she nodded again, looking at her brother in a woebegone fashion, and twisting the fringe of her shawl between her fingers.

'So it is Charles who calls the tune!' said Sir Horace.

'No one could have been more generous,' said Lady Ombersley unhappily. 'We cannot but be sensible of it.'

'Damn his impudence!' said Sir Horace, himself a father. 'What's he done?'

'Well, Horace, you might not know it, because you are always abroad, but poor Ombersley had a great many debts.'

'Everyone knows that! Never knew him when he wasn't under a cloud! You're not going to tell me the boy was fool enough to settle 'em?'

'But, Horace, someone had to settle them!' she protested. 'You can have no notion how difficult things were becoming! And with the younger boys to establish creditably, and the dear girls – it is no wonder that Charles should be so anxious that Cecilia should make a good match!'

'Providing for the whole pack, is he? More fool he! What about the mortgages? If the greater part of Ombersley's inheritance had not been entailed he would have gambled the whole away long since!'

'I do not properly understand entails,' said his sister, 'but I am afraid that Charles did not behave just as he should over it. Ombersley was very much displeased – though I shall always say that to call one's first-born a serpent's tooth is to use quite unbecoming language! It seems that when Charles came of age he might have made everything quite easy for his poor papa, if only he had been in the least degree obliging! But nothing would prevail upon him to agree to break the entail, so all was at a standstill, and one cannot blame Ombersley for being vexed! And then that odious old man died –'

'When?' demanded Sir Horace. 'How comes it about that I never heard a word of this before today?'

'It was rather more than two years ago, and –'

'That accounts for it, then: I was devilish busy, dealing with Angoulême, and all that set. Must have happened at the time of Toulouse, I dare swear. But when I saw you last year you never spoke a word, Lizzie!'

She was stung by the injustice to this, and said indignantly: 'I am sure I don't know how I should have been thinking of such paltry things, with that Monster at large, and the Champ de Mars, and the banks suspending payment, and heaven knows what beside! And you coming over from Brussels without a word of warning, and sitting with me a bare twenty minutes! My head was in a whirl, and if I answered you to the point it is more than I would have bargained for!'

Sir Horace, disregarding this irrelevancy, said, with what for him was strong feeling: 'Outrageous! I don't say Ombersley's not a shocking loose-screw, because there's no sense in wrapping plain facts up in clean linen, but to be cutting a man out of one's will and setting up his son to lord it over him – which I'll be bound he does!'

'No, no!' expostulated Lady Ombersley feebly. 'Charles is fully sensible of what is due to his father! It is not that he is ever lacking in respect, I do assure you! Only poor Ombersley cannot but feel it a little, now that Charles has taken everything into his own hands.'

'A pretty state of affairs!'

'Yes, but one comfort is that it is not generally known. And I cannot deny that in some ways it is by far more pleasant. You would scarcely credit it, Horace, but I do believe there is not an unpaid bill in the house!' A moment's reflection caused her to modify this statement. 'At least, I cannot answer for Ombersley, but all those dreadful household accounts, which Eckington – you remember our good Eckington, Ombersley's agent? – used to pull such a face over; and the fees at Eton and Oxford – *everything*, my dear brother, Charles takes care of!'

'You aren't going to tell me Charles is fool enough to fritter away old Matt Rivenhall's fortune paying all the expenses of this barrack of a house!' exclaimed Sir Horace.

'No. Oh, no! I have not the least head for business, so it is of no use to ask me to explain it to you, but I believe that Charles persuaded his father to – to allow him to administer the estate.'

'Blackmailed him into it, more like!' said Sir Horace grimly. 'Rare times we live in! Mind, I see the boy's point, Lizzie, but, by God, I'm sorry for you!'

'Oh, pray believe it's no such thing!' cried Lady Ombersley, distressed. 'I did not wish you to think – to give you cause to suppose that Charles is ever disagreeable, for indeed he is not, except when he is put out of temper, and one must own that he has a great deal to try his patience! Which is why I can't but feel, dear Horace, that if he does not like me to take charge of Sophia for you, I ought not to tease him!'

'Fiddlesticks!' said Sir Horace. 'And why shouldn't he like it?'

'We – we decided not to give any parties this season, beyond what must be thought necessary. It is a most unfortunate circumstance that Charles's wedding has had to be postponed, on account of a bereavement Miss Wraxton has suffered. One of Lady Brinklow's sisters, and they will not be out of black gloves for six months. You must know that the Brinklows are very particular in all matters of correct conduct. Eugenia goes only to very quiet parties, and – and naturally one must expect Charles to partake of her sentiments!'

'Lord, Elizabeth, a man don't have to wear black gloves for the aunt of a female he ain't even married to!'

'Of course not, but Charles seemed to feel – and then there is Charlbury!'

'What the devil ails him?'

'Mumps,' replied Lady Ombersley tragically.

'He?' Sir Horace burst out laughing. 'Well, what a fellow he must be to have mumps when he should be getting married to Cecilia!'

'Really, Horace, I must say that I think that most unjust of you, for how could he help it? It is so mortifying for him! And, what is more, excessively unfortunate, because I don't doubt that had he been able to attach Cecilia – which I am sure he must have done, for nothing could be more amiable than his disposition, while his manners and address are just what they ought to be! But girls are so foolish, and take romantical notions into their heads, besides all kinds of encroaching fancies – however, I am happy to think that Cecilia is not one of those dreadful modern misses, and of course she will be guided by her parents! But no one can deny that nothing could be more ill-timed than Charlbury's mumps!'

Sir Horace, once more opening his snuff-box, regarded her with an amused and sapient eye. 'And what is Miss Cecilia's particular encroaching fancy?' he enquired.

Lady Ombersley knew that her eldest son would have counselled her to preserve a discreet silence; but the impulse to unburden herself to her brother was too strong to be denied. She said: 'Well, you will not repeat it, I know, Horace, but the fact is that the silly child thinks she is in love with Augustus Fawnhope!'

'One of Lutterworth's boys?' asked Sir Horace. 'I don't think much of that for a match, I must say!'

'Good heavens, don't mention such a thing! The youngest son, too, with not the least expectation in the world! But he is a poet.'

'Very dangerous,' agreed Sir Horace. 'Don't think I ever saw the boy: what's he like?'

'Quite beautiful!' said Lady Ombersley, in despairing accents.

'What, in the style of Lord Byron? That fellow has a great deal to answer for!'

'N-no. I mean, he is as fair as Cecilia is herself, and he doesn't limp, and though his poems are very pretty, bound up in white vellum, they don't seem to *take* very well. I mean, not at all like Lord Byron's. It seems sadly unjust, for I believe it cost a great deal of money to have them printed, and he had to bear the whole – or, rather, Lady Lutterworth did, according to what I have heard.'

'Now I come to think of it,' said Sir Horace, 'I do know the boy. He was with Stuart, in Brussels last year. If you take my advice, you'll marry Cecilia off to Charlbury as quickly as you can!'

'Well, and so I would, if only – that is to say, of course I would not, if I thought she held him in aversion! And you must see, Horace, that it is quite out of my power to do anything of the sort when he is in bed with the mumps!'

Sir Horace shook his head. 'She will marry the poet.'

'Do not say so! But Charles thinks that I should do wisely not to take her where she is bound to meet the young man, which is another reason why we are living in a quiet style for the present. It is of all things the most awkward! Indeed, sometimes I feel that it would be much easier if the wretched creature were quite ineligible – a fortune-hunter, or a merchant's son, or something of that nature! One could then forbid him the house, and forbid Cecilia to stand up with him at balls, only it would not be in the least necessary for we should never meet him in society. But naturally one meets the Fawnhopes everywhere! Nothing could be more provoking! And although I am sure Charles's manner towards him is most repellent, even he acknowledges the impropriety of being so repulsive to him as to offend his family. Almeria Lutterworth is one of my oldest friends!'

Sir Horace, who was already bored with the subject, yawned, and said lazily: 'I daresay there is no occasion for you to be on the fidgets. The Fawnhopes are all as poor as church mice, and very likely Lady Lutterworth desires the match as little as you do.'

'Nothing of the sort!' she replied, quite crossly. 'She is foolish beyond permission, Horace! Whatever Augustus wants he must have! She has given me the most unmistakable hints, so that I scarcely knew where to look, much less what to say, except that Lord Charlbury had requested our leave to address Cecilia, and I believed her to be – well, not indifferent to him! It never entered my head that Augustus was so lost to all sense of propriety as to apply to Cecilia without first approaching Ombersley, yet that is precisely what he has done!'

'Oh, well!' said Sir Horace. 'If she has such a fancy for him, you

had better let her take him. It's not as though she would be marrying beneath her, and if she chooses to be the wife of a penniless
younger son it is quite her own affair.'

'You would not say so if it were Sophia!' said his sister.

'Sophy's not such a fool.'

'Cecilia is not a fool either,' declared Lady Ombersley,
affronted. 'If you have seen Augustus you can not wonder at her!
No one could help feeling a decided partiality for him! I own, I
did myself. But Charles is quite right, as I was soon brought to
acknowledge: it would not answer!'

'Ah, well, when she has her cousin to keep her company it will
divert her, and very likely give her thoughts another direction,'
said Sir Horace consolingly.

Lady Ombersley appeared to be much struck by this suggestion.
Her face brightened; she said: 'I wonder if it might be so? She is
a little shy, you must know, and does not make friends easily, and
since her dear friend, Miss Friston, was married, and has gone to
live in the Midlands, there is really no young female with whom
she is upon terms of intimacy. Now, if we had dear Sophia to
stay with us…' She broke off, obviously turning plans over in
her mind. She was still engaged on this exercise when the door
opened, and her eldest son entered the saloon.

The Honourable Charles Rivenhall was twenty-six years old,
but a rather harsh-featured countenance, coupled with a manner
that combined assurance with a good deal of reserve, made him
give the impression of being some years older. He was a tall,
powerfully-built young man, who looked as though he would
have been better pleased to have been striding over his father's
acres than exchanging civilities in his mother's sitting-room.
He nearly always wore riding-dress in preference to the more
fashionable pantaloons and Hessians; tied his cravat in the plainest
of styles; would permit only a modicum of starch to stiffen his

very moderate shirt-points; wholly disdained such fopperies as seals, fobs, or quizzing-glasses; and offended his tailor by insisting on having his coats cut so that he could shrug himself into them without the assistance of his valet. He had been heard to express the hope that heaven would forbid he should ever be mistaken for one of the dandy-set; but, as his friend, Mr Cyprian Wychbold, kindly pointed out to him, there was not the least need for heavenly intervention in the matter. The dandies, said Mr Wychbold with some severity, were distinguished as much for their polished address as for their exquisite apparel, and were in general an amiable set of men, whose polite manners and winning graces made them acceptable in any drawing-room. As Mr Rivenhall's notion of making himself agreeable in company was to treat with cold civility anyone for whom he felt no particular liking; and his graces – far from winning – included a trick of staring out of countenance those whose pretensions he deprecated, and of uttering blighting comments, which put an abrupt end to social intercourse, he stood in far greater danger (Mr Wychbold said) of being mistaken for a Yahoo.

As he shut the door behind him, his mother looked up, started slightly, and said with a nervous inflection which annoyed her brother: 'Oh! Charles! Only fancy! Your Uncle Horace!'

'So Dassett informed me,' responded Mr Rivenhall. 'How do you do, sir?'

He shook hands with his uncle, drew up a chair, and sat down, civilly engaging Sir Horace in conversation. His mother, fidgeting first with the fringe of her shawl and then with her handkerchief, presently broke in on this interchange to say: 'Charles, you remember Sophia? Your little cousin?'

Mr Rivenhall did not present the appearance of one who remembered his little cousin, but he said in his cool way: 'Certainly. I hope she is well, sir?'

'Never had a day's illness in her life, barring the measles,' said Sir Horace. 'You'll see her for yourself soon; your mother is going to take charge of her while I'm in Brazil.'

It was plain that this way of breaking the news did not recommend itself to Lady Ombersley, who at once hurried into speech. 'Well, of course it is not quite decided yet, though I am sure there is nothing I should like better than to have my dear brother's daughter to stay with me. I was thinking, too, Charles, that it would be so pleasant for Cecilia: Sophia and she are nearly the same age, you know.'

'Brazil?' said Mr Rivenhall. 'That should be very interesting, I daresay. Do you make a long stay there, sir?'

'Oh, no!' replied Sir Horace vaguely. 'Probably not. It will depend upon circumstance. I have been telling your mother that I shall be much in her debt if she can find an eligible husband for my Sophy. It's time she was married, and your mother seems, from what I hear, to be quite a dab in that line. I understand I have to offer you my felicitations, my boy?'

'Thank you: yes,' said Mr Rivenhall, with a slight bow.

'If you should not dislike it, Charles, I own I should be very happy to have Sophia,' said Lady Ombersley placatingly.

He cast her an impatient glance, and replied: 'I beg you will do precisely as you wish, ma'am. I cannot conceive what business it is of mine.'

'Of course I have explained to your uncle that we lead very quiet lives.'

'She won't give a fig for that,' said Sir Horace comfortably. 'She's a good little thing: never at a loss for something to occupy herself with. Just as happy in a Spanish village as in Vienna, or Brussels.'

At this, Lady Ombersley sat up with a jerk. 'Do not tell me you dragged the child to Brussels last year!'

'Of course she was in Brussels! Where the devil should she

have been?' replied Sir Horace testily. 'You wouldn't have had me leave her in Vienna, would you? Besides, she enjoyed it. We met a great many old friends there.'

'The danger!'

'Oh, pooh! Nonsense! Precious little of that with Wellington in command!'

'When, sir, may we have the pleasure of expecting my cousin?' interposed Mr Rivenhall. 'We must hope that she will not find life in London too humdrum after the superior excitement of the Continent.'

'Not she!' said Sir Horace. 'I never knew Sophy when she wasn't always busy with some ploy or another. Give her her head! I always do, and she never comes to any harm. Don't quite know when she'll be with you. She's bound to want to see the last of me, but she'll post up to London as soon as I've sailed.'

'Post up to London as soon as – Horace, surely you will bring her to me!' gasped his sister, quite scandalized. 'A girl of her age, travelling alone! I never heard of such a thing!'

'Won't be alone. She'll have her maid with her – dragon of a woman, she is: journeyed all over Europe with us! – and John Potton as well.' He caught sight of his nephew's raised brows, and felt himself impelled to add: 'Groom – courier – general factotum! Looked after Sophy since she was a baby.' He drew out his watch, and consulted it. 'Well, now that we've settled everything, I must be off, Lizzie. I shall rely upon you to take care of Sophy, and look about you for a match. It's important, because – but I've no time to explain that now! She'll tell you all about it, I expect.'

'But, Horace, we have not settled everything!' protested his sister. 'And Ombersley will be disappointed not to see you! I hoped you would dine with us!'

'No, I can't do that,' he replied. 'I'm dining at Carlton House.

You may give my respects to Ombersley: daresay I shall see him again one of these days!'

He then kissed her in a perfunctory style, bestowed another of his hearty pats upon her shoulder, and took himself off, followed by his nephew. 'Just as if I had nothing more to wish for!' Lady Ombersley said indignantly, when Charles came back into the room. 'And I have not the least notion when that child is to come to me!'

'It doesn't signify,' said Charles, with an indifference she found exasperating. 'You will give orders for a room to be prepared for her, I suppose, and she may come when she pleases. It's to be hoped Cecilia likes her, since I imagine she will be obliged to see the most of her.'

'Poor little thing!' sighed Lady Ombersley. 'I declare I quite long to mother her, Charles! What a strange, lonely life she must lead!'

'Strange certainly; hardly lonely, if she has been acting hostess for my uncle. I must suppose that she has had some older lady to live with her: a governess, or some such thing.'

'Indeed, one would think it must have been so, but your uncle distinctly told me that the governess died when they were in Vienna! I do not like to say such a thing of my only brother, but really it seems as though Horace is quite unfit to have the care of a daughter!'

'Extremely unfit,' he said dryly. 'I trust you will not have cause to regret your kindness, Mama.'

'Oh, no, I am sure I shall not!' she said. 'Your uncle spoke of her in such a way that gave me the greatest desire to welcome her! Poor child, I fear she has not been used to having her wishes or her comfort much considered! I could almost have been angry with Horace when he would keep on telling me that she is a good little thing, and had never been a worry to him! I daresay he has never allowed anyone to be a worry to him, for a more selfish man I believe you could hardly meet! Sophia must have her poor

mother's sweet disposition: I have no doubt of her being a charming companion for Cecilia.'

'I hope so,' said Charles. 'And that reminds me, Mama! I have
just intercepted another of that puppy's floral offerings to my sister.
This billet was attached to it.'

Lady Ombersley took the proffered missive, and looked at it in
dismay. 'What shall I do with it?' she asked.

'Put it on the fire,' he recommended.

'Oh, no, I could not, Charles! It might be quite unexceptionable! Besides – why, it might even contain a message from his
mother for me!'

'Highly unlikely, but if you think that, you had better read it.'

'Of course, I know it is my duty to do so,' she agreed unhappily.

He looked rather contemptuous, but said nothing, and after a
moment's indecision she broke the seal, and spread open the single
sheet. 'Oh, dear, it is a poem!' she announced. 'I must say, it is
very pretty! Listen, Charles! *Nymph, when thy mild cerulean gaze
Upon my restless spirit casts it beam –*'

'I thank you, I have no taste for verse!' interrupted Mr
Rivenhall harshly. 'Put it on the fire, ma'am, and tell Cecilia she
is not to be receiving letters without your sanction!'

'Yes, but do you think I should burn it, Charles? Only think
if this were the only copy of the poem! Perhaps he wants to have
it printed!'

'He is not going to print such stuff about any sister of mine!'
said Mr Rivenhall grimly, holding out an imperative hand.

Lady Ombersley, always overborne by a stronger will, was just
about to give the paper to him when a trembling voice from the
doorway arrested her: 'Mama! Do not!'

Two

Lady Ombersley's hand dropped; Mr Rivenhall turned sharply, a frown on his brow. His sister, casting him a look of burning reproach, ran across the room to her mother, and said: 'Give it to me, Mama! What right has Charles to burn my letters?'

Lady Ombersley looked helplessly at her son, but he said nothing. Cecilia twitched the open sheet of paper from her mother's fingers, and clasped it to her palpitating bosom. This did goad Mr Rivenhall into speech. 'For God's sake, Cecilia, let us have no play-acting!' he said.

'How dare you read my letter?' she retorted.

'I did not read your letter! I gave it to Mama, and you will scarcely say that she had no right to read it!'

Her soft blue eyes swam with tears; she said in a low voice: 'It is all your fault! Mama would never – I hate you, Charles! I hate you!'

He shrugged, and turned away. Lady Ombersley said feebly: 'You should not talk so, Cecilia! You know it is quite improper in you to be receiving letters without my knowledge! I do not know what your Papa would say if he heard of it.'

'Papa!' exclaimed Cecilia scornfully. 'No! It is Charles who delights in making me unhappy!'

He glanced over his shoulder at her. 'It would be useless, I collect, to say that my earnest wish is that you should *not* be made unhappy!'

She returned no answer, but folded the letter with shaking hands, and bestowed it in her bosom, throwing a defiant look at him as she did so. It was met with one of contempt; Mr Rivenhall propped his shoulders against the mantelshelf, dug his hands into his breeches' pockets, and waited sardonically for what she might say next.

She dried her eyes instead, catching her breath on little sobs. She was a very lovely girl, with pale golden locks arranged in ringlets about an exquisitely shaped face, whose delicate complexion was at the moment heightened, not unbecomingly, by an angry flush. In general, her expression was one of sweet pensiveness, but the agitation of the moment had kindled a martial spark in her eyes, and she was gripping her underlip between her teeth in a way that made her look quite vicious. Her brother, cynically observing this, said that she should make a practice of losing her temper, since it improved her, lending animation to a countenance well enough in its way but a trifle insipid.

This unkind remark left Cecilia unmoved. She could hardly fail to know that she was much admired, but she was a very modest girl, quite unappreciative of her own beauty, and would much have preferred to have been fashionably dark. She sighed, released her lip, and sat down on a low chair beside her mama's sofa, saying in a more moderate tone: 'You cannot deny, Charles, that it is your doing that Mama has taken this – this unaccountable dislike to Augustus!'

'Now, there,' said Lady Ombersley earnestly, 'you are at fault, dearest, for I do not dislike him at all! Only I cannot think him an eligible husband!'

'I don't care for that!' declared Cecilia. 'He is the only man for whom I could ever feel that degree of attachment which – in short, I beg you will abandon any notion you may have that I could ever entertain Lord Charlbury's extremely flattering proposal, for I never shall!'

Lady Ombersley uttered a distressful but incoherent protest; Mr Rivenhall said in his prosaic way: 'Yet you were not, I fancy, so much averse from Charlbury's proposal when it was first told you.'

Cecilia turned her lambent gaze upon him, and answered: 'I had not then met Augustus.'

Lady Ombersley appeared to be a good deal struck by the logic of this pronouncement, but her son was less impressionable. He said: 'Don't waste these high flights on me, I beg of you! You have been acquainted with young Fawnhope any time these nineteen years!'

'It was not the same,' said Cecilia simply.

'That,' said Lady Ombersley, in a judicial way, 'is perfectly true, Charles. I am sure he was the most ordinary little boy, and when he was up at Oxford he had the most dreadful spots, so that no one would have supposed he would have grown into such an excessively handsome young man! But the time he spent in Brussels with Sir Charles Stuart improved him out of all knowledge! I own, I never should have known him for the same man!'

'I have sometimes wondered,' retorted Mr Rivenhall, 'whether Sir Charles will ever be the same man again either! How Lady Lutterworth can have reconciled it with her conscience to have foisted upon a public man such a nincompoop to be his secretary I must leave it to herself to decide! All we are privileged to know is that your precious Augustus no longer fills that office! Or any other!' he added trenchantly.

'Augustus,' said Cecilia loftily, 'is a poet. He is quite unfitted for the – the humdrum business of an ambassador's secretary.'

'I do not deny it,' said Mr Rivenhall. 'He is equally unfitted to support a wife, my dear sister. Do not imagine that *I* will frank you in this folly, for I tell you now I will not! And do not delude yourself into believing that you will obtain my father's consent to this most imprudent match, for while I have anything to say you will not!'

'I know well that it is only you who have anything to say in this house!' cried Cecilia, large tear-drops welling over her eyelids. 'I hope that when you have driven me to desperation you may be satisfied!'

From the tightening of the muscles about his mouth it was to be seen that Mr Rivenhall was making a praise-worthy effort to keep his none too amiable temper in check. His mother glanced anxiously up at him, but the voice in which he answered Cecilia was almost alarmingly even. 'Will you, my dear sister, have the goodness to reserve these Cheltenham tragedies for some moment when I am not within hearing? And before you carry Mama away upon the tide of all this rodomontade, may I be permitted to remind you that so far from being forced into a unwelcome marriage you expressed your willingness to listen to what you have yourself described as Lord Charlbury's very flattering offer?'

Lady Ombersley leaned forward to take one of Cecilia's hands in hers, and to squeeze it compassionately. 'Well, you know, my dearest love, that is quite true!' she said. 'Indeed, I thought you liked him excessively! You must not imagine that Papa or I have the least notion of compelling you to marry anyone whom you hold in aversion, for I am sure that such a thing would be quite shocking! And Charles would not do so either, would you, dear Charles?'

'No, certainly not. But neither would I consent to her marriage with any such frippery fellow as Augustus Fawnhope!'

'Augustus,' announced Cecelia, putting up her chin, 'will be remembered long after you have sunk into oblivion!'

'By his creditors? I don't doubt it. Will that compensate you for a lifetime spent in dodging duns?'

Lady Ombersley could not repress a shudder. 'Alas, my love, it is too true! You cannot know the mortification – but we will not speak of that!'

'It was useless to speak to my sister of anything outside the covers of a novel from the lending-library!' said Charles. 'I might have supposed that she would be thankful, in the state to which this family has been reduced, to have been on the point of contracting even a respectable alliance! But no! She is offered not a respectable but a brilliant match, and she chooses to behave like any Bath Miss, swooning and languishing over a poet! A *poet*! Good God, Mama, if the specimen of his talent which you were so ill-advised as to read me – but I have no patience to argue further on that head! If you cannot prevail upon her to conduct herself in a manner worthy of her breeding she had better be sent down to Ombersley, to rusticate for a while, and see if that will bring her to her senses!'

With this terrible threat he strode out of the room, leaving his sister to dissolve into tears, and his mother to recruit her strength through the medium of the vinaigrette.

Between sobs Cecilia animadverted for some moments on the cruelty of fate, which had saddled her with a brother who was as heartless as he was tyrannical, and parents who were totally unable to enter into her feelings. Lady Ombersley, though sympathetic in the main, could not allow this to pass. Without taking it upon herself to answer for her husband's sensibilities, she assured Cecilia that her own were extremely nice, making it perfectly possible for her to appreciate the anguish of a forbidden love.

'When I was a girl, dearest, something of the same nature happened to me,' she said, sighing. 'He was not a poet, of course, but I fancied myself very much in love with him. But it would not

do, and in the end I was married to your Papa, which was thought
to be a splendid match, for in those days he had scarcely began to
run through his fortune, and –' She broke off, realizing that these
reminiscences were infelicitous. 'In short, Cecilia, – and I should
not be obliged to say this to you – persons of our order do not
marry only to please themselves.'

Cecilia was silenced, and could only hang down her head,
dabbing at her eyes with an already damp handkerchief. She knew
herself to have been a good deal indulged through the fondness of
one parent and the cheerful indifference of the other, and was well
aware that in discovering her inclination before permitting Lord
Charlbury to address his suit to her Lady Ombersley had shown
more consideration for her than would have been approved of by
the greater part of her contemporaries. Cecilia might read novels,
but she knew that the spirited behaviour of her favourite heroines
was not for her to imitate. She foresaw that she was doomed
to spinsterhood, and this reflection was so melancholy that she
drooped more than ever, and once more applied her handkerchief
to her eyes.

'Only think how happy your sister is!' said Lady Ombersley,
in a heartening tone. 'I am sure nothing could be more gratifying
than to see her in her own home, with her dear baby, and James
so attentive and obliging, and – and everything just what one
would wish! I declare I did not believe that any love-match could
have turned out better – not that I mean to say that Maria is not
sincerely attached to James! But she had not met him above half a
dozen times when he asked Papa's leave to speak to her, and her
affections were not engaged. Naturally, she felt a strong degree
of liking, or I should never – but Maria was such a good, pretty-
behaved girl! She told me herself that she felt it to be her duty to
accept such a respectable offer, with Papa in such difficulties, and
four more of you to be provided for!'

'Mama, I hope I am not an unnatural daughter, but I had rather be dead than married to James!' declared Cecilia, raising her head. 'He thinks of nothing but hunting, and when they do have company in the evening, he goes to sleep, and *snores!*'

Daunted by this disclosure, Lady Ombersley could find nothing to say for a minute to two. Cecilia blew her nose, and added: 'And Lord Charlbury is even older than James!'

'Yes, but we do not know that he snores, my love,' Lady Ombersley pointed out. 'Indeed, we may be almost certain that he does not, for his manners are so very gentleman-like!'

'A man who would contract the mumps,' declared Cecilia, 'would do anything!'

Lady Ombersley saw nothing unreasonable in this pronouncement, nor was she surprised that his lordship's unromantic behaviour had given Cecilia a distaste for him. She had herself been sadly disappointed, for she had thought him a man of sense, certainly not one to be succumbing to childish ailments at inopportune moments. She could think of nothing to say to palliate his offence, and as Cecilia had apparently no further observations to make, silence reigned uneasily for a time. Cecilia presently broke it, asking rather listlessly whether it was true that her uncle had been in the house that afternoon. Glad of an excuse to talk of more cheerful matters, Lady Ombersley at once told her of the treat in store for her, and had the satisfaction of seeing the cloud lift a little from her daughter's brow. It was not difficult to enlist Cecilia's sympathies on behalf of her cousin: she could scarcely envisage a more horrid fate than to be sent to stay for an indefinite period amongst relatives who were almost strangers, and warmly promised to do all that lay in her power to make Sophia feel herself at home in Berkeley Square. She could conjure up no very clear recollection of her cousin, for it had been some years since they had met; and although she had sometimes thought that to travel about Europe must be exciting, she had also suspected that it might also be extremely uncomfortable, and readily agreed with Lady Ombersley that such an unconventional existence was scarcely an ideal preparation for a London début. The reflection that Sophia's arrival in Berkeley Square must mean some relaxation of the almost conventual life imposed upon the family by Charles's determination to economize sent her away to change her dress for dinner in a far happier frame of mind.

Four of the family sat down at the huge table in the dining-room that evening, his lordship having decided to gratify his wife with one of his rare appearances at his own board. He was the only unconstrained member of the party, for he had a happy disposition which made it possible for him to remain oblivious to the most blatant signs of discontent in his companions. In the same spirit he contrived with amazing ease to be cheerful under the humiliation of being little more than his son's pensioner. He had the greatest dread of being obliged to face unpleasantness, so he never allowed himself to think about unpleasant things, which answered very well, and could be supported in times of really inescapable stress by his genius for persuading himself that any disagreeable necessity forced upon him by his own folly, or his son's overriding will, was the outcome of his own choice and wise decision. While Charles continued to render him the observances of filial respect he was able to forget that the reins of government had been wrenched out of his hands; and when, as sometimes happened, filial respect wore a little thin, at least these regrettable lapses did not last for long, and were not difficult for a man of his sanguine temperament to forget. He bore his son no malice, though he thought him a dull dog; and provided that the luck was running his way, and he was not expected to bear any distasteful part in the management of his young family, he was very well satisfied with his lot.

He could hardly have been unaware of the dissension at present raging in his household, for a request from his wife that he should exercise parental authority over Cecilia had driven him post-haste to Newmarket not a fortnight before. But neither his son's heavy frown, nor his daughter's reddened eyelids, occasioned the slightest comment from him. He appeared to derive no small satisfaction from partaking of a lengthy meal in the company of an anxious wife, an injured daughter, and a glowering son. He said: 'Well, upon my soul, this is very pleasant, to be dining *en famille* in this cosy way! You may tell your cook, Lady Ombersley, that I like this way of serving a duck. I declare I don't get as good at White's!' After that he recounted the latest piece of society gossip, and enquired affably how his children had spent the day.

'If you mean me, Papa,' said Cecilia, 'I have spent the day just as I spend every day. I shopped with Mama; I walked in the Park with my sisters and Miss Adderbury; and I practised my music.'

Her tone did not suggest that she had found these amusements exhilarating, but Lord Ombersley said "Capital!" and turned his attention to his wife. She told him of her brother's visit, and of his proposal that she should assume the charge of Sophia; and Lord Ombersley gave his gracious consent to the scheme, saying that nothing could be better, and congratulating his daughter upon her good luck in so unexpectedly acquiring a charming companion. Charles, who was irritated enough by all this bland insensibility to sympathize with his sister, said dampingly that they had as yet no reason to suppose that Sophia would be in the least charming. But Lord Ombersley said that he entertained no doubts on that head, and added that they must all do their best to make their cousin's stay agreeable. After that, he asked Charles whether he intended to go to the races next day. Charles, who knew that the races referred to were run under the patronage of the Duke of York, and would entail, for that jovial personage's cronies, several evenings spent at Oatlands, playing whist for pound points, looked more forbidding than ever, and said that he was going down to Ombersley Court for a few days.

'To be sure you are!' agreed his father cheerfully. 'I was forgetting that business about the South Hanger. Yes, yes, I wish you will attend to that, my boy!'

'I will, sir,' responded Mr Rivenhall politely. He then glanced across the table at his sister, and asked: 'Do you care to accompany me, Cecilia? I am very willing to take you, if you should like it.'

She hesitated. This might be an olive-branch; on the other hand it might be a singularly futile attempt to wean her mind from thoughts of Mr Fawnhope. The reflection that Charles's absence from town might, with a little contrivance, make it possible for her to meet Mr Fawnhope decided the matter. She shrugged, and said: 'No, I thank you. I do not know what I should do in the country at this season.'

'Ride with me,' suggested Charles.

'I prefer to ride in the Park. If you desire company, I wonder you do not invite the children to go with you: I am sure they would be delighted to oblige you.'

'As you please,' he replied indifferently.

Dinner at an end, Lord Ombersley withdrew from the family circle. Charles, who had no evening engagement, accompanied his mother and sister to the drawing-room, and, while Cecilia strummed idly at the piano, sat talking to his mother about Sophia's visit. Much to her relief, he seemed to be resigned to the necessity of holding at least one moderate party in Sophia's honour, but he strongly advised her against charging herself with the office of finding a suitable husband for her niece.

'Why my uncle, having allowed her to reach the age of – twenty, is it? – without bestirring himself in the matter,' he said, 'must suddenly take it into his head to persuade you to undertake the business, is a matter beyond my comprehension.'

'It does seem odd,' agreed Lady Ombersley. 'I daresay he might not have realized how time flies, you know. Twenty! Why, she is almost upon the shelf! I must say, Horace has been most remiss! There could be no difficulty, I am sure, for she must be quite an heiress! Even if she were a very plain girl, which I do not for moment suppose she can be, for you will allow Horace to be a handsome man, while poor dear Marianne was excessively pretty, though I don't expect that you can remember her – well, even if she *were* plain, it should be the easiest thing in the world to arrange a respectable match for her!'

'Very easy, but you would do well to leave it to my uncle, ma'am,' was all he would say.

At this moment, the schoolroom party came into the room, escorted by Miss Adderbury, a little gray mouse of a woman, who had originally been hired to take charge of Lady Ombersley's numerous offspring when Charles and Maria had been adjudged old enough to leave Nurse's jealous care. It might have been supposed that a twenty-year's residence in the household, under the aegis of a kind-hearted mistress, and the encouragement of her pupils' affection, would long since have allayed Miss Adderbury's nervousness, but this had endured with the years. Not all her accomplishments – and these included, besides a sufficient knowledge of Latin to enable her to prepare little boys for school, the expert use of the globes, a thorough grounding in the Theory of Music, enough proficiency upon the pianoforte and the harp to satisfy all but the most exacting and considerable talent in the correct use of water-colours – made it possible for her to enter the drawing-room without an inward shrinking, or to converse with her employer on terms of equality. Those of her pupils who had outgrown her care found her shyness and her anxiety to please tiresome, but they could never forget her kindness to them in their schoolroom days, and always treated her with something more than civility. So Cecilia smiled at her, and Charles said: 'Well, Addy, and how are you today?' which slight attentions made her grow pink with pleasure, and stammer a good deal in her replies.

Her charges now numbered three only, for Theodore, the youngest son of the house, had lately been sent to Eton. Selina, a sharp-looking damsel of sixteen, went to sit beside her sister on the pianoforte stool; and Gertrude, bidding fair, at twelve, to rival Cecilia in beauty, and Amabel, a stout ten-year-old, cast themselves upon their brother, with loud professions of delight at seeing him, and rather louder reminders to him of a promise he had made them to play at lottery-tickets the very next time he should spend an evening at home. Miss Adderbury, kindly invited by Lady Ombersley to take a seat by the fire, made faint clucking noises in deprecation of this exuberance. She had no hope of being attended to, but was relieved to observe that Lady Ombersley was regarding the group about Charles with a fond smile. Lady Ombersley, in fact, was wishing that Charles, who was so popular with the children, could bring himself to be equally kind to the brother and sister nearer to him in age. There had been a rather painful scene at Christmas, when poor Hubert's Oxford debts had been discovered...

The card-table had been set up, and Amabel was already counting out the mother-of-pearl fishes on its green-baize cloth. Cecilia begged to be excused from joining in the game, and Selina, who would have liked to play but always made a point of following her sister's example, said that she found lottery-tickets a dead bore. Charles paid no heed to this, but as he passed behind the music-stool on his way to fetch the playing-cards from a tall marquetry chest, bent to say something in Cecilia's ear. Lady Ombersley, anxiously watching, could not hear what it was, but she saw, her heart sinking, that it had the effect of making Cecilia colour up to the roots of her hair. However, she rose from the stool, and went to the table, saying, Very well, she would play for a little while. So Selina relented too, and after a very few minutes both young ladies were making quite as much noise as their juniors, and laughing enough to make an impartial observer think that the one had forgotten her advanced years, and the other her lacerated sensibilities. Lady Ombersley was able to withdraw her attention from the table, and to settle down to a comfortable chat with Miss Adderbury.

Miss Adderbury had already heard from Cecilia of Sophia's proposed visit, and was all eagerness to discuss it with Lady Ombersley. She could enter into her ladyship's feelings upon the event, join her in the sighing over the melancholy situation of a girl left motherless at five years old, agree with her plans for Sophia's accommodation and amusement, and, while deploring the irregularity of Sophia's upbringing, feel sure that she would be found to be a very sweet girl.

'I always know I can rely upon you, Miss Adderbury,' said Lady Ombersley. 'Such a comfort to me!'

In what way she was to be relied on Miss Adderbury had no idea, but she did not ask enlightenment, which was just as well, since her ladyship had no idea either, and had merely uttered the gratifying phrase from a general desire to please. Miss Adderbury said: 'Oh, Lady Ombersley! So good – ! So very obliging – !' and was almost ready to burst into tears at the thought of so much confidence being placed in one so unworthy as herself. Most fervently did she hope that her ladyship would never discover that she had nursed a snake in her bosom; and dolefully did she regret the lack of resolution that made it impossible for her to withstand her dear Miss Rivenhall's coaxing. Only two days before she had permitted young Mr Fawnhope to join the walking-party in the Green Park, and – far worse – had made no objection to his falling behind with Cecilia. It was true that Lady Ombersley had not mentioned Cecilia's unhappy infatuation to her, much less laid commands upon her to repulse Mr Fawnhope, but Miss Adderbury was the daughter of a clergyman (mercifully deceased) of stern and rigid morals, and she knew that such quibbling merely aggravated her depravity.

These reflections were interrupted by a further observation made by her ladyship, in a lowered tone, and with a glance cast towards the card-table at the other end of the room. 'I am persuaded that I have no need to tell you, Miss Adderbury, that we had been made a trifle uneasy lately by one of those fancies which young females are subject to. I shall say no more, but you will appreciate how glad I shall be to welcome my niece. Cecilia has been too much alone, and her sisters are not of an age to be the companions which her cousin must be. I am hopeful that in striving to make dear Sophia feel at home amongst us – for the poor little thing will be sadly lost in the middle of such a large family, I daresay – and in showing her how she should go on in London, she will have enough to occupy her to give her thoughts another direction.'

This view of the matter had not until now presented itself to Miss Adderbury, but she grasped it eagerly, and felt sure that all would happen precisely as Lady Ombersley anticipated. 'Oh, yes, indeed!' she declared. 'Nothing could be better! So condescending of your ladyship to – I had collected from dear Miss Rivenhall – but she is such a sweet girl I know she will devote herself to her less fortunate cousin! When do you expect Miss Stanton-Lacy, dear Lady Ombersley?'

'Sir Horace was able to give me no very precise information,' replied Lady Ombersley, 'but I understand that he expects to sail for South America almost immediately. No doubt my niece will be in London very shortly. Indeed, I shall speak to the housekeeper tomorrow about preparing a bedchamber for her.'

Three

But it was not until the Easter holidays were a week old that Sophia arrived in Berkeley Square. The only intelligence received by her aunt during the intervening ten days was a brief scrawl from Sir Horace, conveying the information that his mission was a trifle delayed, but that she would assuredly see her niece before very long. The flowers which Cecilia so prettily arranged in her cousin's room withered, and had to be thrown away; and Mrs Ludstock, a meticulously careful housekeeper, had twice aired the sheets before, in the middle of a bright spring afternoon, a post-chaise-and-four, generously splashed with mud, drew up at the door.

It so happened that Cecilia and Selina had been driving with their Mama in the Park, and had returned to the house not five minutes earlier. All three were just about to ascend the staircase when Mr Hubert Rivenhall came bounding down, uttering: 'It must be my cousin, for there is a mountain of baggage on the roof! Such a horse! By Jupiter, if ever I saw such a bang-up piece of flesh-and-blood!'

This extraordinary speech made the three ladies stare at him in bewilderment. The butler, who had only a minute before withdrawn from the hall, sailed back again, with his attendant satellites, and trod across the marble floor to the front door, announcing, with a bow to his mistress, that he apprehended Miss Stanton-Lacy had that instant arrived. The satellites then threw open the double doors, and the ladies had a clear view, not only of the equipage in the road, but of the awed and inquisitive faces of the younger members of the family, who had been playing at bat-and-ball in the garden of the Square, and were now crowded close to the railings, gazing, in spite of Miss Adderbury's remonstrances, at the animal which had brought Hubert in such pelting haste down the stairs.

Miss Stanton-Lacy's arrival was certainly impressive. Four steaming horses drew her chaise, two outriders accompanied it, and behind it rode a middle-aged groom, leading a splendid black horse. The steps of the chaise were let down, the door opened, and out leaped an Italian greyhound, to be followed a moment later by a gaunt-looking female, holding a dressing-bag, three parasols, and a birdcage. Lastly, Miss Stanton-Lacy herself descended, thanking the footman for his proffered help, but requesting him instead to hold her poor little Jacko. Her poor little Jacko was seen to be a monkey in a scarlet coat, and no sooner had this magnificent fact dawned on the schoolroom party than they brushed past their scandalized preceptress, tore open the garden-gate, and tumbled out into the road, shouting: 'A monkey! She has brought a monkey!'

Lady Ombersley, meanwhile, standing as though rooted to her own doorstep, was realizing, with strong indignation, that the light in which a gentleman of great height and large proportions regarded his daughter had been misleading. Sir Horace's little Sophy stood five feet nine inches in her stockinged feet, and was built on generous lines, a long-legged, deep-bosomed creature, with a merry face, and a quantity of glossy brown ringlets under one of the most dashing hats her cousins had ever seen. A pelisse was buttoned up to her throat, a very long sable stole was slipping from her shoulders, and she carried an enormous sable muff. This, however, she thrust into the second footman's hands so that she was better able to greet Amabel, who was the first to reach her. Her dazed aunt watched her stoop gracefully over the little girl, catching her hands, and saying laughingly: 'Yes, yes, indeed I am your cousin Sophia, but pray won't you call me Sophy? If any one calls me Sophia I think I am in disgrace, which is a very uncomfortable thing. Tell me your name!'

'It's Amabel, and oh, if you please, may I talk to the monkey?' stammered the youngest Miss Rivenhall.

'Of course you may, for I brought him for you. Only be a little gentle with him at first, because he is shy, you know.'

'Brought him for *me?*' gasped Amabel, quite pale with excitement.

'For you all,' said Sophy, embracing Gertrude and Theodore in her warm smile. 'And also the parrot. Do you like pets better than toys and books? I always did, so I thought very likely you would too.'

'Cousin!' said Hubert, breaking in on the fervent assurances of his juniors that their new relative had gauged their tastes with an accuracy utterly unequalled in all their experience of adults. 'Is that *your* horse?'

She turned, surveying him with a certain unselfconscious candour, the smile still lingering on her mouth. 'Yes, that is Salamanca. Do you like him?'

'By Jove, I should think I do! Is he Spanish? Did you bring him from Portugal?'

'Cousin Sophy, what is your dear little dog's name? What kind of a dog is it?'

'Cousin Sophy, can the parrot talk? Addy, may we keep it in the schoolroom?'

'Mama, Mama, Cousin Sophy has brought us a monkey!'

This last shout, from Theodore, made Sophy look quickly round. Perceiving her aunt and her two other cousins in the doorway, she ran up the steps, exclaiming: 'Dear Aunt Elizabeth! I beg your pardon! I was making friends with the children! How do you do? I am so happy to be with you! Thank you for letting me come to you!'

Lady Ombersley was still dazed, still clutching feebly at the fast-vanishing picture of the shy little niece of her imaginings, but at these words that insipid damsel was cast into the limbo of things unregretted and unremembered. She clasped Sophy in her arms, raising her face to the glowing one above her, and saying tremulously: 'Dear, dear Sophy! So happy! So like your father! Welcome, dear child, welcome!'

She was quite overcome, and it was several moments before she could recollect herself enough to introduce Sophy to Cecilia and Selina. Sophy stared at Cecilia, and exclaimed: 'Are you Cecilia? But you are so beautiful! Why don't I remember that?'

Cecilia, who had been feeling quite overpowered, began to laugh. You could not suspect Sophy of saying things like that only to please you; she said exactly what came into her head. 'Well, *I* did not remember either!' she retorted. 'I thought you were a little brown cousin, all legs and tangled hair!'

'Yes, but I am – oh, not tangled, perhaps, but all legs, I assure you, and dreadfully brown! *I* have not grown into a beauty! Sir Horace tells me I must abandon all pretensions – and *he* is a judge, you know!'

Sir Horace was right: Sophy would never be a beauty. She was by far too tall; nose and mouth were both too large, and a pair of expressive gray eyes could scarcely be held to atone entirely for these defects. Only you could not forget Sophy, even though you could not recall the shape of her face, or the colour of her eyes.

She turned again towards her aunt. 'Will your people direct John Potton where he may stable Salamanca, ma'am? Only for tonight! And a room for himself? I shall arrange everything just as soon as I have learnt my way about!'

Mr Hubert Rivenhall made haste to assure her that he would himself conduct John Potton to the stables. She smiled, and thanked him, and Lady Ombersley said that there was room and to spare for Salamanca in the stables, and she must not trouble her head about such matters. But it seemed that Sophy was determined to trouble her head, for she answered quickly: 'No, no, my horses are not to be a charge on you, dear aunt! Sir Horace most particularly charged me to make my own arrangements, if I should be setting up my stable, and indeed I mean to do so! But for tonight it would be so kind in you!'

There was enough here to set her aunt's brain reeling. What kind of a niece was this, who set up her stable, made her own arrangements, and called her father Sir Horace? Then Theodore created a diversion, coming up with the scared monkey clasped in his arms, demanding that she should tell Addy that he might take it to the schoolroom, since Cousin Sophy had given it to them. Lady Ombersley shrank from the monkey, and said feebly: 'My love, I don't think – oh, dear, whatever will Charles say?'

'Charles is not such a muff as to be afraid of a monkey!' declared Theodore. 'Oh, Mama, pray tell Addy we may keep it!'

'Indeed, Jacko will not bite anyone!' Sophy said. 'I have had him with me for close on a week, and he is the gentlest creature! You will not banish him, Miss – Miss Addy? No, I know that is wrong!'

'Miss Adderbury – but we always call her Addy!' Cecilia explained.

'How do you do?' Sophy said, holding out her hand. 'Forgive me! It was impertinent, but I did not know! Do permit the children to keep poor Jacko!'

Between her dismay at having a monkey thrust upon her, and her desire to please this glowing girl, who smiled so kindly down at her, and extended her hand with such frank good-nature, Miss Adderbury lost herself in a morass of half-sentences. Lady Ombersley said that they must ask Charles, a remark which was at once interpreted as permission to take Jacko up to the schoolroom, none of the children thinking so poorly of their brother as to believe that he would raise the least objection to their new pet. Sophy was then led up to the Blue Saloon, where she at once cast her sables on to a chair, unbuttoned her pelisse, and tossed off her modish hat. Her aunt, fondly drawing her down to sit beside her on the sofa, asked if she were tired from the long journey, and if she would like to take some refreshment.

'No, indeed! Thank you, but I am never tired, and although it was a trifle tedious I could not count it as a *journey!*' Sophy replied. 'I should have been with you this morning, only that I was obliged to go first to Merton.'

'Go first to Merton?' echoed Lady Ombersley. 'But why, my love? Have you acquaintances there?'

'No, no, but Sir Horace particularly desired it!'

'My dear, do you always call your papa Sir Horace?' asked Lady Ombersley.

The gray eyes began to dance again. 'No, if he makes me very cross I call him Papa!' Sophy said. 'It is of all things what he most dislikes! Poor angel, it is a great deal too bad that he should be saddled with such a maypole for a daughter, and no one could expect him to bear it!' She perceived that her aunt was looking a little shocked, and added, with her disconcerting frankness: 'You don't like that. I am so sorry, but indeed he is a delightful parent, and I love him dearly! But it is one of his maxims, you know, that one should never allow one's partiality to blind one to a person's defects.'

The startling proposition that a daughter should be encouraged to take note of her father's faults so much horrified Lady Ombersley that she could think of nothing to say. Selina, who liked to get to the root of everything, asked why Sir Horace had particularly desired Sophy to go to Merton.

'Only to take Sancia to her new home,' Sophy explained. 'That was why you saw me with those absurd outriders. Nothing will convince poor Sancia that English roads are not infested with bandits and guerilleros!'

'But who is Sancia?' demanded Lady Ombersley, in some bewilderment.

'Oh, she is the Marquesa de Villacañas! Did Sir Horace not tell you her name? You will like her – indeed, you *must* like her! She is quite stupid, and dreadfully indolent, like all Spaniards, but so pretty and good-natured!' She saw that her aunt was now wholly perplexed, and her straight, rather thick brows drew together. 'You don't know? He did not tell you? Now, how infamous of him! Sir Horace is going to marry Sancia.'

'*What?*' gasped Lady Ombersley.

Sophy leaned forward to take her hand, and to press it coaxingly. 'Yes, indeed he is, and you must be glad, if you please, because she will suit him very well. She is a widow, and extremely wealthy.'

'A Spaniard!' said Lady Ombersley. 'He never breathed a word of this to me!'

'Sir Horace says that explanations are so tedious,' said Sophy excusingly. 'I daresay he might have felt that it would take too long. Or,' she added, a mischievous look in her eyes, 'that I would do it for him!'

'I never heard of such a thing!' said Lady Ombersley, almost roused to wrath. 'Just like Horace! And when, pray, my dear, does he mean to marry this Marquesa?'

'Well,' said Sophy seriously, 'that, I fancy, is why he did not care to explain it all to you. Sir Horace cannot marry Sancia until I am off his hands. It is so awkward for him, poor dear! I have promised to do my best, but I *cannot* engage to marry anyone I don't like! He understands my feelings perfectly: I will say this for Sir Horace, that he is *never* unreasonable!'

Lady Ombersley was strongly of the opinion that these remarks were quite unsuited to her daughters' ears, but she saw no way of stemming them. Selina, still delving to the roots, asked: 'Why cannot your Papa be married until you are, Sophy?'

'On account of Sancia,' replied Sophy readily. 'Sancia says she does not at all wish to be my stepmama.'

Lady Ombersley was smitten to the heart. 'My poor child!' she said, laying a hand on Sophy's knee. 'You are so brave, but you may confide in me! She is jealous of you: I believe all Spaniards have the most shockingly jealous natures! It is too bad of Horace! If I had known this – ! Is she unkind, Sophy? Does she dislike you?'

Sophy went off into a peal of laughter. 'Oh, no, no, no! I am sure she never disliked anyone in all her life! The thing is that if she marries Sir Horace while I am still on his hands everyone will expect her to behave to me like a mama, and she is much too lazy! Then, too, with the best will in the world, I might continue to manage Sir Horace, and his house, and everything that I have been accustomed to do. We have talked it over, and I can't but see that there is a great deal in what she says. But as for jealousy, no indeed! She is much too handsome to be jealous of me, and much too good-natured as well. She says that she has the greatest imaginable affection for me, but share a house with me she will not. I do not blame her: pray do not think I blame her!'

'She sounds a very odd sort of a woman,' said Lady Ombersley disapprovingly. 'And why does she live in Merton?'

'Oh, Sir Horace hired the prettiest villa for her there! She means to live retired until he comes back to England. That,' said Sophy with a gurgle of mirth, 'is because she is excessively idle. She will lie in bed until the morning is half gone, eat a great many sweetmeats, read a great many novels, and be perfectly pleased to see any of her friends who will give themselves the trouble of driving out to visit her. Sir Horace says she is the most restful female of his acquaintance.' She bent to stroke her little dog, which had all the time been sitting at her feet. 'Except Tina here, of course! Dear ma'am, I hope you do not dislike dogs? She is very good, I promise you, and I could not part with her!'

Lady Ombersley assured her that she had no objection to dogs, but was by no means partial to monkeys. Sophy laughed, and said: 'Oh, dear! Was it wrong of me to bring him for the children? Only when I saw him, in Bristol, he seemed to me to be just the thing! And now that I have given him to them, I daresay it will be difficult to persuade them to give him up.'

Lady Ombersley rather thought that it would be impossible, and as there did not seem to be anything more to be said on that subject, and she was feeling quite bemused by her niece's various disclosures, she suggested that Cecilia should escort Sophy up to her room, where she would no doubt like to rest for a while before changing her dress for dinner.

Cecilia rose with alacrity, ready to add her persuasions to her mother's if it should be necessary. She did not suppose that Sophy wished to rest, for the little she had seen of her cousin had been enough to convince her that a creature so full of vitality rarely stood in need of rest. But she felt herself strongly drawn to Sophy, and was anxious to make a friend of her as soon as possible. So when it was discovered that Sophy's maid was unpacking her trunks in her bedchamber, she begged Sophy to come to her own room for a chat. Selina, finding that she was not to be admitted to this tête-à-tête, pouted, but went off, deriving consolation from the reflection that to her would fall the agreeable task of describing to Miss Adderbury every detail of Sophy's conversation in the Blue Saloon.

Cecilia's disposition was shy, and although her manners lacked the forbidding reserve which distinguished those of her elder brother they were never confiding. Yet within a very few minutes she found herself pouring into her cousin's ears some at least of the evils of her situation. Sophy listened to her with interest and sympathy, but the constant recurrence of Mr Rivenhall's name seemed to puzzle her, and she presently interrupted to say: 'I beg your pardon, but this Charles – is he not your brother?'

'My eldest brother,' said Cecilia.

'Well, that is what I collected. But what has he to say to anything?'

Cecilia sighed. 'You will soon discover, Sophy, that nothing may be done in this house without Charles's sanction. It is he who orders everything, arranges everything, and rules everything!'

'Now, let us understand this!' said Sophy. 'My uncle has not died, has he? I am sure Sir Horace never told me so!'

'Oh, no! But Papa – I should not be talking about him, and of course I don't know precisely – but I think poor Papa found himself in difficulties! In fact, I know it was so, for I found my mother in great distress once, and she told me a little, because she was so distracted she hardly knew what she was doing. In general, she would never say a word about Papa to any of us – except Charles, I suppose, and I daresay Maria, now that she is a married lady. Only then my great-uncle Matthew died, and he left all his fortune to Charles, and I don't understand exactly how it was, but I believe Charles did something with mortgages. Whatever it was, it seems to have placed poor Papa quite in his power. And I am very certain that it is Charles who pays for Hubert and Theodore, besides settling all the debts, for that Mama did tell me.'

'Dear me, how very uncomfortable it must be for your Papa!' remarked Sophy. 'My cousin Charles sounds a most disagreeable creature!'

'He is quite *odious!*' said Cecilia. 'I sometimes think he takes a delight in making everyone miserable, for I am sure he grudges us the least pleasure, and is only anxious to marry us to *respectable* men with large fortunes, who are quite middle-aged, and sober, and can do nothing but catch the mumps!'

Since Sophy was far too intelligent to suppose that this embittered speech was a mere generalization she at once pressed Cecilia to tell her more about the respectable man with mumps, and after a little hesitation, and a good deal of circumlocution, Cecilia not only divulged that a marriage between herself and Lord Charlbury had been arranged (though not as yet announced), but favoured her with a word-picture of the Honourable Augustus Fawnhope which must have seemed like the ravings of delirium to anyone who had not been privileged to behold that beautiful young man. But Sophy had already met Mr Fawnhope, and instead of coaxing her cousin to lie down upon her bed with a cooling draught, she said in the most matter-of-fact way: 'Yes, very true. I have never seen Lord Byron, but they tell me that he is nothing to Mr Fawnhope. He is quite the most handsome man I think I ever saw.'

'You know Augustus!' Cecilia breathed, clasping her hands at her palpitating bosom.

'Yes – that is to say, I am acquainted with him. I fancy I danced with him once or twice at the balls in Brussels last year. Was he not attached to Sir Charles Stuart in some capacity or another?'

'One of his secretaries, but Augustus is a poet, and of course he has no head for business, or affairs, which is a circumstance that disgusts Charles more than all the rest, I believe! Oh, Sophy, when we met – it was at Almack's Assembly Rooms, and I was wearing a gown of palest blue satin, embroidered all over with silken rosebuds, and knots of silver twist! – we no sooner saw each other than – He has assured me that it was the same with him! How could I suppose that there would be the least objection? The Fawnhopes, you know! I daresay they have been here since the Conquest, or some such thing! If *I* do not care a button for such things as fortunes and titles, what concern is it of Charles's?'

'None at all,' said Sophy. 'Dear Cecilia, don't cry, I beg of you! Only tell me this! Does your Mama dislike the notion of your marrying Mr Fawnhope?'

'Dearest Mama has such sensibility that I know she must feel for me!' declared Cecilia, obediently drying her eyes. 'She has as good as told me so, but she dare not withstand Charles! That, Sophy, is what governs all in this house!'

'Sir Horace is *always* right!' declared Sophy, rising, and shaking out her skirts. 'I teased him to take me to Brazil, you know, because, to own the truth, I could not imagine how I should contrive to occupy myself in London, with nothing to do but amuse myself in my aunt's house! He assured me that I should find something to be busy with, and you see that he had gauged the matter exactly! I wonder if he knew of all this? My dear Cecilia – oh, may I call you Cecy instead? Cecilia! Such a mouthful! – only trust me! You have fallen into a fit of despondency, and there is not the least need! In fact, nothing could be more fatal, in any predicament! It encourages one to suppose that there is nothing to be done, when a little resolution is all that is wanted to bring matters to a happy conclusion. I must go to my room, and dress for dinner, or I shall be late, and there is nothing more odious than a guest who comes late to meals!'

'But, Sophy, what can you possibly mean?' gasped Cecilia. 'What can *you* do to help me?'

'I have not the least notion, but I daresay a hundred things. Everything you have told me shows me that you are fallen, all of you, into a shocking state of melancholy! Your brother! Good gracious, what were you about to let him grow into such a tyrant? Why, I would not permit even Sir Horace to become so dictatorial, which is a thing the best of men will do, if the females of their families are so foolish as to encourage them! It is not at all good for them, beside making them such dead bores! Is Charles a dead bore? I am sure he must be! Never mind! If he has a fancy for making eligible matches he shall look about him for a husband for me, and that will divert his mind. Cecy, do come with me to my bedroom! Sir Horace desired me to choose mantillas for you and my aunt, and I daresay Jane will have unpacked them by now. How clever it was of me to have selected a white one for you! I am by far too brown-complexioned to wear white, but you will look enchantingly in it!'

She then swept Cecilia off to her own room, where she found the mantillas, carefully wrapped in silver paper, one of which she instantly carried to Lady Ombersley's dressing-room, declaring that Sir Horace had charged her to present it, with his love, to his dear sister. Lady Ombersley was delighted with the mantilla, a particularly handsome black one, and much touched (as she afterwards told Cecilia) by the message that went with it, not one word of which did she believe, but which showed, she said, such thoughtful delicacy in her niece.

By the time Sophy had changed her travelling-dress for an evening-gown of pale green crape, festooned at the bottom with rich silk trimming, and confined at the waist with a cord and tassels, Cecilia had completed her own toilet, and was waiting to escort her downstairs to the drawing-room. Sophy was trying to clasp a necklace of pearls round her throat while the gaunt maid, adjuring her not to be so fidgety, was equally determined to button up the cuffs of her long, full sleeves. Cecilia, tastefully but not strikingly attired in sprigged muslin, with a blue sash, supposed enviously that Sophy had had her gown made in Paris. She was quite right; nearly all Sophy's dresses came from Paris.

'One consolation,' said Cecilia naïvely, 'is that Eugenia will dislike it excessively!'

'Good gracious, who is Eugenia?' exclaimed Sophy, wheeling round upon her dressing-stool. 'Why should she dislike it? I don't think it ugly, do you?'

'Miss Sophy, drat you, *will* you sit still?' interpolated Jane Storridge, giving her a shake.

'No, of course I do not!' responded Cecilia. 'But Eugenia never wears modish gowns. She says there are more important things to think of than one's dresses.'

'What a stupid thing to say!' remarked Sophy. 'Naturally there are, but not, I hold, when one is dressing for dinner. Who is she?'

'Miss Wraxton: Charles is betrothed to her, and Mama sent to warn me a few minutes ago that she is dining here tonight. We had all of us forgotten it in the bustle of your arrival. I daresay she will be in the drawing-room already, for she is always very punctual. Are you ready? Shall we go down?'

'If only my dear Jane would bestir herself a little!' Sophy said, giving her other wrist to her maid, and casting a roguish look into Miss Storridge's disapproving face.

The maid smiled rather grimly, but said nothing. She did up the tiny buttons, draped a gold-embroidered scarf over her mistress's elbows, and gave a little nod of approval. Sophy bent, and kissed her cheek, saying: 'Thank you! Go to bed, and don't think I will let you undress me, for I assure you I will not! Good-night, Jane dear!'

Cecilia, a good deal astonished, said as they descended the stairs together: 'I suppose she has been with you a long time? I fear Mama would stare to see you kiss your maid!'

Sophy lifted her eyebrows at this. 'Indeed? Jane was my

mother's maid, and my own kind nurse when my mother died. I hope I may do nothing worse to make my aunt stare.'

'Oh! Of course she would perfectly understand the circumstances!' Cecilia said hastily. 'Only it looked so odd, you know!'

A decided sparkle in her cousin's fine eyes seemed to indicate that she did not much relish this criticism of her conduct, but as they had by this time reached the drawing-room door she did not say anything, but allowed herself to be ushered into the room.

Lady Ombersley, her two elder sons, and Miss Wraxton were seated in a group about the fire. All looked round at the opening of the door, and the two gentlemen rose to their feet, Hubert gazing at his cousin in frank admiration, Charles looking her over critically.

'Come in, dear Sophy!' Lady Ombersley said, in a welcoming tone. 'You see that I am wearing the beautiful mantilla instead of a shawl! Such exquisite lace! Miss Wraxton has been much admiring it. You will let me introduce Miss Stanton-Lacy to you, my dear Eugenia. Cecilia will have told you, Sophy, that we are soon to have the joy of counting Miss Wraxton one of the family.'

'Yes, indeed!' said Sophy, smiling, and holding out her hand. 'I wish you very happy, Miss Wraxton, and my cousin also.' She turned, having briefly clasped Miss Wraxton's hand, and extended her own to Charles. 'How do you do?'

He shook hands, and discovered that he was being looked at in a manner quite as critical as his own. This surprised him, but it amused him too, and he smiled. 'How do you do? I shall not say that I remember you very well, cousin, for I am sure that neither of us has the least recollection of the other!'

She laughed. 'Very true! Not even Aunt Elizabeth could remember me! Cousin – Hubert, is it? – tell me, if you please, about Salamanca, and John Potton! Did you see both safely bestowed?'

She moved a little aside, to talk to Hubert. Lady Ombersley, who had been anxiously watching her son, was relieved to see that he was looking perfectly amiable, even rather appreciative. A half smile lingered on his lips, and he continued to observe Sophy until his attention was recalled by his betrothed.

The Honourable Eugenia Wraxton was a slender young woman, rather above the average height, who was accustomed to hearing herself described as a tall, elegant girl. Her features were aristocratic, and she was generally held to be a good-looking girl, if a trifle colourless. She was dressed with propriety but great modesty in a gown of dove-coloured crape, whose sober hue seemed to indicate her mourning estate. Her hair, which she wore in neat bands, was of a soft tint between brown and gold; she had long, narrow hands and feet; and rather a thin chest, which, however, was rarely seen, her mama having the greatest objection to such low-cut bodices as (for instance) Miss Stanton-Lacy was wearing. She was the daughter of a Viscount, and, although she was always careful not to appear proud, perfectly aware of her worth. Her manners were gracious, and she took pains to put people at their ease. She had had every intention of being particularly gracious to Sophy, but when she rose to shake hands with her she had found herself looking up into Sophy's face, which made it very difficult to be gracious. She felt just a little ruffled for a moment, but overcame this, and said to Charles in a low voice, and with her calm smile: 'How very tall Miss Stanton-Lacy is! I am quite dwarfed.'

'Yes, too tall,' he replied.

She could not help being glad that he apparently did not admire his cousin, for although she perceived, on closer scrutiny, that Sophy was not as handsome as herself, her first impression had been of a very striking young woman. She now saw that she had been misled by the size and brilliance of Sophy's eyes: her other features were less remarkable. She said: 'Perhaps, a trifle, but she is very graceful.'

Sophy at this moment went to sit down beside her aunt, and Charles caught sight of the fairy-like little greyhound, which had been clinging close to her skirts, not liking so many strangers. His brows rose; he said: 'We seem to have two guests. What is her name, cousin?'

He was holding down his hand to the greyhound, but Sophy said: 'Tina. I am afraid she will not go to you: she is very shy.'

'Oh, yes, she will!' he replied, snapping his fingers.

Sophy found his air of cool certainty rather annoying, but when she saw that he was quite right, and watched her pet making coquettish overtures of friendship, she forgave him, and was inclined to think he could not be as black as he had been painted.

'What a pretty little creature!' remarked Miss Wraxton amiably. 'I am not, in general, fond of pets in the house – my Mama, dear Lady Ombersley, will never have even a cat, you know – but I am sure this must be quite an exception.'

'Mama has a great liking for pet dogs,' said Cecilia. 'We are not usually without one, are we, ma'am?'

'Fat and overfed pugs,' said Charles, with a grimace at his mother. 'I prefer this elegant lady, I confess.'

'Oh, that is not the most famous of Cousin Sophy's pets!' declared Hubert. 'You wait, Charles, until you see what else she has brought from Portugal!'

Lady Ombersley stirred uneasily, for she had not yet broken the news to her eldest son that a monkey in a red coat was now King of the Schoolroom. But Charles only said: 'I understand, cousin, that you have brought your horse with you too. Hubert can talk of nothing else. Spanish?'

'Yes, and Mameluke-trained. He is very beautiful.'

'I'll go bail you're a famous horsewoman, cousin!' Hubert said.

'I don't know that. I have had to ride a great deal.'

The door opened just then, but not, as Lady Ombersley had

expected, to admit her butler, with an announcement that dinner awaited her pleasure. Her husband walked in, announcing that he must just catch a glimpse of his little niece before going off to White's. Lady Ombersley felt that it was bad enough of him to have refused to dine at home in Miss Wraxton's honour without this added piece of casual behaviour, but she did not let her irritation appear, merely saying, 'She is not so very little, after all, my love, as you may see.'

'Good Gad!' exclaimed his lordship, as Sophy rose to greet him. Then he burst out laughing, embraced Sophy, and said: 'Well, well, well! You're almost as tall as your father, my dear! Devilish like him, too, now I come to look at you!'

'Miss Wraxton, Lord Ombersley,' said his wife reprovingly.

'Eh! Oh, yes, how-de-do?' said his lordship, bestowing a cheerful nod on Miss Wraxton. 'I count you as one of the family, and stand on no ceremony with you. Come and sit down beside me, Sophy, and tell me how your father does these days!'

He then drew Sophy to a sofa, and plunged into animated conversation, recalling incidents thirty years old, laughing heartily over them, and presenting all the appearance of one who had completely forgotten an engagement to dine at his club. He was always well-disposed towards pretty young women, and when they added liveliness to their charms, and guessed exactly how he liked to conduct a flirtation, he enjoyed himself very much in their company, and was in no hurry to leave them. Dassett, coming in a few minutes later to announce dinner, took in the situation immediately, and after exchanging a glance with his mistress withdrew again to superintend the laying of another place at the table. When he returned to make his announcement, Lord Ombersley exclaimed: 'What's that? Dinner-time already? I declare, I'll dine at home after all!'

He then took Sophy down on his arm, ignoring Miss Wraxton's

superior claims to this honour, and as they took their places at the dining-table commanded her to tell him what maggot has got into her father's head to make him go off to Peru.

'Not Peru: Brazil, sir,' Sophy replied.

'Much the same, my dear, and just as outlandish! I never knew such a fellow for travelling all over the world! He'll be going off to China next!'

'No, Lord Amherst went to China,' said Sophy. 'In February, I think. Sir Horace was wanted for Brazil because he perfectly understands Portuguese affairs, and it is hoped he may be able to persuade the Regent to go back to Lisbon. Marshal Beresford has become so excessively unpopular, you know. No wonder! He does not know how to be conciliating, and has not a grain of tact.'

'Marshal Beresford,' Miss Wraxton informed Charles, in a well modulated voice, 'is a friend of my father's.'

'Then you must forgive me for saying that he has no tact,' said Sophy at once, and with her swift smile. 'It is perfectly true, but I believe no one ever doubted that he is a man of many excellent qualities. It is a pity that he should be making such a cake of himself.'

This made Lord Ombersley and Hubert laugh, but Miss Wraxton stiffened a little, and Charles shot a frowning look across the table at his cousin, as though he were revising his first favourable impression of her. His betrothed, who always conducted herself with rigid propriety, could not, even at an informal family party, bring herself to talk across the table, and demonstrated her superior upbringing by ignoring Sophy's remark, and beginning to talk to Charles about Dante, with a particular reference to Mr Cary's translation. He listened to her with courtesy, but when Cecilia, following her cousin's unconventional example, joined in their conversation to express her own preference for the style of Lord Byron, he made no effort to snub her, but, on the contrary, seemed rather to welcome her entrance into the discussion. Sophy enthusiastically applauded Cecilia's taste, announcing that her copy of *The Corsair* was so well-worn as to be in danger of disintegrating. Miss Wraxton said that she was unable to give an opinion on the merits of this poem, as her mama did not care to have any of his lordship's works in the house. Since Lord Byron's marital difficulties were amongst the most scandalous *on dits* of the town, it being widely rumoured that he was, at the earnest solicitations of his friends, on the point of leaving the country, this remark at once made the discussion seem undesirably raffish, and everyone was relieved when Hubert, disclaiming any liking for poetry, went into raptures over that capital novel, *Waverley*. Here again Miss Wraxton was unable to edify the company with any measured criticism, but she graciously said that she believed the work in question to be, for a novel, quite unexceptionable. Lord Ombersley then said that they were all very bookish, but Ruff's *Guide to the Turf* was good enough reading for him, and drew Sophy out of the conversation by asking her a great many questions about old friends of his own whom, since they now adorned various Embassies, she might be counted upon to know.

After dinner, Lord Ombersley put in no appearance in the drawing-room, the claims of faro being too insistent to be ignored; and Miss Wraxton very prettily begged that the children might be permitted to come downstairs, adding, with a smile cast upwards at Charles, that she had not had the felicity of seeing her little friend Theodore since he had come home for the Easter holidays. However, when her little friend presently appeared he was carrying Jacko upon his shoulder, which made her shrink back in her chair, and utter an exclamation of protest.

The awful moment of disclosure had come, and, thanks (Lady Ombersley bitterly reflected) to Miss Adderbury's lamentable lack of control over her young charges, at quite the wrong moment.

Charles, at first inclined to be amused, was speedily brought to his senses by Miss Wraxton's evident disapproval. He said that however desirable a denizen of a schoolroom a monkey might be – which was a question to be discussed later – it was no fit creature for his mother's drawing-room, and ordered Theodore, in a tone that invited no argument, to remove Jacko at once. A sullen scowl descended on to Theodore's brow, and for a horrid instant his mother feared that she trembled on the brink of an ugly scene. But Sophy stepped quickly into the breach, saying: 'Yes, take him upstairs, Theodore! I should have warned you that of all things he most dislikes being brought into company! And pray make haste, for I am going to show you a famous game of cards which I learned in Vienna!'

She thrust him out of the room as she spoke, and shut the door on him. Turning, she found Charles eyeing her frostily, and said: 'Am I in disgrace with you for having brought the children a pet you don't approve of? I assure you, he is perfectly gentle: you need not be afraid of him.'

'I am not in the least afraid of him!' snapped Charles. 'Extremely obliging of you to have bestowed him upon the children!'

'Charles! Charles!' said Amabel, tugging at his sleeve. 'She has brought us a parrot too, and it talks capitally! Only Addy would put her shawl over its cage, because she said horrid, rough sailors must have taught it to speak. Do tell her not to!'

'Oh, good God, I am quite undone!' Sophy exclaimed in comical dismay. 'And the man *promised* the wretched bird would say nothing to put anyone to the blush! Now, what is to be done?'

But Charles was laughing. He said: 'You must say your Collect to it every day, Amabel, to put it in a better frame of mind. Cousin, my uncle Horace informed us that you were a good little thing, who would give us no trouble. You have been with us for rather less than half a day: I shudder to think what havoc you will have wrought by the end of a week!'

Four

IT COULD NOT HAVE BEEN SAID THAT LADY OMBERSLEY'S FAMILY dinner-party had been entirely successful, but it gave rise to a good deal of speculation in the minds of most of those who had been present at it. Miss Wraxton, who had seized the opportunity afforded by the rest of the company's sitting down to a round game to draw near to her prospective mother-in-law, and to engage her in low-voiced conversation, returned to her own home quite convinced that however little harm there might be in Sophy she had been very badly brought-up, and stood in need of tactful guidance. She had told Lady Ombersley that she was sorry indeed that the bereavement in her family had postponed her wedding-day, for she felt, in all sincerity, that she could have been both a support and a comfort to her mother-in-law under her present affliction. When Lady Ombersley said, rather defiantly, that she did not feel the visit of her niece to be an affliction, Miss Wraxton smiled at her in a way that showed how well she understood the brave front she was determined to present to the world, pressed her hand, and said that she looked forward to the time when she would be able to relieve dear Lady Ombersley of so many of the duties which now fell to her lot. Since this could only refer to the young couple's scheme of occupying one floor of the family mansion, a profound depression descended upon Lady Ombersley. The arrangement would not be an unusual one, but Lady Ombersley was able to think of many examples where it had been proved a failure, notably in the Melbourne household. Miss Wraxton would certainly not render the Ombersley house hideous by hysterical spasms, or really dreadful scandals, but Lady Ombersley derived small comfort from this knowledge. Almost as insupportable as Lady Caroline Lamb's frenzied behaviour would be Miss Wraxton's determination to exert a beneficent influence over her young brothers- and sisters-in-law; and her conviction that it was her duty to take upon her own shoulders many of the burdens which Lady Ombersley was not at all anxious to relinquish.

Charles, who had enjoyed a few minutes' grave talk with his betrothed before handing her into her carriage at the end of the evening, went to bed with mixed feelings. He could not but acknowledge the justice of his Eugenia's criticisms, but since he was himself of a forthright disposition he was inclined to like Sophy's frank, open manners, and obstinately refused to agree that she put herself forward unbecomingly. He did not think that she put herself forward at all, which made it difficult to see just how it was that she contrived to introduce quite a new atmosphere into the house. She had certainly done this: he was not sure that he approved of it.

As for Sophy herself, she retired to her bedchamber with even more to think about than her hosts. It seemed to her that she had taken up her residence in an unhappy household. Cecilia held Charles accountable for this, which no doubt he was. But Sophy was no schoolroom miss, and it had not taken her more than ten minutes to get Lord Ombersley's measure. Unquestionably Charles had had much to bear from that quarter; and since the rest of his family plainly held him in awe it was not marvellous that a naturally stern and autocratic temper, thus unchecked, should have turned him into a domestic tyrant. Sophy could not believe that he was past reclaim, for not only had Tina made friends with him, but when he laughed his whole personality underwent a change. The worst she yet knew of him was that he had selected for his bride a very tiresome girl. She felt it a pity that so promising a young man should be cast away on one who would make it her business to encourage all the more disagreeable features of his character.

There was no need to worry about the children, she decided, but her quick intelligence had informed her, during the course of the evening, that all was not well with Mr Hubert Rivenhall. She had a strong suspicion that some undisclosed trouble nagged at him. He might forget this in admiration of Salamanca, or in playing an absurd game with his juniors, but when nothing else occupied his mind the trouble crept back into it, and he grew silent, until somebody looked at him, when he instantly began to talk again, in a rattling, over-cheerful style which seemed to satisfy his relations. Sophy, guided by her experience of young officers, thought that he was probably in some foolish scrape which would turn out to be far less serious than he imagined. He ought, of course, to tell his elder brother about it, for no one could doubt, looking at Mr Rivenhall's countenance, that he was competent to deal with any scrape; but since Hubert was obviously afraid to do so it might be a good thing to persuade him to confide in his cousin.

Then there was Cecilia, so lovely, and so helpless! Her affairs might be much more difficult to arrange satisfactorily, for although Sophy, reared in quite a different school, thought it iniquitous to force any girl into a distasteful marriage, she was by no means determined to further the pretensions of Augustus Fawnhope. Sophy, strongly practical, could not feel that Mr Fawnhope would make a satisfactory husband, for he lacked visible means of support, and was apt, when under the influence of his Muse, to forget such mundane considerations as dinner-engagements, or the delivery of important messages. However, he would certainly be preferable to a middle-aged man with mumps, and if Cecilia's passion for him proved to be more than a mere infatuation her friends must busy themselves in finding for him some well-paid and genteel post in which his handsome person and charm of manner would outweigh his erratic habits. Sophy was still trying to think of such a post when she fell asleep.

Breakfast was served, at Ombersley House, in a parlour at the back of the house. Only the three ladies sat down to the table at nine o'clock, for Lord Ombersley, a man of nocturnal habits, never left his room until noon, and his two elder sons had breakfasted an hour earlier, and had gone off to ride in the Park.

Lady Ombersley, whose indifferent health made restful nights rarities in her life, had employed some part of her wakeful hours in planning entertainments for her niece, and as she dipped fingers of dry toast into her tea she propounded a scheme for an evening-party, with dancing. Cecilia's eyes brightened, but she said rather sceptically: 'If Charles will permit it!'

'My dear, you know your brother has no objection to any rational enjoyment. I do not mean that we should give a really large ball, of course.'

Sophy, who had been watching in some awe her aunt's languid consumption of tea-and-toast, said: 'Dear ma'am, I would infinitely prefer that you should not put yourself out for me!'

'I am quite determined to give a party for you,' replied Lady Ombersley firmly. 'I promised your father that I would do so. Besides, I am very fond of entertaining. I assure you, we are not in general so quiet as you find us at present. When I brought dear Maria out we gave a ball, two rout-parties, a Venetian breakfast, and a masquerade! But then,' she added, with a sigh, 'poor cousin

Mathilda was still alive, and she sent out all the invitation-cards, and arranged everything with Gunter's. I miss her sadly: she was carried off by an inflammation of the lung, you know.'

'No, but if that is all that troubles you, ma'am, pray do not give it another thought!' said Sophy. 'Cecy and I will arrange everything, and you shall have nothing to do but choose what dress you will wear, and receive your guests.'

Lady Ombersley blinked at her. 'But, my love, you could not!'

'Indeed I could!' asserted Sophy, smiling warmly at her. 'Why, I have managed all Sir Horace's parties since I was seventeen years old! And that puts me in mind of something I must do at once! Where shall I find Hoare's Bank, Aunt Lizzie?'

'Find Hoare's Bank?' echoed Lady Ombersley blankly.

'What in the world can you want to know *that* for?' asked Cecilia.

Sophy looked a little surprised. 'Why, to present Sir Horace's letter of authorization, to be sure!' she answered. 'I must do so at once, or I may find myself quite at a loss.' She perceived that her aunt and cousin were looking, if anything, rather more bewildered than ever, and lifted her brows. 'But what have I said?' she asked, between amusement and dismay. 'Hoare's, you know! Sir Horace banks with them!'

'Yes, my dear, I daresay he may, but *you* do not have an account with a bank!' expostulated Lady Ombersley.

'No, alas! It is such a bore! However, we settled it that I should draw upon Sir Horace's funds for my needs. And for the expenses of the household, of course, but at this present we have no house,' said Sophy, lavishly spreading butter on her fourth slice of bread.

'My love! Young ladies *never* – ! Why, I myself have never entered your uncle's bank in my life!' said Lady Ombersley, deeply moved.

'No?' said Sophy. 'Perhaps he prefers to settle all the bills himself? Nothing teases Sir Horace more than to be for ever applied to for money! He taught me years ago to understand business, and so we go on very happily.' Her brow wrinkled. 'I hope that Sancia will learn to manage for him. Poor angel! He will very much dislike it if he must study the bills, and pay all the wages.'

'I never heard of such a thing!' said Lady Ombersley. 'Really, Horace – But never mind that! Dear child, you cannot possibly need to draw funds while you are with me!'

Sophy could not help laughing at her aunt's evident conviction that Hoare's Bank must be a haunt of vice, but she said: 'Indeed I shall need funds! You have no notion how expensive I am, ma'am! And Sir Horace warned me most particularly not to allow myself to be a charge on you.'

Cecilia, her eyes round with wonder, asked: 'Does your Papa set no limit to what you spend?'

'No, how could he do so, when he has gone quite out of reach, and can have no notion what I might suddenly need? He knows I shall not outrun the carpenter. But I did not mean to tease you with my affairs! Only, in what part of the town is Hoare's situated, if you please?'

Fortunately, since neither of the other ladies had the smallest idea of the locality of any bank, Mr Rivenhall came into the room at this moment. He was dressed for riding, and had merely looked in to ask his mother if she had any commissions she might desire him to execute in the City, whither he was bound. She had none, but did not hesitate (in spite of his probable disapproval) to divulge to him Sophy's extraordinary wish to be directed to Hoare's Bank. He took this with equanimity, and even bore up wonderfully under the disclosure that she was at liberty to draw on her father's account. He said: 'Unusual!' but he seemed to be more amused than disapproving. 'Hoare's Bank is at Temple Bar,' he added. 'If your need is urgent, I am driving into the City myself this morning, and shall be happy to escort you.'

'Thank you! If my aunt has no objection I shall be glad to go with you. When do you wish to start?'

'I shall await your convenience, cousin,' he replied politely.

This civility augured well for the expedition, and made Lady Ombersley, always inclined to be optimistic, nourish the hope that Charles had taken one of his rare likings to his cousin. He was certainly predisposed in her favour when he found that she did not keep him waiting; and she, for her part, could not think very badly of a man who drove such a splendid pair of horses in his curricle. She took her place beside him in this vehicle; the groom swung himself up behind, as the horses plunged past him; and Sophy, herself no mean whip, preserved a critical but not unappreciative silence while Charles controlled the first ardour of his pair. Reserving her ultimate judgement until she should have seen him with a tandem, or a four-in-hand, she yet felt that she could safely repose confidence in his ability to aid her in the purchase of carriage-horses for her own use, and said presently: 'I must buy a carriage, and don't know whether to choose a curricle or a high-perch phaeton. Which do you recommend, cousin?'

'Neither,' he replied, steadying his horses round a bend in the street.

'Oh?' said Sophy, rather surprised. 'What, then?'

He glanced down at her. 'You are not serious, are you?'

'Not serious? Of course I am serious!'

'If you wish to drive, I will take you in the Park one day,' he said. 'I expect I can find a horse – or even a pair – in the stables quiet enough for a lady to drive.'

'Oh, I fear that would never do!' said Sophy, shaking her head.

'Indeed? Why not?'

'I might excite the horse,' said Sophy dulcetly.

He was momentarily taken aback. Then he laughed, and said: 'I beg your pardon: I had no intention of offending you! But you cannot need a carriage in London. You will no doubt drive out with my mother, and if you should wish to go on some particular errand you may always order one of the carriages to be sent round to the house for your use.'

'That,' said Sophy, 'is very obliging of you, but will not suit me quite so well. Where does one buy carriages in London?'

'You will scarcely drive yourself about the town in a curricle!' he said. 'Nor do I consider a high-perch phaeton at all a suitable vehicle for a lady. They are not easy to drive. I should not care to see any of my sisters making the attempt.'

'You must remember to tell them so,' said Sophy affably. 'Do they mind what you say to them? I never had a brother myself, so I can't know.'

There was a slight pause, while Mr Rivenhall, unaccustomed to sudden attacks, recovered his presence of mind. It did not take him very long. 'It might have been better for you if you had, cousin!' he said grimly.

'I don't think so,' said Sophy, quite unruffled. 'The little I have seen of brothers makes me glad that Sir Horace never burdened me with any.'

'Thank you! I know how I may take that, I suppose!'

'Well, I imagine you might, for although you have a great many antiquated notions I don't think you *stupid*, precisely.'

'Much obliged! Have you any other criticisms you would care to make?'

'Yes, never fly into a miff when you are driving a high-couraged pair! You took that last corner much too fast.'

As Mr Rivenhall was accounted something of a Non-pareil, this thrust failed to pierce his armour. 'What an abominable girl you are!' he said, much more amiably. 'Come! We cannot quarrel all the way to Temple Bar! Let us cry a truce!'

'By all means,' she agreed cordially. 'Let us rather talk about my carriage. Do I go to Tattersall's for my horses?'

'Certainly not!'

'Dear cousin Charles, do you wish me to understand that I have the name wrong, or that there is a superior dealer?'

'Neither. What I wish you to understand is that females do not frequent Tattersall's!'

'Now, is this one of the things you would not like your sisters to do, or would it really be improper in me to go there?'

'Most improper!'

'If you escorted me?'

'I shall do no such thing.'

'Then how shall I manage?' she demanded. 'John Potton is an excellent groom, but I would not trust him to buy my horses for me. Indeed, I would not trust anyone, except, perhaps, Sir Horace, who knows exactly what I like.'

He perceived that she was in earnest, and not, as he had suspected, merely bent on roasting him. 'Cousin, if nothing will do for you but to drive yourself, I will put my tilbury at your disposal, and choose a suitable horse to go between the shafts.'

'One of your own?' enquired Sophy.

'None of my horses are at all suitable for you to drive,' he replied.

'Well, never mind!' said Sophy. 'I shall prefer to have my own phaeton-and-pair.'

'Have you the smallest notion what you would have to pay for a well-matched pair?' he demanded.

'No, tell me! I thought not above three or four hundred pounds?'

'A mere trifle! Your father, of course, would have not the least objection to your squandering three or four hundred pounds on a pair of horses!'

'Not the least, unless I allowed myself to be taken in like a goose, and bought some showy-looking animal for ever throwing out a splint, or a high-stepper found to be touched in the wind at the end of a mile.'

'I advise you to wait until he returns to England, then. He will no doubt choose you the very thing!' was all Mr Rivenhall would say.

Rather to his surprise, Sophy appeared to take this in perfectly good part, for she made no comment, and almost immediately desired him to tell her the name of the street they were driving down. She did not refer again to the phaeton-and-pair, and Mr Rivenhall, realizing that she was merely a little spoilt and in need of a set-down, palliated the severe snub he had dealt her by pointing out one or two places of interest which they passed, and asking her a few civil questions about the scenery of Portugal. Arrived at Temple Bar, he drew up before the narrow entrance to Hoare's Bank, and would have accompanied her inside had she not declined his escort, saying that he would do better to walk his horses, for she did not know how long she might be detained, and there was a sharp wind blowing. So he waited for her outside, reflecting that however unusual it might be for a young and unattached lady to do business in a bank she could not really come to any harm there. When she reappeared, in about twenty minutes' time, some senior official of the Bank came with her, and solicitously handed her up into the curricle. She seemed to be on terms of considerable friendship with this personage, but disclosed, in answer to a somewhat sardonic enquiry made by her cousin as they drove off, that this had been her first meeting with him.

'You surprise me!' said Mr Rivenhall. 'I had supposed he must have dandled you on his knee when you were a baby!'

'I don't think so,' she said. 'He didn't mention it, at all events. Where do we go now?'

He told her that he had some business to transact near St Paul's, adding that he should not keep her waiting above five minutes. If this was a shaft aimed at the length of time she had spent in the Bank he missed his aim, for Sophy said in the most amiable way that she did not mind waiting. This was a much more successful shaft: Mr Rivenhall began to think that in Miss Stanton-Lacy he had met an opponent to be reckoned with.

When he presently drew up in a street beside St Paul's, Sophy held out her hand, saying: 'I will take them.' He therefore put the reins into her hand, for although he did not trust her to control his spirited horses his groom was already at their heads, so that there was no likelihood of any mishap.

Sophy watched him walk into a tall building, and pulled off one of her lavender kid gloves. The east wind was blowing quite strongly: certainly strongly enough to whirl a lady's glove, tossed to it, into the gutter on the farther side of the road. 'Oh, my glove!' exclaimed Sophy. 'Please run quickly, or it will blow quite away! Don't fear for the horses: I can handle them!'

The groom found himself in a quandary. His master would certainly not expect him to leave the grays unattended; on the other hand, someone must rescue Miss Stanton-Lacy's glove, and the street was momentarily deserted. Judging by what he had been able to hear of the lady's conversation, she at least knew enough about driving to be able to hold the grays for a minute. They were standing quite quietly. The groom touched his hat, and strode across the road.

'Tell your master that it is too chilly to keep the horses standing!' Sophy called after him. 'I will tool the curricle round the streets for a few minutes, and come back to take him up when he is ready!'

The groom, who was stooping to pick up the glove, nearly fell over, so swiftly did he spin round. He had an excellent view of Miss Stanton-Lacy driving at a smart pace up the street. He made a gallant but belated attempt to catch the curricle, but it swept round a corner just as the wind blew his hat off, and sent it bowling down the street.

It was nearly half an hour later when the curricle again came into sight. Mr Rivenhall, awaiting it with folded arms, had ample opportunity to observe with what precision his cousin rounded the corner, and how well she handled the reins and whip, but he did not appear to be much gratified, for he watched the approach of the vehicle with a scowl on his brow, and his lips tightly gripped together. Of his groom there was no sign.

Miss Stanton-Lacy, pulling up exactly abreast of Mr Rivenhall, said cheerfully: 'I beg pardon, I have kept you waiting! The thing is that I do not know my way about London, and became quite lost, and was obliged to enquire the directions no less than three times. But where is your groom?'

'I have sent him home!' replied Mr Rivenhall.

She looked down at him, her expressive eyes brimful of amusement. 'How very right of you!' she approved. 'I like a man to think of everything. You could never have quarrelled with me really *well* with that man standing up behind us, and overhearing every word you uttered.'

'How *dared* you drive my horses?' demanded Mr Rivenhall thunderously. He mounted into his seat, and snapped: 'Give me the reins at once!'

She relinquished them, and also the whip, but said disarmingly: 'To be sure, that was not very well-done of me, but you will own that there was no bearing your conduct in talking to me as though I were a silly chit scarcely able to drive a donkey.'

Mr Rivenhall's impatient mouth was once more set so rigidly

that there seemed to be no likelihood of his owning anything at all.

'At least admit that I am able to handle your pair!' said Sophy.

'Well for you that I had taken the edge off them!' he retorted.

'How ungenerous of you!' said Sophy.

It was indeed ungenerous, and he knew it. He said furiously: 'Driving about the City, with not even a groom beside you! Very pretty behaviour, upon my word! It is a pity you have not a little more conduct, cousin! Or are these Portuguese manners?'

'Oh, no!' she replied. 'In Lisbon, where I am known, I could not indulge in such pranks, of course. Dreadful, was it not? I assure you, all the cits were staring at me! But do not put yourself into a pucker on that head! no one knows me in London!'

'No doubt,' he said sardonically, '*Sir Horace* would have applauded such behaviour!'

'No,' said Sophy. 'I think that Sir Horace would have rather expected you to have offered to let me drive your horses. Just so that you could have judged for yourself whether I was capable of handling a spirited pair,' she explained kindly.

'I let no one – *no one* – drive my horses but myself!'

'In general,' said Sophy, 'I think you are very right. It is amazing how swiftly a clumsy pair of hands will spoil the most tender mouth!'

Mr Rivenhall almost audibly ground his teeth.

Sophy laughed suddenly. 'Oh, don't be so out of reason cross, cousin!' she begged. 'You know very well your horses have taken no sort of hurt! Will you put me in the way of choosing a pair for my own use?'

'I will have nothing whatsoever to do with such a mad project!' he said harshly.

Sophy took this with equanimity. 'Very well,' she said. 'Perhaps it would suit you better to find an eligible husband for me. I am very willing, and I understand that you have some talent in that.'

'Have you no delicacy of mind?' demanded Mr Rivenhall.

'Yes, indeed! I daresay it would astonish you to know how much!'

'It would!'

'But with *you*, my dear cousin,' pursued Sophy, 'I know I need have no reserve. Do, pray, find me an eligible husband! I am not at all nice in my notions, and shall be satisfied with the barest modicum of virtues in my partner.'

'Nothing,' stated Mr Rivenhall, showing his cousin, as he swirled round the corner into the Haymarket, how to drive to an inch, 'would afford me greater satisfaction than to see you married to some man who would know how to control your extraordinary quirks!'

'Very creditably performed!' approved Sophy. 'But how would it have been if some dog had strayed into the road, or a poor soul have crossed the street at that moment?'

Mr Rivenhall's sense of humour betrayed him. He was obliged to bite back a laugh before replying: 'I find it a marvellous circumstance, cousin, that no one has yet strangled you!'

He found that he had lost his cousin's attention. Her head was turned away from him, and before he could discover what object of interest had caught her eye she had said quickly: 'Oh, if you please, would you stop? I have seen an old acquaintance!'

He complied with this request, and then saw, too late, who was walking down the street towards them. There could be no mistaking that graceful figure, or those guinea-gold locks, revealed by the doffing of a curly-brimmed beaver. Mr Augustus Fawnhope, perceiving that the lady in the curricle was waving a hand in his direction, halted, took off his hat, and stood with it in his hand, gazing enquiringly up at Sophy.

He was indeed a beautiful young man. His hair waved naturally from a brow of alabaster; his eyes were of a deep blue, a little dreamy, but so exquisitely set under arched brows, of such size and brilliance as to defy criticism; his mouth was moulded in curves to set a sculptor groping for the tools of his art. He was of moderate height, and exact proportions, and had no need to live upon a diet of potatoes steeped in vinegar to preserve his slender figure. Not that it would ever have entered his head to have done so; it was not the least of Mr Fawnhope's charms that he was utterly unconcerned with his appearance. It might have been supposed that he could not be unaware of the admiration this excited, but as he was preoccupied with his ambition to become a major poet, paying very little attention to what was said to him, and none at all to what was said about him, even his ill-wishers (such as Mr Rivenhall and Sir Charles Stuart) were forced to admit that it was very likely that this admiration had not as yet pierced the cloud of abstraction in which he wrapped himself.

But there was more than abstraction in the gaze turned upward to Miss Stanton-Lacy's face, and this circumstance was not lost on Mr Rivenhall, interpreting correctly the doubtful smile hovering on Mr Fawnhope's lips. Mr Fawnhope had not the faintest idea of the identity of the lady stretching down her hand to him in so friendly a fashion. However, he took it in his, and said How-do-you-do, in his soft, vague voice.

'Brussels,' said Sophy helpfully. 'We danced the quadrille at the Duchess of Richmond's ball, do you remember? Oh, are you acquainted with my cousin, Mr Rivenhall? You must know that I am staying with my aunt, in Berkeley Square, for the season. You must come to call upon us: I know she will be delighted!'

'Of course I remember!' said Mr Fawnhope, with less truth than good manners. 'Enchanting to meet again, ma'am, – and so unexpectedly! I shall certainly do myself the pleasure of calling in Berkeley Square.'

He bowed, and stepped back. The grays, to whom Mr Rivenhall's impatience had communicated itself, bounded forward. Mr Rivenhall said: 'How charming for you to have met an old friend so soon after your arrival!'

'Yes, was it not?' agreed Sophy.

'I hope he will have contrived to recall your name before he avails himself of your invitation to visit you.'

Her lips twitched, but she replied with perfect composure: 'Depend upon it, if he does not he will find someone to tell him what it is.'

'You are shameless!' he said angrily.

'Nonsense! You only say so because I drove your horses,' she answered. 'Never mind! I will engage not to do so again.'

'I'll take care of that!' he retorted. 'Let me tell you, my dear cousin, that I should be better pleased if you would refrain from meddling in the affairs of my family!'

'Now, that,' said Sophy, 'I am very glad to know, because if ever I should desire to please you I shall know just how to set about it. I daresay I shan't, but one likes to be prepared for any event, however unlikely.'

He turned his head to look at her, his eyes narrowed, and their expression by no means pleasant. 'Are you thinking of being so unwise as to cross swords with me?' he demanded. 'I shan't pretend to misunderstand you, cousin, and I will leave you in no doubt of my own meaning! If you imagine that I will ever permit that puppy to marry my sister, you have yet something to learn of me!'

'Pooh!' said Sophy. 'Mind your horses, Charles, and don't talk fustian to me!'

Five

'Pretty well, for one morning's work!' said Sophy.

Mr Rivenhall was less satisfied. His mother was dismayed to discover that so far from having taken a liking to his cousin he was appalled to think that they might be obliged to house her for months. 'I tell you frankly, ma'am, it will not do!' he said. 'God knows how long my uncle may be away! I only wish you may not live to regret the day when you consented to take charge of his daughter! The sooner you can fulfil the rest of his expectations, and marry her off to some poor wretch, the better it will be for the rest of us!'

'Good gracious, Charles!' said Lady Ombersley. 'What in the world has she done to put you out?'

He declined to answer this, merely saying that Sophy was pert, headstrong, and so badly brought-up that he doubted whether any man would be fool enough to offer for her. His mother refrained from enquiring further into Sophy's iniquities, but instead seized the moment to suggest that as a prelude to finding a husband for her she should be allowed to give an evening party, with dancing. 'I do not mean a large affair,' she hastened to add. 'Perhaps ten couples, or so – in the drawing-room!'

'By all means!' he said. 'That will make it quite unnecessary for you to invite young Fawnhope!'

'Oh, quite!' she agreed.

'I should warn you, Mama,' he said, 'that we encountered him this morning! My cousin greeted him as an old and valued acquaintance, and begged him to call on her here!'

'Oh, dear!' sighed Lady Ombersley. 'How very unfortunate, to be sure! But I daresay she does know him, Charles, for she was with your uncle in Brussels last year.'

'She!' said Charles witheringly. 'He had no more notion who she was than the Emperor of China! But he will certainly call! I must leave you to deal with *that*, ma'am!'

With these very unfair words he strode out of his mother's room, leaving her to wonder in what way he supposed her to be able to deal with a morning-call paid by a young man of unexceptionable birth, who was the son of one of her oldest friends. She came to the conclusions that he had no more idea than she, and banished the matter from her mind, bending it instead to the far more pleasant problem of whom to invite to the first party she had held in two months.

She was presently interrupted by the entrance of her niece. Remembering Charles's dark words, she asked Sophy, with an assumption of severity, what she had done to vex him. Sophy laughed, and almost stunned her by replying that she had done nothing but steal his curricle, and tool it round the City for half an hour.

'Sophy!' gasped her ladyship. 'Charles's grays? You could never hold them!'

'To own the truth,' admitted Sophy, 'I had the devil's own work to do so! Oh, I beg your pardon! I did not mean to say that, dearest Aunt Lizzie! Don't scold! It comes of living with Sir Horace: I know I say the most shocking things, but I do try to mind my wretched tongue! No, and do not give Charles's pets another thought! He will come about presently. I daresay if he had not engaged himself to marry that tedious girl he would not be so stuffy!'

'Oh, Sophy!' said Lady Ombersley involuntarily. 'I own I cannot like Miss Wraxton, try as I will!'

'Like her! I should think not indeed!' exclaimed Sophy.

'Yes, but one should,' said Lady Ombersley unhappily. 'She is so very good, and I am sure she wishes to be a most dutiful daughter to me, and it is so ill-natured of me not to wish for a dutiful daughter! But when I think that in quite a short time now I shall have her living in the house – But I should not be talking in this style! It is most improper, and you must forget it, if you please, Sophy!'

Sophy paid no heed to this, but echoed: 'Living in the house! You are not serious, ma'am?'

Lady Ombersley nodded. 'There is nothing at all out of the way in such an arrangement, you know, my love. They will have their own apartments, of course, but...' She broke off, and sighed.

Sophy looked at her fixedly for a few moments, but, rather to her surprise, said nothing. Lady Ombersley tried to put these melancholy reflections out of her mind, and began to talk about the party she meant to give. Into these plans her niece entered with enthusiasm, and an efficiency that swept Lady Ombersley quite off her feet. By what stages she arrived at agreement with Sophy on all points she was never afterwards able to explain, either to Charles or to herself, but at the end of an interview which left her feeling bemused but convinced that no one could boast of having a sweeter-natured or more thoughtful niece than Sophy, she had certainly consented not only to allow Sophy and Cecilia to undertake all the necessary arrangements, but also to permit Sir Horace (through his daughter) to defray the cost of the entertainment.

'And now,' Sophy said buoyantly to Cecilia, 'you shall tell me where we must order the cards of invitation, and where you in general go for refreshments. I don't think we should leave that to my aunt's cook, for he would be busy for so many days he would have very little time for anything else, and that would make everything uncomfortable, which I don't at all wish.'

Cecilia regarded her in round-eyed astonishment. 'But Sophy, Mama said it should only be a quiet small party!'

'No, Cecy, it was your brother who said that,' replied Sophy. 'It is going to be a very large party.'

Selina, who was present at this conference, asked shrewdly: 'Does Mama know that?'

Sophy laughed. 'Not yet!' she admitted. 'Do you think she does not care for large parties?'

'Oh, no! Why, there were more than four hundred people invited to the ball she gave for Maria, were there not, Cecilia? Mama enjoyed it excessively, because it was such a capital success, and everyone complimented her on it. Cousin Mathilda told me so.'

'Yes, but the cost of it!' Cecilia said. 'She will not dare! Charles would be so angry!'

'Don't give him a thought!' recommended Sophy. 'It is Sir Horace who will bear the cost, not Charles. Make a list of all your acquaintances, Cecy, and I will make one of those of my friends who are in England, and then we will go out to order the cards. I imagine we shall not need more than five hundred.'

'Sophy,' said Cecilia, in a faint voice, 'are we going to send out *five hundred* invitations without even *asking* Mama?'

Imps of mischief danced in her cousin's eyes. 'Of course we are, dear goose! For once we have despatched them even your horrid brother cannot recall them!'

'Oh, famous, famous!' cried Selina, beginning to skip round the room. '*What* a rage he will be in!'

'*Dare* I?' breathed Cecilia, at once scared and dazzled.

Her sister begged her not to be poor-spirited, but it was Sophy who clinched the matter, by pointing out to her that she would not have to bear the responsibility, and was unlikely to incur much recrimination from her brother, who would have no hesitation in laying the blame at the right door.

Mr Rivenhall, meanwhile, had gone off to visit his betrothed. He arrived at the Brinklows' somewhat cheerless house in Brook Street still seething with indignation, but so thankless and perverse was his disposition that no sooner did he find his sentiments shared and his strictures on his cousin endorsed than he took an abrupt turn in quite another direction, and said much must be forgiven a girl who could handle his grays as Sophy had. From being a female sunk below reproach Sophy became rapidly an unconventional girl whose unaffected manners were refreshing in an age of simpers and high flights.

This was not just to Miss Wraxton's taste. To be driving about the City unattended did not suit her sense of propriety, and she said so. Mr Rivenhall grinned. 'No, very true, but I suppose it was in some sort my fault: I *did* put up her back. There's no harm done: if she could control my grays, as fresh as they were, she's a capital whip. All the same, if I have anything to say to it she is not going to set up her own carriage while she remains in my mother's charge. Good God, we should never know from one moment to the next where she was, for, if I know anything of my abominable cousin Sophy, to drive decorously round the Park would not do for her at all!'

'You take it with a composure that does you the greatest credit, my dear Charles.'

'I didn't!' he interrupted, with a rueful laugh. 'She put me in a thundering rage!'

'I am sure that it is not wonderful that she should have. To drive a gentleman's horses without his leave shows a want of conduct that is above the line of being pleasing. Why, even *I* have never even requested you to let me take the reins!'

He looked amused. 'My dear Eugenia, I hope you never will, for I shall certainly refuse such a request! You could never hold my horses.'

If Miss Wraxton had not been so very well-bred she would at this tactless remark have returned a pretty hot rejoinder, for she prided herself a little on her handling of the ribbons; and, although she did not drive herself in London, owned an elegant phaeton which she used when staying at her home in Hampshire. As it was, she was obliged to pause for a moment before saying anything. During this brief period she swiftly formed the resolve of demonstrating to Charles, and his objectionable cousin, that a lady reared on the strictest principles of propriety could be quite as notable a horsewoman as any hoyden who had spent her girlhood junketing about the Continent. She had several times been complimented on her seat on a horse, and knew her style to be excellent. She said: 'If Miss Stanton-Lacy cares for such things, perhaps she would like to ride with me one afternoon in the Park. That will give her thoughts another direction, diverting them from such foolish notions as setting up her own carriage. Let us make up a party, Charles! Dear Cecilia is not fond of the exercise, I know, or I should solicit her to join us. But Alfred will be pleased to go with me, and you may bring your cousin. Tomorrow? Pray beg her to go with us!'

Mr Rivenhall, an intolerant man, had no affection for his Eugenia's younger brother, and generally made it his business to avoid him, but he was struck by Miss Wraxton's nobility in promoting an engagement which (he guessed) would afford her little pleasure, and at once agreed to it, expressing at the same time his sense of obligation to her. She smiled at him, and said that it must be an object with her to exert herself in his interests. He was a man not much given to the making of graceful gestures, but at this he kissed her hand, and said that he knew well how utterly he could rely upon her in every predicament. Miss Wraxton then repeated the remark she had previously made to Lady Ombersley, that she was particularly sorry that, at this crisis in the Ombersley fortunes, circumstance had intervened to postpone her union with him. She rather thought that the indifferent state of dear Lady Ombersley's health made it impossible for her to manage her household just as Charles could wish. Her kind heart made her perhaps over-tolerant, and the languor induced by an ailing consti-tution rendered her blind to certain defects that could speedily be remedied by a helpful daughter-in-law. Miss Wraxton owned that she had been surprised to learn that Lady Ombersley had allowed herself to be persuaded by her brother – a very odd kind of man, her papa had told her – to assume the charge of his daughter for an unspecified length of time. She passed from this, in the smooth-est fashion, to a gently worded criticism of Miss Adderbury, no doubt an excellent woman, but sadly lacking in accomplishments, or in control over her spirited charges. But this was a mistake: Mr Rivenhall would permit no criticism of Addy, who had guided his own first steps; and as for his uncle, Lord Brinklow's slighting comment made him instantly bristle in defence of his relative. Sir Horace, he informed Miss Wraxton, was a highly distinguished man, with a genius for diplomacy.

'But not, you will own, a genius for rearing a daughter!' said Miss Wraxton archly.

He laughed at that, but said: 'Oh, well! I don't know that there is any real harm in Sophy, after all!'

When Miss Wraxton's invitation was conveyed to Sophy she professed herself happy to accept it, and at once desired Miss Jane Storridge to press out her riding-dress. This garment, when she appeared in it on the following afternoon, filled Cecilia with envy, but slightly staggered her brother, who could not feel that a habit made of pale blue cloth, with epaulettes and frogs, à la Hussar, and sleeves braided half-way up the arm, would win approval from Miss Wraxton. Blue kid gloves and half-boots, a high-standing collar trimmed with lace, a muslin cravat, narrow lace ruffles at the wrists, and a tall-crowned hat, like a shako, with a peak over the eyes, and a plume of curled ostrich feathers completed this dashing toilette. The tightly fitting habit set off Sophy's magnificent figure to admiration, and from under the brim of her hat her brown locks curled quite charmingly; but Mr Rivenhall, appealed to by his sister to subscribe to her conviction that Sophy looked beautiful, merely bowed, and said that he was no judge of such matters.

However that might be, he was no mean judge of a horse, and when he set eyes on Salamanca, being walked up and down the road by John Potton, he did not withhold his praise, but said that he no longer wondered at Hubert's ecstasies. John Potton threw his mistress up into the saddle, and after allowing Salamanca to indulge his playfulness for a few moments Sophy brought him mincing up alongside Mr Rivenhall's bay hack, and they set off at a sedate pace in the direction of Hyde Park. Salamanca was inclined to resent the existence of sedan-chairs, dogs, crossing-sweepers, and took instant exception to a postman's horn, but Mr Rivenhall, accustomed to be on the alert to prevent misadventure when riding with Cecilia through London streets, knew better than to offer advice or assistance to his cousin. She was very well able to control her mount for herself, which, reflected Mr Rivenhall, was just as well, since Salamanca could scarcely have been described as an ideal horse for a lady.

This comment was made by Miss Wraxton, whom they found awaiting them, with her brother, within the gates of the Park. Miss Wraxton, after one glance at Sophy's habit, transferred her gaze

to Salamanca, and said: 'Oh, what a beautiful creature! But surely
he is a little too strong for you, Miss Stanton-Lacy? You should
commission Charles to find a well-mannered lady's horse for you
to ride.'

'I daresay he would be only too delighted, but I have discovered
that his notions and mine on *that* subject are widely separated,'
replied Sophy. 'Moreover, though he is a trifle spirited, there is
not an ounce of vice in Salamanca, and he has what the Duke calls
excellent bottom – has carried me for league upon dreary league
without a sign of flagging!' She leaned forward to pat Salamanca's
gleaming black neck. 'To be sure, he has not yet lashed out at the
end of a long day, which the Duke vows and declares Copenhagen
did, when he dismounted from his back after Waterloo, but I hold
that to be a virtue in him!'

'Indeed, yes!' said Miss Wraxton, ignoring the unbecoming
pretension shown by this careless reference to England's Hero.
'You will let me introduce my brother to you, Miss Stanton-
Lacy. Alfred!'

Mr Wraxton, a pallid young gentleman with a receding chin,
a loose, wet mouth, and a knowing look in his eyes, bowed, and
said he was happy to make Miss Stanton-Lacy's acquaintance. He
then asked her if she had been in Brussels at the time of the great
battle, and added that he had some idea of joining as a Volunteer
at the height of the scare. 'But from one cause and another nothing came of it,' he said. 'Do you know the Duke well? Quite the
great man, ain't he? But perfectly affable, they tell me. I daresay
you are on famous terms with him, for you knew him in Spain,
didn't you?'

'My dear Alfred,' interposed his sister, 'Miss Stanton-Lacy will
think you have less than common-sense if you talk such nonsense.
She will tell you that the Duke has more important things to think
of than all of us poor females who hold him in such admiration.'

Sophy looked rather amused. 'Well, no, I don't think I should say that,' she replied. 'But I was never one of his flirts, if that is what you mean, Mr Wraxton. I am not at all in his style, I assure you.'

'Shall we ride on?' suggested Miss Wraxton. 'You must tell me about your horse. Is he Spanish? Very handsome, but a little too nervous for my taste. But I am spoilt: my own dear Dorcas here is so very well-mannered.'

'Salamanca is not really nervous: he is merely funning,' said Sophy. 'As for manners, I hold him to be unequalled. Would you like to see me put him through his paces? Watch! He was Mameluke-trained, you know!'

'For heaven's sake, Sophy, not in the Park!' said Charles sharply.

She threw him one of her saucy smiles, and set Salamanca caracoling.

'Oh, pray be careful!' exclaimed Miss Wraxton. 'It is very dangerous! Charles, stop her! We shall have everyone staring at us!'

'You won't mind if I shake the fidgets out of his legs!' Sophy called. 'He is itching for a gallop!'

With that, she wheeled Salamanca about, and let him have his head down the stretch of tan that lay beside the carriage-road.

'Yoicks!' uttered Mr Wraxton, and set off in pursuit.

'My dear Charles, what is to be done with her?' said Miss Wraxton. 'Galloping in the Park, and in that habit, which I should blush to wear! I was never more shocked!'

'Yes,' he agreed, his eyes on the diminishing figure in the distance. 'But, by God, she can ride!'

'Of course, if you mean to encourage her in such pranks there is no more to be said.'

'I don't,' he replied briefly.

She was displeased, and said coldly: 'I must confess that I do not admire her style: I am reminded of nothing so much as the equestriennes at Astley's Amphitheatre. Shall we canter?'

In this sedate way they rode side by side down the tan until they saw Sophy galloping back to them, Mr Wraxton still in pursuit. Sophy reined in, wheeled, and fell in beside her cousin. 'How much I enjoyed that!' she said, her cheeks in a glow. 'I have not been on Salamanca's back for over a week. But tell me! Have I done wrong? So many prim persons stared as though they could not believe their eyes!'

'You should not ride in that neck-or-nothing fashion in the Park!' Charles replied. 'I should have warned you.'

'You should indeed! I was afraid it might be that. Never mind! I will be good now, and if anyone speaks of it to you, you will say that it is only your poor little cousin from Portugal, who has been so badly brought-up that there is no doing anything about it.' She leaned forward to speak across him to Miss Wraxton. 'I appeal to you, Miss Wraxton! You are a horsewoman. Is it not insupportable to be held down to a canter when you long to gallop for miles?'

'Most irksome,' agreed Miss Wraxton.

At this moment Alfred Wraxton rejoined them, calling out: 'By Jove, Miss Stanton-Lacy, you will take the shine out of them all! You are nothing to her, Eugenia!'

'We cannot go four abreast,' said Miss Wraxton, ignoring his remark. 'Charles, fall behind with Alfred! I cannot converse with Miss Stanton-Lacy across you.'

He complied with this request, and Miss Wraxton, bringing her mare alongside Salamanca, said with all the tact upon which she plumed herself: 'I am persuaded that you must find our London ways strange at first.'

'Why, I imagine they cannot differ greatly from those of Paris, or Vienna, or even Lisbon!' said Sophy.

'I have never visited those cities, but I believe – indeed I am sure! – that the tone of London is vastly superior,' said Miss Wraxton.

Her air of calm certainty struck Sophy as being so funny that she went into a peal of laughter. 'Oh, I beg your pardon!' she gasped. 'But it is so ridiculous, you know!'

'I expect it must seem so to you,' agreed Miss Wraxton, her calm quite unimpaired. 'I understand that a great deal of licence is permitted on the Continent to females. Here it is not so. Quite the reverse! To be thought bad *ton*, dear Miss Stanton-Lacy, would be very dreadful. I know that you will not take it amiss if I give you a hint. You will of course wish to attend the Assemblies at Almack's, for instance. I assure you, the veriest breath of criticism to reach the ears of the patronesses, and you may say farewell to any hope of obtaining a voucher from them. Tickets may not be purchased without a voucher, you know. It is most exclusive! The rules, too, are very strict, and must not be contravened by a hairsbreadth.'

'You terrify me,' said Sophy. 'Do you think I shall be blackballed?'

Miss Wraxton smiled. 'Hardly, since you will make your début under Lady Ombersley's aegis! She will no doubt tell you just how you should conduct yourself, if her health permits her to take you there. It is unfortunate that circumstances have prevented me from occupying that position which would have enabled me to have relieved her of such duties.'

'Forgive me!' interrupted Sophy, whose attention had been wandering, 'but I think Madam de Lieven is waving to me, and it would be very uncivil not to notice her!'

She rode off as she spoke, to where a smart barouche was drawn up beside the track, and leaned down from her saddle to shake the languid hand held up to her.

'Sophie!' pronounced the Countess. 'Sir Horace told me I should meet you here. You were galloping *ventre à terre*; never do so again! Ah, Mrs Burrell, permit me to present to you Miss Stanton-Lacy!'

The lady seated beside the Ambassador's wife bowed slightly, and

allowed her lips to relax into an infinitesimal smile. This expanded
a little when she observed Miss Wraxton, following in Sophy's
wake, and she inclined her head, a great mark of condescension.

Countess Lieven nodded to Miss Wraxton, but went on talking
to Sophy. 'You are staying with Lady Ombersley. I am a little
acquainted with her, and I shall call. She will spare you to me
perhaps one evening. You have not seen Princess Esterhazy yet, or
Lady Jersey? I shall tell them I have met you, and they will want
to hear how Sir Horace does. What did I promise Sir Horace I
would do? Ah, but of course! Almack's! I will send you a voucher,
ma chère Sophie, but do not gallop in Hyde Park.' She then told
her coachman to drive on, included the whole of Sophy's party in
her light, valedictory smile, and turned to continue her interrupted
conversation with Mrs Drummond Burrell.

'I was not aware that you were acquainted with the Countess
Lieven,' said Miss Wraxton.

'Do you dislike her?' Sophy asked, aware of the coldness in
Miss Wraxton's voice. 'Many people do, I know. Sir Horace calls
her the great *intriguante*, but she is clever, and can be very amusing. She has a *tendre* for him, as I daresay you have guessed. I like
Princess Esterhazy better myself, I own, and Lady Jersey better
than either of them, because she is so much more sincere, in spite
of that restless manner of hers.'

'Dreadful woman!' said Charles. 'She never stops talking! She is
known as Silence, in London.'

'Is she? Well, I am sure, if she knows it, she does not care a bit,
for she dearly loves a joke.'

'You are fortunate in knowing so many of the Patronesses of
Almack's,' observed Miss Wraxton.

Sophy gave her irrepressible chuckle. 'To be honest, I think my
good fortune lies in having such an accomplished flirt for a father!'

Mr Wraxton giggled at this, and his sister, dropping a little behind, brought her mare up on Mr Rivenhall's other side, and said in a low tone, under cover of some quizzing remark made to Sophy by Mr Wraxton: 'It is a pity that men will laugh when her liveliness betrays her into saying what cannot be thought becoming. It brings her too much into notice, and that, I fancy, is the root of the evil.'

He raised his brows. 'You are severe! Do you dislike her?'

'Oh, no, no!' she said quickly. 'It is merely that I have no great taste for that kind of sportive playfulness.'

He looked as though he would have liked to have said something more, but at this moment a very military-looking cavalcade came into sight, cantering easily towards them. It consisted of four gentlemen, whose dashing side-whiskers and soldierly bearing proclaimed their profession. They glanced idly at Mr Rivenhall's party. The next instant there was a shout, and a hurried reining-in, and one of the quartet exclaimed in ringing accents: 'By all that's wonderful, it's the Grand Sophy!'

Confusion and babel followed this, all four gentlemen pressing up to grasp Sophy's hand, and pelting her with questions. Where had she sprung from? how long had she been in England? why had they not been told of her arrival? how was Sir Horace?

'Oh, but, Sophy, you're a sight for sore eyes!' declared Major Quinton, who had first hailed her.

'You have Salamanca still! Lord, do you remember riding him through the Pyrenees when you nearly got snapped up by old Soult?'

'Sophy, what's your direction? Are you living in London now? Where's Sir Horace?'

She was laughing, trying to answer them all, while her horse sidled, and fidgeted, and tossed his head. 'Abroad. Never mind about me! What are you all doing in England? I thought you in France still! Don't tell me you have sold out!'

'Debenham has, lucky dog! I'm on furlough; Wolvey's sta-
tioned in England – what a thing it is to belong to the Gentleman's
Sons! – and Talgarth has become a great man, almost a Tiger! Yes,
I assure you! A.D.C. to the Duke of York. You notice the air of
consequence! But he is all condescension: not the least height in
his manner – yet!'

'Silence, rattle!' said his victim. He was rather older than his
companion, a handsome, dark man, with a decided air of fashion
and a languid manner. 'Dear Sophy, I am tolerably certain that you
cannot have been in London above many days. Not the smallest
rumour of any volcanic disturbance has come to my ears, and you
know how quick I am to get abreast of the news!'

She laughed. 'Oh, that is too bad of you, Sir Vincent! I don't
create disturbances: you know I don't!'

'I know nothing of the kind, my child. When last I saw you,
you were engaged in arranging in the most ruthless fashion
the affairs of the most bewildered family of Belgians I have yet
encountered. They had all my sympathy, but there was nothing I
could do to help them: I know my limitations.'

'Those poor Le Bruns! Well, but *someone* had to help them
out of such a tangle! I assure you, everything was settled *most*
satisfactorily! But come! I forget my manners in all this excitement! Miss Wraxton, do pray forgive me, and allow me to present
to you Colonel Sir Vincent Talgarth; and, beside him, Colonel
Debenham. And this is Major Titus Quinton, and – oh, dear,
ought I to have said your name first, Francis? it is one of the things
I never know, but no matter! – Captain Lord Francis Wolvey!
And this is my cousin, Mr Rivenhall. Oh, and Mr Wraxton, also!'

Miss Wraxton inclined her head politely; Mr Rivenhall,
bowing slightly to the rest of the party, addressed himself to Lord
Francis, saying: 'I don't think I ever met you, but your brother and
I were up at Oxford together.'

Lord Francis at once leaned forward in his saddle to shake him by the hand. 'Now I know who you are!' he announced. 'You are Charles Rivenhall! Thought I couldn't be mistaken! How do you do? Do you still box? Freddy was used to say he never knew an amateur with a more punishing right!'

Mr Rivenhall laughed. 'Did he? He felt it often enough, but I take no credit for that: he was always glaringly abroad!'

Major Quinton, who had been regarding him intently, said: 'Then that is very likely where I have seen you. Jackson's Saloon! You are the fellow Jackson says he might have made into a champion if only you had not been a gentleman!'

This remark naturally beguiled all three men in a sporting conversation. Mr Wraxton hung on the outskirts of it, occasionally interpolating a few words which no one paid any heed to; Sophy smiled benignly to see her friends and her cousin so happily absorbed; and Colonel Debenham, who had excellent manners, and a kind heart, began to make painstaking conversation to Miss Wraxton. By tacit consent, the military gentlemen turned to accompany Mr Rivenhall's party up the track, and the entire cavalcade moved forward at a walking-pace.

Sophy found that Sir Vincent had brought his horse up to walk beside hers, and said suddenly: 'Sir Vincent, you are the very man I need! Let us draw a little ahead!'

'Nothing in this life, enchanting Juno, could afford me more pleasure!' he instantly responded. 'I have no fancy for the Fancy. On no account tell anyone that I said that! It is quite unworthy of me! Are you about to transport me by accepting a heart laid often at your feet, and as often spurned? Something informs me that I indulge my optimism too far, and that you are going to demand of me some service that will plunge me into a morass of trouble, and end in my being cashiered.'

'Nothing of the sort!' declared Sophy. 'But I never knew

anyone, other than Sir Horace, whose judgement I would rather trust when it comes to buying a horse. Sir Vincent, I want to purchase a pair for my phaeton!'

They had by this time considerably outdistanced the rest of the party. Sir Vincent made his roan drop to a walk, and said brokenly: 'Allow me a moment in which to recover my manhood! So that is all the use you have for me!'

'Don't be so absurd!' said Sophy. 'What better use could I have for anyone?'

'Dear Juno, I have told you a great many times, and I shall tell you no more!'

'Sir Vincent,' said Sophy severely, 'you have dangled after every heiress who has come in your way from the day I first met you –'

'Shall I ever forget it? You had lost a front tooth, and torn your dress.'

'Very likely. Though I have not the least doubt that you don't recall the occasion at all, and have this instant made that up. You are a more hardened flirt even than Sir Horace, and you only offer for me because you know I shall not accept your suit. My fortune cannot be large enough to tempt you.'

'That,' acknowledged Sir Vincent, 'is true. But better men than I, my dear Sophy, have been known to cut their coats to suit their cloth.'

'Yes, but I am not your cloth, and you know very well that, indulgent though he may be, Sir Horace would never permit me to marry you, even if I wished to, which I do not.'

'Oh, very well!' sighed Sir Vincent. 'Let us talk of horse-flesh, then!'

'The thing is,' confided Sophy, 'that I was obliged to sell my carriage-horses when we left Lisbon, and Sir Horace had no time to attend to the matter before he sailed for Brazil. He said my cousin would advise me, but he was quite out! He will not.'

'Charles Rivenhall,' said Sir Vincent, looking at her from under drooping eyelids, 'is held to be no bad judge of a horse. What mischief are you brewing, Sophy?'

'None! He has said he will not stir in the matter, and also that it would be improper for me to visit Tattersall's. Is that true?'

'Well, it would certainly be unusual.'

'Then I won't do it: my aunt would be distressed, and she has enough to plague her already. Where else can I buy a pair that will suit me?'

He gazed meditatively ahead between his horse's ears. 'I wonder if you would care to buy two of Manningtree's breakdowns before they come into the open market?' he said presently. 'Quite done-up, poor fellow, and is selling off all his cattle. What's your figure, Sophy?'

'Sir Horace told me not above four hundred, unless I saw a pair it would be a crime not to buy.'

'Manningtree would sell you his match bays for less than that. As handsome a pair as you could wish for: I should buy them myself if I had a feather to fly with.'

'Where may I see them?'

'Leave that to me: I'll arrange it. What's your direction?'

'At Lord Ombersley's house in Berkeley Square: that big one, at the corner!'

'Of course. So he is your uncle, is he?'

'No, but his wife is my aunt.'

'And Charles Rivenhall is therefore your cousin. Well, well! How do you contrive to amuse yourself, my Sophy?'

'I own, I did wonder how I should do so, but I find that the whole family is in a sad tangle, poor dears, and I do hope I may be able to make them more comfortable!'

'I have no particular liking for your uncle, who is one of my esteemed Chief's cronies; on the only occasion when I solicited your beautiful cousin Cecilia to dance with me at Almack's, her forbidding brother forestalled me in a fashion as swift as it was crude – someone ought to tell him that I am only interested in heiresses; and yet my withers are strangely wrung! Almost my heart goes out to the family. Do they tread blindly towards their doom, Sophy, or did they willingly receive a firebrand into their midst?'

She gave a chuckle. 'They tread blindly – but I am *not* a firebrand!'

'No, I used the wrong word. You are like poor Whinyates's rockets: no one knows what you will do next!'

Six

'Is the knocker never still?' demanded Charles of his mother, after the departure of the fourth morning-caller in one day.

'Never!' she replied proudly. 'Since that day when you took dear Sophy riding in the Park, I have received seven gentlemen – no, eight, counting Augustus Fawnhope. Princess Esterhazy, the Countess Lieven, Lady Jersey, and Lady Castlereagh have all left cards; and –'

'Was Talgarth amongst those who called, ma'am?'

She wrinkled her brow. 'Talgarth? Oh, yes! A most amiable man, with side-whiskers! To be sure he was!'

'Take care!' he warned her. '*That* connection will not do!'

She was startled. 'Charles, what can you mean? He seems to be on terms of great friendship with Sophy, and she told me Sir Horace had been acquainted with him for years!'

'I daresay, but if my uncle means to bestow Sophy upon him he is not the man I take him for! He is said to be a gazetted fortune-hunter; and is, besides, a gamester, with more debts than expectations, and such libertine propensities as scarcely render him a desirable catch in the marriage mart!'

'Oh, dear!' said Lady Ombersley, dismayed. She wondered

whether she ought to tell her son that his cousin had gone out driving with Sir Vincent only a day earlier, and decided that no purpose could be served in dwelling on what was past. 'Perhaps I should drop a hint in Sophy's ear.'

'I doubt of its being well-received, ma'am. Eugenia has already spoken with her on this subject. All that my cousin saw fit to reply was that she was quite up to snuff, and would engage not to allow herself to be seduced by Sir Vincent, or anyone else.'

'Oh, *dear!*' said Lady Ombersley again. 'She really should not say such things!'

'Just so, ma'am!'

'But, though I do not wish to offend you, Charles, I cannot help feeling that perhaps it was not quite wise of Eugenia to have spoken to her on such a subject. You know, my dear, she is not in any way related to Sophy!'

'Only Eugenia's strong sense of duty,' he said stiffly, 'and, I may add, Mama, her earnest desire to spare you anxiety, induced her to undertake a task which she felt to be excessively unpleasant.'

'It is very kind of her, I am sure,' said his mother, in a depressed voice.

'Where is my cousin?' he asked abruptly.

She brightened, for to this question she was able to return an unexceptionable answer. 'She has gone for a drive in the barouche with Cecilia and your brother.'

'Well, that should be harmless enough,' he said.

He would have been less satisfied on this point had he known that, having taken up Mr Fawnhope, whom they encountered in Bond Street, the occupants of the barouche were at that moment in Longacre, critically inspecting sporting vehicles. There were a great many of these, together with almost every variety of carriage, on view at the warehouse to which Hubert had conducted his cousin, and although Sophy remained firm in her preference for a phaeton,

Cecilia was much taken with a caned whiskey, and Hubert, having fallen in love with a curricle, forcibly urged his cousin to buy it. Mr Fawnhope, appealed to for his opinion, was found to be missing, and was presently discovered seated in rapt contemplation of a state berlin, which looked rather like a very large breakfast-cup poised upon elongated springs. It was covered with a domed roof, bore a great deal of gilding, and had a coachman's seat perched over the front wheels which was covered in blue velvet with a gold fringe. 'Cinderella!' said Mr Fawnhope simply.

The manager of the warehouse said that he did not think the berlin – which he kept for show purposes – was quite what the lady was looking for.

'A coach for a princess,' said Mr Fawnhope, unheeding. 'This, Cecilia, is what you must drive in. You shall have six white horses to draw it, with plumes on their heads, and blue harness.'

Cecilia had no fault to find with this programme, but reminded him that they had come to help Sophy to choose a sporting carriage. He allowed himself to be dragged away from the berlin, but when asked to cast his vote between the curricle and the phaeton, would only murmur: *'What can little T.O. do? Why, drive a phaeton and two! Can little T.O. do no more? Yes, drive a phaeton and four!'*

'That's all very well,' said Hubert impatiently, 'but my cousin ain't Tommy Onslow, and for my part I think she will do better with this curricle!'

'You cannot scan the lines, yet they have a great deal of merit,' said Mr Fawnhope. 'How beautiful is the curricle! How swift! How splendid! Yet Apollo chose a phaeton. These carriages bewilder me: let us go away!'

'Who is Tommy Onslow? Does he indeed drive a phaeton-and-four?' asked Sophy, her eyes kindling. 'Now, that would be something indeed! What a bore that I have just bought a pair! I could never match them, I fear.'

'You could borrow Charles's grays,' suggested Hubert, grinning wickedly. 'By Jupiter, what a kick-up there would be!'

Sophy laughed, but shook her head. 'No, it would be an infamous thing to do! I shall purchase that phaeton: I have quite made up my mind.'

The manager looked startled, for the carriage she pointed at was not the phaeton he had supposed she would buy – an elegant vehicle, perfectly suited to a lady – but a high-perch model, with huge hind-wheels, and the body, which was hung directly over the front-axle, fully five feet from the ground. However, it was not his business to dissuade a customer from making an expensive purchase, so he bowed, and kept his inevitable reflections to himself.

Hubert, less tactful, said: 'I say, Sophy, it really ain't a lady's carriage! I only hope you may not overturn it round the first corner!'

'Not I!'

'Cecilia,' suddenly pronounced Mr Fawnhope, who had been studying the phaeton intently, 'must never ride in that vehicle!'

He spoke with such unaccustomed decision that everyone looked at him in surprise, and Cecilia turned quite pink with gratification at his solicitude.

'I assure you, I shan't overturn it,' said Sophy.

'Every feeling would be outraged by the sight of so exquisite a creature in such a turn-out as that!' pursued Mr Fawnhope. 'Its proportions are absurd! It was, moreover, built for excessive speed, and should be driven, if driven it must be, by some down-the-road man with fifteen capes and a spotted neckcloth. It is not for Cecilia!'

'Well!' exclaimed Sophy. 'I thought you were afraid I might overturn her in it!'

'I am afraid of that,' replied Mr Fawnhope. 'The very thought of so ungraceful a happening must offend! It *does* offend! It intrudes its grossness upon the sensibilities; it blurs my vision of a porcelain nymph! Let us immediately leave this place!'

Cecilia, wavering between pleasure at hearing herself likened to a porcelain nymph, and affront at having her safety so little regarded, merely said that they could not leave until Sophy had concluded her purchase; but Sophy, a good deal amused, suggested that she should withdraw with her swain to await her in the barouche.

'Y'know,' Hubert said confidentially, when the pair had departed, 'I don't know that I blame Charles for not being able to stomach that fellow! He is quite paltry!'

Within three days of this transaction, Mr Rivenhall, exercising his grays in the Park, paused by the Riding House to take up his friend, Mr Wychbold, sauntering along in all the glory of pale yellow pantaloons, shining Hessians, and a coat of extravagant cut and delicate hue. 'Good God!' he ejaculated. 'What a devilish sight! Get up, Cyprian, and stop ogling all the females! Where have you been hiding yourself this age?'

Mr Wychbold mounted into the curricle, disposing his shapely limbs with rare grace, and replied, with a sigh: 'The call of duty, dear boy! Visiting the ancestral home! I do what I may with lavender-water, but the aroma of the stables and cow-byres is hard to overcome. Charles, much as I love you if I had *seen* that neck-cloth before I consented to let you drive me round the Park – !'

'Don't waste that stuff on me!' recommended his friend. 'What's wrong with your chestnuts?'

Mr Wychbold, one of the shining lights of the Four-Horse Club, sighed mournfully. 'Dead lame! No, not both, but one, which is quite as bad. Would you believe it? I let my sister drive them! Take it as a maxim, Charles, that no woman is to be trusted to handle the ribbons!'

'You haven't yet met my cousin,' replied Mr Rivenhall, with a twisted smile.

'You are mistaken,' said Mr Wychbold calmly. 'I met her at the

Gala night at Almack's, which, dear boy, you might have known, had you not absented yourself from that gathering.'

'Oh, you did, did you? I have no turn for that form of insipidity.'

'Wouldn't have done you any good if you had,' said Mr Wychbold. 'There was no getting near your cousin; at least, there wouldn't have been for you. *I* managed it, but I have a great deal of address. Danced the boulanger with her. Devilish fine girl!'

'Well, it's time you were thinking of getting married: offer for her! I shall be much obliged to you.'

'Almost anything else for your sake, dear boy, but I ain't a marrying man!' said Mr Wychbold firmly.

'I wasn't serious. To be honest with you, if you took such a notion into your head I should do my utmost to dissuade you. She is the most tiresome girl I ever hope to meet. The only thing I know to her credit is that she can drive to an inch. She had the damned impertinence to steal my curricle when my back was turned for five minutes.'

'She drove these grays?' demanded Mr Wychbold.

'She did. Well up to their bits, too. All to force me into buying a phaeton-and-pair for her to lionize in! I shan't do it, but I should rather like to see how she would handle such a turn-out.'

'No wish to raise false hopes,' said Mr Wychbold, who had been watching the approach of a dashing perch-phaeton, 'but can't help thinking that that's just what you're about to do, dear fellow! Though why your cousin should be driving Manningtree's bays beats me!'

'What?' ejaculated Mr Rivenhall sharply. His incredulous gaze fell upon the phaeton, coming towards him at a smart trot. Very much at home in the perilous vehicle, seated high above her horses, with her groom beside her, and holding her whip at exactly the correct angle, was Miss Stanton-Lacy, and if the sight afforded Mr Rivenhall pleasure he vouchsafed no sign whatever of this. He looked at first thunderstruck, and then more than usually grim. As the pace of the bays slackened, and dropped to a walk, he reined in his own pair. The two carriages came to a halt abreast of each other.

'Cousin Charles!' said Sophy. 'And Mr Wychbold! How do you do? Tell me, cousin, what do you think of them? I am persuaded I have a bargain in them.'

'Where,' demanded Mr Rivenhall, 'did you get those horses?'

'Now, Charles, for the lord's sake don't be bird-witted!' implied Mr Wychbold, preparing to descend from the curricle. 'You must see she has Manningtree's match-geldings there! Besides, I told you so, a minute ago. But how is this, Miss Stanton-Lacy? Is Manningtree selling up?'

'So I believe,' she smiled.

'By Jove, you have stolen a march on me, then, for I have had my eye on that pair ever since Manningtree sprang 'em on the town! How did you get wind of it, ma'am?'

'To own the truth, I knew nothing about the matter,' she confessed. 'It was Sir Vincent Talgarth who put me in the way of buying them.'

'That fellow!' interpolated Mr Rivenhall explosively. 'I might have known!'

'Yes, so you might,' she agreed. 'He is quite famous for knowing all the news before others have heard even a rumour. May I take you up, Mr Wychbold? If I have stolen a march on you, the least amends I can make is to offer to let you drive my pair.'

'Don't hesitate to tell me which of my mother's or my horses you would like me to remove from the stables to make room for these!' begged Mr Rivenhall, with savage civility. 'Unless, of course, you are setting up your own stables!'

'Dear Cousin Charles, I hope I know better than to put you to such shocking inconvenience! John Potton here has seen to all that.

You are not to be troubled with my horses! Get down, John: you need not fear to let Mr Wychbold have your place, for if the horses should bolt with me he is better fitted to get them under control again then either of us.'

The middle-aged groom, having favoured Mr Wychbold with a long scrutiny, appeared to be satisfied, for he obeyed without making any comment. Mr Wychbold leaped up lightly into the phaeton; Sophy nodded farewell to her cousin; and the bays moved forward. Mr Rivenhall watched the phaeton smoulderingly for a moment to two, and then lowered his gaze to the groom's countenance. 'What the devil were you about to let your mistress buy a damned dangerous carriage like that?' he demanded.

'Don't you put yourself in a pucker over Miss Sophy, sir!' said John, in a fatherly way. 'Sir Horace himself couldn't stop her, not when she's got the bit between her teeth! Many's the time I've told Sir Horace he should have broke her to bridle, but he never done it, nor tried to.'

'Well, if I have much more –' Mr Rivenhall pulled himself up short, realizing how improper was this interchange. 'Damn your impudence!' he said, and set his grays in motion with a plunge that betrayed the state of his temper.

Mr Wychbold, meanwhile, was most gallantly refusing to take the reins from Miss Stanton-Lacy. 'Dashed if I ever thought I should say so, but it's a pleasure to be driven by a lady who handles 'em as well as you do, ma'am! Very sweet-goers, too: shouldn't be surprised if Charles had had his eye on 'em, which would account for him flying into one of his miffs.'

'No, no, I am sure you wrong him! He has flown into a miff because I bought them against his advice – indeed, in the face of his prohibition! Do you know my cousin well, sir?'

'Known him since we were at Eton.'

'Then tell me! Has he *always* wanted to rule the roast?'

Mr Wychbold considered this, but arrived at no very exact conclusion. 'Well, I don't know,' he said. 'Always one to take the lead, of course, but a man don't come the ruler over his friends, ma'am. At least…' He paused, recalling past incidents. 'Thing is, he's got an awkward temper, but he's a dashed good friend!' he produced. 'Told him times out of mind he ought to watch that devilish unpleasant tongue of his, but the fact is, ma'am, there's no one I'd liefer go to in a fix than Charles Rivenhall!'

'That is a tribute indeed,' she said thoughtfully.

Mr Wychbold coughed deprecatingly. 'Never mentioned the matter to me, of course, but the poor fellow's had a deal to bear, if the half of what one hears is true. Turned him sour. Often thought so! Though why the deuce he must needs get himself engaged to that —' He broke off in considerable confusion. 'Forgotten what I was going to say!' he added hastily.

'Then that settles it!' said Sophy, dropping her hands slightly, and allowing the bays to quicken their pace.

'Settles what?' asked Mr Wychbold.

'Why, Cecilia told me that you were his particular friend, and if *you* think it will not do I need have no scruples. Only fancy, Mr Wychbold, what misery for my dear aunt and those poor children to have that Friday-faced creature setting them all to rights! Living under the same roof, and, you may depend upon it, encouraging Charles to be as disagreeable as he can stare!'

'It don't bear thinking of!' said Mr Wychbold, much struck.

'It must be thought of!' replied Sophy resolutely.

'No use thinking of it,' said Mr Wychbold, shaking his head. 'Betrothal puffed in all the papers weeks ago! Would have been married by now if the girl hadn't had to put up a black ribbon. Very good match, of course: woman of quality, handsome dowry, I daresay, excellent connections!'

'Well,' said Sophy large-mindedly, 'if his *heart* is in the business,

I suppose he must be permitted to have his way, but he shall *not* inflict her upon his family! But I do not think his heart has had anything to say in it, and as for her, she has none! There! That is cutting up a character indeed!'

Mr Wychbold, stirred to enthusiasm, said in a confidential tone: 'Know what, ma'am? Been on the Marriage Mart for two whole years! Fact! Set her cap at Maxstoke last year, but he sheered off. Odds shortened to evens, too, in the clubs, but he got clean away.' He sighed. 'Charles won't. In the Gazette, you know: poor fellow couldn't declare off now if he wanted to!'

'No,' agreed Sophy, her brow creased. '*She* could, however.'

'She *could*, but she won't,' said Mr Wychbold positively.

'We'll see!' said Sophy. 'At all events, I must and I will prevent her making those poor dears miserable! For that is what she does, I assure you! She is for ever coming to Berkeley Square, and casting everyone into the dumps! First it is my aunt, who goes to bed with the head-ache when she has had the creature with her for half an hour; then it is Miss Adderbury, to whom she says the horridest things in that odiously sweet voice she uses when she means to make mischief! She wonders that Miss Adderbury should not have taught the children to read Italian. She is surprised that she makes so little use of the backboard, and tells Charles that she fears little Amabel is growing to be round-shouldered! *Stuff!* She is trying even to persuade him to take their monkey away from the children. But what is worse than all is that she sets him against poor Hubert! That I cannot forgive! She does it in such a shabby way, too! I do not know how I kept my hands from her ears yesterday, for the silly boy had on a new waistcoat – quite dreadful, but he was so proud of it! – and what must she do but draw Charles's attention to it, pretending to chaff Hubert, you know, but contriving to make it appear that he was for ever buying new clothes, and squandering away his allowance on fripperies!'

'What a devilish woman!' exclaimed Mr Wychbold. 'Must say I shouldn't have expected Charles to take that kind of thing tamely! Never one to stand interference!'

'Oh, it is all done with such seeming solicitude that he doesn't see what lies at the root of it – yet!' said Sophy.

'Very bad business,' said Mr Wychbold. 'Nothing to be done, though.'

'That,' said Sophy severely, 'is what people always say when they are too lazy, or perhaps too timorous, to make a push to be helpful! I have a great many faults, but I am not lazy, and I am not timorous – though *that*, I know, is not a virtue, for I was born without any nerves at all, my father tells me, and almost no sensibility. I don't know that I shall, for I have not yet made up my mind just what I should do, but I *may* need your assistance in breaking this foolish engagement.' She perceived, in a quick glance at his face, that he was looking extremely scared, and added reassuringly: 'Very likely not, but one never knows, and it is always well to be prepared. Now I must put you down, for I see Cecilia awaiting me, and she has promised to let me drive her round the Park once she is assured I shan't overturn the phaeton.'

'No fear of that!' said Mr Wychbold, wondering what else this alarming young woman might overturn during her sojourn in Berkeley Square.

He shook hands, told her that if they would but allow females to belong to the Four-Horse Club he should certainly support her candidature, and sprang down from the phaeton, to exchange greetings with Cecilia, who, with Miss Adderbury and the children, were waiting beside the Drive. Gertrude, Amabel, and Theodore naturally asserted their claims to be taken up beside their cousin in preference to their elder sister, but after these had been firmly dealt with Mr Wychbold helped Cecilia to mount into the carriage, bowed, and strolled off.

It had struck Sophy immediately that Cecilia was looking pale, while the little governess was plainly labouring under a considerable degree of suppressed agitation; so, since she believed in getting to the root of any matter without wasting time on circumlocution, she at once demanded bluntly: 'Now, why are you looking as blue as a megrim, Cecy?'

Tina, who during Mr Wychbold's occupation of the passenger's seat, had nestled inconspicuously behind her mistress's feet, now crawled out from beneath the drab rug, and jumped on to Cecilia's knee. Cecilia clasped her mechanically, and stroked her, but said in a tense voice: 'Eugenia!'

'Oh, the deuce take that creature!' exclaimed Sophy. 'Now what has she done?'

'She was walking here with Alfred,' said Cecilia, 'and she came upon us!'

'Well,' said Sophy reasonably, 'I own I do not like her, and Alfred is certainly the horridest little beast in nature, but I see nothing in that to put you so much out of countenance! He cannot have tried to put his arm round your waist if his sister was present!'

'Oh, Alfred – !' said Cecilia contemptuously. 'Not but what he *would* have me take his arm, and then squeezed it in the most odious way, and ogled, and said all the sort of things that make one itch to slap his face. But I care nothing for *him*! You see, Sophy, Augustus was with me!'

'Well?' said Sophy.

'It is true that we had fallen a little way behind Addy, for how can one have any rational conversation with the children chattering all the time? But she was *not* out of sight, and we had *not* stolen down a lonely path – at least, it wasn't one of the more frequented paths, but Addy was there all the time, so what could it signify? – and to say that I was meeting Augustus *clandestinely* is wickedly unjust! Anyone would suppose him to be some hateful adventurer, instead of someone I have known all my life, pretty well! Why shouldn't he walk in the Park? and if he does so, and we meet, pray, why should I not talk to him?'

'No reason at all. Did that repellent girl give you a scold?'

'Not me so much as poor Addy. She is in despair, for Eugenia seems to have said she was betraying Mama's trust, and encouraging me in clandestine behaviour. She was quite odious to me, but she could not say anything very much, because Augustus was with me. She made him walk with her instead, and told Alfred to give me his arm, and I felt smirched, Sophy, *smirched*!'

'Anyone would, who was obliged to take Alfred's arm,' agreed Sophy.

'Not that! But Eugenia's manner! As though she had found me out in something disgraceful! And that is not the worst! Charles is driving here, and not a moment before you came up he went past us with Eugenia seated beside him. He gave the coldest look! She has told him all about it, depend upon it, and now he will be furious with me, and very likely work upon Mama as well, and everything will be so dreadful!'

'No, it won't,' said Sophy coolly. 'In fact, I shouldn't be at all surprised if this turned out to be a very good thing. I cannot explain all that to you now, but I do beg of you, Cecy, not to be so distressed! There is no need: I assure you there is none! Very likely Charles will not say a word to you about this.'

Cecilia turned incredulous eyes towards her. 'Charles not say a word! You don't know him! He was looking like a thunder-cloud!'

'I daresay he was; he very often does, and you are such a goose that you instantly quake like a blancmange,' replied Sophy. 'Presently, I shall set you down, and you will join poor little Addy, and continue your walk. I shall go home, where I am pretty sure to find your brother, for we have driven right round the Park now, and seen no sign of him, and I know he will go back to Berkeley

Square, for I heard him mention to my uncle that somebody called Eckington would be calling there at five o'clock.'

'Papa's agent,' said Cecilia listlessly. 'And I don't see, dearest Sophy, what it signifies, whether you find Charles at home or not, because he won't speak of this to you: why should he?'

'Oh, won't he just?' retorted Sophy. 'Depend upon it, by this time he will have persuaded himself that everything has been my fault from start to finish! Besides, he is furious with me for having bought this turn-out without his help; yes, and for having hired a stable of my own, too! He must be longing for me to come back to the house so that he can quarrel with me without fear of interruption. Poor man! I think I should put you down at once, Cecy.'

'How brave you are!' Cecilia said wonderingly. 'I do not know how you can bear it!'

'What, your brother's tantrums? I see nothing to be afraid of in them!'

Cecilia shuddered. 'It is not being afraid precisely, but I dread people being angry, and thundering at me! I cannot help it, Sophy, and I know it is poor-spirited of me, but my knees shake so, and I feel quite sick!'

'Well, they shan't be made to shake today,' said Sophy cheerfully. 'I am going to spike Charles's guns. Oh, see! There is Francis Wolvey! The very thing! He shall restore you to Addy for me.'

She drew up as she spoke, and Lord Francis, who had been chatting to two ladies in a landaulet, came up to the phaeton, exclaiming: 'Sophy, that's a capital turn-out! 'Servant, Miss Rivenhall! I wonder to see you trust yourself to such a madcap, I do indeed! She overturned me in a gig once. A *gig*!'

'What an unhandsome thing to say!' said Sophy indignantly. 'As though I could have helped it on such a road. Frenada! Oh, dear, what a long time ago it seems, to be sure! I came up with Sir Horace, and stayed with Mrs – Mrs –'

'Scovell,' supplied Lord Francis. 'She was the only lady living at Headquarters that winter, and used to hold loo-parties. Do you remember?'

'Of course I do! And more vividly still the fleas in that dreadful village! Francis, I must pick up John Potton, and be off: will you escort my cousin to meet her little brother and sisters? They are walking with their governess somewhere beside the Drive.'

Lord Francis, upon whom Cecilia's beauty had made a great impression, when he had met her on the occasion of his calling in Berkeley Square, promptly said that nothing could give him more pleasure, and reached up his hands to help her down from the phaeton. He said that he hoped that they would not too speedily encounter the schoolroom-party, and Cecilia, not impervious to his easy, friendly address, and evident admiration, began to look more cheerful. Sophy, well-satisfied, saw them walk off together, and drove on to where her groom awaited her, by the Stanhope Gate. He reported that he had watched Mr Rivenhall pass through it not many minutes earlier, and added, with a dry chuckle, that he looked to be on his high ropes still. 'Damned my impudence Miss Sophy, and fair jobbed at the grays' mouths!'

'Why, what had you said to enrage him?'

'All I said was you hadn't never been broke to bridle, missie, and what with him being in agreement with me, and not able to say so, there was nothing for it but to damn me and drive off. *I* don't blame him! Hot at hand, Miss Sophy, that's what you are!'

Upon her arrival in Berkeley Square, Sophy found that Mr Rivenhall had only just entered the house, having walked round from the mews. He was still wearing his caped driving-coat, and had paused by the table in the hall to pick up and read a note which had been sent by one of his friends. He looked up frowningly as Dassett admitted Sophy, but he did not speak. Tina, who had developed (her mistress considered) an ill-judged passion for his society, frisked gaily up to him, and employed every art known to her to attract his attention. He did indeed glance down at her, but so far from encouraging her advances, said curtly: 'Quiet!'

'Ah, so you are in before me!' remarked Sophy, pulling off her gloves. 'Now, give me your candid opinion of those bays! Mr Wychbold fancies you may have had an eye upon them yourself. Is that so?'

'Quite above my touch, cousin!' he replied.

'No, really? I gave four hundred guineas for them, and think I have a bargain.'

'Were you serious when you gave me to understand that you have set up your own stable?' he demanded.

'Certainly I was serious. A pretty thing it would be if my aunt were obliged to bear the charge of my horses! Besides, I may very likely purchase two more, if I can find a couple to match the bays. I am told that it is all the crack to drive a phaeton-and-four, though I suppose that would mean altering the shafts, which would be a bore.'

'I have no control over your actions, cousin,' he said coldly. 'No doubt if it seems good to you to make a spectacle of yourself in the Park, you will do so. But you will not, if you please, take any of my sisters up beside you!'

'But it doesn't please me,' she said. 'I have already taken Cecilia for a turn round the Drive. You have very antiquated notions, have you not? I saw several excessively smart sporting carriages being driven by ladies of the highest *ton!*'

'I have no particular objection to a phaeton-and-pair,' he said, still more coldly, 'though a perch model is quite unsuited to a lady. You will forgive me if I tell you that there is something more than a little fast in such a style of carriage.'

'Now, who in the world can have been spiteful enough to have put that idea into your head?' wondered Sophy.

He flushed, but did not answer.

'Did you see Cecilia?' asked Sophy. 'She was looking quite ravishing in that new hat your Mama was so clever as to choose for her!'

'I did see Cecilia,' he replied grimly. 'What is more, I, like you, cousin, know just how she had been spending her time! I am going to be extremely plain with you!'

'If you wish to be extremely plain with me,' she interrupted, 'come into the library! It is quite improper in you to be talking of family matters where you may be overheard. Besides, I have something of a decidedly delicate nature to say to you.'

He strode at once to the door into the library, and flung it open. She went past him into the room, and he followed her, shutting the door behind him too soon for Tina, who was left on the other side. This made it necessary for him to open it again, Tina's orders to him to do so being at once shrill and imperative. This trifling anti-climax did nothing to improve his temper, and it was with a very unpleasant edge to his voice that he said: 'We will take the gloves off, Cousin Sophy! Whether or not it was you who arranged an assignation in the Park for my sister with young Fawnhope, I am well aware that you —'

'Isn't Cecilia dashing?' said Sophy approvingly. 'She walked with Fawnhope, and then with Alfred Wraxton, and I left her with Lord Francis! And that, dear Cousin Charles, is what I wanted to speak to you about! Far, *far* be it from me to interfere in the affairs of your family, but I think I ought perhaps to give you a hint. I know it is awkward for you, situated as you are, but you will know how to drop a word in Cecy's ear.'

He was thrown out of his stride by this unexpected gambit, and stared at her. 'What the devil are you talking about?'

'I don't entirely care to mention it,' said Sophy mendaciously, 'but you know how fond I am of Cecy! Then, too, I have been

about the world, and have learnt to take care of myself. Cecy is
such an innocent! There is not a particle of harm in Augustus
Fawnhope, and Francis Wolvey is by far too great a gentleman
to go beyond the line. But you should not encourage so lovely a
girl as your sister to stroll about the Park with the Dishonourable
Alfred, Charles!'

He was so much taken aback that for a moment he did not say
a word. Then he demanded an explanation.

'He is the kind of odious little toad who kisses the housemaids
on the stairs,' replied Sophy frankly.

'My sister is not a housemaid!'

'No, and I do trust she will know how to keep him at arm's
length.'

'May I know whether you have the slightest grounds for bringing this charge against Wraxton?'

'If you mean, have I seen him kiss a housemaid, no, dear
Charles, I have not. If, on the other hand, you mean, has he tried
to kiss me, yes, dear Charles, he has. In this very room, too.'

He looked angry and mortified. 'I am extremely sorry that you
should have been annoyed in such a fashion under this roof,' he
said, getting the words out with an effort.

'Oh, don't mind it! I told you I was able to take care of myself.
But I doubt whether anyone could prevent his – his squeezing and
stroking habits, or convince him that the style of his conversation
is quite improper.'

She had been taking off her pelisse as she spoke, and she now
laid it aside, and sat down on a winged chair beside the fireplace.
After a moment he said, in a milder tone: 'I shall not pretend that I
have any liking for Wraxton, for I have not. So far as it lies within
my power I shall certainly discourage his visits to this house. My
situation is, however, as you said yourself, awkward. I would not,
upon any account, have this come to Miss Wraxton's ears.'

'No, indeed!' she said warmly. 'For you to be telling tales of her brother to Miss Wraxton would be the shabbiest thing!'

He was leaning his arm along the mantelpiece, and had been looking down into the fire, but at that he raised his head and shot a penetrating glance at Sophy. She thought there was a good deal of comprehension in his eyes, but he only said: 'Just so, cousin.'

'Do not refine too much upon it!' she advised him kindly. 'I do not mean to say that Cecy has a *tendre* for him, for she thinks him even more odious than I do.'

'I am well aware that she has no *tendre* for him, I thank you!' he retorted. 'She is infatuated with that puppy, Fawnhope!'

'Of course she is,' said Sophy.

'I am also aware that you have made it your business from the day you entered this house to encourage this folly by every means within your reach! You and Cecilia have been constantly seen in Fawnhope's company; you pretended he was a friend of yours so that he might have an excuse for calling here six days out of the seven; you —'

'In a word, Charles, I have thrown them continually together. I have, and if you had a grain of sense you would have done so weeks before I came to town!'

He was arrested for a moment, and then asked incredulously: 'Do you imagine by doing so you will cure Cecilia? Or that I am likely to believe you have any such intention in mind?'

'Well, I don't know,' she answered, giving the matter some thought. 'One of two things must happen, you know. Either she will grow weary of Augustus — and I must say I do think that very probable, because although he is so handsome, and can be very engaging when he chooses, he is shockingly tiresome, besides forgetting Cecilia's existence just when he should be most solicitous — or she will continue to love him, in spite of his faults. And if that happens, Charles, you will know that it is not an infatuation, and you will be obliged to consent to their marriage.'

'Never!' he said, with considerable violence.

'But you will,' she insisted. 'It would be wicked to try to force her into another marriage, and you would be cruel to attempt it.'

'I shall not force her into any marriage!' he flashed. 'It may interest you to know that I am extremely attached to Cecilia, and that it is for that reason, and not for any whim of my own, that I will not countenance her union with a man of Fawnhope's stamp! As for this glib notion you have that by throwing them together you will make Cecilia tire of him, you were never more mistaken! So far from tiring of his company, Cecilia seizes every opportunity to be alone with him! She is even so lost to all sense of propriety as to make Addy her dupe! Only this afternoon Miss Wraxton came upon her in a secluded path in the Park, alone with Fawnhope, having shaken off the restraint of Addy's presence. Clandestine meetings! Pretty behaviour in Miss Rivenhall of Ombersley, upon my word!'

'My dear Charles,' said Sophy, with unimpaired calm, 'you know very well that you are making that up.'

'I am doing no such thing! Do you imagine I would *make up* such a tale about my sister?'

'To own the truth, I think you would do anything when you are in one of your rages,' she said, smiling. 'There is no secret about her having walked with Fawnhope, but the rest of it springs from your disordered temper. Now, do not say that Miss Wraxton told you it was so, because I am sure she would never have told you such fibs about Cecilia! Shaken Addy off, indeed! She was never out of Addy's sight for a moment! Good gracious, don't you know Cecilia better than to be accusing her of clandestine behaviour? What a very vulgar expression to use, to be sure! Do stop making such a cake of yourself! Next you will be ranting at

Cecy for having allowed a respectable young man whom she has known, I daresay, since they were both children, to walk a little way beside her, under the eye of her governess!'

Again she came under that hard scrutiny. 'Do you know this for a fact?' he asked, in an altered tone.

'Certainly I do, for Cecy told me just what had occurred. It seems that Miss Wraxton said something to Addy which distressed her very much – no doubt she misunderstood it! Miss Wraxton perhaps felt that Addy should have sent Augustus about his business, though how she could have done so I hardly know! But she has a great deal of sensibility, you know, and is readily upset.'

He looked annoyed, and said: 'Addy is not to be blamed; Cecilia is out of her control, and if she should have told my mother of these meetings – well, she was never one to carry tales of any of us!'

She said coaxingly: 'Do show her that you are not angry with her, Charles, and don't mean to turn her off after all these years!'

'Turn her off?' he echoed, astonished. 'What nonsense is this, pray?'

'Exactly what I said to her! Only she has taken it into her head that she is too old-fashioned in her ways to instruct the children, and seems to think she should be able to teach them the Italian tongue, and all sorts of refinements of the same nature.'

There was a slight pause. Mr Rivenhall sat down on the other side of the fireplace, and rather absently began to pull Tina's ears. He was frowning, and presently said, at his curtest: 'I have nothing whatsoever to say in the education of my sisters. It is my mother's business, and I cannot conceive how it could ever belong to anyone else.'

Sophy saw no need to labour this point, and merely agreed with him. He cast her a glance out of narrowed, searching eyes, but she preserved her countenance. He said: 'None of this has anything to do with what I have been saying to you. We did very well, cousin, before you began to turn this house upside-down! I shall be obliged to you if, in the future –'

'Why, what in the world have I done else?' she exclaimed.

He found himself quite unable to put into words the things that she had done, and was obliged to fall back upon her only tangible crime. 'You brought that monkey here, for one thing!' he said. 'No doubt with the kindest of intentions! But it is a most unsuitable animal to have bestowed on the children, and now, of course, they will think themselves ill-used when it is got rid of, as got rid of it must be!'

Her eyes began to dance. 'Charles, you are just trying to be disagreeable! You cannot feed Jacko on bits of apple, and teach him tricks, and warn the children to give him a blanket at night one day, and the next say he must be got rid of!'

He bit his lip, but the rueful grin would not be entirely suppressed. 'Who told you I had done so?'

'Theodore. And also that you carried him down on your shoulder when Miss Wraxton came to call, to show him off to her. I must say, I think that was foolish of you, for you know she does not like pets: she told us so. I am sure there is no reason why she should, and to plague her with them is not kind in you. I never let Tina tease her, you know.'

'You are mistaken!' he said quickly. 'She does not like monkeys, but it is only Lady Brinklow who dislikes dogs!'

'I expect she feels the same,' said Sophy, getting up, and giving her skirts a shake. 'One cannot help observing how often daughters resemble their mothers. Not in face, but in disposition. You must have remarked it!'

He seemed to be somewhat appalled by this. 'No, I have not. I do not think you can be right!'

'Oh, yes, only consider Cecy! She will be just like dear Aunt

Lizzie when she is older.' She saw that the truth of this statement was having its effect upon him, and thought that she had given him enough to ponder for one day. She moved towards the door, saying: 'I must go and change my dress.'

He got up abruptly. 'No, wait!'

She looked over her shoulder. 'Yes?'

He did not seem to know what he wished to say. 'Nothing! It's no matter! Next time you insist on buying horses, you had better tell me what you want! To be employing strangers in the business is most undesirable!'

'But you assured me you would have no hand in it!' Sophy pointed out.

'Yes!' he said savagely. 'Nothing pleases you more than to put me in the wrong, does it?'

She laughed, and went away without answering him. Upstairs, she was pounced on by Cecilia, anxious to know what her fate was to be.

'If he speaks to you at all, it will be to warn you against Alfred Wraxton!' said Sophy, with a gurgle of amusement. 'I told him exactly how that toad conducts himself, and warned him to take care of you!'

'You did not!'

'I did! I have done an excellent day's work, in the most unprincipled way! Oh, tell Addy Charles does not blame her in the least! He won't say a word to my aunt about what happened, and I doubt whether he will say a word to you either. The only person he *may* say a word to is his precious Eugenia. I hope she will induce him to lose his temper.'

Seven

CECILIA WAS QUITE UNABLE TO BELIEVE THAT SHE WAS NOT TO receive one of her brother's scolds, and, when she later came unexpectedly face-to-face with him on a bend in the stair she gave a gasp, and tried to stiffen her unruly knees. 'Hallo!' he said, running an eye over her exquisite ball-dress of gauze over satin. 'You are very smart! Where are you off to?'

'Lady Sefton is calling after dinner to take Sophy and me to Almack's,' she replied thankfully. 'Mama does not find herself equal to it this evening.'

'Taking the shine out of them all!' he said. 'You look very fine!'

'Why do you not accompany us?' she asked, plucking up courage.

'You would not spend the entire evening in Fawnhope's pocket if I did,' he observed dryly.

She lifted her chin. 'I should not under any circumstances spend the entire evening in any gentleman's pocket!'

'No, I believe you would not,' he agreed mildly. 'Not in my line, Cilly? Besides, I am engaged with a party of my own.'

His employment of her almost forgotten nursery-name made her retort with much less constraint: 'Daffy Club!'

He grinned. 'No: Cribb's Parlour!'

'How horrid you are! I suppose you are going to discuss the merits of a Bloomsbury Pet, or a Black Diamond, or – or –'

'A Mayfair Marvel,' he supplied. 'Nothing so interesting: I am going to blow a cloud with a few friends. And what do *you* know of Bloomsbury Pets, miss?'

She threw him a saucy look as she passed him on the way down the staircase. 'Only what I have learnt from my brothers, Charles!'

He laughed, and let her go, but before she had reached the bottom of the flight, leaned over the banisters, and said imperatively: 'Cecilia!' she looked up enquiringly. 'Does that fellow Wraxton annoy you?'

She was nearly betrayed into losing her gravity. She replied: 'Oh, well – ! I daresay I could snub him easily enough, if – well, if I chose to do so!'

'You need not be deterred by any consideration that I know of. I need scarcely say that if Eugenia knew of it she would be the first to condemn his behaviour!'

'Of course,' she said.

Whether he spoke words of censure to Miss Wraxton no one was in a position to know. If he did, they must, Sophy thought, have been mild ones, for she did not appear to be in any way chastened. However, Sophy was granted one satisfaction. When next Miss Wraxton brought up the vexed question of Jacko, confiding to Lady Ombersley that she lived in dread of hearing that the monkey had bitten one of the children, Charles overheard her, and said impatiently: 'Nonsense!'

'I believe a monkey's bite is poisonous.'

'In that case I hope he may bite Theodore.'

Lady Ombersley uttered a protest, but Theodore, already soundly cuffed for hitting a cricket-ball from the Square-garden straight through one of the windows of a neighbouring house, merely grinned. Miss Wraxton, who did not feel that he had been adequately punished for such a piece of lawlessness, had already spoken her mind gravely on the subject. Charles had listened, but all he had said was: 'Very true, but it was a capital hit: I saw it.' This disregard for her opinion rankled with Miss Wraxton, and she now, with the archness which she too often employed when talking to children, read Theodore a playful lecture, telling him that he was fortunate in not being obliged to forfeit his new pet in retribution of his crime. Beyond casting her a glance of resent-ment, he paid no heed, but Gertrude blurted out: 'I believe you don't like Jacko because Sophy gave him to us!'

The truth of this embarrassingly forthright pronouncement struck most of those present with blinding effect. Miss Wraxton's cheeks flew two spots of colour; Lady Ombersley gave a gasp, and Cecilia stifled a giggle. Only Charles and Sophy remained unmoved, Sophy not raising her eyes from the sewing she was engaged on, and Charles saying blightingly: 'A stupid and an impertinent remark, Gertrude. You may return to the school-room, if you cannot conduct yourself more becomingly.'

Gertrude, who had arrived at the age when she cast herself into quite as much confusion as her elders, had already blushed hotly, and now fled in disorder from the room. Lady Ombersley began at once to talk of her projected expedition, with Sophy and Cecilia, to visit the Marquesa de Villacañas at Merton.

'One would not wish to be backward in any attention,' she said, 'so I shall make the effort, and we must hope it will not rain, for that would make it very disagreeable. I wish you will go with us, Charles. Your uncle's affianced wife, you know! I own, I do not care to drive out of town without a gentleman to go with me, though I am sure Radnor is perfectly to be trusted, and I should of course take my footmen.'

'My dear Mama, three able-bodied men should be enough

to protect you on this hazardous journey!' he returned in some amusement.

'Don't tease Charles to go, Aunt Lizzie!' said Sophy, snipping off her thread. 'Sir Vincent vows he will ride there with us, for he has not met Sancia since Madrid days, when her husband was still alive, and they gave splendid parties for all the English officers.'

There was a slight pause before Charles said: 'If you wish it, Mama, I will certainly go with you. I can take my cousin in the curricle, and then you will not be crowded in your carriage.'

'Oh, I mean to go in my phaeton!' Sophy said unconcernedly.

'I thought it was your ambition to drive my grays?'

'Why, would you let me?'

'Perhaps.'

She laughed. 'Oh, no, no! I have no belief in *perhaps!* Take Cecilia!'

'Cecilia would by far rather go in my mother's landaulet. You may take the reins for part of the way.'

She said in a rallying tone: 'This is something indeed! I am overcome, Charles, and fear you cannot be feeling quite the thing!'

'It will be a delightful expedition,' said Miss Wraxton brightly. 'I am almost tempted, dear Lady Ombersley, to beg a place in your carriage!'

Lady Ombersley was too well-bred to betray consternation, but she said a little doubtfully: 'Well, my dear, of course – if Sophy does not think that there might be rather too many of us for the Marquesa! I should not wish to put her out in any way.'

'Not at all!' Sophy replied instantly. 'It is not in your power to put Sancia out, dearest Aunt Lizzie! She will not bestir herself in the least, but will leave everything to her major-domo. He is a Frenchman, and will be delighted to make arrangements for even so small a party as ours. I have only to write Sancia a letter, beg a frank from my uncle, and the thing is done – if she will rouse herself sufficiently to convey my message to Gaston!'

'How interesting it will be to meet a real Spanish lady!' remarked Miss Wraxton.

'For all the world as if Sancia had been a giraffe!' as Sophy afterwards said to Cecilia.

'I wish I had known you meant to accompany my mother!' Mr Rivenhall said, when he presently escorted Miss Wraxton to her carriage. 'I should have offered *you* a place in my curricle. I cannot cry off now, but it is a bore. I should not have said I would go had I not heard that Talgarth was to be of the party. God knows I don't care a jot whom my cousin marries, but I suppose, in the circumstances, we owe it to my uncle not to encourage *that* connection!'

'I am afraid her visit has brought extra cares upon you, my dear Charles. Much must be forgiven to a girl who has never known a mother's care, but I confess I had hoped that under your Mama's guidance she would have tried to conform to English standards of propriety.'

'Not she!' he said. 'It's my belief she delights in keeping us all upon tenterhooks! There is no guessing what she will be at next, while the terms she stands on with every rattle who ever wore a scarlet coat – not that I care for that! But to be encouraging Talgarth to dangle after her is the outside of enough. All very well to say she can look after herself: I daresay she can, but if she is seen too much in his company she will be talked about by every scandal-mongering busybody in town!'

Miss Wraxton, treasuring up these hasty words, was unwise enough to repeat the gist of them to Sophy not forty-eight hours later. During the hour of the fashionable Promenade, when walking in the Park with her maid, she came upon Sophy's phaeton, drawn up to allow Sophy to exchange a few words with the reprehensible Sir Vincent. He had one hand negligently on the step of the phaeton, and she was leaning a little down to say something that seemed to afford them both amusement. She saw Miss Wraxton, and nodded smilingly to her, but looked rather surprised when Eugenia came towards the phaeton, and addressed her. 'How do you do? So this is the carriage I hear so much of! At all events, you have a fine pair of horses, I see. You have driven them tandem! You are to be congratulated: I do not think I would trust myself to do so.'

'You are acquainted with Sir Vincent Talgarth, I believe,' Sophy said.

Sir Vincent received the coldest of bows, and the merest hint of a smile.

'Do you know,' said Miss Wraxton, looking up at Sophy, 'I really think I must ask you to take me up beside you for one turn! I am quite jealous of your prowess, I assure you!'

Sophy signed to John to alight, saying politely: 'Pray come with me, Miss Wraxton! I shall naturally be put on my mettle. Sir Vincent, we meet on Friday, then: you will call for us at Berkeley Square!'

Miss Wraxton, assisted by John Potton, mounted with credible grace into the awkwardly high carriage, and sat down beside Sophy, disposing her skirt neatly, and acknowledging Tina's presence by uttering: 'Dear little doggie!' a form of address which made the little greyhound shiver, and press closer to her mistress. 'I am so happy to have this opportunity of speaking with you, Miss Stanton-Lacy: I had come to think it impossible to find you when you should be alone! You are acquainted with so many people!'

'Yes, am I not fortunate?'

'Indeed, yes!' agreed Miss Wraxton, honey-sweet. 'Though sometimes, dear Miss Stanton-Lacy, when one has a multitude of friends, one is inclined not to be as careful as one should be, perhaps. I wonder if I might venture to put you a little on your guard! In Paris and Vienna I am sure you would be able to tell me how I should go on, but in London I must be more at home than you.'

'Oh, I should never be so impertinent as to tell you how to go on anywhere!' Sophy declared.

'Well, perhaps it would not be necessary,' acknowledged Miss Wraxton graciously. 'My Mama has always been a most careful parent, and very strict in her choice of governesses for her daughters. I have felt so much compassion for you, dear Miss Stanton-Lacy, situated as you are. You must so often have felt the want of a mother!'

'Not at all. Don't waste your compassion on me, I beg! I never wanted a mother while I had Sir Horace.'

'Gentlemen,' said Miss Wraxton, 'are not the same.'

'An unarguable statement. How do you like my bays?'

Miss Wraxton laid a hand on her knee. 'Allow me to speak without reserve!' she begged.

'Short of overturning you I can hardly prevent you,' Sophy replied. 'But you had much better not, you know! I am very unbiddable, and if I were to lose my temper I might do what I should afterwards be sorry for.'

'But I must speak!' Miss Wraxton said earnestly. 'I owe it to your cousin!'

'Indeed! How is this?'

'You will understand that he does not like to mention the matter to you himself. He feels a certain delicacy —'

'I thought you were talking of Charles!' interrupted Sophy. 'Which cousin do you mean?'

'I am talking of Charles.'

'Nonsense! He has no delicate scruples.'

'Miss Stanton-Lacy, believe me, this air of levity is not becoming!' said Miss Wraxton, losing some of her sweetness. 'I do not think you can be aware of what is expected of a woman of quality! Or — forgive me! — how fatal it is to set up the backs of people, and to give rise to such gossip as must be as painful to the Rivenhalls as I am persuaded it would be to you!'

'Now, what in heaven's name comes next?' said Sophy, quite astonished. 'You cannot be so gothic as to suppose that because I drive a high-perch phaeton I give rise to gossip!'

'No, though one would have preferred to have seen you in some vehicle less sporting. But the habits of easy intercourse you are on with so many military gentlemen − rattles in scarlet coats, as Charles divertingly phrases it! − and in particular with that man I saw you conversing with a moment ago, make you appear a little *fast*, dear Miss Stanton-Lacy, which I know you would not wish! Sir Vincent's company cannot give you consequence, indeed, quite the reverse! A certain lady − of the first consideration! − commented to me only today upon his attaching himself to you so particularly.'

'I expect she has an interest there herself,' observed Sophy. 'He is a shocking flirt! And did my cousin Charles desire you to warn me against all these rattles?'

'He did not precisely desire me to do so,' answered Miss Wraxton scrupulously, 'but he has spoken to me on this head, and I know what his sentiments are. You must know that Society will look indulgently upon mere pranks, such as driving off in Charles's curricle, for Lady Ombersley's protection must give you countenance.'

'How fortunate I am!' said Sophy. 'But do you think you are wise to be seen in my company?'

'Now you are quizzing, Miss Stanton-Lacy!'

'No, I am only afraid that you may suffer for being seen in such a vehicle as this, and with so fast a female!'

'Hardly,' Miss Wraxton said gently. 'Perhaps it may be thought a little *odd* in me, for I do not drive myself in London, but I think my character is sufficiently well-established to make it possible for me to do − if I wished − what others might be imprudent to attempt.'

They were by this time within sight of the gate by Apsley House. 'Now let me understand you!' begged Sophy. 'If I were to do something outrageous while in your company, would your credit be good enough to carry me off?'

'Let us say my family's credit, Miss Stanton-Lady. I may venture to reply, without hesitation, yes.'

'Capital!' said Sophy briskly, and turned her horses towards the gate.

Miss Wraxton, losing some of her assurance, said sharply: 'Pray, what are you about?'

'I am going to do what I have been wanting to do ever since I was told I must not, on any account!' replied Sophy. 'It is with me a kind of Bluebeard's chamber.'

The phaeton swung through the gateway, and turned sharply to the left, narrowly escaping collision with a ponderous lozenge-coach. Miss Wraxton uttered a stifled shriek, and clutched the side of the phaeton. 'Take care! Please pull up your horses at once! I do not wish to drive through the streets! Have you taken leave of your senses?'

'No, no, do not be afraid! I am quite sane. How glad I am that you chose to drive with me! Such an opportunity as this might never else have come in my way!'

'Miss Stanton-Lacy, I do not know what you mean, and again I must beg of you to pull up! I am not at all diverted by this prank, and I wish to alight from your phaeton instantly.'

'What, and walk along Piccadilly unattended? You cannot mean it!'

'*Stop!*' commanded Miss Wraxton, in almost shrill accents.

'On no account. Dear me, what a lot of traffic! Perhaps you had better not talk to me until I have weaved my way through all these carts and carriages.'

'For heaven's sake, at least slacken your pace!' Miss Wraxton besought her, in the liveliest alarm.

'I will, when we come to the turning,' promised Sophy,

passing between a wagon and a mail-coach, with a matter of inches to spare. A moan from her companion caused her to add kindly: 'There is no need to be in a fright: Sir Horace made me drive through a gateway until I could be trusted not even to scrape the varnish.'

They were now ascending the rise in Piccadilly. With a strong effort at self-control, Miss Wraxton demanded: 'Tell me at once where you are taking me!'

'Down St James's Street,' replied Sophy coolly.

'What?' gasped Miss Wraxton, turning quite pale. 'You will do no such thing! No lady would be seen driving there! Amongst all the clubs – the object of every town saunterer! You cannot know what would be said of you! Stop this instant!'

'No, I want to see this Bow Window I hear so much of, and all the dandies who sit there. How wretched that Mr Brummell has been obliged to go abroad! Do you know, I never saw him in my life? Are you able to point out the various clubs to me? Shall we recognize White's, or are there other houses with bow windows?'

'This is your notion of raillery, Miss Stanton-Lacy! You are not serious!'

'Yes, I am. Of course, I should not have dared to do it without you sitting beside me, to lend me credit, but you have assured me that your position is unassailable, and I see that I need have no scruple in gratifying my ambition. I daresay your consequence is great enough to make it quite a fashionable drive for ladies. We shall see!'

No argument that Miss Wraxton could advance, and she advanced many, had the power to move her. She drove on inexorably. Wild ideas of springing from the phaeton crossed Miss Wraxton's mind, only to be rejected. It was too dangerous to be attempted. Had she been wearing a veil she might have pulled it over her face, and hoped to have escaped recognition, but her hat

was a perfectly plain one, and bore only a modest bow of ribbon.
She had not even a parasol, and was obliged to sit bolt upright,
staring rigidly ahead of her the length of that disgraceful street. She
did not utter a word until the horses swung round into Pall Mall,
and then she said in a low voice, unsteady with rage and chagrin:
'I will never forgive you! never!'

'How uncharitable of you!' said Sophy lightly. 'Shall I set you
down now?'

'If you dare to abandon me in this locality —'

'Very well, I will drive you to Berkeley Square. I do not know
whether you will find my cousin at home at this hour, but at all
events you may complain of me to my aunt, which I am sure you
must be longing to do.'

'Do not speak to me!' said Miss Wraxton throbbingly.

Sophy laughed.

Outside Ombersley House she broke the silence. 'Can
you get down without assistance? Having cast off my groom,
together with your maid, I must drive the phaeton round to the
stables myself.'

Miss Wraxton, vouchsafing no answer, climbed down, and
walked up the steps to the front door.

It was half an hour later before Dassett admitted Sophy into
the house. She found Mr Rivenhall at that very moment coming
down the stairs, and said at once. 'Ah, so you were at home! I am
so glad!'

He was looking very stern, and replied in a level tone: 'Will you
come into the library for a few minutes?'

She accompanied him there, and began to drag off her driving-
gloves with hands that were not quite steady. Her eyes were still
sparkling, and a not unbecoming flush mantled her cheeks.

'Cousin, what, in God's name, possessed you?' demanded
Mr Rivenhall.

'Oh, has not Miss Wraxton told you? I have realized an ambition!'

'You must be mad! Don't you know how improper it was of you to do such a thing?'

'Yes, indeed I knew, and should never have dared to do it without the protection of Miss Wraxton's presence! Do not look so dismayed! She assured me that even though I did something outrageous in her company her credit was good enough to carry me off! Surely you cannot doubt it!'

'Sophy, she cannot have said such a thing!'

She shrugged, and turned away. 'No? Have it as you will!'

'What had occurred? What reason had you for causing her such mortification?'

'I will leave Miss Wraxton to tell you what she chooses. I have said too much already: I do not like tale-bearers, and will not sink to that level! My actions are no concern of yours, Cousin Charles, and even less are they Miss Wraxton's.'

'What you have just done is very much her concern!'

'True. I stand corrected.'

'It is also my concern to see that you come to no harm while you are a guest in this house. Such conduct as you indulged in this afternoon might do you a great deal of harm, let me tell you!'

'My dear Charles, I am past praying for, as intimate as I am with rakes and rattles!' she flashed.

He stiffened. 'Who said that?'

'You, I understand, but you had too much delicacy to say it to my face. You should have known better than to think I should listen meekly to Miss Wraxton, however!'

'And you should know better than to imagine that I would deliver my strictures through Miss Wraxton, or anyone else!'

She lifted a hand to her cheek, and he saw that it was to dash away a tear-drop. 'Oh, be quiet! Cannot you see that I am too angry to talk with any moderation? My wretched tongue! But though you did not desire Miss Wraxton to scold me for you, you did discuss me with her, did you not?'

'Whatever I may have said I did not mean to be repeated. It was, however, extremely improper of me to have criticized you to Miss Wraxton. I beg your pardon!'

She pulled out her handkerchief from the sleeve of her habit, and blew her nose. Her flush died down; she said ruefully: 'Now I am disarmed. How provoking of you! Why could you not have flown into one of your rages? You are so disobliging! Was it so very bad to have driven down St James's Street?'

'You knew it was, for Miss Wraxton told you so. You have caused her a great deal of distress, Sophy.'

'Oh dear! I do such dreadful things when I lose my temper! Very well, it was wrong of me – very wrong! Must I beg her pardon?'

'You must see that you owe her an apology. If anything she may have said to you angered you, at least she had no such intention. She meant nothing but kindness, and is very much upset by the outcome. Mine is the blame, for having led her to suppose that I wished her to take you to task.'

She smiled. 'That's handsome of you, Charles! I am sorry: I have created an uncomfortable situation. Where is Miss Wraxton? In the drawing-room? Take me up to her, then, and I will do what I may to mend things!'

'Thank you,' he said, opening the door for her.

Miss Wraxton was found to have recovered from her agitation, and to be glancing through the pages of *The Gentleman's Magazine*. She glanced coldly at Sophy, and lowered her eyes again to the periodical. Sophy walked across the room, saying in her frank way: 'Will you forgive me? Indeed, I beg your pardon, and am very sorry! It was shocking conduct!'

'So shocking, Miss Stanton-Lacy, that I prefer not to speak of it.'

'If that means that you will try to forget it, I shall be very grateful to you.'

'Certainly I shall do so.'

'Thank you!' Sophy said. 'You are very kind!'

She turned and went quickly to the door. Mr Rivenhall was holding it, and detained her for a moment, saying in a much warmer voice than she had yet heard him use: 'If anyone should mention the affair to me, I shall say that having bought those bays of yours against my advice you were well served, for they got away with you!'

She smiled, but said: 'I wish you will do what you can to undo any harm I may have caused.'

'My dear girl, don't refine too much upon it! There is no need, I assure you.'

She cast him a look of gratitude, and left the room.

'You were not very generous, were you, Eugenia?' said Mr Rivenhall.

'I consider her behaviour unpardonable.'

'It is unnecessary to tell me so: you made it plain enough that you thought so.'

Her bosom swelled. 'I did not think to hear you take her part against me, Charles!'

'I have not done so, but the fault was not all hers. You had no right to take her to task, Eugenia, much less to repeat whatever ill-considered words I may have uttered! I am not surprised she was so angry: I have a temper myself!'

'You do not seem to consider the agony of mortification I have been obliged to suffer! What Mama would say if she knew —'

'Oh, enough, enough!' he said impatiently. 'You make too much of it! Let us, for heaven's sake, forget it!'

She was offended, but she saw that to persist would lower her in his eyes. It annoyed her to think that she had shown to less advantage than Sophy in the little scene that had been enacted. She forced herself to smile, and to say magniloquently: 'You are right: I have allowed myself to be too much moved. Please assure your cousin that I shall not think of the matter again!'

She had her reward, for he grasped her hand at once, saying: 'That is more like you! I knew I could not be mistaken in you!'

Eight

THE TWO LADIES DID NOT MEET AGAIN UNTIL THE DAY OF THE
expedition to Merton, Miss Wraxton, convinced that she had
become notorious, having decided to pay a long deferred visit to
her elder sister, who lived in Kent, and was famous for turning
her guests to good account. Eugenia was not fond of running
Lady Ealing's errands, or of playing with her numerous offspring,
but she was strongly of the opinion that she would be wise to
absent herself from London until the inevitable whisperings
had died down. The Rivenhalls thus enjoyed immunity from
her punitive descents upon them for seven whole days, which
was felt by almost all to be an advantage far outweighing the
ills of Sophy's indiscretion. This did not reach the ears of Lady
Ombersley, but was naturally known to the younger members of
the household, some of whom were much shocked, while others,
notably Hubert and Selina, considered that their cousin had taken
a splendid lark. No apparent repercussions followed her exploit,
and although she was obliged to endure much chaffing from
her young relatives, even this very soon took a turn in another
direction. A much more fruitful topic for jests presented itself in
the shape of young Lord Bromford, who swam suddenly into the

Rivenhall's ken, and was regarded by them as so much manna dropped from heaven.

Lord Bromford, who was almost unknown to the Polite World, had but lately, upon the death of his father, succeeded to a modest barony. He was the only surviving child of his parents, every one of his brothers and sisters (varying in number, according to popular report, from seven to seventeen) having died in infancy. It may have been for this reason that his mother had from the start deemed him unfit to be wrested from her care. No other reason was observable; although, as Sophy fairmindedly pointed out to her cousins, a florid complexion and a full habit of body were not infallible signs of a robust constitution. He had been educated at home, and although there had been a project afoot to send him up to Oxford, a providential chill had intervened to save him from the perils of University life. It was well known to Lord Bromford that his heir's lungs were delicate, and it was only necessary for Lady Bromford to point out to him every day for several weeks the evils that would accrue from exposing Henry to the rigours of Oxford to induce him to give his consent to an alternative plan. Henry, accompanied by a clerical gentleman in whom Lady Bromford reposed the greatest confidence, was sent to Jamaica, on a visit to his uncle, the governor. The climate was said to be beneficial to persons with weak lungs, and it was not until Henry had been four days at sea that his mama discovered that the island was periodically devastated by hurricanes. It was then too late to recall Henry, who proceeded on his voyage, being extremely sea-sick, but arriving at Port Royal without any trace of the cough which had cast his mama into such a fever of anxiety. No hurricane occurred during his visit to sweep him away, and when he returned to England, a few months before attaining his majority, he was so stout that his mama was able to congratulate herself on the success of her scheme. She did not immediately perceive that his eighteen-month sojourn apart from her had had the effect of making him occasionally disinclined to submit to her benevolent rule. On her advice, he changed his socks, wound mufflers round his neck, swathed his legs in warm rugs, and eschewed all harmful forms of sustenance; but when she advised him not to subject his person to the racket of London, he said, after due consideration, that he rather thought he should like to live in London; and when she proposed a very eligible match for him, he said he was much obliged to her, but had not yet made up his mind what sort of female he wished to marry. He did not argue: he merely turned his back on the eligible match, and took up his residence in London. His mother began to tell her friends that Henry could be led, but not driven; his valet, a plain-spoken man, said that his lordship was as obstinate as a pig.

He had been upon the town for some time before the Rivenhalls were more than vaguely aware of his existence. His intimates (whom Hubert stigmatized as a dull set of gudgeons) were not amongst their particular friends, and it was not until he met Sophy at Almack's, and stood up with her in a country dance, that the full glory of his personality burst upon them. For Lord Bromford, impervious alike to Cecilia's beauty, and to the eligibility of his mama's choice, had made up his mind that Sophy would make him a suitable wife. He called in Berkeley Square, and at a moment when Hubert and Selina were with Lady Ombersley. He stayed for half an hour, imparting information to his hosts on such varied topics as the vegetation in Jamaica, and the effect of paregoric draughts upon the human system, and the Rivenhalls listened to him in stunned indignation until Sophy entered the room. Then the scales fell from before their eyes, and they perceived why his lordship had honoured them with a morning-call, and their boredom changed to unholy glee. Sophy's beau became in a trice the solid foundation upon which a lively set of young persons built the most preposterous of fabrications. No street-singer could lift his voice in the Square but what Hubert or Cecilia would declare it to be Lord Bromford, serenading Sophy; when he was confined to his house for three days with an internal disorder he was held to have fought a duel for the sake of her fine eyes; and the serial story of his adventures in the West Indies, conceived, added to, and improved upon by three fertile brains, grew so outrageous as to draw protests from Lady Ombersley and Miss Adderbury. But Lady Ombersley, though she might deprecate such an excess of high spirits, could not help but be amused by the determination shown by Lord Bromford in his pursuit of her niece. He was for ever calling in Berkeley Square on the most slender of pretexts; he daily promenaded in the Park only to waylay Sophy, and be taken up into her phaeton; he even purchased a showy hack, and rode solemnly up and down the Row every morning in the hope that she might be exercising Salamanca there. More wonderful still, he prevailed upon his mama to cultivate the acquaintance of Lady Ombersley, and to invite Sophy to go with her to one of the Concerts of Ancient Music. He was impervious to snubs, and when his mama hinted to him that Sophy would scarcely make a suitable wife for a serious man, being wholly given over to frivolity, he said that he was confident that he would be able to direct her thoughts into more sober channels.

The cream of the jest, thought the young Rivenhalls, was that Charles, in general so impatient of pretensions, was, for inscrutable reasons, encouraging his lordship. Charles said that there was a great deal of good in Lord Bromford. He said that Lord Bromford's conversation showed him to be a sensible man, and that his descriptions of Jamaica were extremely interesting. Only Selina (who was growing up, Charles said, to be disagreeably pert) ventured to observe that Lord Bromford's entrance into the house seemed to be the signal for Charles's departure for his club.

What with his lordship's courtship, the plans for the ball, the stream of visitors to the house, even Sophy's indiscretion, life in Berkeley Square had become all at once full of fun and excitement. Even Lord Ombersley was aware of it. 'By God, I don't know what's come over you all, for the place was used to be as lively as a tomb!' he declared. 'I'll tell you what, Lady Ombersley: I daresay I can prevail upon York to look in on your party. Nothing formal, y'know, but he's fixed in Stableyard for the present, and will very likely be pleased enough to drop in for half an hour.'

'Prevail upon the Duke of York to come to my party?' echoed Lady Ombersley, in the greatest astonishment. 'My dear Ombersley, you must be out of your senses! Ten, or perhaps twelve couples, getting up a dance in the drawing-room, and a couple of card-tables set out in the Crimson Saloon! I beg you will do no such thing!'

'Ten or twelve couples? No, no, Dassett would not be talking of red carpets and awnings for such a paltry affair as that!' said his lordship.

These ominous words struck a chill into his wife's soul. Beyond fixing the date for the party, and warning Cecilia not to forget to send a card to a very dull girl, who was her Goddaughter, and must be invited, she had not as yet thought much about the engagement. She now nerved herself to ask her niece how many people were expected on the fatal night. The answer almost brought on one of her spasms. She was obliged to drink a little hartshorn and water, thoughtfully pressed into her hand by Cecilia, before she could recover herself sufficiently to protest. She sat, alternately sipping the hartshorn, and sniffing her vinaigrette, and moaning that she shuddered to think what Charles would say. It took Sophy twenty minutes to convince her that since he was not to be asked to defray the expenses of the entertainment, it was no concern of his; and even then

Lady Ombersley dreaded the inevitable moment of discovery, and could scarcely see him walk into the room without giving a nervous start.

Fortunately for the success of the expedition, the truth had not dawned upon Charles when the Ombersley party set out to visit the Marquesa de Villacañas at Merton. The omens seemed to be propitious: the Marquesa had written a very pretty letter to Lady Ombersley, expressing her pleasure in the proposed meeting, and begging her to bring with her as many of her interesting children as would care to come; the sun shone, and the day was warm, with no threat of April showers; and Miss Wraxton, who had returned to the metropolis in time to share in the treat, was in her most amiable humour, not even excluding Sophy from her good graces. At the last moment, Hubert suddenly announced his intention of accompanying the party, saying that he too wanted to see the giraffe. Sophy frowned him down, and as his mother had not caught what he said, but at once began to express her delight in having his company, the awkward moment passed unnoticed. Mr Rivenhall, having greeted Sir Vincent Talgarth with perfect civility, was standing exchanging conversation with him while the three ladies who were to drive in the landaulet arranged themselves in it, Miss Wraxton begging to be allowed to take the back seat, and Cecilia insisting that she should not. Everything seemed to be in train for a day of enjoyment, when Mr Fawnhope came round the corner of the Square, saw the cavalcade, and at once crossed the road towards it.

Mr Rivenhall's face hardened; he shot an accusing look at Sophy, but she shook her head. Mr Fawnhope, shaking hands with Lady Ombersley, asked whither she was bound. She told him, Merton, and he said elliptically: 'Statutes, *Nolumus leges Angliae mutari.*'

'Very likely,' said Lady Ombersley almost tartly.

Miss Wraxton, who could never resist the temptation to display her superior education, smiled quite kindly at Mr Fawnhope, and said: 'Very true. King John, you know, is said to have slept at the Priory the night before he signed the Great Charter. It is a very historic spot, for we are told that it was the scene of the murder of Cenulph, King of Wessex. It has, of course, more recent historic associations,' she added, but repressively, for these more recent historic associations regrettably included a quite unmentionable female.

'Nelson!' said Mr Fawnhope. 'Romantic Merton! I will go with you.' He then climbed into the carriage, and took his place beside Cecilia, smiling seraphically at Lady Ombersley, and saying: 'Now I know what it is I wish to do. I had no notion when I got up this morning, but was filled with a vast discontent. I will go to Merton.'

'You cannot wish to go to Merton!' said Lady Ombersley, very much put-out, and hoping that Charles would not put her to the blush by saying something cutting to this tiresome young man.

'Yes,' said Mr Fawnhope. 'There will be verdure, and that, I think, is what my soul craves. *I, with my fair Cecilia, to Merton now will go, Where softly flows the Wandle, and daffodils that blow* – What an ugly word is Wandle! How displeasing to the ear! Why do you frown at me? May I not go with you?'

This sudden change from rapt poet into cajoling boy threw Lady Ombersley off her balance, and she replied in a mollified voice: 'I am sure we should be pleased to take you, Augustus, but we are going to visit the Marquesa de Villacañas, and she will not be expecting you.'

'Now there,' said Mr Fawnhope, 'is a beautiful name! Villacañas! It is most rich! A Spanish lady, with "*garments gay and rich as maybe, Decked with jewels had she on!*"'

'I'm sure I don't know,' replied Lady Ombersley crossly.

Sophy, much amused by Mr Fawnhope's utter imperviousness

to hints that he was not wanted, said laughingly: 'Yes, pearls worth a king's ransom. She even loves an English man: my father!'

'How splendid!' said Mr Fawnhope. 'I am so glad I came!'

Short of ordering him point-blank to get out of the carriage, there seemed to be no way of getting rid of him. Lady Ombersley cast her eldest son a despairing glance, and Cecilia an imploring one; and Miss Wraxton smiled in a reassuring way that was designed to show how perfect was her comprehension and how firm her resolve to keep an eye on Cecilia.

'Who is this Adonis?' Sir Vincent asked Mr Rivenhall. 'He and your sister, seated side by side, quite take one's breath away!'

'Augustus Fawnhope,' replied Mr Rivenhall curtly. 'Cousin, if you are ready, I will hand you up!'

Lady Ombersley, gathering that she had received a tacit consent to Mr Fawnhope's presence, told her coachman to start. Sir Vincent and Hubert fell in behind the carriage, and Mr Rivenhall said to Sophy: 'If this is your doing – !'

'I promise you it is not. If I thought that he had the smallest notion of your hostility, I should say that he had rolled you up, Charles: horse, foot, and guns!'

He was obliged to laugh. 'I doubt if he would have the smallest notion of anything less violent than a blow from a cudgel. How you can tolerate the fellow – !'

'I told you that I was not at all nice in my ideas. Come, don't let us talk of him! I have sworn an oath to heaven not to quarrel with you today.'

'You amaze me! Why?'

'Don't be such an ape!' she begged. 'I want to drive your grays, of course!'

He took his place beside her in the curricle, and nodded to the groom to stand away from the grays' heads. 'Oh, that! When we are clear of the town, you shall do so.'

'That,' said Sophy, 'is a remark calculated, I daresay, to make me lose my temper at the outset. I shall not do it, however.'

'I don't doubt your skill,' he said.

'A handsome admission. It cost you an effort to make it, perhaps, and that makes it the more valuable. But the roads are so good in England that not much skill is required. You should see some of the tracks in Spain!'

'Deliberate provocation, Sophy!' said Mr Rivenhall.

She laughed, disclaimed, and began to ask him about hunting. Once beyond the narrow streets he let his horses lengthen their stride, and overtook, and passed, the landaulet. Miss Wraxton was seen to be conversing amicably with Mr Fawnhope, while Cecilia was looking bored. The reason was explained by Hubert, who rode beside the curricle for a little way, and disclosed that the subject under discussion was Dante's *Inferno*. 'And this I will say for Fawnhope!' he added handsomely, 'he knows that Italian stuff much better than your Eugenia, Charles, and can go on at it for hours, never at a loss! What's more, there's another fellow, called Uberti, or some such thing, and he knows him too. Sad stuff, if you ask me, but Talgarth – I say, he's a bang-up fellow, isn't he? – says he's devilish well-read. Cecilia don't like it above half. Jupiter, I should laugh if Eugenia were to cut her out with the poet!'

Receiving no encouragement from his brother to expatiate on this theme, he fell behind again to rejoin Sir Vincent. Mr Rivenhall handed over the reins to Sophy, observing as he did so that he was glad not to be sitting in the landaulet.

She refrained from making any comment, and the rest of the drive passed very pleasantly, no controversial topics arising to mar the good relations between them.

The house procured for the Marquesa by Sir Horace was a spacious Palladian villa, prettily situated in charming gardens, and with a bluebell wood attached, which, though fenced off from the pleasure grounds, could be reached through some graceful iron gates, brought from Italy by a previous owner. A few shallow steps led up from the carriage-sweep to the front door, and this, upon the approach of the curricle, was flung open, and a thin man, dressed in black, came out of the house, and stood bowing on the top step. Sophy greeted him in her usual friendly fashion, and at once asked where Mr Rivenhall could stable his horses. The thin man snapped an imperative finger and thumb, rather in the manner of a conjuror, and a groom seemed to spring up out of nowhere, and ran to the grays' heads.

'I'll see them stabled, Sophy, and come in presently with my mother,' Mr Rivenhall said.

Sophy nodded, and walked up the steps, saying: 'There are two more in the party than you were expecting, Gaston. You won't mind that, I daresay.'

'It makes nothing, mademoiselle,' he replied grandly. 'Madam awaits you in the salon.'

The Marquesa was discovered reclining upon a sofa in a drawing-room facing the south lawn. The early spring sunshine was not overpowering, but the blinds had been drawn a little way across the windows to exclude it. As these were green, like the upholstery on the chairs, a subaqueous light dimly lit the apartment. Sophy immediately flung back the curtains, exclaiming as she did so: 'Sancia, you cannot go to sleep when your visitors are almost at the door!'

A faint moan came from the sofa. 'Sophie, my complexion! Nothing so injurious as sunshine! How often have I said it!'

Sophy walked over to her, and bent to kiss her. 'Yes, dearest Sancia, but my aunt will think you quite odd if you lie there in darkness while she gropes her way to you by guess. Do get up!'

'*Bien entendido* I get up when your aunt approaches,' said the Marquesa, with dignity. 'If she is at the door, it shall be now, I grudge no exertion.'

In proof of this statement, she disentangled a singularly beautiful embroidered shawl from about her feet, dropped it on the floor, and allowed Sophy to help her to rise.

She was an opulent brunette, dressed more in the French style than the English, and with her luxuriant black locks covered only by a mantilla, draped over a high comb. Her gown was of gauze over satin, drawn in tightly below her full breasts, and revealing a good deal more of her shape than Lady Ombersley was likely to think seemly. This, however, was slightly concealed by the various scarves and shawls which she draped round herself as protection against treacherous draughts. The mantilla was pinned to her low corsage by a large emerald brooch; more emeralds, set in massive gold, dangled from the lobes of her ears; and she wore her famous pearls, twisted twice round her throat, and hanging almost to her waist. She was extremely handsome, with large, sleepy brown eyes, and a creamy complexion, delicately tinted by the hand of an artist. She was little more than thirty-five, but her plumpness made her appear to be older. She did not look in the least like a widow, which was the first thought that occurred to Lady Ombersley when she presently entered the room, and took the languid hand held out to her.

'*Com' está?*' the Marquesa said, in her rich, lazy voice.

This terrified Hubert, who had been assured that she spoke excellent English. He cast a burning look of reproach at Sophy, who at once intervened, calling her future stepmother to order. The Marquesa smiled placidly, and said: '*De seguro!* I speak French and English, and both very well. Also German, but that not so well, yet better than most people. It is a profound happiness to meet the sister of Sir Horace, though you do not, I find, resemble him, *señora. Válgame!* are these then all your sons and daughters!'

Lady Ombersley made haste to reassure her, and to perform the necessary introductions. The Marquesa lost interest in these before very long, but smiled in a general way upon her guests, and begged them all to sit down. Sophy told her that in Sir Vincent she beheld an old acquaintance, so she gave him her hand, and said that she remembered him perfectly. No one believed her, least of all Sir Vincent; but when she had been reminded of a certain evening on the Prado, she began to laugh, and said yes, now indeed she did remember him, *pechero* that he was! She then, having had time to assimilate the perfection of Cecilia's features, complimented Lady Ombersley on her beauty, which, she said, was in the best English style, and much admired upon the Continent. Apparently feeling that something was due to Miss Wraxton, she smiled kindly at her, and said that she also was very English. Miss Wraxton, who did not grudge Cecilia her beauty (for she had been brought up to think beauty only skin-deep), replied that she feared that she was not above the ordinary, and that in England the fashion was for dark women.

This subject having been pretty well thrashed out, silence fell, the Marquesa lying back against the cushions in one corner of the sofa, and Lady Ombersley wondering what topic of conversation would interest this lethargic lady. Mr Fawnhope, who had retired to the brocade-covered window-seat, sat gazing out upon the verdure his soul craved; Hubert regarded his hostess with a fascinated eye; and Mr Rivenhall, adapting himself to his company, picked up a periodical from the table at his elbow, and casually flicked over the pages. It was left to Miss Wraxton, with her fine social sense, to fill the breach, which she did by telling the Marquesa that she was a great admirer of *Don Quixote*.

'All the English are,' responded the Marquesa. 'And they will none of them say the name correctly. In Madrid, when the English army was there, every officer told me that he so much admired Cervantes, though mostly it was not true. But we have also Quevedo, and Espinel, and Montelban, to name only a few. In poetry, too —'

'*El Fenix de España*,' interpolated Mr Fawnhope, suddenly entering into the conversation.

The Marquesa looked approvingly at him. 'That is so. You are familiar with the works of Lope de Vega? Sophie,' she said, breaking into her own tongue, 'this young man with the face of an angel reads Spanish!'

'Very indifferently,' said Mr Fawnhope, quite unmoved by this embarrassing description of his face.

'We will talk together,' said the Marquesa.

'Certainly not,' said Sophy firmly. 'At least, not if you mean to do so in Spanish.'

Fortunately for the success of the party, Gaston came in at this moment to announce that refreshments were laid out in the dining-room. It was soon discovered that however indolent a hostess the Marquesa might be her maître d'hôtel left nothing to chance. A profusion of succulent foreign dishes awaited the guests, garnished with aspic, or spread with subtle sauces, and served with various light wines. Jellies, trifles, syllabubs, puptons of fruit, and coffee creams in cups of almond paste rounded off what the Marquesa called a light *merienda*. From the sparing way in which Miss Wraxton partook of a few of the delicacies it was not difficult to see that she considered such lavish hospitality vulgar; but Hubert, making a hearty meal, began to think the Marquesa a very good sort of woman after all. When he saw how many coffee creams, Italian rusks, and brandy-cherries she herself consumed, in the most negligent fashion, his manner towards her became tinged with respect bordering on awe.

The repast at an end, Gaston bent to his mistress's ear, and reminded her that the gate into the wood had been unlocked. She said: 'Ah, yes! The bluebell wood! So pretty! These young people would like to wander through it, *señora*, while you and I repose ourselves a little.'

It would never have occurred to Lady Ombersley to suggest a siesta to a visitor, but since she invariably dozed during the afternoon she had no real fault to find with this programme, and accompanied the Marquesa into the drawing-room. Here she at first endeavoured to engage the Marquesa in talk of her brother, but without much success. The Marquesa said: 'It is not amusing to be a widow, and, besides, I prefer England to Spain, since it is now very impoverished there. But to be *madrastra* to Sophie – ! No, and a thousand times no!'

'We are all very fond of my dear niece,' said Lady Ombersley, bristling.

'I also, but she is too fatiguing. One does not know what next she will do, or, which is worse by far, what she will make one do that one does not wish at all.'

Lady Ombersley found herself quite unable to resist the temptation of indulging in a little gentle malice. 'My dear ma'am, I am sure my niece could never persuade you to exert yourself in any way disagreeable to you!'

'But yes!' said the Marquesa simply. 'It is plain that you do not know Sophie. To withstand her is much, much more fatiguing still!'

Meanwhile, the subject of this exchange was arranging a flower in Hubert's button-hole, in the formal garden. Mr Rivenhall had gone off in the direction of the stables, and the four others were wending their way, through the shrubbery, towards the bluebell wood, Mr Fawnhope having been visited by inspiration which only the sight of Cecilia in the wood could, he said, bring to fruition. So far, he had only achieved one line of his poem, but he felt it to be promising. '*When amidst bluebells my Cecilia treads,*' he murmured.

'Quite Carolinian!' remarked Miss Wraxton.

Mr Fawnhope's verse was at all times derivative, but he liked being told so no better than any other poet, so he took his Cecilia's hand and would have led her away had not Miss Wraxton been on the alert to prevent just such a happening. With determination she stayed beside the lovers, and presently, by a happy reference to Cowper, succeeded in diverting Mr Fawnhope's attention from Cecilia to herself. Sir Vincent, finding solace for boredom in amusement at this situation, bided his time, and was presently rewarded. Cecilia, unable to bear a part in the elevated discussion in progress (for she was no great reader), began to drop behind. Sir Vincent fell in beside her, and in a very short space of time coaxed her out of her crossness, and, indeed, out of the wood as well. He said that profound as was his admiration for Miss Wraxton's intellect he found her conversation oppressive. Woods and blue-stockings, he said, exercised a lowering effect upon his spirits. He thought the ground was damp: certainly unfit walking for a delicately nurtured lady. He took Cecilia instead to inspect the dovecot, and since he was skilled in the art of flirtation, and she was lovely enough to make a little dalliance a pleasant way of whiling away a dull afternoon, they contrived to pass an agreeable hour together.

While all this was going on, Sophy was walking in the shrubbery with Hubert. She had not failed to notice that during the past few days he had swung between exaggeratedly high spirits, and fits of black depression. She had mentioned the matter to Cecilia, but Cecilia had merely said that Hubert had always been moody, and had not seemed to be inclined to think any more about it. But Sophy could not see anyone in the grip of care without instantly wishing to discover the cause, and, if possible, to rectify it. She thought she was now on good enough terms with him to venture to broach the matter to him, and so, it seemed, she was, although he could not be said to confide in her, he did not, as she had been afraid he might, mount upon a high horse. Yes, he confessed, he was a trifle worried, but it was no great matter, and he expected to have put it all behind him in a very few days' time.

Sophy, who had led the way to a rustic seat, now obliged him to sit down beside her on it. Tracing a pattern on the gravel path with the point of her parasol, she said: 'If it is money – and it nearly always is: it is the most odious thing! – and you do not care to ask your papa for it, I expect I could help you.'

'Much good it would be to ask my father!' said Hubert. 'He hasn't a feather to fly with, and what is so dashed unjust, when you consider, the only time I ever applied to him he went into a worse rage than Charles does!'

'Does Charles go into a rage?'

'Oh, well – ! Not, not precisely, but I don't know but what I'd liefer he did!' replied Hubert bitterly.

She nodded. 'Then you don't wish to approach him. Do pray, tell me!'

'Certainly not!' said Hubert, on his dignity. 'Devilish good of you, Sophy, but I haven't come to *that* yet!'

'Come to what?' she demanded.

'Borrowing money from females, of course! Besides, there's no need. I shall come about, and before I go up to Oxford again, thank the lord!'

'How?'

'Never mind, but it can't fail! If it does – but it will not! I may have a father who – well, no sense in talking of *him*! And I may have a dashed disagreeable brother, holding so tightly to the purse-strings that you'd think he was a Jew, but fortunately for me I've a couple of good friends – whatever Charles may say!'

'Oh!' said Sophy, digesting this information. Disagreeable Charles might be, but she was shrewd enough to suspect that if he condemned any of Hubert's friends there might be much to be said in his defence. 'Does he dislike your friends?'

Hubert gave a short laugh. 'Lord, yes! Just because they are knowing 'uns, and kick up a lark every now and then, he proses like a Methodist, and – Here, Sophy, you won't start talking to Charles, will you?'

'Of course I shall do no such thing!' she said indignantly. 'Why, what a creature you must think me!'

'No, I don't, only – Oh, well, it don't signify! I shall be as merry as a grig in a week's time, and I don't mean to get into a fix again, I can tell you!'

She was obliged to be satisfied with this assurance, for he would say no more. After taking another turn round the shrubbery, she left him, and went back to the house.

She found Mr Rivenhall seated under the elm tree on the south lawn, with Tina, who was sleeping off a large repast, at his feet. 'If you want to see a rare picture, Sophy,' he said, 'peep in at the drawing-room window! My mother is sound asleep on one sofa, and the Marquesa on another.'

'Well, if that is their notion of enjoyment I don't think we should disturb them,' she replied. 'It would not be mine, but I do *try* to remember that some people like to spend half their days doing nothing at all.'

He made room for her to sit down beside him. 'No, I fancy idleness is not your besetting sin,' he agreed. 'Sometimes I wonder whether it would not be better for the rest of us if it were, but we have agreed not to quarrel today, so I shall not pursue that thought. But, Sophy, what is my uncle about to be marrying that woman?'

She wrinkled her brow. 'She is very good-natured, you know, and Sir Horace says he likes reposeful females.'

'I am astonished that you have sanctioned so unsuitable a match.'

'Nonsense! I have nothing to say to it.'

'I imagine you have everything to say to it,' he retorted. 'Don't play off the airs of an innocent to me, cousin! I know you well enough to be tolerably certain that you rule my uncle with a rod of iron, and have probably guarded him from dozens of Marquesas in your time!'

She laughed. 'Well, yes,' she admitted. 'But, then, they would none of them have made the poor angel at all comfortable, and I do think perhaps Sancia may. I have long made up my mind to it that he should marry again, you know.'

'Next you will say that this match is of your making!'

'Oh, no! There is never the least need to make matches for Sir Horace!' she said frankly. 'He is the most susceptible creature imaginable, and, which is so dangerous, if a pretty woman will but weep on his shoulder he will do anything she wants!'

He did not reply, and she saw that his attention was fixed on Cecilia and Sir Vincent, who had that instant come round a corner of the clipped yew hedge. A slight frown descended on to his brow, which made Sophy say severely: 'Now, don't take one of your pets because Cecy flirts a little with Sir Vincent! You should be thankful to see her taking interest in some other man than Mr Fawnhope. But there is no pleasing you!'

'I am certainly not pleased with *that* connection!'

'Oh, you have no cause to feel alarm! Sir Vincent is only interested in heiresses, and has no intention of offering for Cecy.'

'Thank you, it is not on that score that I feel alarm,' he answered.

She could say no more, for by this time the other couple had come up to them. Cecilia, who was looking prettier than ever, described how Sir Vincent had been so obliging as to find a servant who gave him some maize for the pigeons. She had fed them, and her cousin thought she had taken far more delight in encouraging them to take maize from between her lips than in listening to Sir Vincent's practised compliments.

They were soon joined by Hubert. He shot Sophy a glance so pregnant with mischief that in spite of his high shirt-points, his elaborate neckcloth, and his fashionable waistcoat he looked very much more like a schoolboy than the town-beau he fancied himself. She could not imagine what mischief he could have found to perform in the little time since she had left him, but before she could speculate very seriously on this problem her attention was diverted by the Marquesa, who appeared at the drawing-room window, and made signs indicative of her desire that they should all come into the house. Civility obliged even Mr Rivenhall to obey the summons. They found the Marquesa so much refreshed by her nap as to have become quite animated. Lady Ombersley had awakened from slumber, uttering the mystic words: *Lotion of the Ladies of Denmark*, which had operated so powerfully upon her hostess as to make her sit bolt upright upon her sofa, exclaiming: 'But no! Better distilled water of green pineapples, I assure you!' By the time the party on the south lawn entered the house the two elder ladies had thoroughly explored every path known to them that led to the preservation of the complexion, and if they differed on such points as the value of raw veal laid on the face at night to remove wrinkles, they found themselves at one over the beneficial effects of chervil water, and crushed strawberries.

It now being at least two hours since the light *merienda* had been consumed, the Marquesa stood in urgent need of further sustenance, and warmly invited her guests to partake of tea and angel cakes. It was then that Lady Ombersley became aware of the absence of Miss Wraxton and Mr Fawnhope from the gathering, and demanded to know where they were. Cecilia replied, with a shrug, that they were no doubt quoting poetry to each other in the wood; but when twenty minutes passed without their putting in an appearance not only Lady Ombersley, but her elder son also, became a trifle restive. Then it was that Sophy remembered Hubert's look of mischief. She glanced across at him, and saw his expression was so unconcerned as to be wholly incredible. In deep foreboding she made an excuse to change her seat to one beside his, and whispered, under cover of the general conversation: 'You dreadful creature, what have you done?'

'Locked them into the wood!' he whispered in return. 'That will teach her to play propriety!'

She had to bite back a laugh, but managed to say, with suitable severity: 'It will not do! If you have the key, give it to me so that no one will observe you!'

He said: 'What a spoil-sport you are!' but soon found an opportunity to drop it into her lap, for although it had seemed, at the time, a splendid idea to lock the gate into the wood, he had been realizing for some minutes that to release the imprisoned couple without scandal might prove to be rather more difficult.

'It is so unlike dear Eugenia!' said Lady Ombersley. 'I cannot think what they can be about!'

'*En verdad*, it is not difficult to imagine!' remarked the Marquesa, rather amused. 'So beautiful a young man and so romantic a scene!'

'I will go and look for them,' said Mr Rivenhall, getting up, and walking out of the room.

Hubert began to look a little alarmed, but Sophy exclaimed suddenly: 'I wonder if one of the gardeners can have locked the gate again, thinking that we had all left the wood? Excuse me, Sancia!'

She overtook Mr Rivenhall in the shrubbery, and called out: 'So stupid! Sancia, you know, lives in dread of robbers and has trained all her servants never to leave a gate or a door unlocked! One of the gardeners, supposing us all to have gone back to the house, locked the gate into the wood. Gaston had the key: here it is!'

A bend in the gravel walk brought the gates into the wood within view. Miss Wraxton was standing by them, and it was plain to the meanest intelligence that she was in no very amiable humour. Behind her, seated upon a bank, and absorbed in metrical composition, was Mr Fawnhope, to all appearances divorced from the world.

As Mr Rivenhall fitted the key into the lock, Sophy said: 'I am so sorry! It is all the fault of Sancia's absurd terrors! Are you very bored and chilled, Miss Wraxton?'

Miss Wraxton had endured a trying half-hour. Upon finding herself shut into the wood, she had first asked Mr Fawnhope if he could not climb over the fence, and when he had replied, quite simply, that he could not, she had requested him to shout. But the ode that was burgeoning in his head had by this time taken possession of him, and he had said that the sylvan setting was just the inspiration he needed. After that, he sat down on the bank, and drew out his notebook and a pencil, and whenever she begged him to bestir himself to procure her release, all he said, and that in a voice that showed how far away were his thoughts, was 'Hush!' Consequently she was in a mood ripe for murder when the rescue party at last arrived on the scene, and was betrayed into an unwise accusation. 'You did this!' she flung at Sophy, quite white with anger.

Sophy, who felt sorry for her being discovered in so ridiculous a situation, replied soothingly: 'No, it was a foolish servant, who thought we had all gone back to the house. Never mind! Come and drink some of Sancia's excellent tea!'

'I don't believe you. You are unprincipled, and vulgar, and –'

'Eugenia!' said Mr Rivenhall sharply.

She gave an angry sob, but said no more. Sophy went into the wood to rouse Mr Fawnhope from his abstraction, and Mr Rivenhall said: 'It was nothing but an accident, and there is no need to be so put-out.'

'I am persuaded your cousin did it to make me a laughingstock,' she said in a low voice.

'Nonsense!' he replied coldly.

She saw that he was by no means in sympathy with her, and said: 'I need hardly tell you that my aim was to prevent your sister spending the whole afternoon in that odious young man's company.'

'With the result that she spent it in Talgarth's company,' he retorted. 'There was no reason for you to be so busy, Eugenia. My mother's presence, not to mention my own, made your action – I shall say *unnecessary!*'

It might have been supposed that these words of censure filled Miss Wraxton's cup to the brim, but upon entering the drawing-room she found that she had still to endure the Marquesa's comments. The Marquesa favoured the company with a disquisition on the licence allowed to young English ladies, contrasting it with the strict chaperonage of Spanish damsels; and everyone, with the exception of Mr Rivenhall, who was markedly silent, felt for Miss Wraxton in her chagrin, and made great efforts to placate her, Sophy going so far as to give up her place in the curricle to her on the homeward journey. She was insensibly mollified, but when, later, she tried to justify her actions to her betrothed, he cut her short, saying too much noise had been made already over a trivial occurrence.

'I cannot believe that any of the servants were responsible,' she insisted.

'You would do better to pretend to believe it, however.'

'Then you do not think so either!' she exclaimed.

'No, I think Hubert did it,' he replied coldly. 'And if I am right, you have my cousin to thank for speedily releasing you.'

'Hubert!' she cried. 'Why should he do such an ungentlemanly thing, pray?'

He shrugged. 'Possibly for a jest, possibly because he resented your interference in Cecilia's affairs, my dear Eugenia. He is much attached to his sister.'

She said in a deeply mortified tone: 'If that is so, I hope you mean to take him to task!'

'I shall do nothing so ill-judged,' responded Mr Rivenhall, at his most blighting.

Nine

SHORTLY AFTER THIS NOT ENTIRELY SUCCESSFUL DAY IN THE COUNTRY Mr Rivenhall announced his intention of going down to Ombersley for a spell. His mother had no objection to advance, but realizing that the dread moment of disclosure had now come, said, with an assumption of calm she was far from feeling, that she hoped he would come back to London in time to attend Sophy's party.

'Is it so important?' he asked. 'I have no turn for dancing, Mama, and such an evening as you will no doubt pass is of all things most insipid!'

'Well, it is rather important,' she confessed. 'It would be thought rather strange if you were absent, dear Charles!'

'Good heavens, Mama, I have been absent from all such affairs in this house!'

'As a matter of fact, this party is to be a little larger than we first thought it would be!' she said desperately.

He bent one of his disconcerting stares upon her. 'Indeed! I had collected that some twenty persons were to be invited?'

'There – there will be a few more than that!' she said.

'How many more?'

She became intent on disentangling the fringe of her shawl from the arm of her chair. 'Well, we thought perhaps it would be best – since it is our first party for your cousin, and your uncle particularly desired me to launch her upon society – to give a set ball, Charles! And your father promises to bring the Duke of York to it, if only for half an hour! It seems he is well-acquainted with Horace: I am sure it is most gratifying!'

'How many persons, ma'am, have you invited to this precious ball?' demanded Mr Rivenhall, ungratified.

'Not – not above four hundred!' faltered his guilty parent. 'And they will not all of them come, dear Charles!'

'Four hundred!' he exclaimed. 'I need not ask whose doing this is! And who, ma'am, is to foot the bill for this entertainment?'

'Sophy – that is to say, your uncle, of course! I assure you the cost is not to come upon you!'

He was not in the least soothed by this, but, on the contrary, rapped out: 'Do you imagine I will permit that wretched girl to pay for parties in this house? If you have been mad enough, ma'am, to consent to this scheme –'

Lady Ombersley prudently sought refuge in tears, and began to grope for her smelling-salts. Her son eyed her in a baffled way, and said with painstaking restraint: 'Pray do not cry, Mama! I am well aware whom I have to thank for this.'

An interruption, welcome to Lady Ombersley, occurred in the shape of Selina, who bounced into the room, exclaiming: 'Oh, Mama! When we gave the ball for Cecilia, did we –' She then perceived her eldest brother, and broke off short, looking extremely conscious.

'Go on!' said Mr Rivenhall grimly.

Selina gave her head a slight toss. 'I suppose you know all about Sophy's ball: well, I am sure I don't care, for you cannot stop it now that all the cards of invitation have gone out, and three hundred and eighty seven persons have accepted! Mama, Sophy says that when she and Sir Horace held a great reception in Vienna, Sir Horace warned the police-officers of it, so that they were able to keep the street clear, and tell the coachmen where to go, and so-on. Did we not do the same for Cecilia's ball?'

'Yes, and the link-boys as well,' replied Lady Ombersley, emerging briefly from her handkerchief, but retiring into its protection again immediately.

'Yes, Mama, and the champagne!' said Selina, determined to discharge the whole of her errand. 'Should it be ordered from Gunters, with all the rest? Or –'

'You may inform your cousin,' interrupted Mr Rivenhall, 'that the champagne will be provided from our own cellars!' He then turned his shoulder on his young sister, and demanded of his parent: 'How does it come about that Eugenia has not mentioned this affair to me? Has she not been invited to your ball?'

One desperately enquiring eye emerged from the handkerchief, wildly seeking enlightenment of Selina.

'Good gracious, Charles!' said that damsel, shocked. 'Can you have forgotten the bereavement in Miss Wraxton's family? I am sure if she has told us once she has told us a dozen times that propriety forbids her to attend any but the most quiet parties!'

'This, too, is my cousin's work, I collect!' he said, his lips tightening. 'I must say, ma'am, I might have expected, if you were bent on this folly, that you would have sent a card to my promised wife!'

'Of course, Charles, of course!' said Lady Ombersley. 'If it has not been done, it is a foolish oversight! Though it is perfectly true that Eugenia has told us that while she is in black gloves –'

'Oh, Mama, don't!' cried Selina impetuously. 'You know she will cast a damper over everything, with that long face of hers, just like a horse –'

'How dare you?' interrupted Mr Rivenhall furiously.

Selina looked a little frightened, but muttered: 'Well, she *does*, whatever you may choose to think, Charles!'

'More of my cousin's work, no doubt!'

Selina flushed, and cast down her eyes. Mr Rivenhall turned to his mother. 'Be so good as to tell me, ma'am, in what manner this affair is arranged between you and Sophy! Does she give you a draft on my uncle's bank, or what?'

'I – I don't precisely know!' said Lady Ombersley. 'I mean, it has not been discussed yet! Indeed, Charles, I did not know myself until the just the other day that so many people had been invited!'

'Well, *I* know, Mama!' said Selina. 'The bills are all sent to Sophy, and you will not be troubled with them at all!'

'I thank you!' Charles said, and walked abruptly out of the room.

He found his cousin in the small saloon at the back of the house which was generally known as the Young Ladies' Room. She was engaged in compiling some kind of a list, but she looked up at the opening of the door, and smiled at Charles. 'Are you looking for Cecilia? She has gone out to do some shopping in Bond Street, with Miss Adderbury.'

'No, I am not looking for Cecilia!' he answered. 'My business is with you, cousin, and will not take me long. I am informed that my mother is giving a ball in your honour on Tuesday, and by some extraordinary piece of mismanagement the bills for this have been sent to you. Will you be so obliging as to find them, and give them to me?'

'On your high ropes again, Charles?' she said, lifting her brows. 'This is Sir Horace's ball, not my aunt's: there is no mismanagement.'

'Sir Horace may be master in his own house – though that I doubt! – but he is not master in this one! If my mother chooses to hold a ball, she may do so, but in no circumstances will the charge fall upon my uncle. It is intolerable that you should have persuaded my mother to consent to such a scheme! Give me what bills you have, if you please!'

'But I do not please,' replied Sophy. 'Neither Sir Horace nor you, dear cousin, is the master in this house. I have my Uncle Ombersley's consent to what I have done.' She saw with satisfaction that she had utterly taken him aback, and added: 'If I were you, Charles, I would go for a nice walk in the Park. I have always found that there is nothing so beneficial to the temper as exercise in the fresh air.'

He controlled himself with a strong effort. 'Cousin, I am in earnest! I cannot and I will not tolerate such a situation as this!'

'But no one has asked you to tolerate anything at all,' she pointed out. 'If my uncle and aunt are satisfied with my arrangements, pray what have you to say to them?'

He said through shut teeth: 'I think I told you once before, cousin, that we did very well here before you came to upset all our comfort!'

'Yes, you did, and what you meant, Charles, was that until I came no one dared to flout you. You should be grateful to me – or at any rate, Miss Wraxton should, for I am sure you would have made an odious husband before I came to stay with your Mama.'

This put him in mind of a complaint he could with justice make. He said stiffly: 'Since you have brought up Miss Wraxton's name, I shall be much obliged to you, cousin, if you will refrain from telling my sisters that she has a face like a horse!'

'But, Charles, no blame attaches to Miss Wraxton! She cannot help it, and that, I *assure* you, I have always pointed out to your sisters!'

'I consider Miss Wraxton's countenance particularly well-bred!'

'Yes, indeed, but you have quite misunderstood the matter! I *meant* a particularly well-bred horse!'

'You meant, as I am perfectly aware, to belittle Miss Wraxton!'

'No, no! I am very fond of horses!' Sophy said earnestly.

Before he could stop himself he found that he was replying to this. 'Selina, who repeated this remark to me, is *not* fond of horses, however, and she —' He broke off, seeing how absurd it was to argue on such a head.

'I expect she will be, when she has lived in the same house with Miss Wraxton for a month or two,' said Sophy encouragingly.

Mr Rivenhall, restraining an impulse to box his cousin's ears, flung out of the room, slamming the door behind him. At the foot of the stairs he encountered Lord Bromford, who was handing his hat and overcoat to a footman. Mr Rivenhall, seeing how he might, in some measure, be revenged on Sophy, greeted him with a great affability, asked him if he meant to attend Tuesday's ball, and, upon hearing that his lordship was much looking forward to the engagement, said: 'Have you come to bespeak my cousin's hand to the cotillion? You are wise! She will certainly be besieged with solicitations! Dassett, you will find Miss Stanton-Lacy in the Yellow Saloon! Take his lordship up to her!'

'Do you think I should?' said Lord Bromford anxiously. 'It was not danced in Jamaica, you know, but I have been taking lessons, and two of the steps I know tolerably well. Will there be waltzing? I do not waltz. I do not think it seemly. I hope Miss Stanton-Lacy does not waltz. I do not like to see a lady doing so.'

'Everyone waltzes nowadays,' said Mr Rivenhall bent on his fell intent. 'You should take lessons in that too, Bromford, or you will be quite cut out!'

'I do not think,' said Lord Bromford, having considered the matter gravely, 'that one should sacrifice one's principles to gratify a female's whim. I do not think the quadrille objectionable, although I am aware that there are many who do not permit it to be danced in their houses. In the country dance I am prepared to take my part. There is authority for the exercise of dancing, by which I mean to signify the round, or country-dance, in the works of the Ancients. Plato, you know, recommended that children should be taught to dance, and several classic writers deemed it an excellent recreation after serious study.'

But at this point Mr Rivenhall bethought him of a pressing engagement, and fled the house. Lord Bromford followed the butler upstairs to the drawing-room, Dasset having his own views on the impropriety of ushering single gentlemen into the Young Ladies' Room. When Sophy, duly chaperoned by Selina, joined him there, he lost no time in begging her to dance the cotillion with him. Sophy, trusting that one of her Peninsula friends would come to her rescue, said how sorry she was to be obliged to refuse him. She was, she said, already engaged. His face fell, and he looked even a little offended, exclaiming. 'How can this be, when your cousin told me to make haste to be first with you?'

'My cousin Charles? Did he indeed?' said Sophy appreciatively. 'Well, no doubt he did not know that my hand has been claimed these past three days. Perhaps we may stand up together for one of the country-dances.'

He bowed, and said: 'I have been telling your cousin that we have good authority for indulging in country-dances. They cannot, I believe, be considered harmful. The waltz, on the other hand, I cannot approve of.'

'Oh, you do not waltz? I am so glad – I mean, one does not think of your indulging in anything so frivolous, Lord Bromford!'

He appeared to be pleased by this; he settled himself deeper in his chair, and said: 'You raise an interesting thesis, ma'am. One is familiar with the phrase. *A man may be known by the company he keeps*: can it be that he may also be known by the dances he permits himself to indulge in?'

Since neither lady had any views to advance on this subject, it was fortunate that his question was purely rhetorical. He began to expand the topic, and was only interrupted by the arrival of Mr Wychbold, who came first to offer to escort Sophy and her cousins to witness a wild beast show, and second to beg the honour of partnering her in the cotillion. She was obliged to deny him, but with regret, for Mr Wychbold was a notable dancer, performing every step in the cotillion with grace and elegance.

However, when Tuesday dawned she had acquired a far from contemptible partner in Lord Francis Wolvey. The fact that he had first applied for Miss Rivenhall's hand she bore with great fortitude, saying that in Christian charity to all other young females Cecilia should lose no time in disposing of herself in wedlock.

It was plain from the outset that the ball was to be one of the season's successes. Even the weather favoured it. From dawn till dinner-time Ombersley House was the scene of restless activity, and the road outside noisy with the wheels of tradesmen's carts, and the whistling of innumerable errand-boys. Mr Rivenhall arrived from the country just as two men in shirtsleeves and leather breeches were erecting an awning across the flag-way to the road; and another, wearing a baize apron, laying a red carpet down the steps, under Dassett's lofty supervision. Inside the house, Mr Rivenhall almost collided with a footman, staggering in the direction of the ballroom with a gigantic potted palm clasped to his bosom, and avoided him only to be faintly screamed at by the housekeeper, who was carrying a pile of the best table-damask to the dining-room. Dassett, who had followed Mr Rivenhall into the house, informed him, with satisfaction, that they would sit down thirty to dinner at eight o'clock. He added that her ladyship was laid down upon her bed in preparation for the revels, and that his lordship had personally selected the wines to be served at dinner. Mr Rivenhall, who seemed to be resigned rather than delighted, nodded, and asked whether any letters awaited him.

'No, sir,' replied Dassett. 'I should mention that the band of

Scots Greys will play during supper, Miss Sophy being acquainted with the Colonel, who will be amongst the dinner-guests. A vast improvement, if I may say so, sir, on the Pandean pipes, which have become quite common since we had them for Miss Cecilia's ball last year. Miss Sophy, I venture to say, is a lady as knows precisely how things should be done. A great pleasure, if I may be pardoned the liberty, to work for Miss Sophy, for she thinks of everything, and I fancy there will be no hitch to mar the festivities.'

Mr Rivenhall grunted, and went off to his own apartments. When he next appeared, it was to join the rest of his family in the drawing-room a few minutes only before eight o'clock. His two young sisters, who were deriving much entertainment from hanging over the banisters of the staircase leading to the schoolroom floor, informed him in penetrating whispers that he looked so smart they could not believe that there would be any other gentleman to rival him. He looked up, laughing, for although he had a good figure, and was dressed with propriety in black satin knee-breeches, a white waistcoat, striped stockings, and a waisted coat with very long tails, he knew that he would be sartorially outshone by half the male guests. But his little sisters' wholehearted admiration certainly softened his mood, and after promising faithfully to send a servant up to the schoolroom with ices later on, he went on to the drawing-room and was even able to bring himself to compliment his sister and cousin on their gowns.

Sophy had chosen a dress of her favourite pomona-green crape, which she wore over a slip of white satin. It had tiny puff-sleeves of lace and seed-pearls, and was lavishly trimmed with lace. Particularly fine diamond drops hung from her ears; her pearl necklace was clasped round her throat; and an opera-comb was set behind the elaborate knot of hair on the crown of her head. Jane Storridge had brushed and pomaded her side-curls until they glowed richly chestnut in the candlelight. Green-striped satin slippers, long gloves, and a fan of frosted crape on ivory sticks completed her toilet. Lady Ombersley, while approving of this striking ensemble, could not forbear gazing at Cecilia with eyes misty with maternal pride. All the youth and beauty of the Upper Ten Thousand would be present at her ball tonight, she reflected, in a large-minded spirit, but there was not a girl amongst them who would not be cast into the shade by Cecilia, a dream-princess in white spider-gauze, glinting a little when she moved, and the light caught the silver acorns embroidered on the delicate material. Cecilia's curls, with only a silver ribbon threaded through them, were like spun gold; her eyes a clear, translucent blue; her mouth a perfect bow. Beside Sophy she seemed ethereal; her father, surveying her with easy affection, said she made him think of a fairy: Queen Mab, or Titania, was it? He needed Eugenia Wraxton to set him right.

He was to have her. Miss Wraxton, after prolonged consideration, had decided to attend Sophy's ball, gaining her mama's consent by assuring her that she should certainly not take part in any dancing. She was the first of the dinner-guests to arrive, and was attended by her brother Alfred, who ogled Cecilia and Sophy through his quizzing-glass, paying them such extravagant compliments as to bring a faint flush to Cecilia's cheeks, and a sparkling look into Sophy's eyes. Miss Wraxton, who was attired in discreet lavender crape, and had come determined to please, and to be pleased, also complimented the cousins on their appearance. Her remarks, however, were in far better taste, and won a warm look from Charles. At the first opportunity, he engaged her attention, going over to put a chair for her, and saying: 'I had not dared to hope that you would be present tonight. Thank you!'

She smiled, and pressed his hand slightly. 'Mama did not quite like it, but she agreed that it would be proper for me to come, in the circumstances. I shall not dance, I need hardly say.'

'I am delighted to hear it: you present me with a capital excuse for following your example!'

She looked gratified, but said: 'No, no, you are to do your duty, Charles! I insist upon it!'

'The Marquesa de Villacañas!' announced Dassett.

'Good God!' ejaculated Charles, under his breath.

The Marquesa came into the room, magnificent, and decidedly exotic, in gold satin, casually adorned with ruby or emerald brooches, chains, and necklaces. An immensely high Spanish comb was in her hair, with a mantilla draped over it; an aroma of heavy perfume hung about her; and a very long train swept the floor behind her. Lord Ombersley drew a deep breath, and moved forward to greet with real enthusiasm a guest so worthy of his notice.

Mr Rivenhall forgot that he was not on speaking-terms with his abominable cousin, and said in her ear: 'How in the world did you rouse her to so much effort?'

She laughed. 'Oh, she wished in any event to spend a few days in London, so all I had to do was to engage a suite of rooms for her at the Pulteney Hotel, and to charge Pepita, her maid, most straitly, to send her to us tonight.'

'I am astonished that she could be brought even to contemplate so much exertion!'

'Ah, she knew I would go myself to fetch her if she failed!'

More guests were arriving; Mr Rivenhall moved away to assist his parents in receiving them; the big double drawing-room began to fill up; and at only a few minutes past eight o'clock Dasset was able to announce dinner.

The guests assembled for dinner were of a quality to fill any hostess's bosom with pride, including as they did a great many members of the diplomatic set, and two Cabinet Ministers, with their wives. Lady Ombersley could cram her rooms with as many

members of the nobility as she cared to invite, but since her husband took little interest in politics, Government circles were rather
beyond her reach. But Sophy, barely acquainted with the very
well-born but equally undistinguished people who made up the
larger part of the Polite World, had been bred up in Government
circles, and, from the day when she first did up her hair and let
down her skirts, had been entertaining celebrated persons, and
was on the friendliest of terms with them. Her, or perhaps Sir
Horace's, acquaintances preponderated at her aunt's board, but
not even Miss Wraxton, on the watch for signs of presumption in
her, could find any fault with her demeanour. It might have been
expected, since all the arrangements for the party had been hers,
that she would have put herself forward more than was becoming,
but so far from doing so she seemed to be in a retiring mood,
bearing no part in greeting guests upstairs, and confining her conversation at table, most correctly, to the gentlemen on her either
side. Miss Wraxton, who had labelled her a hoyden, was obliged
to own that her company manners at least were above reproach.

The ball, which began at ten o'clock, was held in the huge room
built for the purpose at the back of the house. It was lit by hundreds
of candles in a great crystal chandelier hanging from the ceiling,
and since this had been unswathed from its holland covering three
days before so that both footmen and the pantry-boy could wash
and polish its lustres, it sparkled like a collection of mammoth diamonds. Masses of flowers were arranged in set pieces at either end
of the room, and an excellent orchestra had been engaged, quite
regardless (Mr Rivenhall bitterly reflected) of expense.

The room, large as it was, soon became so crowded with
elegant persons that it seemed certain that the function would
receive the final accolade, in being voted a sad crush. No hostess
could desire more.

The ball opened with a country-dance, in which Mr Rivenhall, in honour bound, stood up with his cousin. He performed his part with propriety, she hers with grace; and Miss Wraxton, watching from a route-chair at one side of the room, smiled graciously upon them both. Mr Fawnhope, a most beautiful dancer, had led Cecilia into the same set, a circumstance that considerably annoyed Mr Rivenhall. He thought that Cecilia should have reserved the opening dance for some more important guest, and he derived no satisfaction from overhearing more than one tribute to the grace and beauty of such an arresting couple. Nowhere did Mr Fawnhope shine to more advantage than in a ballroom, and happy was the lady who stood up with him. Envious eyes followed Cecilia, and more than one dark beauty wished that, since Mr Fawnhope, himself so angelically fair, unaccountably preferred gold hair to black, she could change her colouring to suit his fancy.

Lord Bromford, one of the earliest arrivals, failed, owing to Mr Rivenhall's sense of duty, to secure Sophy's hand for the first dance, and as a waltz followed the country-dance it was some time before he was able to stand up with her. While waltzing was in progress he stood watching the performers, and in due course gravitated to Miss Wraxton's side, and entertained her with an exposition of his views on the waltz. With these she was to some extent in sympathy, but she expressed herself more moderately, saying that while she herself would not care to waltz, the dance could not be altogether frowned on now that it had been sanctioned at Almack's.

'I did not see it danced at Government House,' said Lord Bromford.

Miss Wraxton, who was fond of reading books of travels, said: 'Jamaica! How much I envy you, sir, your sojourn in that interesting island! I am sure it must be one of the most romantic places imaginable.'

Lord Bromford, whose youth had never been charmed by tales

of the Spanish Main, replied that it had much to recommend it, and went on to describe the properties of its medicinal springs, and the great variety of marbles to be found in the mountains, all of which Miss Wraxton listened to with interest, telling Mr Rivenhall later that she thought his lordship had a well-informed mind.

It was half-way through the evening when Sophy, breathless from an energetic waltz with Mr Wychbold, was standing at the side of the room, fanning herself, and watching the couples still circling round the floor while her partner went to procure a glass of iced lemonade for her, was suddenly accosted by a pleasant-looking gentleman, who came up to her, and said with a smile: 'My friend, Major Quinton, promised that he would present me to the Grand Sophy, but the wretched fellow goes from one set to the next, and never spares me a thought! How do you do, Miss Stanton-Lacy? You will forgive my informality, won't you? It is true that I have no business here, for I was not invited, but Charles assures me that had I not been believed to be still laid upon a bed of sickness I must have received a card.'

She looked at him in that frank way of hers, summing him up. She liked what she saw. He was a man in the early thirties, not precisely handsome, but with a pleasing countenance redeemed from the commonplace by a pair of humorous gray eyes. He was above the medium height, and had a good pair of shoulders, and an excellent leg for a riding-boot.

'It is certainly too bad of Major Quinton,' Sophy said smilingly. 'But you know what a rattle-pate he is! Ought we to have sent you a card? You must forgive us! I hope your illness was not of a serious nature?'

'Alas, merely painful and humiliating!' he replied. 'Would you believe that a man of my age could fall a victim to so childish a complaint, ma'am? – Mumps!'

Sophy dropped her fan, exclaiming: 'What did you say? *Mumps?*'

'Mumps,' he repeated, picking up the fan, and giving it back to her. 'I do not wonder at your astonishment!'

'Then you,' said Sophy, 'are Lord Charlbury!'

He bowed. 'I am, and I perceive that my fame has gone before me. I own, I should not have chosen to figure in your mind as the man with mumps, but so, I see, it is!'

'Let us sit down,' said Sophy.

He looked amused, but accompanied her at once to a sofa against the wall. 'By all means! But may I not get you a glass of lemonade?'

'Mr Wychbold – I expect you are acquainted with him – has already gone to do so. I should like to talk to you for a little while, for I have heard a great deal about you, you know.'

'Nothing could please me more, for *I* have heard a great deal about you, ma'am, and it has inspired me with the liveliest desire to meet you!'

'Major Quinton,' said Sophy, 'is a shocking quiz, and I daresay has given you quite a false notion of me!'

'I must point out to you, ma'am,' he retaliated, 'that we are both in the same case, for you know *me* only as a man with mumps, and at the risk of sounding like a coxcomb I must assure you that *that* must have given *you* an equally false notion of *me!*'

'You are perfectly right,' said Sophy seriously. 'It did give me a false notion of you!' Her eyes followed Cecilia and Mr Fawnhope round the room; she drew a breath, and said: 'Things may be a trifle difficult.'

'That,' said Lord Charlbury, his eyes following hers, 'I had already realized.'

'I cannot conceive,' said Sophy, with strong feeling, 'what can have possessed you, sir, to contract mumps at such a moment!'

'It was not done by design,' said his lordship meekly.

'Nothing could have been more ill-judged!' said Sophy.

'Not ill-judged!' he pleaded. 'Unfortunate!'

Mr Wychbold came up just then with Sophy's lemonade. 'Hallo, Everard!' he said. 'I didn't know you were fit to be seen yet! How are you, dear boy?'

'Bruised in spirit, Cyprian, bruised in spirit! My sufferings under the complaint that struck me down were as nothing to what I now undergo. Shall I ever live it down?'

'Oh, I don't know!' replied Mr Wychbold consolingly. 'Dashed paltry thing to happen to one, of course, but the town's memory ain't long. Why, do you remember poor Bolton taking a toss into the Serpentine, clean over his horse's head? No one talked of anything else for almost a week. Poor fellow had to rusticate for a while, but it blew over, y'know!'

'Must it be rustication?' Lord Charlbury asked.

'On no account!' said Sophy decidedly. She waited until Mr Wychbold's attention was claimed by a lady in puce satin, and then turned towards her companion, and said forthrightly: 'Are you a very good dancer, sir?'

'Not, I fancy, above the average, ma'am. Certainly not to compare with the exquisite young man we are both watching.'

'In that case,' said Sophy, 'I would not, if I were you, solicit Cecilia to waltz!'

'I have already done so, but your warning is unnecessary: she is engaged for every waltz, and also the quadrille. The most I can hope for is to stand up with her in a country-dance.'

'Don't do it!' Sophy advised him. 'To be trying to talk to anyone when you should be attending to the figure is always fatal, believe me!'

He turned his head, and gave her back a look as frank as her own. 'Miss Stanton-Lacy, you are plainly aware of my circumstances. Will you tell me in what case I stand, and who is the Adonis monopolizing Miss Rivenhall?'

'He is Augustus Fawnhope, and he is a poet.'

'That has an ominous ring,' he said lightly. 'I know the family, of course, but I think I have not previously encountered this sprig.'

'Very likely you might not, for he was used to be with Sir Charles Stuart, in Brussels. Lord Charlbury, you look to me like a sensible man!'

'I had rather I had a head like a Greek coin,' he remarked ruefully.

'You must understand,' said Sophy, disregarding this frivolity, 'that half of the young ladies in London are in love with Mr Fawnhope.'

'I can readily believe it, and I grudge him only one of his conquests.'

She would have replied, but they were interrupted. Lord Ombersley, who had gone away after dinner, now reappeared, accompanied by an elderly and immensely corpulent man in whom no one had the least difficulty in recognizing a member of the Royal Family. He was, in fact, the Duke of York, that one of Farmer George's sons who most nearly resembled him. He had the same protuberant blue eye, and beaky nose, the same puffy cheeks, and pouting mouth, but he was a much larger man than his father. He appeared to be in imminent danger of bursting out of his tightly stretched pantaloons, he wheezed when he spoke, but he was plainly a genial prince, ready to be pleased, standing on very little ceremony, and chatting affably to anyone who was presented to him. Both Cecilia and Sophy had this honour. His Royal Highness's appreciation of Cecilia's beauty was quite as broadly expressed as Mr Wraxton's had been, and no one could doubt that had he met her in some less public spot it would not have been many minutes before the ducal arm would have been round her waist. Sophy aroused no such amorous tendency in him, but he talked very jovially to her, asked her how her father did, and opined, with a loud laugh, that by this time Sir Horace was enjoying himself amongst all the Brazilian beauties, the dog that he was! After that, he exchanged greetings with several friends, circulated about the room for a while, and finally withdrew to the library with his host and two other of his intimates for a rubber of whist.

Cecilia, escaping from the Royal presence with burning cheeks (for she hated to be the target of fulsome compliments), was intercepted by Mr Fawnhope, who said with great simplicity: 'You are more beautiful tonight than I had thought possible!'

'Oh, do not!' she exclaimed involuntarily. 'How insufferably hot it is in this room!'

'You are flushed, but it becomes you. I will take you on to the balcony.'

She made no demur, though this large term merely described the veriest foothold built outside each one of the twelve long windows of the ballroom, and fenced in with low iron railings. Mr Fawnhope parted the heavy curtains that veiled the window at the far end of the room, and she passed through them into a shallow embrasure. After a slight struggle with the bolt, Mr Fawnhope succeeded in opening the double window, and she was able to step out on to the narrow ledge. A chill breeze fanned her cheeks; she said: 'Ah, what a night! The stars!'

'*The evening star, love's harbinger!*' quoted Mr Fawnhope, somewhat vaguely scanning the heavens.

This idyll was rudely interrupted. Mr Rivenhall, having observed the retreat of the young couple, had followed them, and now stepped through the brocade curtains, saying harshly: 'Cecilia, are you lost to *all* sense of propriety? Come back into the ballroom at once!'

Startled, Cecilia turned quickly. Already agitated by the

unexpected encounter with Lord Charlbury, her nerves betrayed her into a hasty rejoinder. 'How dare you, Charles?' she said, in a trembling voice. 'Pray, what impropriety am I guilty of in seeking the fresh air in the company of my affianced husband?'

She took Mr Fawnhope's hand as she spoke, and confronted her brother with her chin up, and her cheeks very much flushed. Lord Charlbury, who had drawn back the curtain with one hand, stood perfectly still, as pale as she was red, steadfastly regarding her.

'Oh!' cried Cecilia faintly, snatching her hand from Mr Fawnhope's to press it to her cheek.

'May I know, Cecilia, if what you have just announced is the truth?' asked his lordship, not a trace of emotion in his well-bred voice.

'Yes!' she uttered.

'The devil it is not!' said Mr Rivenhall.

'You must permit me to offer you my felicitations,' said Lord Charlbury, bowing. He then let the curtain fall, and walked away the length of the ballroom in the direction of the doors.

Sophy, about to take her place with Major Quinton in the set which was forming, deserted her partner with a word of excuse, and overtook his lordship in the anteroom. 'Lord Charlbury!'

He turned. 'Miss Stanton-Lacy! Will you tender my apologies to Lady Ombersley for my not taking formal leave of her? She is not at present in the ballroom.'

'Yes, never mind that! What has occurred to make you leave so early?'

'I came, ma'am, with one purpose only in mind. It has been rendered useless for me to stay by your cousin's announcement a moment since that she is betrothed to young Fawnhope.'

'What a goose she is!' remarked Sophy cheerfully. 'I saw her go apart with Augustus, and I saw Charles follow her. Depend upon it, this is all his doing! I could box his ears! Do you ever ride in the Park?'

'Do I *what*?' he asked, bewildered.

'Ride in the Park!'

'Certainly I do, but –'

'Then do so tomorrow morning! Not too early, for I daresay I shall not be in bed until four o'clock! At ten, then; don't fail!'

She waited for no answer, but went back into the ballroom, leaving him to stare after her in considerable surprise. At any other time he would have smiled at her odd, abrupt ways, but he was a man in love, labouring under a crushing blow, and although he could maintain his calm manner it was at present beyond his power to feel any amusement.

Ten

IT WAS WITH NO REAL EXPECTATION OF MEETING SOPHY THAT LORD Charlbury had a horse saddled next morning, and betook himself to Hyde Park, for it seemed to him that a young lady who had danced the night through would not be very likely to be found riding in the Park by ten o'clock next day. But he had not cantered once round the Row when he saw a magnificent black horse coming towards him, and recognized Sophy on its back. He reined in, and pulled off his hat, exclaiming: 'I made sure you would still be abed, and fast asleep! Are you made of iron, Miss Stanton-Lacy?'

She pulled Salamanca up, sidling and prancing. 'Pooh!' she said, laughing at him. 'Did you think me such a poor creature as to be prostrated by one ball, sir?'

He turned his horse, and fell in beside her. John Potton followed at a discreet distance. Lord Charlbury complimented Sophy on Salamanca, but was cut short.

'Very true, he is a superb horse, but we have not met to talk of horses. *Such* a kick-up as there has been in Berkeley Square! Charles, of course – all Charles! The most diverting thing of all – do be diverted! indeed, there is no need for that grave face! – is that Augustus Fawnhope was quite as much taken aback as you or Charles!'

'Are you telling me that he does not *wish* to marry Cecilia!' demanded Charlbury.

'Oh – ! In some misty future! Certainly not immediately! I expect, you know, being a poet, he would much prefer to be the victim of a hopeless passion!' said Sophy merrily.

'Coxcomb!'

'If you like. I danced one waltz with him last night, when you had left us, and I do think I was very helpful, for I suggested to him a number of genteel occupations of a gainful nature, and promised to look about me for some great man in need of a secretary.'

'I hope he was grateful to you,' said Charlbury heavily.

'Not in the least! Augustus does not want to be any man's secretary, for he has a soul quite above such mundane matters as acquiring a respectable competence. I showed him what his future would be, in the prettiest way imaginable! Love in a cottage, you know, and a dozen hopeful children prattling at his knee.'

'You are a most unaccountable girl!' he exclaimed, looking at her in a good deal of amusement. 'Did this picture appal him?'

'Of course it did, but he is very chivalrous, and has now made up his mind to an early marriage. For anything I know he may be planning a flight to the Border.'

'What!' ejaculated his lordship.

'Oh, have no fear! Cecilia is by far too well brought-up to consent to such a scandalous thing! Let us have just one gallop! I know it is wrong, but there seem to be only nursemaids in the Park this morning. Good God, I am quite at fault! There is Lord Bromford, on that fat cob of his! I must tell you that he left the ball at midnight, because late hours are injurious to his health. Now we *must* gallop, or he will join us, and tell us about Jamaica!'

They flew down the track, Salamanca always just ahead of

Charlbury's rat-tailed gray, and so rousing Lord Charlbury to enthusiasm. 'By God, that's a capital horse!' he said. 'I do not know how you contrive to hold him, ma'am! Surely he is too strong for you?'

'I daresay, but he has charming manners, you see. Now we will proceed more soberly! Should you object very much to telling me whether you still desire to marry my cousin? You may snub me, if you choose!'

He replied rather ruefully: 'Will you think me contemptible if I tell you, yes?'

'Not at all. You would be foolish to refine too much upon what happened last night. Only consider! Instead of first fixing your interest with Cecilia, you applied to my uncle for leave to address her –'

'It is usual to do so!' he pointed out.

'It may be punctilious, but it is the greatest folly imaginable, particularly if you mean to contract mumps before you have even had time to offer for her!'

'It would, I collect, be useless to assure you that I did *not* mean to contract mumps! I had reason to believe that my suit would not be distasteful to her.'

'I expect she was very well-disposed towards you,' agreed Sophy cordially. 'But she had not then seen Augustus Fawnhope. At least, she had, but it seems that he was covered in spots at that time, so no one could expect her to fall in love with him.'

'I don't find the reflection precisely comforting, Miss Stanton-Lacy.'

'Call me Sophy! Everyone does, and we are going to become excessively friendly.'

'Are – are we?' he said. 'I mean, I am delighted to hear you say so, of course!'

She laughed. 'Oh pray don't be alarmed! If you still wish

to marry Cecilia – and I must tell you that although I thought otherwise before I had met you, I have now made up my mind to it that you would suit capitally – I will show you just how you must go on.'

He could not help smiling. 'I am much obliged to you! But if she loves young Fawnhope –'

'You must, if you please, consider for a moment!' said Sophy earnestly. 'Only think how it was! No sooner had you declared yourself to my uncle than you contracted a ridiculous complaint. *She* was informed that she was to become your wife – quite gothic, and most ill-judged! – and along came Augustus Fawnhope, looking, you will own, like a prince out of a fairy-tale, and what must he do but turn his back on all the poor females who were setting their caps at him, and fall in love with Cecilia's beauty! My dear sir, he wrote poems in her praise! He calls her a nymph, and says that her eyes put the stars to shame, and such stuff as that!'

'Good God!' said his lordship.

'Exactly so! You cannot wonder that she was swept off her feet. I daresay you had never so much as thought of calling her a nymph!'

'Miss Stanton – Sophy! Even to win Cecilia, I cannot write poetry, and if I could I'll be dashed if I would write such – Well, in any event I have no turn in that direction!'

'Oh, no, you must not attempt to outshine Augustus in that line!' said Sophy. 'Your strength lies in being precisely the kind of man who can procure one a chair when it has come on to rain.'

'I beg your pardon?'

'Can you not?' she asked, turning her head to look at him with raised brows.

'I expect I could, but –'

'Believe me, it is by far more important than being able to turn a verse!' she told him. 'Augustus is quite unable to do so. I know, because he failed miserably at the Chelsea Gardens. I thought he would, which is why I made him escort Cecilia and me there on a day when you could see it would come on to pour. Our muslins were soaked, and I daresay we should have died of an inflammation of the lung had not one of my old friends procured a hackney to convey us home. Poor Cecy! she became almost cross with Augustus!'

He burst out laughing. 'Major Quinton spoke nothing but the truth about you!' he declared. 'I am already terrified of you!'

She smiled, but said: 'Well, you need not be, for I mean to help you.'

'That is what terrifies me.'

'Nonsense! You are trying to quiz me. We have established that you can procure chairs in a rainstorm; I am also of the opinion that when you invite a party to supper at the Piazza the waiters do not fob you off with a table in a draught.'

'No,' he agreed, regarding her with a fascinated eye.

'Augustus, of course, is not in a position to invite us to supper at the Piazza, because my aunt would certainly not permit us to accept, but he did once entertain us to tea here, in the Park, and I could not but see that he is just the kind of man whom the waiters serve last. I feel sure I can rely upon you to see to it that everything goes without the least hitch when you invite us to the theatre, and to supper afterwards. You will be obliged, of course, to invite my aunt as well, but –'

'For heaven's sake!' he interrupted. 'You cannot suppose that in the situation in which we now stand Cecilia would consent to make one of a party of my making!'

'Certainly I do,' she replied coolly. 'What is more, you will invite Augustus.'

'No, that I will not!' he declared.

'Then you will be a great gaby. You must understand that

Cecilia has been driven into announcing that she means to marry Augustus! You were not there to engage her affections; Augustus was sighing verses to her left eyebrow; and to clinch the matter my cousin Charles behaved in the most tyrannical fashion, forbidding her to think of Augustus, and fairly ordering her to marry you! I assure you, it would have been wonderful indeed if she had not made up her mind to do no such thing!'

He rode in silence beside her for some moments, frowning between his horse's ears. 'I see,' he said at last. 'At least – Well, at all events, you don't advise me to despair!'

'I don't suppose,' said Sophy honestly, 'that I should ever advise anyone to despair, for I can't bear such poor-spirited conduct!'

'What *do* you advise me to do?' he asked. 'I seem to be wholly in your hands!'

'Withdraw your suit!' said Sophy.

He looked sharply at her. 'No! I mean to make a push –'

'You will call in Berkeley Square this afternoon,' said Sophy, with an utmost patience, 'and you will request the favour of a few minutes alone with Cecilia. When you see her –'

'I shall not see her. She will deny herself!' he said bitterly.

'She will see you, because I shall tell her she owes it to you to do so. I wish you will not keep on interrupting me!' He begged pardon meekly, and she continued: 'When you see her, you will assure her that you have no desire to distress her, that you will never mention the matter again to her. You will be excessively noble, and she will feel that you sympathize with her, and if you can convey to her also the sense of your heart being broken, however well you contrive to conceal it, so much the better!'

'I am strongly of the opinion that Major Quinton grossly understated the case!' said his lordship, with feeling.

'Very likely. Gentlemen can never see when a little duplicity is needed. You, I have no doubt, if I left you to your own devices, would storm and rant at Cecilia, so that all would end in a quarrel, and you would find it quite impossible to visit the house, even! But if she knows that you will not enact her tragedies she will be perfectly pleased to see you as often as you care to come to Berkeley Square.'

'How can I visit in Berkeley Square when she is betrothed to another man? If you imagine that I'll play the love-lorn suitor in the hope of arousing pity in Cecilia's breast you were never more at fault! As well be a lap-dog!'

'Much better,' said Sophy. 'You will visit in Berkeley Square to see me. You cannot too suddenly seem to transfer your interest in my direction, of course, but it would be an excellent start if you were to find an opportunity of telling Cecilia today how droll and entertaining you think me.'

'Do you know,' he said seriously, 'you are the most startling female it has ever been my fortune to meet? You will observe that I do not say good or ill fortune, for I haven't the smallest notion which it will prove to be!'

She laughed. 'But will you do what I tell you?'

'Yes,' he replied. 'To the best of my poor ability. But I wish I knew the extent of the dark scheme you are revolving in your head.'

She turned her head to look at him, her expressive eyes questioning, and at the same time acknowledging a hit. 'But I have told you!'

'I have a notion there is more to it than what you have told me.'

She looked mischievous, but would only shake her head. They had reached the Stanhope Gate again, and she reined in, holding out her hand. 'I must go now. Pray don't be afraid of me! I never do people any harm – indeed I don't! Goodbye! At about four o'clock, mind!'

She reached Berkeley Square to find the house in a state of considerable uneasiness, Lord Ombersley, informed by his wife of

Cecilia's overnight announcement, having flown into a passion of exasperation at the folly, ingratitude, and selfishness of daughters, and Hubert and Theodore between them having chosen this singularly inappropriate moment to allow Jacko to escape from the schoolroom. Sophy was met on her arrival by various distracted persons, who lost no time in pouring their woes or grievances into her ears. Cecilia, shaken by the interview with her father, wanted to carry her off instantly to the seclusion of her bedchamber; Miss Adderbury wished to explain that she had repeatedly warned Mr Hubert not to excite the monkey; Theodore desired to impress upon everyone that it had all been Hubert's fault; Hubert demanded that she should help him to recover the monkey before its escape came to Charles's ears; and Dassett, having observed with disfavour the enthusiasm with which both footmen entered into the chase, delivered himself of an icily civil monologue, the gist of which seemed to be that Wild Animals roaming at large in a Nobleman's Residence were not what he had been accustomed to, or what he could bring himself to tolerate. As this speech contained a dark threat to Inform His Lordship instantly, it appeared to Sophy that her most pressing duty was to soothe Dassett's feelings, half a dozen persons having informed her that Lord Ombersley was in a dreadful temper. So she told Cecilia that she would come to her room presently, and considerably mollified the butler by rejecting the services of the footmen. Cecilia, who besides her interview with Lord Ombersley, had endured a few moments with her elder brother, and half an hour with Lady Ombersley, was in no mood for monkeys, and said, rather hysterically, that she supposed she might have expected that Jacko would be thought of more importance than herself. Selina, who was thoroughly enjoying the atmosphere of drama and impending doom that hung over the house, hissed: 'H'sh! Charles is in the library!' Cecilia retorted that she did not care where he was, and rushed upstairs to her bedroom.

'What a commotion!' exclaimed Sophy, amused.

Her voice, penetrating the shut library door, reached the sharp ears of Tina, who, during her absence from the house, had attached herself to Mr Rivenhall. She at once demanded to be allowed to rejoin her mistress, and her insistence brought Mr Rivenhall upon the scene, for he was obliged to open the door for her. Perceiving that a large part of his family appeared to be assembled in the hall, he somewhat coldly enquired the reason. Before anyone could answer him, Amabel, in the basement, gave a warning shriek, Jacko suddenly erupted into the hall from the nether regions, gibbered at the sight of Tina, and swarmed up the window curtains to a place of safety well out of anyone's reach. Amabel then came storming up the basement-stairs, closely followed by the housekeeper, who at once lodged an impassioned protest with Mr Rivenhall. The dratted monkey, she said, had wantonly destroyed two of the best dishclothes, and had scattered a bowl of raisins all over the kitchen-floor.

'If that damned monkey cannot be controlled,' said Mr Rivenhall, making no apology for the violence of his language, 'it must be got rid of!'

Theodore, Gertrude, and Amabel at once burst into a spirited accusation against Hubert, who, they averred, had wantonly teased Jacko. Hubert, conscious of a rent coat-pocket, retired into the background, and Mr Rivenhall, eyeing his juniors with revulsion, walked forward to the window, and held up his hand, saying calmly: 'Come along!'

Jacko's reply to this, though voluble, was incomprehensible. His general attitude, however, was contumacious, so that everyone was surprised when, upon Mr Rivenhall's repeating his command, he began to descend the curtain. Tina, in wholehearted agreement with Dassett and the housekeeper on the undesirability of monkeys in noblemen's residences, caused a slight set-back

by barking, but Sophy snatched her up and muffled her before
Jacko had had time to retreat again to the top of the window. Mr
Rivenhall, acidly requesting his audience to refrain from making
any noise or sudden movement, again commanded Jacko to come
down. Jacko, satisfied that Tina was under strong guard, reluctantly descended, allowed himself to be seized, and clasped both
skinny arms round Mr Rivenhall's neck. Unimpressed by this
mark of affection, Mr Rivenhall detached him, handed him over
to Gertrude, and warned her not to permit him to escape again.
The schoolroom party then withdrew circumspectly, scarcely
able to believe that their pet was not to be wrested from them;
and Sophy, smiling warmly upon Mr Rivenhall, said: 'Thank
you! There is some magic in you which makes all animals trust
you, I think. When I am most vexed with you I cannot but
remember it!'

'The only magic, cousin, lay in not alarming an already
frightened animal,' he replied dampingly, and went back into the
library, and shut the door.

'Phew!' uttered Hubert, emerging from the embrasure at the
head of the basement-stairs. 'Sophy, only look what that dashed
brute has done to my new coat!'

'Give it to me! I'll mend it for you – and for heaven's sake, you
wretched creature, don't kick up any more larks today!' said Sophy.

He grinned at her, stripped off the coat, and handed it to her.
'What *did* happen last night?' he asked. 'Don't know when I've seen
my father in such a taking! Is Cecilia going to marry Fawnhope?'

'Ask her!' Sophy advised him. 'I will have your coat ready for
you in twenty minutes: come to my room then, and you shall
have it!'

She ran up the stairs and, without waiting to change her riding-
habit, sat down by the window to repair the rent caused by Jacko's
fury. She was a deft needlewoman, and had mended half the tear

with her tiny stitches when Cecilia came to her room. Cecilia was strongly of the opinion that Hubert might have found someone else to do his mending, and begged her to put it aside. This, however, Sophy refused to do, merely saying: 'I can listen to you while I work, you know. What a goose you were last night, Cecy!'

This brought Cecilia's chin up. She enunciated with great clarity: 'I am betrothed to Augustus, and if I may not marry him I will marry no one!'

'I daresay, but to make such an announcement in the middle of a ball!'

'Sophy, I thought *you* would feel for me!'

It occurred to Sophy suddenly that the fewer people to sympathize with Cecilia the better it would be, so she kept her head bent over her work, and said lightly: 'Well, and so I do, but I still think it was a ridiculous moment to choose for making such an announcement!'

Cecilia began to tell her again what provocation had been supplied by Charles; she agreed, but absently, and appeared to be more exercised with the set of Hubert's coat than with Cecilia's wrongs. She shook it out, smoothed the darn she had made, and, when Hubert came knocking at the door, cut Cecilia short to jump up and restore the garment to him. The end of all this was that when, at four o'clock, Lord Charlbury sent up his card, with a request to see Miss Rivenhall, Cecilia, almost forced to accede to his wishes, found in him her only sympathizer. One glance at her pale face, and tragic mouth, banished from his mind all notion of duplicity. He stepped quickly forward, took the hand so shrinkingly held out to him, and said in a deeply concerned voice: 'Do not look so unhappy! Indeed, I have not come to distress you!'

Her eyes filled with tears; her hand slightly returned the pressure of his before it was withdrawn; and she managed to say something in a suffocated voice, about his kindness, and her own regret. He obliged her to be seated, himself took a chair near to hers, and said: 'My sentiments have undergone no change: indeed, I believe it to be impossible that they should! But I have been told – I have understood – that yours were never engaged. Believe me, if you cannot return my regard, I honour you for having the courage to say so! That you should be constrained to accept my suit, when your heart is given to another, is a thought wholly repugnant to me! Forgive me! I think you have had to bear a great deal on *this* head which I never intended, or indeed, dreamed – But I have said enough! Only let me assure you that I will do all that lies in my power to put an end to such intolerable promptings!'

'You are all consideration – all goodness!' Cecilia uttered. 'I am so sorry that – that expectations which it is not in my power to fulfil should have been raised! If my gratitude for a sensibility which permits you to feel for me in my present predicament, for a chivalry which –' Her voice became wholly suspended by tears; she could only turn away her face, and make a gesture imploring his understanding.

He took her hand, and kissed it. 'Say no more! I always thought the prize beyond my reach. Though you deny me that nearer relationship which I so ardently desire, we may continue friends? If there is any way in which I can serve you, will you tell me of it? That would be a happiness indeed!'

'Oh, do not say so! You are too good!'

The door opened. Mr Rivenhall came into the room, checked an instant on the threshold, when he saw Charlbury, and looked as though he would have retired again. Charlbury rose, however, and said: 'I am glad you are at home, Charles, for I believe I can settle this business better with you than with anyone. Your sister and I have agreed that we shall not suit.'

'I see,' said Mr Rivenhall, dryly. 'There seems to be nothing

I can profitably say, except that I am sorry. I conclude that you wish me to inform my father that there is to be no engagement?'

'Lord Charlbury has been everything that is most kind – most magnanimous!' whispered Cecilia.

'That I can believe,' responded Mr Rivenhall.

'Nonsense!' Charlbury said, taking her hand. 'I shall leave you now, but I hope I may still visit this house, on terms of friendship. Your friendship I must always value, you know. Perhaps I may not dance at your wedding, but I shall wish you very happy, upon my honour!'

He pressed her hand, released it, and went out of the room, followed by Mr Rivenhall, who escorted him downstairs to the hall, saying: 'This is a damnable business, Everard. She is out of her senses! But as for marrying that puppy – no, by God!'

'Your cousin tells me it is all my fault for having wilfully contracted mumps!' Charlbury said ruefully.

'Sophy!' Mr Rivenhall ejaculated, in anything but loving accents. 'I do not think we have had a day's peace since that girl entered the house!'

'I shouldn't think you would,' said his lordship, reflectively. 'She is the oddest female I ever met, but I own I like her! Do you not?'

'No, I do not!' said Mr Rivenhall.

He saw Charlbury off the premises, and turned back into the house just as Hubert came down the stairs, in long bounds. 'Hallo, where are you off to in such haste?' he enquired.

'Oh, nowhere!' Hubert answered. 'Just out!'

'When do you go up to Oxford again?'

'Next week. Why?'

'Do you care to go with me to Thorpe Grange tomorrow? I must go down, and shall stay a night, I daresay.'

Hubert shook his head. 'No, I can't. I'm off to stay with Harpenden for a couple of nights, you know.'

'I didn't. Newmarket?'

Hubert flushed. 'Dash it, why should I not go to Newmarket, if I choose?'

'There is no reason why you should not, but I could wish that you would choose your company more wisely. Are you set on it? We could ride over from Thorpe, if you liked.'

'Very good of you, Charles, but I'm promised to Harpenden, and can't fail now!' Hubert said gruffly.

'Very well. Don't draw the bustle too much!'

Hubert hunched his shoulder. 'I knew you would say that!'

'I'll say something else, and you may believe it! I can't and I won't be saddled with your racing debts, so don't bet beyond your means!'

He waited for no answer, but went upstairs again to the drawing-room, where he found his sister still seated where he had left her, weeping softly into a shred of a handkerchief. He tossed his own into her lap. 'If you must be a watering-pot, take mine!' he recommended. 'Are you satisfied? You should be! It is not every girl who can boast of having rejected a man like Charlbury!'

'I do not boast of it!' she retorted, firing up. 'But I care nothing for wealth and position! Where my affections are not engaged –'

'You might care for worth of character, however! You could search England without finding a better fellow, Cecilia. Don't flatter yourself you have found one in your poet! I wish you may not live to regret this day's work.'

'I am aware that Lord Charlbury has every amiable quality,' she said, in a subdued voice, and mopping her wet cheeks with his handkerchief. 'Indeed, I believe him to be the finest gentleman of my acquaintance, and if I am crying it is from sorrow at having been obliged to wound him!'

He walked over to the window, and stood looking out into the square. 'It is useless now to remonstrate with you. After your announcement last night it is not very likely that Charlbury would desire to marry you. What do you mean to do? I may tell you now that my father will not consent to your marriage with Fawnhope.'

'Because you will not let him consent! Can you not be content, Charles, with making a marriage of convenience yourself, without wishing me to do the same?' she cried hotly.

He stiffened. 'It is not difficult to perceive my cousin's influence at work!' he said. 'Before her arrival in London, you would not have spoken so to me! My regard for Eugenia —'

'If you *loved*, Charles, you would not talk of your *regard* for Eugenia!'

It was at this inappropriate moment that Dassett ushered Miss Wraxton into the room. Cecilia whisked her brother's handkerchief out of sight, a tide of crimson flooding her cheeks; Mr Rivenhall turned away from the window, and said with a palpable effort: 'Eugenia! We did not expect this pleasure! How do you do!'

She gave him her hand, but turned her gaze upon Cecilia, saying: 'Tell me it is not so! I was never more shocked in my life than when Alfred told me what had occurred last night!'

Almost insensibly the brother and sister drew closer together. 'Alfred!' repeated Mr Rivenhall.

'He told me, when he drove home after the ball, that he could not choose but overhear what Cecilia had said to you, Charles. And Lord Charlbury! I could not believe it to have been possible!'

Loyalty, as much as the ties of affection, kept Mr Rivenhall ranged on the side of his sister, for he looked to be very much annoyed, which indeed he was, for he thought it inexcusable of Cecilia to have placed him in such a situation. He said repressively: 'If you mean that Cecilia and Lord Charlbury have made up their minds to it they would not suit, you are quite correct. I do not know what business it is of Alfred's, or why he must run to you with what he — overhears!'

'My dear Charles, he knows that what concerns your family must be also my concern!'

'I am much obliged to you, but I have no wish to discuss the matter.'

'Excuse me! I must go to my mother!' Cecilia said.

She escaped from the room; Miss Wraxton looked significantly at Mr Rivenhall, and said: 'I do not wonder you are vexed. It has been a sadly mismanaged business, and I fancy we have not far to seek for the influence that prompted dear Cecilia to behave in a way so unlike herself!'

'I have not the smallest conjecture as to your meaning.'

His tone, which was forbidding, warned her that she would be wise to turn the subject, but her dislike of Sophy had become such an obsession with her that she was impelled to continue.

'You must have noticed, dear Charles, that our sweet sister has fallen quite under the sway of her cousin. I cannot think it will lead to anything but disaster. Miss Stanton-Lacy doubtless has many excellent qualities, but I have always thought that you were right in saying she had too little delicacy of mind.'

Mr Rivenhall, who had decided that Sophy was to blame for his sister's conduct, said without an instant's hesitation: 'You are mistaken: I never made any such remark!'

'Did you not? Something of that nature I think you once said to me, but it hardly signifies! It is a thousand pities that dear Lady Ombersley was forced to receive her as a guest at this precise time. Every time I enter the house I am conscious of a change in it! Even the children —'

'It is certainly by far more lively,' he interrupted.

She gave vent to rather an artificial laugh. 'It is certainly less *peaceful*!' She began to smooth the wrinkles from her gloves. 'Do you know, Charles, I have always so much admired the *tone* of this house? Your doing, I know well! I cannot but feel a little

melancholy when I see that ordered calm – a certain dignity, I
should say – shattered by wild spirits. Poor little Amabel, I thought
the other day, is growing quite out of hand! Of course, Miss
Stanton-Lacy encourages her unthinkingly. One must remember
that she herself has had a strangely irregular upbringing!'

'My cousin,' said Mr Rivenhall, with finality, 'has been
extremely kind to the children, and is a great favourite with my
mother. I must add that it is a pleasure to see my mother's spirits
so much improved by Sophy's presence. Have you any errands in
this part of the town? May I escort you? I must be in Bond Street
in twenty minutes' time.'

In face of so comprehensive a snub as this it was impossible for
Miss Wraxton to say more. Her colour rose, and her lips tight-
ened, but she managed to suppress an acid retort, and to say with
the appearance at least of complaisance: 'Thank you, I have to call
at the library for Mama. I came in the barouche, and shall be glad
to take you up as far as your destination.'

Since this was Jackson's Boxing Saloon, she could hardly have
been expected to have been pleased, for she did not care for sport
of any kind, and considered boxing a peculiarly low form of it.
But apart from quizzing Mr Rivenhall archly for his obvious
preference for a horrid prizefighter's society than for her own, she
made no comment.

Cecilia, meanwhile, had fled, not to Lady Ombersley, but to
her cousin, whom she discovered seated before her dressing-table,
scanning a slip of paper. Jane Storridge was putting away her habit,
but when Cecilia came into the room she seemed to feel that she
was not wanted, for she gave an audible sniff, picked up Sophy's
riding-boots, and went away with them under her arm.

'What do you suppose this can be, Cecy?' asked Sophy, still
studying with knit brows the paper in her hand. 'Jane says she
found it by the window, and thought it must be mine. What a

funny name! *Goldhanger, Bear Alley, Fleet Lane.* I do not know the writing, and cannot conceive how – Oh, how stupid! It must have fallen out of the pocket of Hubert's coat!'

'Sophy!' said Cecilia, 'I have had the most dreadful interview with Charlbury!'

Sophy laid the paper down. 'Good gracious, how is this!'

'I find my spirits utterly overborne!' declared Cecilia, sinking into a chair. 'No one – *no one* – could have behaved with more exquisite sensibility! I wish you had not persuaded me to see him! Nothing could have been more painful!'

'Oh, do not give him a thought!' said Sophy bracingly. 'Let us rather think what is to be done about fixing Augustus in some genteel occupation!'

'How can you be so heartless?' demanded Cecilia. 'When he was so kind, and I could not but see how much I had grieved him!'

'I daresay he will recover speedily enough,' Sophy replied, in a careless way. 'Ten to one he will fall in love with another female before the month is out!'

Cecilia did not look as though she found this prophecy consoling, but after a moment she said: 'I am sure I wish he may, for to be ruining a man's life is no very pleasant thing, I can tell you!'

'Do you think it will rain? Dare I wear my new straw hat? I have a mind to flirt with Charlbury myself: I liked him.'

'I wish you may succeed,' said Cecilia, a trifle stiffly. 'I do not think him a man at all given to flirting, however. The tone of his mind is too nice for such a pastime as that!'

Sophy laughed. 'We'll see! Do tell me which hat I should wear! The straw is so ravishing, but if it were to come on to mizzle –'

'I don't care which hat you wear!' snapped Cecilia.

Eleven

THE REST OF THE DAY PASSED UNEVENTFULLY, SOPHY DRIVING Cecilia in Hyde Park in her phaeton, setting her down to enjoy a stroll with Mr Fawnhope, encountered by previous arrangement by the Riding House, and taking up in her stead Sir Vincent Talgarth, who only deserted her when he perceived the Marquesa de Villacañas's barouche drawn up beside the rails that separated Rotten Row from the carriageway. The Marquesa, who was attracting no little attention by the number and height of the curled ostrich plumes in her hat, welcomed him with her lazy smile, and told Sophy that she found the shops in London wholly inferior to those in Paris. Nothing she had seen in Bond Street that day had tempted her to undo her purse-strings. But Sir Vincent knew of a modiste in Bruton Street who might be trusted to recognize at a glance the style and quality of such a customer, and he offered to escort the Marquesa to her establishment.

Sophy knit her brows a little over this, but before she had time to think much on the subject her attention was claimed by Lord Bromford. Civility obliged her to invite him to take a turn about the Park in her phaeton. He got up beside her, and after telling her how much enjoyment he had derived from the Ombersley ball, made her a formal offer of marriage. Sophy declined this, without hesitation and without embarrassment. Lord Bromford, disconcerted only for a minute, said that his ardour had made him too precipitate, but that he did not despair of a happy issue. 'When your parent returns to these shores,' he pronounced, 'I shall formally apply to him for leave to address you. You are very right to insist upon so much propriety, and I must beg your pardon for having contravened the laws of etiquette. Only the strong passion under which I labour – and I must tell you that not the most forceful representations of my mother, a Being to whom I, in filial duty, tender the most profound respect, have had the power to alter my decision – only, as I have said, this passion could have induced me to forget –'

'I think,' said Sophy, 'that you should take your seat in the House of Lords. Have you done so?'

'It is strange,' responded his lordship, swelling slightly, 'that you should ask me that question, for I am upon the point of doing so. I shall be presented by a sponsor no less distinguished for his high lineage than for his forensic attainments, and I trust –'

'I have no doubt at all that you are destined to become a great man,' said Sophy. 'No matter how lengthy, or how involved your periods, you *never* lose yourself in them! How charming the foliage is on those beech trees! Do you know any tree to rival the beech? I am sure I do not!'

'Certainly a graceful tree,' conceded Lord Bromford, patronizing the beech. 'Hardly, however, to rank in majesty with the mahogany, which grows in the West Indies; or in usefulness with the lancewood. I wonder, Miss Stanton-Lacy, how many persons are aware that the lancewood supplies the shafts for their carriages?'

'In the southern provinces of Spain,' countered Sophy, 'the cork oak grows in great profusion.'

'Another interesting tree to be found in Jamaica,' said his lordship, 'is the ballata. We have also the rosewood, the ebony, the
lignum vitae –'

'The northern parts of Spain,' said Sophy defiantly, 'are more
remarkable for the many varieties of shrubs which grow there,
including what we call the jarales, and the ladanum bush, and –
and – Oh, there is Lord Francis! I shall have to put you down,
Lord Bromford!'

He was reluctant, but since Lord Francis was waving to Sophy,
and showed every desire to speak to her, he was unable to demur.
When the phaeton drew up, he climbed ponderously down from
it, and Lord Francis leaped equally nimbly up into it, saying:
'Sophy, that was a capital ball last night! What a lovely creature
your cousin is, to be sure!'

Sophy set her horses in motion again. 'Francis, *does* the cork oak
grow in the southern provinces in Spain?'

'Lord, Sophy, how should I know? You were in Cadiz! Can't
you recall? Who cares for cork oaks, in any event?'

'I hope,' said Sophy warmly, 'that when you have done with
being the worst flirt in Europe, Francis, you will win a *very*
beautiful wife, for you deserve one! Do you know anything about
the ballata?'

'Never heard of it in my life! What is it? A new dance?'

'No, it's a tree, and it grows in Jamaica. I hope she will be as
good-natured as she is beautiful.'

'Trust me for that! But, y'know, Sophy, it ain't like you to be
boring on and on about trees! What's come over you?'

'Lord Bromford,' sighed Sophy.

'What, that prosy fellow you had up beside you just now? He
told Sally Jersey last night how valuable guinea-grass was for horses
and cattle: heard him! Never saw poor Silence so silenced!'

'I wish she had given him one of her set-downs. I must put

you down when we reach the Riding House, for Cecilia will be waiting for me.'

Cecilia and her swain were found at the appointed spot. Lord Francis sprang down from the phaeton, and it was he who handed Cecilia up into it, Mr Fawnhope having become rapt in contemplation of a clump of daffodils, which caused him to throw out a hand, murmuring: '"*Daffodils that come before the swallow dares!*"'

Cecilia's spirits did not appear to have derived much benefit from her meeting with her lover. His plans for their future maintenance seemed to be a trifle vague, but he had an epic poem in his head, which might win him fame in a night, he thought. While this was in preparation, he would not object, he said, to accepting a post as a librarian. But as Cecilia was unable to imagine that her father or her brother would feel any marked degree of satisfaction in giving her in marriage to a librarian, this very handsome concession on Mr Fawnhope's part merely added to her despondency. She had gone so far as to suggest to him that he should embrace the profession of Politics, but he had only said: 'How sordid!' which did not augur well for this excellent scheme. When he had added that since the death of Mr Fox, ten years earlier, there was no leader a man of sensibility could attach himself to, this remark had only served to show her how very improbable it was that his politics would find more favour with her family than his poetic aspirations.

Sophy, gathering the gist of all this from Cecilia's somewhat elliptical remarks, took up a buoyant attitude, saying: 'Oh, well! We must find a great man who is willing to become his patron!' which gave Cecilia a poor notion of her understanding.

Sophy was able to restore to Hubert the scrap of paper which had fallen from his pocket before going down to dinner that evening. Until this moment she had not thought much about it, but his manner of receiving it from her was so strange that it set up in her head various speculations which he was far from desiring. He almost snatched it from her hand, exclaiming: 'Where did you find this?' and when she explained, in the most temperate manner, that she thought it must have fallen out of the pocket of the coat she had mended for him, he said: 'Yes, it is mine, but I did not know I had put it there! I cannot tell you what it signifies, but pray do not mention it to anyone!'

She could only assure him that she had no intention of doing so, but he appeared to be so much discomposed that some inevitable reflections were set up in her brain. These did not come to fruition until she saw him upon his return from his visit to his friend Mr Harpenden, when his demeanour was so much that of a man who had received some stunning blow that she seized the earliest opportunity that offered of asking him if anything were amiss. Mr Rivenhall, who had left London twenty-four hours earlier for Thorpe Grange, the estate in Leicestershire which he had inherited from his great-uncle, had not yet returned to London; but Hubert made it plain to his cousin that even had his elder brother been in London, not the direst necessity would have induced him to apply to him.

'He has not minced matters! He told me in round terms that he would not – Oh well! no matter for that!'

'I daresay,' said Sophy, in her calm way, 'that Charles might very likely say more than he meant. I wish you will tell me what has gone awry, Hubert! My conjecture is that you have lost perhaps a large sum at Newmarket?'

'If that were all!' he exclaimed unguardedly.

'Well, if it is not all, I wish you will tell the full sum of it, Hubert!' she said, with one of her friendly smiles. 'I assure you, you are quite safe in my hands, for Sir Horace brought me up to think there was nothing more odious than to be the kind of person who blabbed secrets abroad. But I know that you are in trouble of some sort, and I do think I ought, if you will tell me nothing, to drop a hint in your brother's ear, for ten to one you will make bad much worse if you go on in this way, with no one to advise you!'

He turned pale. 'Sophy, you would not – !'

Her eyes twinkled. 'No, of course I would not!' she admitted. 'You are so *very* loth to tell me anything that I am quite forced to ask you. Is it anything to do with a woman? What Sir Horace would call a bit of muslin, perhaps?'

'*Sophy!* Upon my word – ! No! Nothing of that sort!'

'Money, then?'

He did not answer, and after a moment she patted the sofa on which she sat invitingly, and said: 'Do, pray, come and sit down! I don't suppose it is by half as bad as you fear.'

He gave a short laugh, but after a little more persuasion sat down beside her, and sank his head in between his clenched fists. 'I shall come about. If the worst comes to the worst, a man may always enlist!'

'True,' she agreed. 'But I know something of the Army, and I do not think that life in the ranks would suit you at all. Besides, it would very much distress my aunt, you know!'

It was not to be supposed that a young gentleman of Hubert's order would readily confide his difficulties into the ears of a female, and that female not quite as old as he was himself, but after a good deal of coaxing Sophy managed to extract his story from him. It was not a very coherent tale, and she was obliged to prompt him several times during its recital, but in the end she gathered that he had fallen into the clutches of a moneylender. There had been some trouble over debts contracted during the previous year at Oxford, the full sum of which he had not dared to disclose to his brother, hoping, in the immemorial way of youth, to be able to discharge them himself. He had knowing friends who knew all the gaming-houses in London; quite a brief run of luck at French hazard, or roulette, would have set all to rights; but when, during the Christmas vacation, he had sought this method of recuperating his fortunes only the most unprecedented bad luck had attended his efforts. He still shuddered whenever he recalled those ruinous, and, indeed, terrifying evenings, a circumstance which led his sapient cousin to infer that gaming held little attraction for him. Faced with large debts of honour, already in hot water with his formidable brother for far smaller debts, what could he do but jump into the river, or go to the Jews? And even so, he assured Sophy, he would never have gone near a curst moneylender had he not felt certain of being able to pay the shark off within six months.

'You mean, when you come of age next month?' Sophy asked.

'Well, no,' he admitted, colouring. 'Though I fancy that was what old Goldhanger thought, when he agreed to lend me the money. I never told him so, mind! All I said was that I was certain of coming into possession of a large sum, and I *was*, Sophy! I did not think it could possibly fail! Bob Gilmorton – he is a particular friend of mine! – knows the owner well, and he swore to me the horse could not lose!'

Sophy, who had an excellent memory, instantly recognized the name of Goldhanger as being the one she had read on the scrap of paper discovered in her bedroom, but she made no comment on this, merely enquiring whether the perfidious horse had lost his race.

'Unplaced!' said Hubert, with a groan.

She nodded wisely. 'Sir Horace says that if ever you trust to a horse to set your fortune to rights he always is unplaced,' she observed. 'He says also that if you game when your pockets are to let you will lose. It is only when you are very *well-breeched* that you may expect to win. Sir Horace is *always* right!'

Declining to argue this point, Hubert spoke for several embittered minutes on the running of his horse, casting such grave aspersions upon the owner, the trainer, and the jockey as must have rendered him liable to prosecution for slander had they been uttered to anyone less discreet than his cousin. She let him run on, listening sympathetically, and only when he had talked himself to a standstill did she bring him back to what she thought a far more important point.

'Hubert, you are not of age,' she said. 'And I know that it is quite illegal to lend money to minors, because when young Mr – well, never mind the name, but we knew him well! – when a young man of my acquaintance got into just such a fix, he came to Sir Horace for advice, and that is what Sir Horace said. I believe there are excessively heavy penalties for doing such a thing.'

'Well, I know that,' Hubert answered. 'Most of 'em won't do it, but – well, the thing is that a friend of mine knew of this fellow, Goldhanger, and gave me his direction, and – and told me what I should say, and the sort of interest I should have to pay – not that that seemed to matter *then*, because I thought –'

'Is it very heavy?' Sophy interrupted.

He nodded. 'Yes, because, though I lied about my age he knew, of course, that I'm not yet twenty-one, and – and he had me pretty well at his mercy. And I thought I should have been able to have paid it all off after that race.'

'How much did you borrow, Hubert?'

'Five hundred,' he muttered.

'Good gracious, did you lose all that at cards?' she exclaimed.

'No, but I wanted a hundred to lay on that curst screw, you see,' he explained. 'It was of no use only to borrow enough to pay my debts, because how was I to pay back Goldhanger?'

Sophy could not help laughing at this ingenious method of finance, but as Hubert looked rather hurt she begged pardon, and said: 'It is evident to me that your Mr Goldhanger is an infamous rascal!'

'Yes,' Hubert said, looking a little haggard. 'He's an old devil, and I was a fool ever to go near him. I didn't know as much about him then as I do now, of course, but still, as soon as I saw him – But it's too late to be repining over that!'

'Yes, much too late, besides there is no need to be in despair! I am certain that you have nothing to fear, because he must know he cannot recover his money from a minor, and would never dare to sue you for it.'

'Dash it, Sophy, I must pay the fellow back what I owe him! Besides, there's worse. He insisted on my giving him a pledge, and – and I did!'

He sounded so guilty that several hair-raising possibilities flashed through Sophy's mind. 'Hubert, you did not pledge a family heirloom, or – or something of that nature, did you?'

'Good God, no! I'm not as bad as *that!*' he cried indignantly. 'It was mine, and I shouldn't call it an heirloom, precisely, though if ever it was discovered that I had lost it I daresay there would be the deuce of a kick-up, and I should be abused as though I were a pickpocket! Grandfather Stanton-Lacy left it to me: stupid sort of thing, *I* think, because men don't wear 'em nowadays. He did, of course, and my mother says the sight of it brings him back to her as nothing else could, because she never saw him without it on his hand – so you may judge what would happen if she knew I had pledged it! It's a ring, you know: a great, square emerald, with diamonds all round it. Fancy wearing such a thing as that! Why, one would look like Romeo Coates, or some wealthy cit trying to lionize! Mama always kept it, and I never knew it had been left to me until I went to a masquerade last year, and she gave it to me to wear, and told me it was mine. And when Goldhanger demanded I should give him a pledge, I – I couldn't think of anything else, and – well, I knew where Mama kept it, and I took it! And don't tell me I stole it from her, because it was no such thing, and she only kept it because I had no use for it!'

'No, no, of course I know you would not steal anything!' Sophy said hastily.

He studied his knuckles with rapt interest. 'No. Mind, I don't say I ought to have taken it from my mother's case, but – it *was* my own!'

'Well, naturally you ought not!' said Sophy. 'I daresay she would be vexed with you, so we must recover it at once.'

'I wish I might, but there's no chance of that now! I don't know what to do! When that horse failed, I was ready to blow my brains out! I shan't do so, because I don't suppose it would mend matters, besides creating a dashed scandal.'

'What a good thing you told me the whole! I know exactly what you should do. Make a clean breast of the business to your brother! He will very likely give you a tremendous scold, but you may depend upon his helping you out of this fix.'

'You don't know him! Scold, indeed! Depend upon it, he would make me come down from Oxford, and thrust me into the Army, or some such thing! I'll try everything before I apply to him!'

'Very well, I will lend you five hundred pounds,' said Sophy.

He flushed. 'You're a great gun, Sophy – no, but I don't mean that! – a capital girl! I'm devilish grateful, but of course I could not borrow money from you! No, no, pray don't say any more! It is out of the question! Besides, you don't understand! The old bloodsucker made me sign a bond to pay him fifteen per cent interest a month!'

'Good God, you never agreed to such an iniquitous thing!'

'What else could I do! I had to have the money to pay my gaming debts, and I knew it was useless to go to Howard and Gibbs, or any of those fellows, for they would have shown me the door.'

'Hubert, I am persuaded there is nothing he can do to extort one penny of interest from you! Why, in law he could not even recover the principal! Only let me lend you five hundred pounds, and take it to him, and insist upon his restoring to you the bond you signed, and your ring! Tell him that if he does not choose to accept the principal he may do his worst!'

'And have him inform at Oxford against me! I tell you, Sophy, he is an out-and-out villain! He would do me all the harm that lay in his power! He is not a regular moneylender: in fact, I'm pretty certain he's what they call a lock, or a fence: a receiver, you know. What's more, he would refuse to give me back the ring, and even if I brought him to book he would have sold it, I expect.'

Nothing that Sophy could urge had the power to move him. He was plainly in considerable dread of Mr Goldhanger, and since she found this incomprehensible she could only suppose that some darker threat than had been disclosed to her was being held over his head. She made no attempt to discover what this might be, for she felt reasonably certain that it would not have impressed her. Instead, she asked him what he intended to do to extricate himself from his difficulties, if he would neither apply to his brother nor accept a loan from her. The answer was not very definite, Hubert being young enough still to cherish youth's ineradicable belief in timely miracles. He said several times that he had a month left to him before he need do anything desperate, and while agreeing reluctantly that he might in the end be forced to go to his brother evidently felt that something would happen to make this unnecessary. With an attempt at lightheartedness, he begged Sophy not to trouble her head over it, and as she perceived that it would be useless to continue arguing with him she said no more.

But when he had left her she sat for some time with her chin in her hand, pondering the matter. Her first impulse, which was to place the whole affair in the hands of Sir Horace's lawyer, she regretfully discarded. She was well-enough acquainted with

Mr Meriden to know that he would most strenuously resist her determination to pay five hundred pounds into a moneylender's hands. Any advice he might be expected to give her could only lead to the disclosure of Hubert's folly, which was naturally unthinkable. Her mind flitted through the ranks of her friends, but they too had to be discarded, for the same reason. But since she was not one to abandon any project she had once decided on she did not for as much as an instant entertain the idea of leaving her young cousin to settle his difficulties for himself. There seemed to be no other course open to her but to confront the villainous Mr Goldhanger herself. This decision was not reached without careful consideration, for although she was not in the least afraid of Mr Goldhanger she was perfectly well-aware that young ladies did not visit usurers, and that such conduct would be thought outrageous by any person of breeding. However, since she could perceive no reason why anyone, except perhaps Hubert, should ever know anything at all about it, she came to the conclusion that to hang back from missish scruples would be stupid and spiritless: not the sort of behaviour to be expected of Sir Horace Stanton-Lacy's daughter.

Having made up her mind to intervene in Hubert's affairs, it was characteristic of her that she wasted no time in further heart-burnings. It was also characteristic of her that she made no attempt to persuade herself that she might with propriety draw upon Sir Horace's funds to defray Hubert's debt. In her view, which he would undoubtedly have shared, it was one thing to spend five hundred pounds on a ball to launch herself into London society, and quite another to force him into an act of generosity towards a nephew of whose very existence he was in all probability oblivious. Instead, she unlocked her jewel-case, and, after turning over its contents, abstracted from it the diamond ear-rings Sir Horace had bought for her at Rundell and Bridge only a year earlier. They were singularly fine stones, and it cost her a slight pang to part with them; but the rest of her more valuable jewelry had been left to her by her mother, and although she had not the smallest recollection of this lady her scruples forbade her to part with her trinkets.

Upon the following day, she contrived to excuse herself from accompanying Lady Ombersley and Cecilia to a silk warehouse in the Strand, and instead, sallied forth quite unaccompanied to those noted jewellers, Rundell and Bridge. The shop was empty of customers when she arrived, but the sight of a young lady of commanding height and presence, and dressed, moreover, in the first style of elegance, brought the head salesman hurrying forward, all eagerness to oblige. He was an excellent man of business who prided himself on never forgetting the face of a valued customer. He recognized Miss Stanton-Lacy at a glance, set a chair for her with his own august hands, and begged to be told what he might have the honour of showing her. When he discovered the true nature of her business he looked thunderstruck, but swiftly concealed his amazement, and, by a flicker of the eyelids, conveyed to an intelligent underling an order to summon on to the scene Mr Bridge himself. Mr Bridge, gliding into the shop, and bowing politely to the daughter of a patron who had bought many expensive trinkets of him (though mostly for quite a different class of female), begged Sophy to go with him into his private office at the back of the show-room. Whatever he may have thought of her wish to dispose of ear-rings carefully chosen by herself only a year before he kept to himself. A civil enquiry for Sir Horace having elicited the information that he was at present in Brazil, Mr Bridges, putting two and two together, instantly resolved to buy the ear-rings back at a handsome figure, instead of resorting, as had been his first intention, to the time-honoured custom of explaining to his client just why the price of diamonds had fallen so low. He had no intention of selling the ear-rings again; he would put them by until the return of Sir Horace from Brazil. Sir Horace, he shrewdly suspected, would repurchase them; and his gratification at being able to do so reasonably would no doubt find expression, in the future, in buying a great many more expensive trifles from the jewellers who had behaved in so gentlemanly a way towards his only daughter. The transaction, therefore, between Miss Stanton-Lacy and Mr Bridges was conducted on the most genteel lines possible, each party being perfectly satisfied with the bargain; Mr Bridges, the soul of discretion, kept Miss Stanton-Lacy in his private office until two other customers had left the shop. He fancied that Sir Horace might not wish it to be known that his daughter had been reduced to selling her jewelry. Without a blink he agreed to pay Sophy five hundred pounds in bills; without a blink he counted them out on the table before her; and without the least diminution in respect did he presently bow her out of the shop.

The bills stuffed into her muff, Sophy next hailed a hackney, and desired the coachman to drive her to Bear Alley. The vehicle she selected was by no means the first or the smartest which lumbered past her, but it was driven by the most prepossessing jarvey. He was a burly, middle-aged man, with a rubicund and jovial countenance, in whom Sophy felt that she might repose a certain degree of confidence, this belief being strengthened by the manner in which he received her order. After eyeing her shrewdly, and stroking his chin with one mittened hand, he gave it as his opinion that she had mistaken the direction, Bear Alley not being, to his way of thinking, the sort of locality to which a lady of her quality would wish to be taken.

'No, is it a back-slum?' asked Sophy.

'It ain't the place for a young lady,' repeated the jarvey, declining to commit himself on this point. He added that he had daughters of his own, begging her pardon.

'Well, back-slum or not, that is where I wish to go,' said Sophy. 'I have business with a Mr Goldhanger there, who, I daresay, is a great rogue; and you look to me just the sort of man I may trust not to drive off, and leave me there.'

She got up into the hackney; the jarvey shut the door upon her; climbed back on to the box, and, after expressing to the ambient air his desire to be floored if ever he should be so betwattled again, besought his horse to get up.

Bear Alley, which led eastward from the Fleet Market, was a narrow and malodorous lane, where filth of every description lay mouldering between the uneven cobbles. The shadow of the great prison seemed to brood over the whole district, and even the people who trod the streets, or lounged on doorsteps, had a depressed look not entirely attributable to their circumstances. The coachman enquired of a man in a greasy muffler whether he knew Mr Goldhanger's abode, and was directed to a house half-way up the alley, his informant hesitating palpably before answering, and seemingly disinclined to enter into any sort of conversation.

A dingy hackney, once a gentleman's coach, attracted little notice, but when it drew up, and a tall, well-dressed young woman alighted, holding up her flounced skirts to avoid soiling them against a pile of garbage, several loafers and two small, ragged boys drew near to stare at her. Various comments were made, but these were happily phrased in such cant terms as were quite incomprehensible to Sophy. She had been stared out of countenance in too many Spanish and Portuguese villages to be in any way discomposed by the attention she was attracting, and after running a critical eye over her audience beckoned to one of the small boys, and said with a smile: 'Tell me, does a man called Goldhanger live here?'

The urchin gaped at her, but when she held out a shilling to him, caught his breath sharply, and, stretching out a claw of a hand, uttered: 'Fust floor!' He then grabbed the coin and took to his heels before any of his seniors could relieve him of it.

The glimpse of largesse made the crowd converge on Sophy, but the jarvey climbed down from the box, his whip in his hand, and genially invited anyone who had a fancy for a little of the home-brewed to come on. No one accepted the invitation, and Sophy said: 'Thank you, but pray do not start a brawl! I wish you will wait for me here, if you please.'

'If I were you, missie,' said the jarvey earnestly, 'I'd keep out of a ken like this here, that's what I'd do! You don't know what might happen to you!'

'Well, if anything happens to me,' responded Sophy cheerfully, 'I shall give a loud scream, and you may come in and rescue me. I shall not, I think, keep you waiting for very long.'

She then picked her way through the kennel, and entered the house which had been pointed out to her. The door stood open, and a flight of uncarpeted stairs lay at the end of a short passage. She went up them, and found herself on a small landing. Two doors gave on to this, so she knocked on them both, in an imperative way. There was a pause, and she had an unpleasant feeling that she was being watched. She looked round, but there was no one in sight, and it was only when she turned her head again that she saw that an unmistakable eye was regarding her through a small hole in one of the panels of the door at the back of house. It disappeared instantly, there was the sound of a key turning in a lock, and the door was slowly opened to reveal a thin, swarthy individual, with long greasy curls, a semitic nose, and an ingratiating leer. He was dressed in a suit of rusty black, and nothing about him suggested sufficient affluence to lend as much as five hundred pence to anyone. His hooded eyes rapidly took in every detail of Sophy's appearance, from the curled feathers in her high-crowned hat to the neat kid boots upon her feet.

'Good-morning!' said Sophy. 'Are you Mr Goldhanger?'

He stood, a little bent, before her, wiping his hands together. 'And what would you be wanting with Mr Goldhanger, my lady?' he asked.

'I have business with him,' replied Sophy. 'So if you are he please do not keep me standing in this dirty passage any longer! I cannot conceive why you do not at least sweep the floor!'

Mr Goldhanger was considerably taken aback, a thing that had not happened to him for a very long time. He was accustomed to receiving all sorts and conditions of visitors, from furtive persons who stole into the house under cover of darkness and spilled strange wares upon the desk under the light of one oil lamp, to haggard-eyed young men of fashion seeking relief from their immediate obligations, but never before had he opened his door to a self-possessed young lady who took him to task for not sweeping the floors.

'I wish you will stop staring at me in that foolish way!' said Sophy. 'You have already peered at me through that hole in the door, and you must by now have convinced yourself that I am not a law-officer in disguise.'

Mr Goldhanger protested. The insinuation that he would not welcome a visit from a law-officer seemed to wound him. However, he stood back to allow Sophy to enter the room, and invited her to take a chair on one side of the large desk which occupied the centre of the floor.

'Yes, but I shall be obliged to you if you will first dust it,' she said.

Mr Goldhanger performed this office with one of his long coat-tails. He heard the key grate behind him, and turned sharply to see his visitor removing it from the lock.

'You won't object to my locking the door, I daresay,' said Sophy. 'I don't in the least desire to be interrupted by any of your acquaintances, you see. And since I should much dislike to be spied on you will permit me to stuff my handkerchief into that Judas of yours.' She removed one hand from her large swansdown muff as she spoke, and poked a corner of her handkerchief into the hole.

Mr Goldhanger had the oddest feeling that the world had begun to revolve in reverse. For years he had taken care never to get into any situation he was unable to command, and his visitors were more in the habit of pleading with him than of locking the door, and ordering him to dust the furniture. He could see no particular harm in allowing Sophy to retain the key, for although she was a large young woman he had no doubt of being able to wrest it from her, should such a need arise. The instinct of his race made him prefer, whenever possible, to maintain a manner of the utmost urbanity, so he now smiled, and bowed, and said that my lady was welcome to do what she pleased in his humble abode. He then betook himself to the chair on the other side of the desk, and asked what he might have the honour of doing for her.

'I have come on a very simple matter,' responded Sophy. 'It is merely to recover from you Mr Hubert Rivenhall's bond, and the emerald ring given you as a pledge.'

'That,' said Mr Goldhanger, smiling more ingratiatingly than ever, 'is indeed a simple matter. I shall be delighted to oblige you, my lady. I need not ask whether you have brought with you the funds, for I am sure such a business-like young lady –'

'Now, that is excellent!' interrupted Sophy cordially. 'I find that so many persons imagine that if one is a female one has no head for business, and that, of course, leads to a sad waste of time. I must tell you at once that when you lent five hundred pounds to Mr Rivenhall you lent money to a minor. I expect I need not explain to you what *that* means.'

She smiled in the most friendly way as she spoke these words, and Mr Goldhanger smiled back at her, and said softly: 'What a well-informed young lady, to be sure! If I sued Mr Rivenhall for my money I could not recover it. But I do not think Mr Rivenhall would like me to sue him for it.'

'Of course he would not,' Sophy agreed. 'Moreover, although it was extremely wrong of you to have lent him any money, it seems unjust that you should not at least recover the principal.'

'Most unjust,' said Mr Goldhanger. 'There is also a little matter of the interest, my lady.'

Sophy shook her head. 'No, I shan't pay you a penny in interest, which may perhaps teach you a lesson to be more careful in future. I have with me five hundred pounds in bills, and when you have handed me the bond and the ring I will give them to you.'

Mr Goldhanger could not help laughing a little at this, for although he had not very much sense of humour he could not but be tickled at the thought that he would forgo his interest at the command of a young lady. 'I think I prefer to keep the bond and the ring,' he said.

'I expect you would prefer it,' said Sophy.

'You should consider, my lady, that I could do Mr Rivenhall a great deal of harm,' Mr Goldhanger pointed out. 'He is up at Oxford, isn't he? Yes, I don't think they would be pleased there if they knew of his little transaction with me. Or –'

'They would not be at all pleased,' said Sophy. 'It would be a trifle awkward for you, though, would it not? But perhaps you could persuade them that you had no notion that Mr Rivenhall was under age.'

'Such a clever young lady!' smiled Mr Goldhanger.

'No, but I have a great deal of common-sense, which tells me that if you refuse to give up the bond and the ring the best course for me to pursue would be to drive at once to Bow Street and lay the whole matter before the magistrate there.'

The smile faded: Mr Goldhanger watched her through narrowed eyelids. 'I don't think you would be wise to do that,' he said.

'Don't you? Well, I think it is the wisest thing I could possibly do, and I have a strong feeling that they would like to have news of you in Bow Street.'

Mr Goldhanger shared this feeling. But he did not believe that Sophy meant what she said, his clients having the most providential dislike to publicity. He said: 'I think my Lord Ombersley would prefer to pay me my money.'

'I daresay he would, and that is why I have told him nothing about it, for I think it nonsensical to be blackmailed by such a creature as you, all for the want of a little courage!'

This unprecedented point of view began to engender in Mr Goldhanger a dislike for his guest. Women, he knew, were unpredictable. He leaned forward in his chair, and tried to explain to her some of the more disagreeable consequences that would befall Mr Rivenhall if he repudiated any part of his debt. He spoke well, and it was a sinister little speech that seldom failed to impress his hearers. It failed today.

'All this,' said Sophy, cutting him short, 'is nonsense, and you must know that as well as I do. All that would happen to Mr Rivenhall would be that he would get a great scold, and be in disgrace with his father for a while, and as for being sent down from Oxford, no such thing! They will never know anything about it there, because it is my belief that you do worse things than lending money at extortionate rates to young men, and once I have been to Bow Street, ten to one they will contrive to put you in prison on quite another charge! What is more, the instant it becomes known to the law-officers that you lent money to a minor you will be unable to recover a penny of it. So pray do not talk any more to me in that absurd way! I am not in the least afraid of you, or of anything you can do.'

'You are very courageous,' said Mr Goldhanger gently. 'Also

you have much common-sense, as you told me. But I too have common-sense, my lady, and I do not think that you came to see me with the consent, or even the knowledge of your parents, or your maid, or even of Mr Hubert Rivenhall. Perhaps you would indeed inform against me at Bow Street: I do not know, but perhaps you may never be granted the opportunity. Now I should not like to be harsh to such a beautiful young lady, so shall we agree to a little compromise? You will give me the five hundred pounds you have brought with you, and those pretty pearls you wear in your ears, and I will hand you Mr Rivenhall's bond, and we shall both of us be satisfied.'

Sophy laughed. 'I imagine you would be more than satisfied!' she said. 'I will give you five hundred pounds for the bond and the ring, and nothing more.'

'But perhaps you have loving parents who would be willing to give me much, much more to have you restored to them, alive, my lady, and unhurt?'

He rose from his chair as he spoke, but his objectionable guest, instead of displaying decent alarm, merely withdrew her right hand from her muff. In it she held a small but eminently service-able pistol. 'Pray sit down again, Mr Goldhanger!' she said.

Mr Goldhanger sat down. He believed that no female could stand loud reports, much less pull triggers, but he had seen quite enough of Sophy to be reluctant to put this belief to the test. He begged her not to be foolish.

'You must not be afraid that I don't know how to handle guns,' Sophy told him reassuringly. 'Indeed, I am a very fair shot. Perhaps I ought to tell you that I have lived for some time in Spain, where of course they have a great many unpleasant people, such as ban-dits. My father taught me to shoot. I am not such a fine shot as he is, but at this range I would engage to put a bullet through any part of you I chose.'

'You are trying to frighten me,' said Mr Goldhanger queru-
lously, 'but I am not frightened of guns in women's hands, and I
know very well it is unloaded!'

'Well, if you move out of that chair you will discover that it is
loaded,' said Sophy. 'At least, you will be dead, but I expect you
will know how it happened.'

Mr Goldhanger gave an uneasy laugh. 'And what would
happen to *you*, my lady?' he asked.

'I don't suppose that anything very much would happen to me,'
she replied. 'And I cannot conceive how that should interest you
when you were dead. However, if it does, I will tell you just what
I should say to the law-officers.'

Mr Goldhanger, forgetting his urbanity, said testily that he did
not desire to hear it.

'You know,' said Sophy, frowning slightly, 'I cannot help
thinking that it might be a very good thing if I were to shoot you
in any event. I did not mean to when I first came because naturally
I cannot approve of murder, but I see that you are a very evil man,
and I cannot help wondering if a really courageous person would
not shoot now, and so rid the world of someone who has done a
great deal of harm in it.'

'Put that silly gun away, and we will talk business!' Mr
Goldhanger besought her.

'There is nothing more to talk about, and I feel much more
comfortable with the gun in my hand. Are you going to give me
what I came for, or shall I go to Bow Street, and inform them
there that you tried to kidnap me?'

'My lady,' said Mr Goldhanger, on a whining note, 'I am only
a poor man! You —'

'You will be much richer when I have paid you back your five
hundred pounds,' Sophy pointed out.

He brightened, for it had really seemed for a few minutes as though he might be forced to forgo even this sum. 'Very well,' he said. 'I do not wish any unpleasantness, so I will give back the bond. The ring I cannot give back, for it was stolen from me.'

'In that event,' said Sophy. 'I shall certainly go to Bow Street, because I am persuaded they will not believe there, any more than I do, that it was stolen. If you have not got it, you must have sold it, and *that* means you may be prosecuted. I enquired of a most respectable jeweller only this morning what the law is with regard to pledged articles.'

Mr Goldhanger, revolted by this unwomanly knowledge of the law, cast her a glance of loathing, and said: 'I have not sold it!'

'No, and it was not stolen from you either. I expect it is in one of the drawers of this desk, together with the bond, for I can't imagine why you should have bought such a handsome piece of furniture, unless it was to lock valuables away in it. And it may even be that you keep a gun of your own in it, so perhaps I should warn you that if you pulled the trigger quicker than I did, I left a letter at my home to inform my – parents precisely where I had gone to, and what my purpose was.'

'If I had a daughter like you, I would be ashamed to own her!' said Mr Goldhanger, with real feeling.

'Nonsense!' said Sophy. 'You would probably be very proud of me, and would have taught me how to pick pockets. And if you had a daughter like me she would have scrubbed your floors for you, and washed your shirt, so you would have been a deal better off then you are now. Pray do not keep me waiting any longer, for I am quite tired of talking to you, and, indeed, have found you a dead bore from the outset!'

Mr Goldhanger had been called a villain, a bloodsucker, a cheat, a devil, a ghoul, and innumerable other hard names, but never had anyone told him that he was a dead bore, and never had any of his victims looked at him with such amused contempt. He would have liked to have closed his long, bony fingers round Sophy's throat, and choked the life slowly out of her. But Sophy held a gun, so instead he unlocked the drawer in his desk, and sought in it with a trembling hand for what he wanted. He thrust a ring and a scrap of paper across the desk, and said: 'The money! Give me my money!'

Sophy picked the bond up, and read it; then she put it, with the ring, into her muff, and withdrew from this convenient receptacle a wad of bills, and laid it on the desk. 'There it is,' she said.

Mechanically, he began to count the bills, Sophy rose. 'And now, if you please, will you be so obliging as to turn your chair round with its back to the door?'

Mr Goldhanger almost snarled at her, but he complied with this request, saying over his shoulder: 'You need not be afraid! I am very glad to see you go!' he added, quivering with fury: 'Doxy!'

Sophy chuckled. Fitting the key into the lock, and turning it, she said: 'Well, I really believe I would rather be a doxy than a turnip dressed up in a sheet to frighten silly boys!'

'Turnip?' repeated Mr Goldhanger, stupefied. '*Turnip – ?*'

But his unwelcome guest had gone.

Twelve

HUBERT WAS ON HIS WAY UPSTAIRS TO HIS ROOM THAT EVENING when he met his cousin, coming down from the schoolroom. She said: 'Hubert! The very person I wanted! Wait, I have something for you!' She then went into her own room, and came back in a minute or two, looking mischievous, and said: 'Shut your eyes, and stretch out your hand!'

'Now, Sophy, is this something horrid?' he demanded suspiciously.

'Of course it is not!'

'Well, you look as though you meant to hoax me,' he said, but he obediently shut his eyes, and held out one hand. Sophy placed his ring, and his bond in it, and told him he might now open his eyes. He did so, and suffered so severe a shock that he dropped the ring. '*Sophy!*'

'What a careless creature you are!' she remarked. 'Don't neglect to burn that silly piece of paper! I very nearly did it myself, for I am sure it would be just like you to leave it in your pocket, but then I thought you would like to see for yourself that it really had been recovered.'

He bent to pick the ring up. 'B – but, Sophy, how – who – how came this into your hands?'

'I had it from Mr Goldhanger, of course.'

He gave a gasp. 'Had it from – You did not go to that old devil's house! You *could* not have done so!'

'Yes, I did. What should stop me?'

'Good God!' he ejaculated. He grasped her wrist, and said sharply. 'Why did he give it up to you? Do you tell me you paid the money I owed him?'

'Oh, don't give that a thought! I happened to have five hundred pounds by me, and you will pay me back sometime, I expect. There is no need to look so shocked, you silly boy!'

'Sophy, I cannot *bear* it!' he said, in a strangled voice. 'Besides he lent it to me at fifteen per cent per month, and I know well he would never have parted with my bond for a penny less than was his due! Sophy, tell me the truth!'

'I have done so. Of course, he did not like it very much, but he was obliged to do what I wanted, because I told him I should go to Bow Street if he refused. I think you were very right about him, Hubert! He is probably in league with every thief in London, for the instant I made that threat I could see how uneasy I had made him, so very likely he does not at all wish to be brought under the notice of the magistrates.'

'Goldhanger allowed himself to be frightened into giving up these things? *Goldhanger?*' he said incredulously.

'Well, what else could he do? I told him it was nonsensical to suppose that anything very dreadful would happen to you, if the whole matter *was* laid bare; and he knew that if I did go to Bow Street he would never be able to recover a penny of his money.'

'*You* with that slimy villain! Were you afraid, Sophy?' he asked wonderingly.

'No, not a bit.' She added apologetically: 'You know, I haven't the least sensibility! Sir Horace says it is quite shocking, and *most* unfeminine. But, to own the truth, I thought Goldhanger a

ridiculous person. I was by far more afraid of El Moro! He was one
of the guerrilleros, and a dreadful rogue! He and his men broke into
the house one night when Sir Horace was away – but never mind
that! People who are for ever recounting their adventures are the
most tedious persons imaginable!'

'Sophy, he might have done you some mischief –'

'Yes, but I had my pistol with me, so he very soon thought
better of that notion!' she explained.

'Sophy, Sophy, what am I to do?' he exclaimed.

'Nothing: there is nothing left to be done. I must go, or I shall
be late for dinner. Don't forget to burn that paper!'

She vanished into her room, cutting short his stammered
thanks and protestations, and since he did not see her alone again
that night he was unable to repeat them. He was engaged with
a party of his own, but his friends found him in an unconvivial
mood. His thoughts were, indeed, in a sad turmoil, and although
his relief at being rid of his debt to Goldhanger had been at first
overwhelming, it was succeeded, as soon as he had had time to
think the matter over, by a most uncomfortable feeling of guilt.
That Sophy, a mere female (and younger than himself), should
not only have paid off his debt, but should also have visited on
his behalf such a person as Goldhanger, made him squirm in his
chair. Blue Ruin did little to clear his intellect, and when he
sought Berkeley Square in the early hours of the morning he was
no nearer a solution of this new difficulty than he had been at the
start of the evening, the only coherent thought in his head being
that in some undiscovered way he must instantly pay his cousin
five hundred pounds.

Mr Rivenhall returned from Leicestershire on the following day, arriving in Berkeley Square at a somewhat infelicitous
moment. Jane Storridge, whose vigilance Sophy had not sufficiently taken into account, had not only discovered that the

diamond drops were missing from her mistress's jewel-case, but had raised such a hue and cry in the servant's quarters that Mrs Ludstock, the housekeeper, felt herself called upon to inform Lady Ombersley that while she was sure she did not know what servants were coming to these days she would take her dying oath that none of the maids under her control had touched Miss Sophy's ear-rings; and, further, that anybody might be pardoned for thinking that a lady's maid worthy of the name would take better care of her mistress's valuables than Miss Storridge seemed to suppose was necessary. With the gist of these remarks Dassett also wished to be identified, and so pregnant with unuttered offence was his manner that Lady Ombersley became quite flustered, realizing that she stood upon the brink of a domestic disaster. She sent for Jane Storridge, and Mr Rivenhall arrived in time to hear the end of a dialogue between the three servants so icily civil, so bristling with veiled innuendo as to terrify poor Lady Ombersley. Before he had the opportunity of demanding an explanation, Sophy herself came in, in her walking-dress, saying that she and Cecilia were going out to do some shopping, and had her aunt any commissions for her? Lady Ombersley greeted her with relief, and at once asked her why she had not disclosed the loss of her ear-rings.

Sophy did not start, but a very slight flush rose to her cheeks. She replied with perfect composure: 'I have not lost any ear-rings, dear ma'am. What is this?'

'Oh, my love, your maid says that your diamond drops are gone from your case, and I would not have had such a thing happen for the world!'

Sophy bent to kiss her cheek. 'Aunt Lizzie, I am so sorry! It is quite my fault for having been so stupid as to forget to tell Jane! They are not lost: I took them to the jeweller to be cleaned, and reset. One of the hooks was a little loose. How foolish of you to

have worried her ladyship, Jane, before first asking me if I knew
where the ear-rings were!'

'Cleaned?' cried Miss Storridge. 'Why, Miss Sophy, as though
I did not take all your jewels to Rundell and Bridge to be cleaned
when we first came to London!'

'Yes, but I thought on the night of our ball that those drops
looked quite dull,' responded Sophy. 'Go away now, Jane: her
ladyship has been plagued enough!'

She was aware of her cousin's eyes upon her face, and a
swift glance in his direction had informed her that there was an
uncomfortably searching expression in them. However, he said
nothing, so she got rid of her maid, ascertained that her aunt
had no commissions for her to execute, and went off, devoutly
trusting that neither she nor Mr Rivenhall would notice the
continued absence of her diamond ear-rings.

But on the following day, just as she had sat down to a light
luncheon with Lady Ombersley, Cecilia, Selina, and Hubert, Mr
Rivenhall walked into the room, and handed her a small package.
'Your ear-rings, cousin,' he said briefly. 'I think you will find that
they have now been cleaned to your satisfaction.'

For once in her life, Sophy was bereft of all power of speech.
Fortunately, he did not seem to expect her to say anything, for
he turned away to carve himself a slice of ham, and began to talk
to his mother, desiring to know whether she wished to spend any
part of the summer in Brighton that year. Lady Ombersley referred
this question to Sophy. Brighton did not agree with her constitution, but the Regent had made the resort so fashionable that any
number of distinguished persons would flock there in June, and if
Sophy wished it she would certainly hire a house there for some
part of the season.

Cecilia, who had her own reasons for wanting to remain
in town, said: 'Oh, Mama, you know you are never well in

Brighton! Pray do not let us go! I am sure there is nothing more stupid than those parties at the Pavilion, and the excessive heat in the rooms quite knocks you up!'

Sophy at once disclaimed any wish to visit the place, and the rest of the meal was spent in discussing the rival attractions of Ombersley, Thorpe Grange, and Scarborough, with some reminiscences from Lady Ombersley on a summer she had spent at Ramsgate before the Regent's patronage of Brighton had quite cast this resort into the shade.

When they rose from the table, Hubert, who had been trying unavailingly for some time to get his cousin alone, blurted out: 'Are you busy, Sophy? Would you care to stroll in the garden for a while?'

'Thank you! By and by, perhaps! Charles, may I have a word with you at your convenience?'

He met her direct gaze unsmilingly. 'By all means! Now, if you wish.'

Lady Ombersley looked vaguely surprised; Selina exclaimed: 'Secrets! Are you hatching a plot, I wonder? Shall we like it?'

'Nothing so exciting,' replied Sophy lightly. 'Merely, Charles executed a commission for me.'

She accompanied him across the hall to the library. She was never one to beat about the bush, and no sooner had he shut the door than she said, without preamble: 'Now, if you please, tell me what this means! How did you know that I had sold my ear-rings, and why have you – as I suppose – bought them back for me?'

'I bought them back because I can think of only two reasons why you should have disposed of them.'

'Indeed! And what may they be, Cousin Charles?'

'I have never been permitted to see the bills for your ball, but I have some experience in these matters, and I can possibly guess at a rough total. If that is your explanation, you can want none from me. The arrangement was repugnant to me from the outset, as well you know.'

'My dear Charles, I have a great many expenses of which you know nothing at all! You are being absurd, you know!'

'I do not think that you have any expenses which your father would be unprepared to meet.'

She was silent for a moment. Then she said: 'You have not yet told me what is the second of the reasons that occurred to you.'

He looked at her under frowning brows. 'My fear is that you have lent the money to Hubert.'

'Good gracious! Banish it!' she exclaimed, laughing. 'Pray, why should I do such a thing?'

'I hope you have not. The young fool was at Newmarket with a set of fellows I could wish at Jericho. Did he lose a large sum there?'

'Surely he would tell you if he had, rather than me!'

He walked over to his desk, and rather absently tidied some paper that lay on it. 'It may have been that he was afraid to,' he said. He looked up. 'Was that it?'

'I needed the money for reasons into which I will not take you,' she replied. 'I must point out to you, Charles, that you have not yet answered my other question. How did you guess that I had sold the ear-rings?'

'It was not a conjecture: I knew.'

'How is this possible? You were not hidden in the shop, I assume!'

'No, I was not. But I called in Brook Street on my way home yesterday, and saw Miss Wraxton.' He hesitated, and again looked across at his cousin. 'You must understand that Miss Wraxton felt it to be her duty to tell me that she feared you might be in some difficulty! She was in Rundell and Bridge's with Lady Brinklow when you were transacting this sale. It appears that Bridge had not properly closed the door into his office; Miss Wraxton recognized your voice, and could not help but overhear something you said to Bridge.'

Her hand, which was lying on the back of a chair, closed tightly on the polished wood, but relaxed again after a moment. She said, in a voice from which all emotion had been banished: 'There is no end to Miss Wraxton's solicitude. How very obliging of her to have interested herself in my affairs! I expect it was delicacy that forbade her to speak to me rather than to you.'

He flushed. 'You must remember that I am betrothed to Miss Wraxton. In the circumstances, she thought it her duty to mention the matter to me. She felt that she did not stand upon such terms with you as could make it possible for her to ask you for an explanation.'

'Well, that is certainly true,' said Sophy. 'Neither of you, my dear cousin, stands upon such terms with me! And if you have any notion of asking me for an explanation of anything I choose to do, let me tell you that you may go to the devil!'

He smiled. 'Then perhaps it is as well that Eugenia did not venture to address you on this head, for she would have been much shocked at being told to go to the devil! Do you always talk like your father when you lose your temper, Sophy?'

'No, not invariably. I beg your pardon! But it was quite intolerable!'

'I daresay, but I should not have asked you for an explanation had you not sought this interview.'

'You should have paid no heed to Miss Wraxton! As for repurchasing my ear-rings, good God, what a fix you have placed me in!'

As she spoke, the door opened behind her, and Hubert came into the room. He was looking extremely white, but perfectly determined, and he said jerkily: 'I beg pardon, but I have been wanting to speak to you all day, Sophy, and – and to Charles! So I have come!'

Mr Rivenhall said nothing, nor did he cast him more than one of his penetrating glances, but Sophy turned, and held out her hand. 'Yes, pray come in, Hubert!' she said, smiling at him.

He took her hand, and pressed it a little convulsively. 'Cecilia told me about your ear-rings, and all the kick-up – Sophy, was it *that*? For if it was, and, indeed, in any event! I can't and I won't stand it! I had rather by far tell Charles the whole!'

Her hand returned the pressure of his before releasing it. She said in her calm way: 'Well, you know, Hubert, I always thought you made a mistake not to tell Charles, for Mr Wychbold told me once that there was no one he would liefer go to in a fix. And if *he* could trust him, how much more reason must *you* have to do so! I am persuaded you will do much better without me, so I will leave you.'

She did not look at Mr Rivenhall to see what effect her words might have had on him, but walked immediately out of the room.

There had been an effect; Mr Rivenhall said quietly: 'I think I know what it is, but tell me! Newmarket?'

'It is worse than that! Oh, yes, I lost at Newmarket, but that's the least part of it!' Hubert said.

Mr Rivenhall nodded to a chair. 'Sit down. What's the worst part of it?'

Hubert did not avail himself of this invitation. Apprehension made him assume a belligerent tone that in no way expressed his feelings. 'You may as well know that I didn't tell you the whole of my debts, last year!'

'Young fool!' commented his brother, without heat.

'I know that, but you said – Oh, well, it doesn't signify talking of that now!'

'You should know I don't mean all I say when I am angry. However, if my tongue's to blame, I'm sorry for it. Go on!'

'I know I ought to have told you,' Hubert muttered. 'And I wish to God I had, instead of –' He broke off, drew a breath, and started again. 'I thought I might be able to come about. I – you won't like this! You need not tell me it was wrong, for I know that! But other fellows –'

'Well, I won't tell you it was wrong, then. But let me know what it was, for I am quite in the dark as yet!'

'I went with – a man I know – to a – place in Pall Mall. And another in St James's Place. Roulette, and French Hazard! And I lost the devil of a sum of money!'

'Oh, my God!' Mr Rivenhall exclaimed sharply. 'Have we not had enough of that in this family?'

The bitterness in his voice, grown suddenly harsh, made Hubert wince, and retire behind a barrier of sullenness. 'Well, I knew you would be in a rage, but I don't see that it was so very bad! I wish I had not had such infamous luck, but everyone plays, after all!'

It seemed for a moment as though his brother would have returned a stinging answer, but he checked himself, and walked over to the window instead, and stood frowning out. After a pause, he said abruptly: 'Do you know the sum of my father's gaming debts?'

Hubert was surprised, for the subject had never before been mentioned between them. He replied: 'No. That is, I do know that they must have been rather heavy, of course, but I never heard the exact sum.'

Mr Rivenhall told him.

There was a stunned silence. Hubert broke it at last. 'But – but – My *God*, Charles! You're – you're not bamming me, are you?'

Mr Rivenhall gave a short laugh.

'But – Charles, *you* did not pay all that?'

'Hardly. I settled some part, but the estate is still grossly encumbered. I need not take you into all that. Now that my father has given the management into my hands I have a reasonable hope of being able to tow the family out of the river Tick. But compounding with creditors, spending my life contriving ways and means with our man of business is the very devil!'

'Good God, I should rather think it would be! Listen, Charles, I'm damned sorry I should have added to it all!'

Mr Rivenhall came back to the desk. 'Yes, I know. Your debt is no great matter, but if gaming is in your blood as well –'

'Well, it ain't! You needn't fear for that, for I don't care for cards above half, and I can assure you I had no pleasure in going to those damned hells!' He took a turn about the room, a frown slowly gathering on his brow. He stopped suddenly, and exclaimed: 'Why didn't you tell me? Dash it, I'm not a child! You should have told me.'

Mr Rivenhall looked at him, half smiling. 'Yes, perhaps I should,' he said mildly. 'But the fewer people to know the better. Even my mother does not know the whole.'

'Mama! No, indeed! I should think not! But I had a right to be told, instead of being allowed to go on as though – It is just like you, Charles, to shoulder everything, and to suppose no one can do the least thing but yourself! I daresay there might be a dozen ways in which I could help you! It seems to me that I ought to come down from Oxford at once, and find an eligible post somewhere, or join the Army – no, that won't do, because you would have to buy me a commission, and even if I didn't join a cavalry regiment, or the Guards –'

'It certainly will not do!' interrupted his brother, amused, and rather touched. 'You'll oblige me by staying where you are! We are not on our last legs yet. Why, you bacon-brained young idiot, what do you suppose my object is but to see that you, and Theodore, and the girls don't suffer through my father's curst folly? If you choose to help me to run the estate, you may do so, and I shall be grateful, for Eckington is growing past it. I can't be rid of him, for he has been with us so long that I daresay he would break his heart, but he is of very little use, and I've no great degree of confidence in young Badsey yet. Have you a head for business?'

'I don't know, but I'll precious soon learn!' replied Hubert, with determination. 'When I come down for the Long Vacation, you may teach me. And mind, Charles! No keeping me in the dark!'

'No, very well. But you are still keeping *me* a little in the dark, you know. When did you lose all this money? Not lately, surely?'

'At Christmas. Well, I had better make a clean breast of the whole! I went to a rascally moneylender, and I borrowed five hundred from him, for six months. I thought I should have won every penny back, and more beside, at Newmarket. But the damnable screw was unplaced!' He saw his brother's expression, and said: 'You need not look like that! I swear I shall never do so again as long as I live! Of course I ought to have come rather to you, but –'

'You should have come to me, and that you did not must have been far more my fault than yours!'

'Oh, well, I don't know that!' Hubert said uncomfortably. 'I expect if I had been rather better acquainted with you I should have done so. Sophy said I should do so from the start, and, lord, if I'd had the least notion of what she meant to do I would have run to you straight away!'

'Then you did not apply to her for that money?'

'Good God, no! Charles, you *can't* think I would borrow money from Sophy?'

'I didn't think it. But neither did I think we were so ill-acquainted that – Well, never mind that! How did Sophy know of this, and if you did not borrow the money from her, why did she sell her ear-rings?'

'She guessed I was all to pieces. She made me tell her, and when I said I had rather not say a word to you, she offered to lend me the money. Of course I refused! But she knew where Goldhanger lived, and, without telling me what she meant to do, she went to see him herself, and got back my note of hand, and my ring. I had to pledge Grandfather Stanton-Lacy's emerald, you see. I don't know how she did it, for she swears she did not pay the old devil a penny of the interest. She is the most redoubtable girl! But I couldn't stand *that*, as you may suppose!'

'Sophy went to a moneylender?' repeated Mr Rivenhall incredulously. 'Nonsense! She cannot have done such a thing!'

'Well, she ain't one to tell fibs, and that's what she said!' declared Hubert.

Not many minutes later, Sophy, reading in the Yellow Parlour, was interrupted by the entrance of Mr Rivenhall, who came in, and closed the door behind him, saying bluntly: 'I seem to be very much in your debt, cousin. Yes, Hubert has told me the whole. I hardly know what I can say to you.'

'You are not at all in my debt,' replied Sophy. 'You have given me back my ear-rings! There is nothing to be said, in fact! You know that Miss Wraxton is in the drawing-room, with your mother? Lord Bromford, too, which is why I have sought refuge here.'

'There is a great deal to be said,' he replied, disregarding. 'I wish to God you had told me!'

'I am persuaded you could not seriously expect me to betray Hubert's confidence to you. You must not think, however, that I encouraged him to keep you in the dark. I advised him most earnestly to tell you the fix he was in, but he seemed to be in such dread of doing so that I might not persist.' She saw a slightly rigid look on his face, and added: 'I believe it is often so, between brothers, where there is a considerable disparity of age. And you are very formidable, upon occasion, are you not?'

'It seems so, indeed. Don't imagine I am not grateful to you,

Sophy! I don't know by what means you discovered the coil he had tangled himself in —'

'Oh, it was not so difficult! The poor boy has been looking quite hagridden ever since I came to London! After his return from Newmarket, it was plain to be seen that something of a disastrous nature must have befallen him. He did not wish to confide in me, but a threat to tell you of my suspicions brought the whole stupid story out.'

He looked at her, his eyes hard and bright. 'I know well it is I who should have noticed there was something preying on Hubert's mind!'

He was evidently deeply mortified; she said: 'You have many other things to think about, perhaps. Men do not notice as quickly as women do. I am very glad that he has told you all. Don't refine too much upon it! I am quite sure that he has had a lesson he will be in no danger of forgetting.'

'I believe you are right. I used to think him as volatile as — well, I was used to think him volatile, but he has given me reason to indulge the hope that I was mistaken! But, Sophy, I don't yet know the whole of this deplorable business! Whom did you employ in it?'

'No one, upon my honour!' she assured him at once. 'I considered the matter from every aspect, and although I was much inclined, at first, to consult my father's lawyer, I soon saw that it would not do. There was no one I could apply to without divulging Hubert's part in the business. So I set about it myself.'

'Sophy, you cannot have gone to this creature yourself!'

'Yes, I did. Oh, I know it was dreadfully fast and bold of me, but I thought nobody would ever know! And then, too, I could not but reflect how much you must dislike Hubert's affairs becoming known outside our immediate circle.'

She saw that he was looking at her in patent disbelief, and raised her brows enquiringly.

'Hubert has told me enough about Goldhanger to make it perfectly plain to me what sort of a man he is!' he said. 'Do not tell me he willingly relinquished a note of hand and a valuable pledge to you for no more than the bare principal!'

She smiled. 'Most unwillingly! But only consider at what a disadvantage he stood! He had lent his money to a minor and he could not recover a penny of it, at law. I fancy he was glad to see back his principal. The instant I said I would go to Bow Street – a shot drawn at a venture, too! – I could see that I had discomposed him. My dear Charles, what Hubert found to alarm him in such a creature I cannot imagine. A bogey to frighten children!'

He was watching her closely, his brows knit. 'This sounds to me pure fantasy, Sophy! From what I collect, this was no accredited moneylender, but an out-and-out villain! Do you tell me he made no effort to extort his interest from you?'

'No, he tried to frighten me into paying him, or giving him my pearl ear-rings. But Hubert had warned me with what manner of person I should have to deal, and I took the precaution of carrying my pistol with me.'

'*What?*'

She was surprised, and again raised her brows. 'My pistol,' she repeated.

His mortification found expression in disbelief. 'This must be nonsense! I wish you will tell me the truth! You do not ask me to believe that you carry a pistol about your person! I tell you now that I do not believe it!'

She got up quickly, a sparkle in her eye. 'Indeed? Wait! I shall not be gone above a minute or two!'

She whisked herself out of the room, only to reappear very soon afterwards with her silver-mounted gun in her hand. 'Do you not believe it, Charles? Do you not?' she demanded.

He stared at the weapon. 'Good God! *You?*' He held out his

hand, as though he would have taken it from her, but she withheld it.

'Take care! It is loaded!'

He replied impatiently: 'Let me see it!'

'Sir Horace,' said Sophy provocatively, 'told me always to be careful, and never to give it into the hands of anyone I was not perfectly satisfied could be trusted to handle it.'

For an astounded moment, Mr Rivenhall, who was no mean shot, stared at her. The pent-up emotions in his breast got the better of him. He flung over to the fireplace, and ripped down from the overmantel an invitation-card which had been stuck into a corner of a large, gilded mirror. 'Hold that up, stand there, and give me that gun!' he commanded.

Sophy laughed, and obeyed, standing quite fearlessly with her back to one wall, and holding the card out by one corner. 'I warn you, it throws a trifle left!' she said coolly.

He was white with anger, an anger that had very little to do with her slighting reference to his ability to handle a pistol, but even as he levelled the gun, he seemed in some measure to recollect himself, for he lowered his arm again, and said: 'I cannot! Not with a pistol I don't know!'

'Faintheart!' mocked Sophy.

He cast her a glance of dislike, stepped forward to twitch the card out of her hand, and stuck it against the wall under the corner of a picture. In great interest, Sophy watched him walk away to the other end of the room, turn, jerk up his arm, and fire. An explosion, deafening in the confined space of the room, shattered the stillness, and the bullet, nicking one edge of the card, buried itself in the wall.

'I told you that it threw left,' Sophy reminded him, critically surveying his handiwork. 'Shall we reload it so that I can show you what *I* can do?'

They looked at one another. The enormity of this conduct suddenly dawned on Mr Rivenhall, and he began to laugh. 'Sophy, you – you *devil!*'

That made Sophy laugh too, so when a startled crowd of persons burst into the room a minute to two later, they found only a scene of unbridled mirth. Lady Ombersley, Cecilia, Miss Wraxton, Lord Bromford, Hubert, one of the footmen, and two housemaids all clustered in the doorway, evidently in the expectation of beholding the results of a shocking accident. 'I could murder you, Sophy!' said Mr Rivenhall.

'Unjust! Did *I* tell you to do it?' she countered. 'Dear Aunt Lizzie, do not look so alarmed! Charles was – was merely satisfying himself that my pistol was in order!'

By this time the eyes of most of the company had discovered the rent in the wall. Lady Ombersley, clutching Hubert's arm for support, faintly enunciated: 'Are you *mad*, Charles?'

He looked a little guiltily at the havoc he had wrought. 'I must be, I suppose. The damage can soon be made good, however. It *does* throw left, Sophy. I would give much to see you fire it! What a pity I cannot take you to Manton's!'

'Is that Sophy's pistol?' asked Hubert, much interested. 'By Jupiter, you are an out-and-outer, Sophy! But what possessed you to fire it here, Charles? You *must* be mad!'

'It was naturally, an accident,' pronounced Lord Bromford. 'A man in his senses, which we cannot doubt Lord Rivenhall to be, does not, of intent, fire a pistol in the presence of ladies. My dear Miss Stanton-Lacy, you have sustained a severe shock to the nerves! It could not be otherwise. Let me beg you to repose yourself for a while!'

'I am not such a poor creature!' Sophy replied, her eyes still brimming with laughter. 'Charles will bear me out, if there is any truth in him, that I neither squeaked nor jumped! Sir

Horace nipped such bad habits in the bud by soundly boxing my ears!'

'I am sure you are always an example to us all!' said Miss Wraxton acidly. 'One can only envy you your iron composure! I, alas, am made of weaker stuff, and must confess to have been very much startled by such an unprecedented noise in the house. I do not know what you can have been about, Charles. Or is it indeed Miss Stanton-Lacy's pistol, and was she exhibiting her skill to you?'

'On the contrary, it was I who shot disgracefully wide of my mark. May I clean this for you, Sophy?'

She shook her head, and held out her hand for the gun. 'Thank you, but I like to clean and load it myself.'

'Load it?' gasped Lady Ombersley. 'Sophy, you do not mean to load that horrid thing again, *surely*?'

Hubert laughed. 'I said she was a redoubtable girl, Charles! I say, Sophy, do you always keep it loaded?'

'Yes, for how can one tell when one may need it, and what is the use of an empty pistol? You know, what a delicate business it is, too! I daresay Charles can do it in a trice, but I cannot!'

He gave the gun into her hand. 'If we go down to Ombersley this summer, we must have a match, you and I,' he said. As their hands met, and she took the gun, he grasped her wrist, and held it for a moment. 'An infamous thing to have done!' he said, in a slightly lowered tone. 'I beg your pardon – and I thank you!'

Thirteen

It was not to be supposed that this incident would be pleasing to Miss Wraxton. A degree of understanding seemed to be existent between Mr Rivenhall and his cousin which was not at all to her taste, for although she was not in love with him, and, indeed, would have considered such an emotion very far beneath her station, she had made up her mind to marry him, and was feminine enough to resent his paying the least attention to any other female.

Fortune had not smiled upon Miss Wraxton. She had been contracted, in schoolroom days, to a nobleman of impeccable lineage, and respectable fortune, who had been carried off by an attack of small-pox before she was of an age to be formally affianced to him. Several eligible gentlemen had shown faint tendencies to dangle after her during her first two seasons upon the Marriage Mart, for she was a handsome girl with a handsome portion; but for unaccountable reasons none of them had come up to scratch, as her elder brother rather vulgarly phrased it. Mr Rivenhall's offer had been made at a moment when she had begun to fear that she might be left upon the shelf, and had been thankfully received. Miss Wraxton, reared in the strictest propriety, had never taken any undesirably romantic notions into her head, and had had no hesitation informing her Papa that she was willing to receive Mr Rivenhall's addresses. Lord Brinklow, who held Lord Ombersley in the greatest aversion, would certainly not have entertained Mr Rivenhall's offer for as much as a minute had it not been for the providential death of Matthew Rivenhall. But the old Nabob's fortune was something not to be despised even by the most sanctimonious of peers. Lord Brinklow had informed his daughter that Charles Rivenhall's suit carried his blessing with it; and Lady Brinklow, a sterner moralist even than her spouse, had clearly indicated to Eugenia where her duty lay, and by what means she might hope to detach Charles from his unregenerate family. An apt pupil, Miss Wraxton had thereafter lost no opportunity of pointing out to Charles, in the most tactful way, the delinquencies and general undesirability of his father, and his brothers and sisters. She was actuated by the purest of motives; she considered that the volatility of Lord Ombersley and Hubert was prejudicial to Charles's interest; she heartily despised Lady Ombersley, and as heartily deprecated the excessive sentiment which made Cecilia contemplate marriage with a penniless younger son. It seemed to her that to detach Charles from his family must be her first object, but sometimes she was seduced into playing with the notion of reclaiming the Ombersley household from the abyss of impropriety into which it had fallen. Becoming engaged to Mr Rivenhall at a moment when he was exacerbated by his father's excesses, her gentle words had fallen on fruitful soil. A naturally joyless nature, reared on bleak principles, could perceive only the most deplorable tendencies in a lively family's desire for enjoyment. Charles, wrestling with mountainous piles of bills, was much inclined to think that she was right. It was only since Sophy's arrival that his sentiments seemed to have undergone a change. Miss Wraxton could not deceive herself into under-rating Sophy's ruinous influence upon Charles's character; and since she was not, in spite of her learning, very wise, she tried to counteract it in a variety of ways that served merely to set up his back. When she enquired whether Sophy had offered him an explanation of her visit to Rundell and Bridge, and, in justice to his cousin, he felt himself obliged to tell her some part of the truth, her evil genius had inspired her to point out to him the total unreliability of Hubert's character, his resemblance to his father, and the ill-judged nature of Sophy's admittedly good-natured conduct in the affair. But Mr Rivenhall was already writhing under the lash of his own conscience, and since, with all his faults, he was not one to burk a clear issue, these remarks found no favour with him. He said: 'I blame myself. That any hasty words of mine should have made Hubert feel that anything would be preferable to confiding his difficulties to me must be an everlasting reproach to me! I have to thank my cousin for showing me how much I have erred! I hope I may do better in the future. I had no intention – but I see now how unsympathetic I must have appeared to him! I'll take good care poor little Theodore does not grow up in the belief that he must at all costs conceal his peccadilloes from me!'

'My dear Charles, I assure you this is an excess of sensibility!' Miss Wraxton said soothingly. '*You* are not to be held accountable for the behaviour of your brothers!'

'You are wrong, Eugenia: I am six years older than Hubert, and since I know – none better! – that my father would never concern himself with any one of us, it was my duty to take care of the younger ones! I do not scruple to say this to you, for you know how we are circumstanced!'

She replied without hesitation: 'I am persuaded you have always done your duty! I have seen how you have tried to introduce into your father's household more exact standards of conduct, a greater notion of discipline, and of management. Hubert can have been in no doubt of your sentiments upon this occasion, and to *condone* his behaviour – which I must think quite shocking! – would be most improper. Miss Stanton-Lacy's intervention, which was, of course, meant in the kindest way, sprang from impulse, and cannot have been dictated by her conscience. Painful though it might have been to her, there can be no doubt that it was her duty to have told you the whole, and immediately! To have paid off Hubert's debts in that fashion was merely to encourage him in his gaming propensities. I fancy that a moment's reflection must have convinced her of this, but, alas, with all her good qualities I fear that Miss Stanton-Lacy is not much given to the indulgence of rational thought!'

He stared at her, an odd expression in his eyes which she was at a loss to interpret. 'If Hubert had confided in you, Eugenia, would you have come to me with his story?' he asked.

'Undoubtedly,' she replied. 'I should not have known an instant's hesitation.'

'Not an instant's hesitation!' he repeated. 'Although it was a confidence made in the belief that you would not betray it?'

She smiled at him. 'That, my dear Charles, is a great piece of nonsense. To be boggling at such a thing as that when one's duty is so plain is what I have no patience with! My concern for your brother's future career must have convinced me that I had no other course open to me than to divulge his wrong-doing to you. Such ruinous tendencies must be checked, and since your father, as you have said, does not concern himself with –'

He interrupted her without apology. 'These sentiments may do honour to your reason, but not to your heart, Eugenia! You are a female: perhaps you do not understand that a confidence reposed in you must – *must!* – be held sacred! I said that I wished she had told me, but it was untrue! I could not wish anyone to betray a confidence! Good God, would I do so myself?'

These rapidly uttered words brought a flush to her cheek; she said sharply: 'I collect that Miss Stanton-Lacy – I presume she is also a female! – does understand this?'

'Yes,' he replied. 'She does. Perhaps that is one of the results of her upbringing! It is an excellent one! Perhaps she knew what must be the result of her action; perhaps she only went to Hubert's rescue from motives of generosity: I don't know that; I have not enquired of her! The outcome has been happy – far happier than would have been the case had she divulged all to me! Hubert is too much of a man to shelter behind his cousin: he confessed the whole to me!'

She smiled. 'I am afraid your partiality makes you a trifle blind, Charles! Once you had discovered that Miss Stanton-Lacy had sold her jewelry you were bound to discover the rest! Had I not been in a position to apprise you of this circumstance, I wonder if Hubert would have confessed?'

He said sternly: 'Such a speech does you no credit! I do not know why you should be so unjust to Hubert, or why you should so continually wish me to think ill of him! I *did* think ill of him, and I have been proved wrong! Mine has been the fault: I treated him as though he were still a child, and I his mentor. I should have done better to have taken him into my counsels. None of this would have happened had he and I been better friends. He said to me, *Had we been better acquainted – !* You may judge of my feelings upon hearing *that* from my brother!' He gave a short laugh. 'A leveller indeed! Jackson himself could not have floored me more completely!'

'I fear,' said Miss Wraxton, at her sweetest, 'that if you mean to use boxing-cant I can never hope to understand you, Charles. No doubt your cousin, with her superior knowledge, would appreciate such language!'

'I should not be at all surprised!' he retorted, nettled.

Not all her training could prevent her saying: 'You seem to cherish an extraordinary regard for Miss Stanton-Lacy!'

'I!' he ejaculated, thunderstruck. 'For Sophy? Good God! I thought my sentiments towards her were sufficiently well-known! I wish to heaven we were rid of her, but I suppose I need not be so prejudiced as to be blind to her good qualities!'

She was mollified. 'No, indeed, and I hope I am not either! What a pity it is that she will not entertain Lord Bromford's suit! He is an excellent man, with a good understanding, and such sobriety of judgment as must, I fancy, exercise a beneficial effect upon any female.' She saw that he was looking at her with a good deal of amusement, and added: 'I had thought that you were inclined to encourage his suit?'

'It is nothing to me whom Sophy marries!' he said. 'She would never take Bromford, though! Well for him!'

'I am afraid Lady Bromford feels as you do,' Miss Wraxton said. 'She and Mama are acquainted, you know, and I have had some conversation with her on this subject. She is a most excellent woman! She has been telling me of the delicacy of Lord Bromford's constitution, and of her fear for him. I could not but feel for her! One cannot but agree with her that your cousin would never make him a good wife!'

'The very worst!' he said, laughing. 'God knows why such a fellow should have taken it into his head to fall in love with Sophy! You may imagine how Cecilia and Hubert roast her over it! As for the tales they make up of his adventures in the West Indies, even my mother has been thrown into whoops! He is the most absurd oddity!'

'I cannot agree with you,' she said. 'And even though I did, I could not listen with anything but pain to a man's sensibility being made a mock of.'

This reproof had the effect of making Mr Rivenhall recollect an engagement in the neighbourhood which necessitated his instant departure. He had never before found himself so little in accord with his betrothed.

On the other hand, never before had he been in such charity with his cousin, a happy state of affairs which lasted for very nearly a week. It inspired him to gratify an expressed wish of hers to see Kemble act. While making no secret of the fact that he found the great player's affections insupportable, his odd mispronunciations ruining his most brilliant histrionic flights, he took a box at Covent Garden, and escorted Sophy there, with Cecilia and Mr Wychbold. Sophy was a trifle disappointed in an actor of whom she had heard so much praise, but the evening passed very agreeably, ending at the fashionable hotel in Henrietta Street, known as the Star. Here, Mr Rivenhall, proving himself to be an excellent host, had ordered a private dining-room, and a most elegant supper. His mood was so amiable as even to preclude his making a slighting remark about Kemble's acting. Mr Wychbold was chatty and obliging, Cecilia in her best looks, and Sophy lively enough to set the ball of conversation rolling gaily at the outset. In fact, Cecilia said, when she later bade her brother good-night, that she had not been so much diverted for months.

'Nor I,' he responded. 'I cannot think why we do not go out more often together, Cilly. Do you suppose our cousin would care to see Kean? I believe he is appearing in a new play at the Lane.'

Cecilia could feel no doubts on this head, but before Mr Rivenhall had had time to put a half-formulated plan into execution he had been forestalled, and the better understanding set up between him and Sophy had begun noticeably to wane. Lord Charlbury, obedient to the commands of his instructress, begged Lady Ombersley to honour him by bringing her daughter and her niece to a little theatre-party of his making. Mr Rivenhall bore up perfectly well under this, but when it leaked out, later, that Mr Fawnhope had made one of the party, his equanimity suffered a severe set-back. Nothing, it seemed, could have excelled the evening's delights! Even Lady Ombersley, who had been decidedly disturbed by the unexpected presence of Mr Fawnhope, succumbed to the combined attentions of her host, and of her old friend, General Retford, who had certainly been invited to entertain her. The play, *Bertram*, was pronounced to have been most affecting; Kean's acting was beyond praise; and quite the most delightful supper-party at the Piazza had wound up the evening. Much of this Mr Rivenhall gathered from his mother, but some of it he had from Cecilia, who was at immense pains to tell him how much she had enjoyed herself. She said that Sophy had been in high spirits, but failed to mention that Sophy's spirits had taken the form of flirtation with her host. Cecilia was naturally glad to find that her rejected suitor was not nursing a broken heart, and almost equally glad to think that she herself had no turn for a form of amusement that showed her otherwise charming cousin in a very poor light. As for Lord Charlbury's volunteering to show Sophy how his father, a sad rake, had been used to take snuff from a lady's wrist, and Sophy's instantly holding out her hand, that, thought Cecilia, was the outside of enough! She was happy to reflect that Augustus would never behave in such an audacious fashion. He had certainly no notion of doing so that evening. The tragedy he had witnessed had fired him with an ambition to write a lyrical drama, and although it would have been impossible to have found fault with his manners as a guest, Cecilia had a strong suspicion that his thoughts were otherwise.

Bad as this evening had been, there was worse, in Mr Rivenhall's estimation, to follow. Until Lord Charlbury's emergence from a sickroom, Sophy's most frequent cavalier (or, as Mr Rivenhall preferred savagely to dub him, her cicisbeo) had been Sir Vincent Talgarth. But Lord Charlbury was soon seen to have supplanted Sir Vincent. He met her on horseback in the Park in the mornings; he was to be observed seated in her phaeton at the hour of the promenade; he stood up with her for two dances at Almack's; took her in his own curricle to a military review; and even acted as her escort on a visit to Merton. His lordship made no secret of the fact that he had enjoyed his expedition enormously, his sense of humour being much tickled by the Marquesa's rich and languorous personality. He told Sophy that he would have been happy to have remained for twice as long in her company. Any lady, he declared, who, overcome by the fatigue of entertaining morning-callers, closed her eyes, and went to sleep under their startled gaze, was something quite out of the ordinary, and worthy of being cultivated. She smiled, and agreed to it, but she was secretly a little dismayed. It had been a shock to her to find Sir Vincent seated with the Marquesa. He had not been her only visitor – the Marquesa's brief sojourn at the Pulteney had drawn to her several gentlemen who had enjoyed her hospitality in Madrid – but he was all too plainly her most assiduous visitor. Major Quinton had been there too, as well as Lord Francis Wolvey, and Mr Fawnhope. Mr Fawnhope's presence was easily explained: he rather thought of writing a tragedy about Don John of Austria, whose brief but glorious career seemed to him eminently suited to lyric drama. He had already composed some moving lines for his hero to utter upon his fevered deathbed, and he thought that the Marquesa might reasonably be expected to be in a position to divulge to him many details of Spanish life and customs that would prove invaluable to him in the writing of his masterpiece. In the event, the Marquesa's knowledge of the customs obtaining in her country in the sixteenth century was considerably less than his own, but she was not to discourage a handsome young man from visiting her, so she smiled sleepily upon him, and invited him to come again, when she had no other company to engage her attention.

Sophy, who had never connected Mr Fawnhope with any manly attribute, was quite surprised to discover that he had ridden out to visit the Marquesa on a pure-bred mare she would not herself have disdained to possess. He rode back to London, behind her phaeton, and handled the pretty, playful creature well, she noticed. She confided to Lord Charlbury that she thought it would be to his advantage if Cecilia were never to see her poet upon a horse.

He sighed. 'Do not think, dear Sophy, that I have not a great deal of pleasure in your society, but where is all this leading me? Do you know, for I do not?'

'I depend upon its leading you just where you would wish to be,' she replied seriously. 'Pray trust me! Cecilia by no means likes to see you dancing attendance on me, I can assure you!'

Cecilia was not the only one to derive no pleasure from this spectacle. Mr Rivenhall, possibly because he still cherished hopes that a match might be made up between Charlbury and his sister, regarded it with the greatest dislike; and Lord Bromford, finding himself quite cut out, developed such a degree of hostility towards his rival as made it almost impossible for him to meet him even with the appearance of complaisance.

'It seems to me a very extraordinary circumstance,' he told his chief sympathizer, 'that a man who has been dangling after one female – as the common phrase runs! – for more weeks than I care to enumerate should be so fickle as to transfer his attentions to another in so short a time! I confess, I have no comprehension of such conduct. Had I, dear Miss Wraxton, not been about the world a little, and learnt something of the frailty of mankind, I must have been totally at a loss! But I do not scruple to tell *you* that I never liked Charlbury above half. *His* conduct does not astonish me. I am only grieved, and I may add, surprised, to see Miss Stanton-Lacy so taken-in!'

'No doubt,' said Miss Wraxton pleasantly, 'a lady who had been used to live upon the Continent must be expected to regard these

matters in rather a different light from that in which such poor
stay-at-homes as myself must look upon them. I believe that *flirting*
is quite a pastime amongst foreign ladies.'

'My dear ma'am,' said his lordship, 'I must tell you that I am
by no means an advocate of travel for ladies. It does not seem to
me to be a necessary thing for the education of the weaker sex,
although for a man I think it to be indispensable. I should not be
astonished to learn that Charlbury had never set foot outside this
island, which is a circumstance that makes me wonder more than
ever at Miss Stanton-Lacy's partiality for his society.'

Lord Bromford's hostility was perfectly well known to its
object. Charlbury, cantering along the Row with Sophy, said to
her once: 'If I come out of this masquerade with a whole skin I
may think myself fortunate! Are you determined I shall be slain,
Sophy, you wretch?'

She laughed. 'Bromford?'

'He or Charles. Of the two, I hope it may be he who calls
me out. I daresay he cannot hit a haystack at twelve yards, but
Rivenhall I know to be a capital shot.'

She turned her head to look at him. 'Do you think so indeed?
Charles?'

He returned her look, his own eyes quizzing her. 'Yes, Madam
Innocence! Doubtless because of the slight upon his sister! Tell
me – you are always frank! – do you make a practice of setting
everyone to partners wherever you go?'

'No,' she replied. 'Not unless I am persuaded it would be better
for them!'

He laughed and laughed, and was still laughing when they
encountered Mr and Miss Rivenhall, riding side by side towards
them.

Sophy greeted her cousins with unaffected pleasure, altogether
refraining from expressing her surprise at seeing Cecilia indulging

in a form of exercise she was not much addicted to. She and Charlbury turned their horses to ride with the Rivenhalls, and she made no objection when, after a little way, Mr Rivenhall obliged her to fall behind the other two, and proceed at a sedate pace down the track. She said: 'I like that bay of yours, Charles.'

'You may like him,' returned Mr Rivenhall disagreeably, 'but you are not going to ride him!'

She cast him a sidelong look, brimful of mischief. 'No, dear Charles?'

'Sophy,' said Mr Rivenhall, descending rapidly from the autocratic to the merely threatening, 'if you dare to have your saddle put upon my Thunderer, I will strangle you, and throw your body into the Serpentine!'

She gave the gurgle of laughter that never failed to bring his twisted grin into being. 'Oh, no, Charles, would you indeed? Well, I do not blame you! If ever I find you astride Salamanca, I shall certainly shoot you – and *I* can make allowance for a gun that throws a little left!'

'Yes?' said Mr Rivenhall. 'Well, my dear cousin, when we go down to Ombersley I shall derive much satisfaction from watching your marksmanship! You shall show me what you can do with my duelling pistols. They do not throw left, or even right: I am rather nice in the choice of my weapons!'

'Duelling pistols!' said Sophy, much impressed. 'I had not thought it of you, Charles! How many times have you been *out*? Do you always kill your man?'

'Rarely!' he retorted. 'Duelling has gone sadly out of fashion, dear Sophy! I am so sorry to be obliged to disappoint you!'

'No,' she said, shaking her head. 'I had no *real* expectation of hearing that you had done anything so dashing!'

That made him laugh. He flung up a hand, in the gesture of a swordsman acknowledging a hit. 'Very well, Sophy! *Touché!*'

'Do you fence?'

'Indifferently. Why?'

'Oh, merely that it is something I have never learnt!'

'Good God, how is this! I had thought Sir Horace *must* have taught you how to handle a small-sword!'

'No,' said Sophy, making her mouth prim. 'And he has not taught me how to box either, so there are two things, Charles, which you must be able to do better than I can!'

'You quite outstrip me,' he agreed suavely. 'Particularly in the art of dalliance!'

She instantly disconcerted him by making an attack direct. 'Dalliance, Charles? You do not, I hope, accuse me of *flirting*?'

'Do I not?' he said grimly. 'Enlighten me, I beg, on the nature of your dealings with Charlbury!'

She showed him an innocent face. 'But, Charles, how is this? Surely I could not be mistaken! All is at an end between him and Cecilia! You cannot suppose it possible that I would encourage his advances if that were not so!'

The bay horse broke into a canter, and was checked. Mr Rivenhall said furiously: 'Foolery! Don't try to humbug me, Sophy! Charlbury and you – ! Why, what a gull you must think me!'

'Oh, no!' Sophy assured him soulfully. 'But there is nothing I would not do to oblige Sir Horace, and I would far rather marry Charlbury than Bromford!'

'It sometimes seems to me,' said Mr Rivenhall, 'that *delicacy* is a virtue utterly unknown to you!'

'Yes, tell me about it!' she said, with immense cordiality.

He did not avail himself of this invitation, but said in a biting tone: 'I should warn you, perhaps, that Charlbury's determined pursuit is fast making you the talk of the town. Whether you care a button for that I know not, but since my mother is responsible for you I must own that I should be grateful to you if you would behave with a little more discretion!'

'You told me once before of something else I could do if ever I should wish to please you,' remarked Sophy thoughtfully. 'I must say, I hope I never shall wish to, for, try as I may, I *cannot* recall what it was!'

'You have been determined, have you not, to make me dislike you, from the very day we met?' he shot at her.

'Not at all: you did so without the least encour-agement!'

He rode beside her in silence for a few moments, saying at last, in a stiff voice: 'You are mistaken. I do not dislike you. That is to say, there have been many times when I have liked you very well. Nor need you imagine that I forget how much I stand in your debt.'

She interrupted him. 'You do not! Let me hear no more of that, if you please! Tell me about Hubert! I heard you tell my aunt that you had received a letter from him. Is he well?'

'Perfectly, I imagine. He only wrote to desire me to send him a book he had left behind.' He grinned suddenly. 'And to tell me of his determination to attend all his lectures! If I did not think that *that* resolution must fail, I would post up to Oxford immediately! Such virtue could only end in his seeking relief in the most shock-ing excesses. Let me say one thing to you, Sophy! I have never said it: we were interrupted before I could do so, and I have never found the opportunity since! I must always be grateful to you for showing me, as you did, how much at fault I had been in my dealings with Hubert.'

'That is nonsense, but I could show you, if you would permit me, how much at fault you are in your dealings with Cecilia!' she said.

His face hardened. 'Thank God! On that subject we are not likely to agree!'

She said no more, but allowed Salamanca to break into a canter, and to overtake Lord Charlbury and Cecilia.

She found them conversing comfortably, the constraint Cecilia had felt upon finding herself obliged to ride alone in his company having been speedily banished by the friendly ease of his manners. Neither by word nor by look did he remind her of what lay between them, but began to talk to her at once on some unexceptionable subject that he knew would interest her. This made a pleasant change for her, Mr Fawnhope's conversation being, at present, almost wholly confined to the scope and structure of his great tragedy. To listen to a poet arguing with himself – for she could scarcely have been said to have borne any part in the discussion – on the merits of blank verse as a dramatic medium was naturally a privilege of which any young lady must be proud, but there could be no denying that to talk for half an hour to a man who listened with interest to anything she said was, if not precisely a relief, certainly a welcome variation in her life. Not for nothing had his lordship endured the world for ten more years than his youthful rival. Mr Fawnhope's handsome face and engaging smile might dazzle the female eye, but Mr Fawnhope had not yet learnt the art of conveying to a lady the gratifying impression that he considered her a fragile creature, to be cherished, and in every way considered. Lord Charlbury might be constitutionally incapable of addressing her as Nymph, or of comparing bluebells unfavourably with her eyes, but Lord Charlbury would infallibly provide a cloak for her if the weather were inclement, lift her over obstacles she could well climb without assistance, and in every way convince her that in his eyes she was a precious being whom it was impossible to guard too carefully.

It would have been too much to have said that Cecilia was regretting her rejection of his lordship's suit, but when Sophy and

Charles joined her she was certainly conscious of a faint feeling of dissatisfaction at having her tête-à-tête interrupted.

She tried to discuss the matter in a dispassionate way with Sophy, later, but found it curiously hard to utter any of the sentiments she had persuaded herself she felt. Finally, she bent her head over a piece of embroidery, and asked her cousin whether Lord Charlbury had yet offered for her.

Sophy laughed at this. 'Good God, no, you goose! Charlbury has no serious intentions towards me.'

Cecilia kept her eyes lowered. 'Indeed? I should have said that he showed the most decided partiality for you.'

'My dear Cecy, I would not tease you by adverting to this subject, but I am persuaded that what Charlbury wears on his sleeve is not his heart. I should not wonder at it if he were to end his days a bachelor.'

'I do not think it,' said Cecilia, snipping her silk. 'And nor, I fancy, do you, Sophy. He will offer for you, and – and I hope you will accept him, because if one were not in love with another I cannot imagine any gentleman one would prefer to him.'

'Well, we shall see!' was all Sophy would say.

Fourteen

THE NOTION OF WRITING A TRAGEDY HAVING TAKEN STRONG
possession of Mr Fawnhope's mind, he appeared to banish from
it any immediate plan for seeking remunerative employment. On
several occasions he arrived in Berkeley Square, quite impervious
to Mr Rivenhall's brutal snubs, carrying in his pocket the latest
instalment of his play, which he read to Cecilia and to Sophy, and
once even to Lady Ombersley, who complained afterwards that
she had not understood a word of it. He seemed to spend a good
many afternoons at Merton as well, but when Sophy questioned
him about Sancia's other guests he could never remember with
any clarity who had been present. But Sir Vincent, when he came
to call in Berkeley Square, made no secret of the fact that he was
very often at Merton. Sophy, a blunt creature, told him roundly
that she mistrusted him, and would thank him to remember that
Sancia was betrothed to Sir Horace.

Sir Vincent laughed gently, and pinched her chin, holding it an
instant too long, and tilting up her face. 'Will you, Sophy?' he said,
quizzing her. 'But when I offered to run in your harness you would
have none of me! Be reasonable, Juno! If you reject me, you cannot
expect me to respond docilely to your hand on my rein!'

She put up her hand to grasp his wrist. 'Sir Vincent, you shall not serve Sir Horace a backhanded turn!' she said.

'Why not?' he asked coolly. 'Do you think he would not do the same to me? You are such a splendid innocent, adorable Juno!'

Since Mr Rivenhall chose this inauspicious moment to walk into the drawing-room Sophy was unable to say more. Without embarrassment, Sir Vincent released her, and moved forward to greet his host. His reception was frosty; he was given no encouragement to prolong his visit; and no sooner had he taken leave, and parted, than Mr Rivenhall gave his cousin, without reserve, the benefit of his opinion of her behaviour in encouraging a notorious rake to practise familiarities with her. Sophy listened to him with an air of great interest, but if he had hoped to abash her he was disappointed, for all she said in reply was: 'I think your scolds are capital, Charles, for you are never at a loss for a word! But would you call me an *incorrigible* flirt?'

'Yes, I would! You encourage every scarlet coat you have ever met to haunt the house! You set the town talking with your shameless conduct in keeping Charlbury dangling after you, and not content with that you allow a fellow like Talgarth to behave to you as though you had been an inn-servant!'

She opened her eyes at him. '*Charles!* Is that what you do? Pinch their chins? Well, I was never more astonished! I don't think you should!'

'Don't try my temper too far, Sophy!' he said dangerously. 'If you knew how my hands itch to box your ears, you would take care!'

'Oh, I am sure you never would!' she said, smiling. 'You know Sir Horace did not teach me how to box, and how unfair it would be! Besides, why should you care a button what I do? I am not one of your sisters!'

'Thank God for it!'

'Yes, indeed, for you are the horridest brother, you know! Do stop making a cake of yourself! Sir Vincent is a sad case, but he would never do me any harm, I assure you. *That* would be quite against his code, for he knew me when I was a little girl, and he is a friend of Sir Horace's. I must say, he is the oddest creature! Sancia, it is perfectly plain, he does not hold to be in the least sacred.' Her brow creased. 'I am much afraid of what he may do in that direction. I wonder if I ought to say I will marry him after all?'

'What!' exclaimed Mr Rivenhall. 'Marry that fellow? Not while you are under this roof!'

'Yes, but I cannot help thinking that perhaps I owe it to Sir Horace,' she explained. 'I own, it would be a sacrifice, but I am sure he trusts me to take care of Sancia while he is away, and I don't at all perceive how I am to prevent Sir Vincent from stealing her affections, unless I marry him myself. He has so much address, you know!'

'You appear to me,' said Mr Rivenhall scathingly, 'to have taken leave of your senses! You will scarcely expect me to believe that you would entertain the thought of marriage with that man!'

'But, Charles, I find you most unreasonable!' she pointed out. 'Not a week ago you said that the sooner I was married and out of this house the better pleased you would be, but when I said perhaps I might marry Charlbury you flew into a passion, and now you will not hear of poor Sir Vincent either!'

Mr Rivenhall made no attempt to answer this. He merely cast a darkling glance at his cousin, and said: 'Only one thing could surprise me, and that would be to learn that Talgarth had offered for you!'

'Well, you must be surprised,' said Sophy placidly, 'because he has done so a score of times. It is become a habit with him, I think. But I know what you mean, and you are right: he would be very much disconcerted if I took him at his word. I might, of course, become engaged to him, and cry off when Sir Horace returns, but it seems rather a shabby thing to do, don't you think?'

'Extremely so!'

She sighed. 'Yes, and he is so clever that I daresay he would guess what I was about. I might, I suppose, remove to Merton, and that would certainly make it awkward for Sir Vincent. But Sancia would not like that at all, I fear.'

'She has my sympathy!'

Sophy looked at him. Under his amazed and horrified gaze, large tears slowly welled over her eyelids, and rolled down her cheeks. She did not sniff, or gulp, or even sob: merely allowed her tears to gather and fall.

'*Sophy!*' ejaculated Mr Rivenhall, visibly shaken. He took an involuntary step towards her, checked himself, and said, rather disjointedly: 'Pray do not! I did not mean – I had no intention – You know how it is with me! I say more than I mean, when – Sophy, for God's sake do not cry!'

'Oh, do not stop me!' begged Sophy. 'Sir Horace says it is my *only* accomplishment!'

Mr Rivenhall glared at her. '*What!*'

'Very few persons are able to do it!' Sophy assured him. 'I discovered it by the veriest accident when I was only seven years old. Sir Horace said I should cultivate it, for I should find it most useful.'

'You – you –' Words failed Mr Rivenhall. 'Stop at once!'

'Oh, I have stopped!' said Sophy, carefully wiping the drops away. 'I cannot continue if I don't keep sad thoughts in my mind, such as you saying unkind things to me, or –'

'I do not believe you felt the slightest inclination to cry!' declared Mr Rivenhall roundly. 'You did it only to set me at a disadvantage! You are, without exception, the most abominable, shameless – Don't start again!'

She laughed. 'Very well, but if I am so horrid, perhaps it would be better for me to go to stay with Sancia.'

'Understand this!' said Mr Rivenhall. 'My uncle left you expressly to my mother's care, and in this you will remain until such time as he returns to England! As for these nonsensical notions about the Marquesa, *you* are not to be held responsible for anything she may choose to do!'

'Where the well-being of the persons to whom one is attached is concerned, one cannot say that one is not responsible,' said Sophy simply. 'One should make a push to be of service. Yet I do not perceive what I should do in this event. I wish it had been possible for Sancia to have stayed in Sir Horace's own house!'

'At Ashtead? How should that serve?'

'It is not so near to town,' she pointed out.

'Sixteen or seventeen miles only, I daresay!'

'More than twice as far away as Merton, however. But it is useless to repine over that. Sir Horace says the place is in disrepair, quite unfit to live in. He means to set it all to rights when he comes back to England. I only wish it may not be too late!'

'Why should it be too late?' asked Mr Rivenhall, wilfully misunderstanding her. 'I assume Lacy Manor does not stand entirely empty! Does not my uncle leave some servants in charge?'

'Only the Claverings, and, I suppose, a man to look after the gardens, and the farm. But that, you know very well, is not what I meant!'

'If you take my advice,' said Mr Rivenhall, 'you will not meddle in the Marquesa's affairs!' He added caustically: 'Or in anyone else's! – And spare yourself the trouble of telling me that you do not mean to take my advice, for that I know already!'

Sophy folded her hands in her lap, and began to twiddle her thumbs, so absurd an expression of docility on her face that he was obliged to smile.

But as the season advanced he smiled less and less frequently. Since she had not yet been presented at Court, Sophy was not invited to the Regent's grand fête at Carlton House, but there was scarcely another society event which she did not grace. In honour bound, Mr Rivenhall accompanied his mother and her two charges to many of these functions, but as he was obliged to spend a considerable part of his time watching his sister dancing with Mr Fawnhope, and his cousin flirting outrageously with Charlbury, it was scarcely surprising that he should have been goaded into saying that he would be thankful when July saw the Ombersley household safely bestowed at Ombersley Court. He also expressed the wish that Sophy would choose between her various suitors, so that he might one day return to a house empty of visitors. Miss Wraxton said hopefully that perhaps Sir Horace would not be much longer absent from England, but as the one letter so far received from this erratic gentleman had not mentioned any prospect of a speedy return from Brazil, he was unable to set much store by this.

'If,' said Miss Wraxton, casting down her eyes in pretty bashfulness, 'she should still be with dear Lady Ombersley in September, Charles, I think I must beg her to be one of my bridesmaids. It would be only civil!'

He agreed to it, but only after a moment's pause. 'I trust that by then my uncle may have returned. God knows what mischief she will find to plague me – us – with at Ombersley, but no doubt she will discover something!'

But when July came there was no question of Ombersley. Mr Rivenhall, fulfilling an old promise, took his three younger sisters to Astley's Amphitheatre to celebrate Gertrude's birthday, and within a week of this dissipation Dr Baillie had been called in to prescribe for Amabel.

She had begun to show signs of ill-health almost at once, and although the doctor repeatedly assured Mr Rivenhall later that there was no saying where she might have contracted fever, he continued obstinately to blame himself. It was evident that the little girl was very ill, her head aching continually, her feverishness increasing alarmingly at night. The dread spectre of typhus raised its head, and not all Dr Baillie's assurances that Amabel's complaint was a milder form of this scourge, neither so infectious nor so dangerous, could allay Lady Ombersley's fears. Miss Adderbury, with Selina and Gertrude, was sent off incontinent to Ombersley; and Hubert, staying for the first few weeks of the Long Vacation with relatives in Yorkshire, warned by express not to venture near Berkeley Square until all danger should be past. Lady Ombersley would have banished Cecilia and Sophy too could she have prevailed upon either of them to have listened to her prayers, but they were adamant. Sophy said that she had had much experience of far deadlier fevers than Amabel's, and had never caught any worse infection than the measles; and Cecilia, hanging affectionately over her mother, told her that nothing short of force would detach her from her side. Poor Lady Ombersley could only cling to her and weep. Her constitution was not strong enough to enable her to support with fortitude the illnesses of her children. With all the wish in the world to tend Amabel with her own hands, she could not bear the sight of the child's discomfort. Her sensibility overcame her resolution; the very sight of the hectic flush on Amabel's cheeks brought on one of her worst spasms, so that Cecilia had to help her from the sickroom to her own bed, and to send her maid to beg Dr Baillie to visit her before he should leave the house. Lady Ombersley could not forget the tragic death under similar circumstances, of the little daughter who had followed Maria into the world, and from the start of Amabel's illness abandoned hope of her recovery.

It was felt to be unfortunate that Mr Rivenhall should also have gone to stay with his aunt in Yorkshire, for his presence always exercised a calming effect upon his mother in times of stress; and Amabel, as the fever waxed, often cried for Charles to come to her. It was hoped that a man's voice might soothe her, so her father was introduced into her room, and tried clumsily to coax her into rationality. He was not afraid of infection, the doctor having told him that it was rare for an adult person to contract the disease, but although he was much affected by the sight of his little daughter's condition, he had never paid much attention to his children, and now failed to quiet her. Indeed, his tears flowed so freely that he was obliged to leave the room.

Dr Baillie, dubiously eyeing old Nurse, shook his head and sent Mrs Pebworth to Berkeley Square. Mrs Pebworth, a voluminous female, with a watery eye, and mountainous bonnet, smiled fondly upon the two young ladies who received her, and bade them, in a husky voice, to have no fears, since the little dear would be safe in her charge. Within twelve hours of her arrival, she was addressing vituperative remarks to the closed door of the mansion, having been, at the orders of Miss Stanton-Lacy, shown off the premises by the redoubtable Jane Storridge. A nurse, Sophy bluntly informed Dr Baillie, who refreshed herself continually from a square bottle, and slept the night through in a chair by the fire while her patient tossed and moaned, they could well dispense with. So, when Mr Rivenhall, posting south immediately on receipt of the tidings from London, arrived in Berkeley Square, it was to find his mother suffering from nervous palpitations, his father seeking relief at White's or Wattier's, his sister snatching an hour's sleep on her bed, and his cousin in command of the sickroom.

When trouble descended upon the household, Lady Ombersley forgot all Charles's disagreeable ways, and was much inclined to think him her only support. Her joy at seeing him walk into her dressing-room was only alloyed by her fear that he might catch the typhoid. She was reclining on the sofa, but heaved herself up to cast her arms about his neck, exclaiming: 'Charles! Oh, my dear son, thank God you are come! It is so terrible, and I know she will be taken from me, like my poor little Clara!'

A burst of tears ended this speech, and for some minutes he was fully occupied in soothing the agitation of her spirits. When she was calmer, he ventured to question her on the nature of Amabel's complaint. Her replies were disjointed, but she said enough to convince him that the case was desperate, and the illness contracted perhaps at Astley's Amphitheatre. He was so much appalled that he could say nothing for several moments, but got up abruptly from the chair by the sofa, and strode over to stare out of the window. His mother, wiping her eyes, said: 'If only I were not so wretchedly weak! You know, Charles, how I must long to be beside my child! But the sight of her, so wasted, so flushed, brings on my worst palpitations, and if she recognizes me at all she cannot help but be distressed! They will scarcely allow me to enter the room!'

'It is not fit for you,' he said mechanically. 'Who nurses her? Is Addy here?'

'No, no, Dr Baillie thought it wiser to send the other children off to Ombersley! He sent us a dreadful creature – at least, I never saw her, but Cecilia said she was a drunken wretch! – and Sophy sent her packing. Old Nurse is in charge, and you know how she is to be trusted! And the girls help her, so that Dr Baillie assures me I need feel no uneasiness on that head. He says that dearest Sophy is a capital sick-nurse, and that the disease is running its proper course, but oh, Charles, I cannot persuade myself that she will be spared!'

He came back to her side at once, and devoted himself to the task of comforting her alarms with more patience than might have been expected in one of his hasty temper. When he could escape, he did so, and went upstairs to find his sister. She had just got up from her bed, and was coming out of her room as he reached the landing. She was looking pale, and tired, but her face lit up at sight of him, and she exclaimed in a hushed voice: 'Charles! I knew we might depend upon your coming! Have you been to my mother? She has felt the need of your presence so much!'

'I have this instant come from her dressing-room. Cilly, Cilly, she tells me Amabel began to ail within a few days of that accursed evening at Astley's!'

'Hush! Come into my room! Amabel is in the Blue Spare-room, and you must not talk so loud just here! We thought that too, but Dr Baillie says it could hardly be so. Recollect that the other two are well! Addy sent up word only yesterday.' She softly closed the door of her bedroom. 'I must not stay above a minute: Mama will be needing me.'

'My poor girl, you look fagged to death!'

'No, no, I am not! Why, there is hardly anything that I do, so that it chafes me dreadfully sometimes, when I see Sophy and that good, kind maid of hers carrying all the burden on their shoulders! For Nurse is growing too old to be able to manage, you know, and it affects her sadly to see poor little Amabel so uncomfortable. But if one of us is not continually with Mama she frets herself into one of her spasms – you know her way! But now you are here you will relieve me of that duty!' She smiled, and pressed his hand. 'I never thought to be so glad to see anyone! Amabel too! She so often calls for you, and wonders where you can be! If I had not known that you would come, I must have sent for you! You are not afraid of infection?' He made an impatient gesture. 'No, I was sure you would not think of that. Sophy is out walking – Dr Baillie impresses on us the need for exercise in the fresh air, and we are very obedient, I assure you! Nurse sits with Amabel during the afternoon.'

'May I see her! It would not agitate her?'

'No, indeed! It must soothe her, I believe. If she is awake, and – and herself, would you care to come to her room now? You will find her wretchedly altered, poor little thing!'

She led him to the sickroom, and went softly in. Amabel was restless, and very hot, fretfully rejecting any suggestions for her relief, but when she saw her favourite brother her heavy eyes brightened perceptibly, and a faint smile came into her little flushed face. She held out her hand, and he took it, and spoke gently and cheerfully to her, in a way that seemed to do her good. She did not wish to let him go, but at a sign from Cecilia he disengaged his hand from the feeble clutch on it, promising to come back again presently if Amabel would be a good girl, and swallow the medicine Nurse had ready for her.

He was a good deal shocked by her appearance, and found it difficult to believe Cecilia's assurance that when the fever had passed the patient would speedily recover her lost weight. Nor could he feel that old Nurse was competent to have the command of a sickroom. Cecilia agreed to this, but comforted him by saying that it was Sophy who was in command.

'Dr Baillie says that no one could manage better, and, indeed, Charles, you would not doubt it could you but see how good Amabel is with her! She has such resolution, such firmness! Poor Nurse does not like to force the little dear to do what she does not wish to, and then, too, she has old-fashioned notions that will not do for Dr Baillie. But our cousin, he says, may be trusted to obey his directions implicitly. Oh, you could not wrest her away from Amabel! It would be fatal, for she frets if Sophy is too long absent from her room.'

'We are very much obliged to Sophy,' he said. 'But it is not right that she should be doing such work! Setting aside the risk of infection, she did not come to us to act as sick-nurse!'

'No,' Cecilia said. 'She did not, of course, but – but – I don't know how it is, but she seems to be so much a part of our family that one does not consider such things as that!'

He was silent, and she left him, saying that she must go to their mother. When, later, he saw Sophy, and attempted to remonstrate with her, she cut him very short.

'I am delighted you are come home, my dear Charles, for nothing could do Amabel more good. Your poor Mama, too, needs the support of your presence. But if you mean to talk in that nonsensical style I shall soon be wishing you a thousand miles off!'

'You have your own engagements,' he persisted. 'I daresay I must have seen as many as a dozen cards of invitation on the mantelpiece in the Yellow Saloon! I cannot think it right that you should forgo all your amusements for the sake of my little sister!'

Her eyes laughed at him. 'No, indeed! What a shocking thing that I should be obliged to forgo a few balls! How shall I survive it, I wonder? How delightful it would be in me to be demanding my aunt's chaperonage at parties with the house in this upset! Now, pray do not let me hear any more on this head, but instead of vexing yourself with such absurdities, try what you may do to divert my aunt's mind! You know her nervous disposition, and how the least thing upsets her constitution! The charge of keeping her soothed and calm falls upon poor Cecy, for your Papa, if you will not be offended with me for saying so, is not of the smallest use in such a crisis at this!'

'I know it,' he responded. 'I will do what I may; I can well imagine how arduous a task Cecilia finds it. Indeed, I was shocked to see her looking so fagged!' He hesitated, and then said, a little stiffly: 'Miss Wraxton, perhaps, might be of service there. I would not suggest her entering Amabel's room, but I am sure, if she would sit with my mother sometimes it must be of benefit! The tone of her mind is such that –' He broke off, perceiving a change in his cousin's expression and said with some asperity: 'I am aware that you dislike Miss Wraxton, but even you will allow that her calm good sense must be of value in this predicament!'

'My dear Charles, do not eat me! I have no doubt it is just as you say!' Sophy replied. 'Try if she will come to this house!'

More she would not say, but it was not long before Mr Rivenhall had discovered that his betrothed, while sympathizing most sincerely with his family on their affliction, had no intention of exposing her person to the dangers of infection. She told him, clasping his hand fondly, that her mama had most expressly forbidden her to enter the house until all danger should be past. It was true: Lady Brinklow herself told Mr Rivenhall so. Upon learning that he had had the imprudence to visit Amabel, she became visibly alarmed, and begged him not to repeat the visit. Miss Wraxton added the weight of her own counsel. 'Indeed, Charles, it is not wise! There can be no need for you to run such a risk, moreover. Gentlemen in sickrooms are quite out of place!'

'Are you afraid that I may take the disease, and convey it to you?' he asked, in his blunt way. 'I beg your pardon! I should not have come to call upon you! I will not do so again until Amabel is well.'

Lady Brinklow hailed this decision with obvious relief, but it was going too far for her daughter, who at once assured Mr Rivenhall that he was talking nonsense, and must always be a welcome caller in Brook Street. He thanked her, but took his leave of her almost immediately.

His opinion of her was not improved by finding, upon his return to Berkeley Square, that Lord Charlbury was sitting with his mother. It soon transpired that he was a regular visitor to the house, and, whatever his motive might be, Mr Rivenhall could not but honour him for his indifference to the danger of infection.

Another regular caller was Mr Fawnhope, but since his only

object in coming was to see Cecilia, Mr Rivenhall was easily able to refrain from succumbing to any feelings of gratitude towards him for his intrepid visits. But Cecilia was looking so worn and anxious that, with rare restraint, he curbed his bitter tongue, and made no reference whatsoever to her lover's frequent presence in the house.

Had he but known it, Mr Fawnhope's visits were affording Cecilia quite as little pleasure as he could have desired. It was midway through the second week of Amabel's illness, and that she was very seriously unwell Dr Baillie did not waste his time denying to her nurses. Cecilia had no inclination towards any form of dalliance, and no interest in poetic drama. She carried up to the sickroom a remarkably fine bunch of grapes, saying in a low tone to Sophy that Lord Charlbury had brought them for Amabel, having sent all the way to his country seat for them. He was said to possess some of the finest succession-houses in the country, besides a pinery which, he promised, should yield the best of its fruits to Amabel, as soon as they should become ripe enough to be eaten.

'How very kind! said Sophy, setting the dish upon a table. 'I did not know Charlbury had called: I had thought it was Augustus.'

'They were both here,' Cecilia replied. 'Augustus wished to give me a poem he has written, on a sick child.'

Her tone was non-committal. Sophy said: 'Dear me! I mean, how charming! Was it pretty?'

'I daresay it may have been. I find I do not care for poems on such a subject,' Cecilia said quietly.

Sophy said nothing. After a moment, Cecilia added: 'Although it was impossible for me to return Lord Charlbury's regard, I must always be sensible of the delicacy of his behaviour, and the extreme kindness he has shown us in our trouble. I – I wish you may be brought to reward him, Sophy! You are in general above-stairs, and so cannot know the many hours he has spent with my mother, talking to her, and playing at backgammon with her, only, I am persuaded, to relieve us a little of that duty.'

Sophy could not help smiling at this. 'Not to relieve me, Cecy, for he must know that the care of my aunt does not fall upon me! If a compliment is intended, you must certainly take it to yourself.'

'No, no, it is mere goodness of heart! That he has an ulterior motive I will not credit.' She smiled, and added quizzingly: 'I could wish that your *other* beau would do half as much!'

'Bromford? Do not tell me he has ventured within a hundred paces of the house! I should certainly not believe you!'

'No, indeed! And I have it from Charles that he avoids him as though he too were infected. Charles makes a jest of it, but Eugenia's conduct he does not mention.'

'It would be too much to expect of him.'

A movement from the bed put an end to the conversation, nor was the subject again referred to by the cousins. Amabel's illness, reaching its climax, banished all other thoughts from their heads. For several days, the gravest fears possessed the minds of all those who continually saw the invalid; and old Nurse, obstinately refusing to believe in new-fangled diseases, brought on one of Lady Ombersley's worst attacks of nervous spasms by confiding in her that she had recognized the complaint from the start as being typhus. It took the combined exertions of Lady Ombersley's son, daughter, and physician to disabuse her mind of this hideous conviction; while his lordship, to whom she had communicated it, sought relief in the only way that seemed to him possible, and, in consequence, not only had to be escorted home from his club, but suffered so severe a recrudescence of his gout that he was unable to leave his room for several days afterwards.

But Amabel survived the crisis. The fever began to abate; and although its ravages left her listless and emaciated, Dr Baillie was able to assure her mother that, provided that there was no relapse, he now entertained reasonable hopes of her complete recovery. He handsomely gave Sophy much of the credit for the improvement in the little girl's condition; and Lady Ombersley, shedding tears, said that she shuddered to think where they would any of them have been without her dearest niece.

'Well, well, she is a very capable young lady, and so too is Miss Rivenhall,' said the doctor. 'While *they* are with Miss Amabel you may be easy, ma'am!'

Mr Fawnhope, ushered into the room five minutes later, was the first recipient of the glad tidings, and instantly dashed off a little lyric in commemoration of Amabel's emergence from danger. Lady Ombersley thought it particularly touching, and begged to be given a copy; but since it dealt more with the pretty picture of Cecilia bending over the sickbed than with Amabel's sufferings, it quite failed to please the person for whom it was intended. With far more gratitude did Cecilia receive an exquisite bouquet of flowers brought by Lord Charlbury for her small sister. She saw him only to thank him. He did not importune her to remain in his company, but said, upon her excusing herself immediately: 'Indeed I understand! I had not hoped to have been granted even a minute of your time. It was like you to have come downstairs. If only I could be sure that I have not interrupted your too hard-earned rest!'

'No, no!' she said, scarcely able to command her voice. 'I was sitting with my sister, and when your flowers were brought up to her room I could not help but run down to tell you of her delight in them. Too good, too kind! Forgive me! I must not stay!'

It had been hoped that when the invalid began to mend the constant attendance on her of her sister or her cousin might become less necessary, but it was soon found that she was too weak to be patient, and became fretful if left for too long in the care of Nurse or Jane Storridge. Mr Rivenhall, softly entering the sickroom one evening shortly after midnight, was shocked to discover not Nurse but Sophy seated by the small fire that was kept burning in the grate. She was sewing by the light of a branch of candles, but she looked up when the door opened, and smiled, and laid a finger to her lips. A screen was drawn between the candles and the bed, so that Mr Rivenhall could only dimly perceive his sister. She seemed to be sleeping. He closed the door soundlessly, and trod over to the fire, whispering: 'I understood Nurse was to sit up with her at night. How is this? It is not fit for you, Sophy!'

She glanced at the clock on the mantelpiece, and began to fold up her work. Nodding towards the door that stood ajar into the dressing-room, she replied in a low tone: 'Nurse is laid down upon the sofa there. Poor soul, she is knocked-up! Amabel is very restless tonight – has been so all day. Don't be alarmed! It is an excellent sign when a patient becomes peevish, and hard to manage. But she has been so much in the habit of getting her own way with Nurse that she will not mind her as she should. Sit down: I am going to heat some milk for her to drink, and, if you will, you may coax her to do so when she wakes.'

'You must be tired to death!' he said.

'No, not at all: I was asleep all the afternoon,' she returned, setting a small saucepan on the hob. 'Like the Duke, I can sleep at any hour! Poor Cecy can never get a wink during the day, so we have decided that she must not attempt to sit up at night.'

'You mean that you have decided it,' he said.

She only smiled and shook her head. He said no more, but sat watching her as she knelt by the fire, her attention on the milk slowly heating on the hob. After a few minutes, Amabel began to stir. Almost before her feeble, plaintive cry of 'Sophy!' had been uttered, Sophy had risen to her feet, and moved to the bedside. Amabel was hot, thirsty, uncomfortable, and disinclined to believe that anything could do her good. To be raised, so that her pillows could be shaken and turned, made her cry; she wanted Sophy to bathe her forehead, but complained that the lavender-water stung her eyes when she did so.

'Hush, you will shock your visitor if you cry!' Sophy said, smoothing her tangled curls. 'Do you know there is a gentleman come to see you?'

'Charles?' Amabel asked, forgetting her woes for a moment.

'Yes, Charles, so you must let me tidy you a little, and straighten the sheets. There! Now, Charles, Miss Rivenhall will be pleased to receive you!'

She removed the screen, so that the candlelight fell on the bed, and nodded to Charles to sit down beside his sister. He did so, holding the claw-like little hand in his, and talking to the child in a cheerful way that succeeded in diverting her until Sophy brought a cup of milk to the bedside. The sight of this at once made her peevish. She wanted nothing; it would make her sick to swallow any milk; why would not Sophy leave her in peace?

'I hope you don't mean to be so unkind as to refuse it, when I have come especially to hold the cup for you,' Charles said, taking it from his cousin. 'A cup with roses on it, too! Now, where had you this! I am sure I do not recognize it!'

'Cecilia gave it to me for my very own,' Amabel replied. 'But I don't wish for any milk. It is the middle of the night, not the proper time for drinking milk!'

'I hope Charles has admired your real roses,' said Sophy, sitting down on the edge of the bed, and raising Amabel to rest against her shoulder. 'We are so jealous, Charles, Cecy and I! Amabel has such a fine beau that we are cast quite into the shade. Only look at the bouquet he brought her!'

'Charlbury!' he said, smiling.

'Yes, but I like your posy best,' Amabel said.

'Of course you do,' said Sophy. 'So take a sip of the milk he is offering you! I must tell you that a gentleman's feelings are very easily wounded, my dear, and *that*, you know, would never do!'

'Very true,' Charles corroborated. 'I shall be thinking that you have a greater regard for Charlbury than for me, and that will very likely make me fall into a melancholy.'

That made her laugh weakly, and so, between nonsense and coaxing, she was persuaded to drink nearly all the milk. Sophy laid her gently down again, but nothing would do but that both Charles and Sophy should stay beside her.

'Yes, but no more talking,' Sophy said. 'I am going to tell you about another of my adventures, and if your interrupt me I shall lose the thread.'

'Oh, yes, tell about the time you were lost in the Pyrenees!' begged Amabel drowsily.

Sophy did so, her voice sinking as the little girl's eyelids began to droop. Mr Rivenhall sat still and silent on the other side of the bed, watching his sister. Presently Amabel's deeper breathing betrayed that she slept. Sophy's voice ceased; she looked up, and met Mr Rivenhall's eyes. He was staring at her, as though a thought, blinding in its novelty, had occurred to him. Her gaze remained steady, a little questioning. He rose abruptly, half-stretched out his hand, but let it fall again, and, turning, went quickly out of the room.

Fifteen

UPON THE FOLLOWING DAY, SOPHY DID NOT ENCOUNTER HER cousin. He visited Amabel at an hour when he knew Sophy to be resting, and was not at home to dinner. Lady Ombersley feared that something had occurred to vex him, for although his manner towards her was unfailingly patient, and he abated none of his solicitude for her comfort, his brow was clouded, and he replied to many of her remarks quite at random. He submitted, however, to the penance of a hand at cribbage with her; and when the game was interrupted by the arrival of Mr Fawnhope, with a copy of his poem for Lady Ombersley, and a posy of moss-roses for Cecilia, he was sufficiently master of himself to greet the visitor, if not with enthusiasm, at least with civility.

Mr Fawnhope, having written some thirty lines of his tragedy the previous day, with which he was not dissatisfied, was in a complaisant humour, neither chasing an elusive epithet, nor brooding over an infelicitous line. He said everything that was proper, and, when all enquiries into the invalid's condition were exhausted, conversed on various topics so much like a sensible man that Mr Rivenhall found himself quite in charity with him, and was only driven from the room by Lady Ombersley's request to the poet to read aloud to her his lyric on Amabel's deliverance from danger. Even this abominable affectation could not wholly dissipate the kindlier feelings with which he regarded Mr Fawnhope, whose continued visits to the house gave him a better opinion of the poet than was at all deserved. Cecilia could have told him that Mr Fawnhope's intrepidity sprang more from a sublime unconsciousness of the risk of infection than from any deliberate heroism; but since she was not in the habit of discussing her lover with her brother, he continued in a happy state of ignorance, himself too practical a man to comprehend the density of the veil in which a poet could wrap himself.

He never again visited the sickroom at a moment when he might expect to find his cousin there, and when they met at the dinner-table his manner towards her was so curt as to border on the brusque. Cecilia, knowing how very much obliged to Sophy he thought himself, was astonished, and more than once pressed her cousin to tell her whether they had quarrelled. But Sophy would only shake her head, and look mischievous.

Amabel continued to mend, although slowly, and with many set-backs, and all the irrational fidgets of a convalescent. For twelve hours nothing would do for her but to have Jacko brought to her room. Only Sophy's forcible representations prevented Mr Rivenhall from posting down to Ombersley Court to bring back the indispensable monkey, so anxious was he that nothing should be allowed to retard his little sister's recovery. But Tina, hitherto excluded, to her great indignation, from attendance on her mistress in the sickroom, made an excellent substitute for Jacko, and was only too content to curl up on the quilt under Amabel's caressing hand.

At the beginning of the fourth week of the illness, Dr Baillie began to talk of the propriety of removing his patient into the country. But here he encountered an unexpected and obstinate opposition from Lady Ombersley. He had once mentioned to her the possibility of a relapse, and this had taken such strong possession of her mind that no inducement could serve to make her consent to Amabel's going out of reach of his expert care. She represented to him the unwisdom of restoring Amabel to the society of her sisters and her noisy brother, soon to be enjoying his summer holiday at Ombersley. The little girl was still languid, disinclined for any exertion, and wincing at sudden sounds: she would do better in London, under his eye, and in the fond care of her mama. Now that all danger was past, Lady Ombersley's maternal instinct could assert itself. She, and she alone, should bear the charge of her youngest daughter's convalescence. In the event, to lie upon the sofa in Mama's dressing-room, to drive sedately out with her in the barouche, just suited Amabel's present humour, and so it was settled, both Cecilia and Sophy disclaiming any desire to leave London for the country.

Town was very thin of company, but the weather was not so sultry as to make the streets disagreeable. The month was showery, and few were the days when even the most modish young lady cared to venture forth without a pelisse, or a shawl.

Others beside the Ombersley family had chosen to remain in town until August. Lord Charlbury was still to be found in Mount Street; Mr Fawnhope in his rooms off St James's; Lord Bromford, deaf to the entreaties of his mother, refused to retire into Kent; and the Brinklows found several excellent excuses for remaining in Brook Street. As soon as all danger of infection was over, Miss Wraxton was once more to be seen in Berkeley Square, gracious to everyone, even caressing towards Lady Ombersley and Amabel, and very full of wedding-schemes. Mr Rivenhall found pressing business to attend to on his estates; and if Miss Wraxton chose to assume that his frequent absences from town were accounted for by his desire to set his house in order for her reception, she was quite at liberty to do so.

Cecilia, less robust than her cousin, did not recover so quickly from the anxiety and exertion of her four weeks' incarceration. She was a good deal pulled-down, and had lost a little of her bloom. She was rather silent, too, a fact that did not escape her brother's eye. He taxed her with it, and, when she returned an evasive answer, and would have left the room, detained her, saying: 'Don't go, Cilly!'

She waited, looking enquiringly at him. After a moment, he asked abruptly: 'Are you unhappy?'

Her colour rose, and her lips trembled in spite of herself. She made a protesting gesture, turning away her face, for it was impossible to explain to him the turmoil raging in her own heart.

To her surprise, he took her hand, and pressed it, saying awkwardly, but in a softened tone: 'I never meant you to be unhappy. I did not think – You are such a good girl, Cilly! I suppose, if your poet will but engage on some respectable profession, I must withdraw my opposition, and let you have your way.'

Amazement held her motionless, only her startled eyes flying to his face. She allowed her hand to lie in his, until he released it, and turned away, as though he did not choose to meet her wide gaze.

'You thought me cruel – unfeeling! No doubt I must have seemed so, but I have never desired anything but your happiness! I cannot be glad of your choice, but if your mind is made up, God forbid I should have any hand in parting you from one whom you sincerely love, or in promoting your marriage to a man you cannot care for!'

'Charles!' she uttered faintly.

He said over his shoulder, and with some difficulty: 'I have come to see that nothing but misery could result from such a union. You at least shall not be subjected to a lifetime of regret! I will speak to my father. You have resented my influence with him: *this* time it shall be exerted in your favour.'

At any other moment his words must have prompted her to have enquired into their unexpressed significance, but shock seemed to suspend her every faculty. She found not a word to say, and experienced the greatest difficulty in preventing herself from bursting into tears. He turned his head, and said, with a smile: 'What an ogre I must appear to you, to have so taken your breath away, Cilly! Don't stare at me so unbelievingly! You shall marry your poet: my hand on it!'

She put out her own mechanically, managed to speak two words: 'Thank you!' and ran out of the room, unable to say more, or to control her emotion.

She sought the seclusion of her own bedchamber, her thoughts in such disorder that it was long before her agitation had at all subsided.

Never had opposition been withdrawn at so inopportune a moment; never had a victory seemed more empty! Almost without her knowledge, her sentiments, during the past weeks, had been undergoing a change. Now that her brother had accorded her his permission to marry the man of her choice, she discovered that her feeling for Augustus had been no more than the infatuation Charles had always thought it. Opposition had fostered it, leading her into the fatal error of almost publicly announcing her unalterable determination to marry Augustus or no one. Lord Charlbury, so superior to Augustus in every way, had accepted her rejection of his suit, and had turned his attention elsewhere; and whatever unacknowledged hope she might have cherished of seeing his affections reanimate towards her must now be quite at an end. To confess to Charles that he had been right from the start, and she most miserably mistaken, was impossible. She had gone too far; nothing now remained to her but to accept the fate she had insisted on bringing on herself, and, for pride's sake, to show a smiling face to the world.

She showed it first to Sophy, resolutely begging her to felicitate her upon her happiness. Sophy was thunderstruck. 'Good God!' she exclaimed, stupefied. 'Charles will *promote* this match?'

'He does not wish me to be unhappy. He never wished it. Now that he is convinced that I am in earnest he will place no bar in my way. Indeed, he was so good as to promise that he would speak to Papa for me! That must decide it: Papa always does what Charles desires him to.' She saw that her cousin was regarding her fixedly, and continued quickly: 'I have never known Charles kinder! He spoke of the misery of being forced into a marriage against one's inclination. He said *I* should not spend a lifetime of regret. Oh, Sophy, can it be that he no longer cares for Eugenia? The suspicion cannot but obtrude!'

'Good gracious, he never did care for her!' replied Sophy scornfully. 'And if he has but just discovered it, *that* is no reason for –' She broke off, darting a swift glance at Cecilia, and perceiving much more than her cousin would have wished. 'Well! This is a day of miracles indeed!' she said. 'Of course I felicitate you with all my heart, dearest Cecy! When is your betrothal to be announced?'

'Oh, not until Augustus is settled in – in some respectable occupation!' Cecilia answered. 'But *that* will not be long, I am persuaded! Or his tragedy may take, you know.'

Sophy agreed to this without a blink, and listened with an assumption of interest to Cecilia's various schemes for the future. That these were couched in somewhat melancholy terms she allowed to pass without comment, merely repeating her congratulations, and wishing her cousin every happiness. But behind these mendacities her brain was working swiftly. She perfectly understood the fix Cecilia was in, and never for an instant thought of wasting her breath in expostulation. Something far more drastic than expostulation was needed in this case, for no lady who had entered into an engagement in the teeth of parental opposition could be expected to cry off from it the instant she had gained the sanction she had so insistently demanded. Willingly could Sophy have boxed Mr Rivenhall's ears. To remain adamant when opposition could only strengthen his sister's resolve had been bad enough; to withdraw his opposition at a moment when Charlbury was in a fair way to ousting the poet from her affections was an act of such insanity that it put Sophy out of all patience with him. Thanks to Alfred Wraxton's predilection for gossip, Cecilia's secret engagement to Mr Fawnhope was widely known. She had, moreover, been at some pains to display to Society her determination to wed him. It would need something very drastic indeed to induce so gently-bred a girl to fly in the face of all convention. If Mr Rivenhall had agreed to the match Sophy could not suppose that the official announcement would be long delayed; once this had appeared in the Gazette nothing, she thought, would prevail upon Cecilia to brand herself a jilt. It was even doubtful if she could be induced to cry off before the announcement had been made, for she presumably had a greater dependence on the strength of Mr Fawnhope's attachment than her shrewder cousin could share, and her tender heart would shrink from giving such pain to one who had been so faithful a lover.

As for Mr Rivenhall's extraordinary change of face, this was not perhaps so inexplicable to Sophy as to his sister; but although the sentiments which had prompted it could not but gratify her, she was unable to deceive herself into thinking that he had any intention of terminating his engagement to Miss Wraxton. It was not to be expected of him: careless of appearances he might be, but no man of his breeding could offer such an affront to a lady. Nor could Sophy suppose that Miss Wraxton, surely aware of the tepid nature of his regard for her, would herself put an end to an alliance that held so little prospect of future happiness for either of the contracting parties. Miss Wraxton's talk was all of her approaching nuptials, and it was quite evident that marriage to a man with whom she scarcely shared a thought was preferable to her than a continued existence as a spinster.

Sophy, cupping her chin in her hands, sat weaving her toils undismayed by a situation which would certainly have daunted a less ruthless female than herself. Those who knew her best would have taken instant alarm, knowing that, her determination once taken, no consideration of propriety would deter her from embarking on schemes which might well prove to be as outrageous as they were original.

'Surprise is the essence of attack.'

The phrase, once uttered by a General in her presence, came into her head. She pondered it, and found it good. Nothing short of surprise would wrench Charles or Cecilia from the paths of convention, so surprise they should have in full measure.

The immediate outcome of all this cogitation was an interview with Lord Ombersley, caught on his return to Berkeley Square from a day at the races. His lordship, firmly led into his own sanctum, scented danger, and made haste to inform his niece that he was pressed for time, having a dinner-engagement that must be kept within the hour.

'Never mind that!' said Sophy. 'Have you seen Charles this day, sir?'

'Of course I have seen Charles!' replied his lordship testily. 'I saw him this morning!'

'But not since then? He has not spoken to you of Cecilia's affairs?'

'No, he has not! And I'll tell you this, Sophy! I want to hear no more of Cecilia's affairs! My mind's made up: I won't have her marrying this poet-fellow!'

'My dear sir,' said Sophy, warmly clasping his hand, 'do not budge from that stand! I must tell you that Charles is about to counsel you to sanction the engagement, and you must not!'

'What?' ejaculated his lordship. 'You're certainly out there, Sophy! Charles won't hear of it, and for once he's right! What should get into the silly chit to make her reject as good as man as you may find – I was never more incensed! To whistle Charlbury, with all his fortune, down the wind – !'

His niece firmly drew him to the sofa, and obliged him to sit down on it beside her. 'Dear Uncle Bernard, if you will only do precisely as I bid you she will marry Charlbury!' she assured him. 'But you must promise me most faithfully not to permit Charles to overbear your judgement!'

'But, Sophy, I keep telling you –'

'Charles has told Cecilia that he will no longer withhold his consent.'

'Good God, has he taken leave of his senses too? You must be mistaken, girl!'

'Upon my honour, I am not! It is the stupidest thing, and will very likely wreck everything, unless you can be trusted to remain firm. Now, my dear uncle, never mind why Charles has taken this start! Only attend to me! When Charles speaks to you about this, you must refuse to entertain the notion of Cecy's marrying Augustus Fawnhope. In fact, it would be an excellent stratagem if you were to say that you are of the same mind as ever, and mean her to marry Charlbury!'

Lord Ombersley, slightly bewildered, entered on a feeble expostulation. 'Much good that would do, when Charlbury has withdrawn his offer!'

'It is of no consequence at all. Charlbury is still extremely desirous of marrying Cecilia, and, if you choose, you may tell her so. She will say that she means to marry her tiresome Augustus, because she is in honour bound to do so. You may rave at her as much as you please – as much as you did when she first made her resolve known to you! But the important thing, dear sir, is that you should remain adamant! I will do the rest.'

He looked suspiciously at her. 'Now, Sophy, this won't do! It was you who helped her to live in that damned poet's pocket, for Charles told me so!'

'Yes, and only see with what splendid results! She no longer has any real desire to wed him, and has come to see how superior Charlbury is! If Charles had not meddled, all would have gone just as you would have wished!'

'I don't understand a word of this!' complained his lordship.

'Very likely not: it has in great measure been due to poor little Amabel's illness.'

'But,' persisted her uncle, painstakingly attempting to follow the thread of her argument, 'if she is now willing to listen to Charlbury, why the devil don't he renew his suit?'

'I daresay he would, if I would let him. It would be useless. Only consider it, sir, in what a fix poor Cecy finds herself! She has kept Augustus dangling after her for months, has sworn she will wed him or none! You have only to consent to the alliance and she must feel herself bound to marry him! At all costs any formal announcement must be stopped! You may do this, and I beg you will! Do not listen to anything Charles may say to you!' Her expressive eyes laughed at him. 'Be as disagreeable to Cecilia as you were before! Nothing could serve the purpose better!'

He pinched her cheek, 'You rogue! But if Charles has changed his mind – You know, Sophy, I am no hand at argument!'

'Then do not argue with him! You have only to fly into a towering passion, and *that*, I know, you are well able to do!'

He chuckled, seeing in this pronouncement a compliment. 'Yes, but if they give me no peace –'

'My dear sir, you may seek refuge at White's! Leave the rest to me! If you will but do your part, I fancy I cannot fail to do mine. I have only this to add! – On no account must you divulge that I have been speaking to you on this matter! Promise!'

'Oh, very well!' said his lordship. 'But I'll tell you what, Sophy! I'd as lief take young Fawnhope into my family as that sour creature Charles must needs bring into it!'

'Oh, certainly!' she responded coolly. '*That* could never answer! I have known it since first I came to London, and I now entertain a reasonable hope of terminating that entanglement. Only do your part, and we may all come about!'

'Sophy!' exclaimed her uncle explosively. 'What the devil do you mean to be about now?'

But she would only laugh, and whisk herself out of the room.

The upshot of this interview staggered the household. For once Mr Rivenhall failed to bend his parent to his will. His representations to Lord Ombersley of the enduring nature of Cecilia's passion fell quite wide of the mark, and were only productive of an outburst of rage that surprised him. Knowing that his heir would speedily out-argue him, and dreading nothing so much as a struggle against a will far stronger than his own, Lord Ombersley scarcely allowed him an opportunity to open his mouth. He said that however high-handed Charles might be in the management of the estates, he was still not his sisters' guardian. He added that he had always considered Cecilia more than half-promised to Charlbury, and would not consent to her marriage with another.

'Unfortunately, sir,' said Charles dryly, 'Charlbury no longer affects my sister. His eyes are turned in quite another direction.'

'Pooh! Nonsense! The fellow haunts the place!'

'Exactly so, sir! Encouraged by my cousin!'

'Don't believe a word of it!' said his lordship. 'Sophy wouldn't have him.' Charles gave a short laugh. 'And if he did offer for her, I still wouldn't permit Cecilia to marry that nincompoop of hers, and so you may tell her!'

Mr Rivenhall did tell her, but as he added consolingly that he had little doubt of being able to talk his father round to his way of thinking, he was not surprised at her calm manner of receiving the news. Not even a tirade from Lord Ombersley, delivered over the dinner-table, quite shattered her composure, although she had the greatest dislike of angry voices, and could not help wincing a little, and changing colour.

The person to be least affected by the parental dictate was Mr Fawnhope. When informed that it would not be possible immediately to send the notice of the betrothal to the society journals, he blinked, and said vaguely: 'Were we about to do so? Did you tell me? I might not have been attending. I am in a great worry about Lepanto, you know. It is useless to deny that battle-scenes upon the stage are never felicitous, yet how to avoid it? I have been pacing the floor the better part of the night, and am no nearer to solving the problem.'

'I must tell you, Augustus, that it is unlikely that we shall be married this year,' said Cecilia.

'Oh, yes, very unlikely!' he agreed. 'I don't think I should think of marriage until the play is off my hands.'

'No, and we must remember that Charles stipulates that you should find some respectable employment before the engagement is announced.'

'That quite settles it, then,' said Mr Fawnhope. 'The question is how far one might, with propriety, employ the methods of the Greek dramatists to overcome the difficulty.'

'Augustus!' said Cecilia, in a despairing voice. 'Is your play more to you than I am?'

He looked at her in surprise, perceived that she was in earnest, and at once took her hand, and kissed it, and said, smiling at her: 'How absurd you are, my beautiful angel! How could anything or anyone be more to me than my Saint Cecilia? It is for your sake that I am writing the play. Should you dislike the notion of a chorus, in the Greek style?'

Lord Charlbury, finding that his rival continued, even without the excuse of enquiring after Amabel's condition, to visit in Berkeley Square, took fright and demanded an explanation of his preceptress. He was driving her down to Merton in his curricle at the time, and when she told him frankly what had occurred, he kept his eyes fixed on the road ahead, and for several moments said nothing. At last, with a palpable effort, he produced: 'I see. When may I expect to see the announcement?'

'Never,' replied Sophy. 'Don't look so hagged, my dear Charlbury! I assure you, there is no need. Poor Cecy has discovered these many weeks that she mistook her own heart!'

At that he turned his head quickly to look at her. 'Is this so indeed? Sophy, don't trifle with me! I own, I had thought – I had hoped – Then I shall try my fortune once more, before it is too late!'

'Charlbury, for a sensible man you say the stupidest things!' Sophy told him. 'Pray, what do you imagine must be her answer in this predicament?'

'But if she no longer loves Fawnhope – if she perhaps regrets turning me off – ?'

'She does, of course, but it is one of those things which appear to be so easy until one considers a little more deeply. Do so! If your situations were reversed – you the impoverished poet, Augustus, the man of fortune – perhaps she might be brought to listen to you. But it is not so! Here is her poet, whom she has declared she will marry in despite of all her family – and you will allow that he has been uncommonly faithful to her!'

'He – ! If he has a thought to spare for anything beyond his trumpery verses I will own myself astonished!'

'He has not, of course, but you will scarcely expect my cousin to believe that! He has attached himself to her to the exclusion of every other female since before I came to England, and that, you know, must rank in the eyes of the world as devotion of no common order! You, my poor Charlbury, labour under all the disadvantages of rank and fortune! How heartless Cecilia must be to cast off her poet to wed you! You may depend upon it that this circumstance weighs with her! Her disposition is tender: she will not, without good reason, inflict pain upon one whom she believes loves her with all his heart. There is only one thing to be done: we must give her good reason for doing so.'

He knew her well enough to feel a considerable degree of uneasiness. 'For God's sake, Sophy, what now do you mean to do?'

'Why, make her feel that it is you who are to be pitied, to be sure!'

Uneasiness changed to the deepest foreboding. 'Good God! How?'

She laughed. 'I daresay it will suit you better not to know, Charlbury!'

'Now, Sophy, listen to me!'

'No, why should I? You say nothing to the point, and, besides, here we are already, and there is no time to enter upon a discussion! You must continue to trust me, if you please!'

The curricle was already bowling up the sweep to the Marquesa's door. 'The lord knows I don't, and never have!' he retorted.

They found the Marquesa alone, and surprisingly wide-awake. She welcomed Sophy affectionately, yet with a little constraint, and soon disclosed that she had only returned two days since from Brighton, where she had been sojourning for a fortnight.

'Brighton!' exclaimed Sophy. 'You told me nothing of this, Sancia! Pray, what took you there so suddenly?'

'But, Sophie, how should I tell you anything when you shut yourself up in a sickroom, and do not visit me any more?' complained the Marquesa. 'To remain always in one place – *majadero*!'

'Very true, but you had the intention of living retired until Sir Horace's return. I daresay you may have had tidings of him –'

'No, I assure you! Not one word!'

'Oh!' said Sophy, slightly disconcerted. 'Well, he had a pros-
perous voyage, and I daresay he will be with us again at any time
now. For it is not likely that at this time of year they will encounter any very unfavourable weather, you know. Has the Duke of
York been staying with his brother?'

The Marquesa opened her sleepy eyes wide. 'But, Sophie, how
should I know? They are alike, the royal princes: gross and – what
is it? – *embotado*! I do not know one from the other.'

Sophy was obliged to be satisfied. Her escort, when they drove
away, asked curiously: 'Why were you put out, Sophy? Must not
the Marquesa follow the rest of the world to Brighton?'

She sighed. 'Not if Sir Vincent Talgarth was there also, which
is what I fear. I never saw her so animated!'

'Disappointing! She won my heart originally by falling asleep
under my eyes!'

She laughed, and said no more, a slight abstraction possessing
her until she was set down in Berkeley Square, and found Mr
Rivenhall awaiting her return in considerable ill-humour. This
instantly revived her, and she had no hesitation in informing him,
upon demand, where she had been.

'You did not go alone!'

'By no means: Charlbury drove me there.'

'I see? First you must set the town talking with Talgarth, and
now with Charlbury! Famous!'

'I do not perfectly understand you,' said Sophy, as one inno-
cently seeking enlightenment. 'I thought your objection to Sir
Vincent was that he has the name for being a great rake. Surely
you do not suspect Charlbury of this! Why, you were even desirous at one time of wedding your sister to him.'

'I am even more desirous that my cousin should not earn for
herself the reputation of being *fast*!'

'Why?' asked Sophy, looking him in the eye. He made her no answer, and, after a moment, she said: 'What right have you, Charles, to take exception to what I may choose to do?'

'If your own good taste –'

'What right, Charles?'

'None!' he said. 'Do as you please! It can be of no consequence to me! You have an easy conquest in Everard! I had not thought him so fickle. Take care you do not lose your other suitor through encouraging this flirtation – for that is all I believe it to be!'

'Bromford? Now, what a shocking thing that would be! You do right to put me on my guard! Charlbury lives in dread of being called out by him.'

'I might have known I should meet with nothing but levity in you!'

'If you will scold me so absurdly. I am not always so.'

'Sophy – !' He took a hasty step towards her, his hand going out, but almost immediately dropping to his side again. 'I wish you had never come amongst us!' he said, and turned away, to lean his arm along the mantelpiece, and stare down at the empty grate.

'That is not kind, Charles.'

He was silent.

'Well, you will be rid of me soon, I daresay. I depend upon seeing Sir Horace at any time now. You will be glad!'

'I must be glad.' The words were uttered almost inaudibly, and he did not raise his head, or make any movement to prevent her leaving the room.

The exchange had taken place in the library. She stepped out into the hall just as Dassett opened the front door to admit Mr Wychbold, very natty in a driving-coat of innumerable capes, shining Hessians, and an enormous nosegay stuck into his buttonhole. He was in the act of laying his tall beaver-hat down upon a marble-topped table, but at the sight of Sophy he used it to lend flourish to his bow. 'Miss Stanton-Lacy! Very obedient servant, ma'am!'

She was surprised to see him, for he had been out of town for some weeks. As she shook hands, she said: 'How delightful this is! I did not know you were in London! How do you do?'

'Only reached town today, ma'am. Heard of your troubles from Charlbury: never more shocked in my life! Came at once to enquire!'

'That is like you! Thank you, she is almost well now, although dreadfully thin, poor little dear, and languid still! You are the very person I wished to see! Are you driving yourself? Must you instantly see my cousin, or will you take me for a turn round the Park?'

He was driving his phaeton, and there could be only one answer to her request. With the greatest gallantry he bowed her out of the house, warning her, however, that she would encounter none but cits in the Park at this season.

'And what, sir, would you have me say to Mr Rivenhall?' asked Dassett, fixing his disapproving eye on a point above Mr Wychbold's left shoulder.

'Oh, tell him I called, and was sorry to find him from home!' replied Mr Wychbold, with an insouciance the butler found offensive.

'Have you been out in your own phaeton, ma'am?' Mr Wychbold asked, as he handed Sophy in the carriage. 'How do your bays go on?'

'Very well. I have not been driving them today, however, but have been to Merton with Charlbury.'

'Oh – ah!' he said, with a slight cough and a sidelong look.

'Yes, making myself the talk of the town!' Sophy said merrily. 'Who told you so? The arch-enemy?'

He set his pair in motion, nodding gloomily. 'Came smash up

to her in Bond Street on my way here. Felt obliged to stop. She
has put off her black ribands!'

'And means to marry Charles next month!' said Sophy, who,
having reached habits of easy intercourse with Mr Wychbold,
never stood upon ceremony with him.

'Told you so,' he pointed out, with a certain melancholy
satisfaction.

'So you did, and I replied that I might need your good offices.
Do you make a prolonged stay in town, or are you off again
immediately?'

'Next week. But, y'know, ma'am, there ain't anything to be
done! Pity, but there it is.'

'We shall see. What do you think would happen if you were
to tell Charles one day that you had seen me driving off in a post-
chaise and four with Charlbury?'

'He would plant me a facer,' responded Mr Wychbold, without
hesitation. 'What's more: shouldn't blame him!'

'Oh!' said Sophy, disconcerted. 'Well, I am sure I don't wish
him to do that. But if it were true?'

'Wouldn't believe me. No need for you to go off with
Charlbury. Not the kind of fellow to engage in such freaks, either.'

'I know that, but it might be contrived. He would not plant
you a facer if you only asked him *why* I was leaving town with
Charlbury for my escort, would he?'

After giving this his consideration, Mr Wychbold admitted that
he might be spared the facer on these terms.

'Will you do it?' Sophy asked him. 'If I were to send you word
to your lodgings, would you make certain that Charles knows of
it? Is he not always at White's in the afternoon?'

'Well, you may generally find him there, but I would not say
always,' replied Mr Wychbold cautiously. 'Besides, I shan't see
you driving off!'

'You may, if you choose to give yourself the trouble of walking round to Berkeley Square!' she retorted. 'If you have word from me, you will know it to be true, and may tell Charles with a clear conscience. I'll take care he knows of it when he comes home, but sometimes he does not come in to dinner. And that would ruin everything! Well, no! not everything, perhaps, but I have always found it to be an excellent scheme to kill two birds with one stone whenever it may be possible!'

Mr Wychbold gave this his profound consideration. Having turned all the implications of Sophy's words over in his brain, he said suddenly: 'Know what I think?'

'No, tell me!'

'No wish to throw a rub in the way, mind!' Mr Wychbold said. 'Not a particular friend of mine, Charlbury. Very good sort of a fellow, I believe, but he don't happen to have come much in my way.'

'But what do you think?' demanded Sophy, impatient of this divagation.

'Think Charles may very likely call him out,' said Mr Wychbold, 'Come to think of it, bound to! Devilish fine shot, Charles! Just thought I would mention it!' he added apologetically.

'You are right, and I am very much obliged to you for putting me in mind of such a possibility!' said Sophy warmly. 'I would not for the world place Charlbury in jeopardy! But there will not be the least need for such a measure, you know.'

'Ah, well!' said Mr Wychbold comfortably. 'Daresay he won't do more than drop him a few times, then! Draw his claret, I mean!'

'Fisticuffs? Oh no! surely he would not!'

'Well, he will,' said Mr Wychbold, without hesitation. 'Last time I saw Charles, don't scruple to tell you he was in such a miff with Charlbury he said it would be wonderful if he did not plant him a flush hit one of these days! Devil of a fellow with his fives,

is Charles! Don't know how Charlbury displays: shouldn't think
he would be a match for Charles, though.' Waxing enthusiastic,
he added: 'Prettiest fighter, for an amateur, I ever saw in my life!
Excellent science and bottom, never any trifling or shifting! No
mere flourishing, and very rarely abroad!' he recollected himself
suddenly, and broke off in some confusion, and begged pardon.

'Yes, never mind that!' said Sophy, her brow creased. 'I must
think of this, for it won't do at all. If I make Charles angry, which,
I own, I wish to do –'

'No difficulty in that,' interpolated Mr Wychbold encouragingly. 'Very quick temper! Always has had!'

She nodded. 'And would be only too glad of an excuse to hit
someone, I have no doubt. Of course, I see how I could prevent
him doing Charlbury a mischief.' She drew a breath. 'Resolution
is all that is needed!' she said. 'One should never shrink from the
performance of unpleasant tasks to obtain a laudable object, after
all! Mr Wychbold, I am very much obliged to you! I now see just
what I must do, and I should not be at all surprised if it answered
both purposes to admiration!'

Sixteen

Miss Wraxton, learning of Mr Rivenhall's consent to his sister's marriage to Mr Fawnhope, was so genuinely shocked that she could not forbear remonstrating with him. With her customary good sense, she pointed out the evil consequences of such a match, begging him to consider well before he abetted Cecilia in her folly. He heard her in silence, but when she had talked herself out of arguments he said bluntly: 'I have given my word. I cannot but agree with much of what you have said. I do not like the match, but I will have no hand in forcing my sister into a marriage she does not desire. I believed that she must soon recover from what seemed to me a mere infatuation. She has not done so. I am forced to acknowledge that her heart is engaged: not her fancy only.'

She raised her brows, her expression one of faint distaste. 'My dear Charles! This is not like you! I daresay I have not far to seek for the influence which prompts you to utter such a speech, but I own that I scarcely expected you to repeat sentiments so much at variance with your disposition, and – I must add – your breeding.'

'Indeed! You will have to explain your meaning more fully, if I am to understand you, Eugenia, for I am quite abroad!'

She said gently: 'Surely not! We have so often conversed on this head! Are we not agreed that there is something very unbecoming in a daughter's setting up her will in opposition to her parents?'

'In general, yes.'

'And in *particular*, Charles, when it comes to be a question of her marriage. Her parents must be the best judges of what will be most proper for her. There is something very forward and disagreeable in a girl's *falling in love*, as the common phrase is. No doubt underbred persons make quite a practice of it, but I fancy a man of birth and upbringing would prefer to see rather more restraint in the lady he marries. The language you have adopted – forgive me, dear Charles! – surely belongs more to the stage than to your mother's drawing-room!'

'Does it?' he said. 'Tell me, Eugenia! Had I offered for your hand without the consent of your father, would you have entertained my suit?'

She smiled. 'We need not consider absurdities! You, of all men, would not have done so!'

'But if I had?'

'Certainly not,' she replied, with composure.

'I am obliged to you!' he said satirically.

'You should be,' she said. 'You could scarcely have wished the future Lady Ombersley to have been a female without reserve or filial obedience!'

His eyes were very hard and keen. 'I begin to understand you,' he said.

'I knew you would, for you are a man of sense. I am no advocate, I need scarcely say, for a marriage where there is no mutual esteem. That could hardly prosper! Certainly, if Cecilia holds Charlbury in distaste, it would have been wrong to have compelled her to marry him.'

'Generous!'

'I hope so,' she said gravely. 'I should not wish to be other than generous towards your sisters – towards all your family! It must be one of my chief objects to promote their welfare, and I assure you I mean to do so!'

'Thank you,' he said, in a colourless tone.

She turned a bracelet upon her arm. 'You are inclined to regard Miss Stanton-Lacy with indulgence, I know, but I think you will allow that her influence in this house has not been a happy one, in many respects. Without her encouragement, I venture to think that Cecilia would not have behaved as she has.'

'I don't know that. You would not say that her influence was not a happy one had you seen her nursing Amabel, supporting both my mother and Cecilia in their anxiety! That is something I can never forget.'

'I am sure no one could wish you to. One is glad to be able to praise her conduct in that emergency without reserve.'

'I owe it to her also that I stand now upon such easy terms with Hubert. *There* she has done nothing but good.'

'Well, on that point we have always differed, have we not?' she said pleasantly. 'But I have no wish to argue with you on such a subject! I only hope that Hubert continues to go on well.'

'Very well. I might almost say *too* well, for what must the ridiculous fellow do but think himself in honour bound to make up some lost study during this vacation! He is gone off on a reading-party!' He laughed suddenly. 'If he does not fall into a melancholy through all this virtue, I must surely expect to hear that he is in some shocking scrape soon!'

'I'm afraid you are right,' she agreed seriously. 'There is an instability of purpose that must continuously distress you.'

He stared at her incredulously, but before he could speak, Dassett had ushered Lord Bromford into the room. He at once went forward to shake hands, greeting this new guest with more amiability than was usual, but saying: 'I fear you are out of luck: my cousin has gone out driving.'

'I was informed of it at the door – How do you do, ma'am? – but I considered it proper to step upstairs to felicitate you upon your sister's happy recovery,' replied his lordship. 'I have had occasion to call in our good Baillie – excellent man! – and he swore upon his honour there was not the least lingering danger of infection.'

Judging from the curl of Mr Rivenhall's lip that he was about to make a sardonic rejoinder, Miss Wraxton intervened rather hastily. 'Have you been indisposed, dear Lord Bromford? This is sad hearing! No serious disorder, I must hope?'

'Baillie does not consider it so. He thinks the season has been uncommonly sickly: such inclement weather, you know, and very likely to produce affections of the throat, to which I am peculiarly susceptible. My mother has been, you may imagine, quite in a worry, for my constitution is delicate – it would be idle to deny that it is delicate! I was obliged to keep to my room above a week.'

Mr Rivenhall, leaning his broad shoulders against the mantelpiece, drove his hands into the pockets of his breeches, and presented all the appearance of a man willing to be amused. Lord Bromford did not recognize the signs, but Miss Wraxton did, and was cast into an agony of apprehension. She once more hurried into speech. 'Sore throats have been very prevalent, I believe. I do not wonder that Lady Bromford was anxious. You were well-nursed, I know!'

'Yes,' he concurred. 'Not that my complaint was of such a nature as to – In short, even Mama owns herself to have been moved by the devotion of Miss Stanton-Lacy to her little cousin!' He bowed to Mr Rivenhall, who graciously inclined his head in acknowledgement of the courtesy, only spoiling the effect by a peculiarly saturnine grin. 'I have been put in mind of certain lines from *Marmion*, in this connection.'

Miss Wraxton, who had heard enough of Sophy's perfections in a sickroom, could only be grateful to Mr Rivenhall for interpolating: 'Yes, we know them well!'

Lord Bromford, who had started to repeat *O woman, in our hours of ease!* was thrown a little out of his stride by this, but recovered directly, and pronounced: 'Any doubts that might have been nourished of the true womanliness of Miss Stanton-Lacy's character, must, I venture to say, have been lulled to rest.'

At this moment, Dassett reappeared to announce that Lady Brinklow's carriage was at the door. Miss Wraxton, who had only been set down in Berkeley Square while her parent executed a commission in Bond Street, was obliged to take her leave. Lord Bromford said that since neither Lady Ombersley nor her niece was at home he would not trespass longer upon the premises, and within a very few minutes Mr Rivenhall was able to have his laugh out in comfort. Lord Bromford, who was a favourite with Lady Brinklow, was offered a seat in the landaulet, and beguiled the short drive to Brook Street with an exact account of the symptoms of his late indisposition.

Mr Rivenhall, for all his resolve to hold his cousin at arm's length, could not resist the temptation of recounting this passage to her. She enjoyed the joke just as he had known she would, but put an abrupt end to his amusement by exclaiming involuntarily: 'How well he and Miss Wraxton would suit! Now, why did I never think of that before?'

'Possibly,' said Mr Rivenhall frostily, 'you may have recalled that Miss Wraxton is betrothed to me!'

'I don't think *that* was the reason,' said Sophy, considering it. She lifted an eyebrow at him. 'Offended, Charles?'

'Yes!' said Mr Rivenhall.

'Oh, Charles, I wonder at you!' she said, with her irrepressible gurgle of mirth. 'So *untruthful!*'

As she beat a strategic retreat upon the words, he was left to glare at the unresponsive door.

He told his mother roundly that Sophy's conduct went from bad to worse, but the full measure of her iniquity did not burst upon him until two days later, when, upon ordering his groom to harness his latest acquisition to his tilbury, he was staggered to learn that Miss Stanton-Lacy had driven out in this equipage not half an hour earlier.

'Taken my tilbury out?' he repeated. His voice sharpened. 'Which horse?' he demanded.

The groom shook visibly. 'The – the young horse, sir!'

'You – harnessed – the young horse for Miss Stanton-Lacy to drive?' said Mr Rivenhall, giving his words such awful weight as almost to deprive his henchman of all power of speech.

'Miss said – miss was sure – you would have no objection, sir!' stammered this unfortunate. 'And seeing as how she has twice driven the grays, sir, and me not having no orders contrary – and her saying as all was right – I thought she had your permission, sir!'

Mr Rivenhall, in a few pungent words, swept this illusion from his mind, adding a rider which summarily disposed of any pretensions his groom might have cherished of being able to think at all. The groom, not daring to venture on an explanation of the circumstances, waited in miserable silence for his dismissal. It did not come. Mr Rivenhall was a stern master, but also a just one, and even in his wrath he had a very fair notion of the means his unprincipled cousin must have employed to gain her ends. He checked himself suddenly, and rapped out: 'Where has she gone? To Richmond? Answer!'

Seeing the culprit quite unable to collect his wits, Lord Ombersley's own groom intervened, saying obsequiously: 'Oh no, sir! No, indeed! My lady and Miss Cecilia set out in the barouche an hour ago for Richmond! And Miss Amabel with them, sir!'

Mr Rivenhall, who knew that a visit had been arranged to a cousin who lived at Richmond, stared at him with knit brows. It had certainly been agreed that Sophy was to have accompanied her aunt and cousins, and he was at a loss to imagine what could have caused her to change her mind. But this was a minor problem. The young chestnut she had had the temerity to drive out was a headstrong animal, quite unaccustomed to town-traffic, and certainly unfit for a lady to handle. Mr Rivenhall could control him, but even so notable a whip as Mr Wychbold had handsomely acknowledged that the brute was a rare handful. Mr Rivenhall, thinking of some of the chestnut's least engaging tricks, felt himself growing cold with apprehension. It was this fear that lent the edge to his anger. A certain degree of anger he must always have felt at having his horse taken out without his permission, but nothing to compare with the murderous rage that now consumed him. Sophy had behaved unpardonably – and that her conduct was strangely unlike her he was in no mood to consider – and might even now be lying upon the cobbles with a broken neck.

'Saddle Thunderer, and the brown hack!' he commanded suddenly. 'Quick!'

Both grooms flew to carry out this order, exchanging glances that spoke volumes. No ostlers, trained to change coach-horses in fifty seconds, could have worked faster; and while a couple of stable-hands still stood gaping at such unaccustomed doings, Mr Rivenhall, followed at a discreet distance by his groom, was riding swiftly in the direction of Hyde Park.

He had judged correctly, but it was perhaps unfortunate that he should have come up with his cousin just as the young chestnut, first trying to rear up between the shafts at the sight of a small boy flying a kite, made a spirited attempt to kick the floor-boards out of the carriage. Mr Rivenhall, who had almost believed that he could forgive all if only he should find his cousin unharmed, found that he had been mistaken. Pale with fury, he dismounted, dragged the bridle over Thunderer's head, thrust it into the groom's hand, with a brief order to him to lead the horse home, swung himself into the tilbury, and possessed himself of the reins. For several moments he was fully occupied with his horse, and Sophy had leisure to admire his skill. She did not think she had managed so very badly herself, for, with the best will in the world to do so, the chestnut had not bolted with her, but she did not pretend to Mr Rivenhall's mastery over a high-couraged, half-broke animal. Assuaging Mr Rivenhall's wrath formed no part of her schemes, but in spite of herself she exclaimed: 'Ah, you are a capital whip! I never knew how good until today!'

'I don't need you to tell me so!' he flashed, face and voice at curious variance with his steady hands. 'How dared you do this? How dared you? If you had broken your neck you would have come by your deserts! That you have not broken my horse's knees I must think a miracle!'

'Pooh!' said Sophy, atoning for her previous error by laying this promising faggot upon the smouldering fire.

The result was all that she had hoped it might be. The drive back to Berkeley Square did not occupy very many minutes, but Mr Rivenhall crammed into them every pent-up exasperation of the past fortnight. He tore his cousin's character to shreds; condemned her manners, her morals, and her upbringing; expressed his strong desire to have the schooling of her, and, in the same breath, pitied the man who should be fool enough to marry her; and fervently looked forward to the day when he should be relieved of her unwelcome presence in his home.

It was doubtful whether Sophy could have stemmed the tide of this eloquence. In the event, she made no attempt to do so, but sat with folded hands, and downcast eyes, beside her accuser. That his rage had been fanned, quite irrationally, to white heat by finding her unhurt she had no doubt at all. There had been moments during her escapade when she had doubted her ability to bring either herself or the horse off safely. She had never been more glad to see her cousin; and one glance at his face had been enough to assure her that he had suffered a degree of anxiety out of all proportion to the concern even the keenest whip might be expected to feel for his horse. He might say what he pleased: she was not deceived.

He set her down in Berkeley Square, telling her roughly that she might alight without his assistance. She obeyed him, and without so much as waiting to see her admitted into the house he drove off towards the mews.

That was shortly after noon. Mr Rivenhall did not return to the house, and, as soon as she was satisfied that there was no fear of his walking in on her, his wholly unchastened cousin first summoned the under-footman to her, and sent him on an errand to the nearest livery-stables; and then sat down to write several careful notes. By two o'clock, John Potton, puzzled but unsuspicious, was trotting down to Merton with one of these in his pocket. Had he been privileged to know its contents he might not have ridden so cheerfully out of London.

'*Dearest Sancia*,' Sophy wrote. '*I find myself in the most dreadful predicament, and most earnestly beg of you to join me at Lacy Manor immediately. Do not fail me, or I shall be utterly ruined! Ashtead lies only ten miles from Merton, so you need not fear to be fatigued. I leave London within the hour, and wholly depend upon you. Ever your devoted Sophy.*'

Upon the footman's return from his errand, he was gratified to receive half-a-guinea for his pains, and set forth again with alacrity to deliver two sealed letters. One of these he left at Mr Wychbold's lodging; the other he carried from Lord Charlbury's house to Manton's Shooting Gallery, and thence to Brooks's Club, where he finally ran his quarry to earth. Lord Charlbury, summoned to the hall to receive the billet in person, read it in considerable astonishment, but handsomely rewarded the bearer, and charged him to inform Miss Stanton-Lacy that he was entirely at her disposal.

Meanwhile, Miss Stanton-Lacy, who had thoughtfully given her too zealous maid a holiday, instructed a startled housemaid to pack her night-gear in a portmanteau, and sat down to write two more letters. She was still engaged on this task when Lord Charlbury was shown into the saloon. She looked up, smiling, and said: 'I knew I might depend on you! Thank you! Only let me finish this note!'

He waited until the door had closed behind Dassett before demanding: 'What in heaven's name is amiss, Sophy? Why must you go to Ashtead?'

'It is my home: Sir Horace's house!'

'Indeed! I was not aware – But so suddenly! Your aunt – your cousin – ?'

'Don't tease me!' she begged. 'I will explain it to you on the way, if you will be so good as to give me your escort! It is not far – may be accomplished in one stage, you know!'

'Of course I will escort you!' he replied at once. 'Is Rivenhall away from home?'

'It is impossible for me to ask him to go with me. Pray let me finish this note for Cecilia!'

He begged pardon, and moved away to a chair by the window. Good manners forbade him to press her for an explanation she was plainly reluctant to offer, but he was very much puzzled. The mischievous look had quite vanished from her eyes; she seemed to be in an unusually grave mood: a circumstance that threw him off his guard, and made him only anxious to be of service to her.

The note to Cecilia was soon finished, and closed with a wafer. Sophy rose from the writing-table, and Charlbury ventured to ask whether she desired him to drive her to Ashtead in his curricle.

'No, no, I have hired a post-chaise! I daresay it will be here directly. You did not come in your curricle?'

'No, I walked from Brooks's. You are making a stay in the country?'

'I hardly know. Will you wait while I put on my hat and cloak?'

He assented, and she went away, returning presently with Tina frisking about her in the expectation of being taken for a walk. The hack-chaise was already at the door, and Dassett, quite as mystified as Lord Charlbury, had directed a footman to strap Miss Stanton-Lacy's portmanteau on to the back. Sophy gave her two last notes into his hand, directing him to be sure that Mr and Miss Rivenhall received them immediately upon their return to the house. Five minutes later she was seated in the chaise beside Charlbury, and expressing the hope that the threatened rain-storm would hold off until they reached Lacy Manor. Tina jumped up into her lap, and she then told his lordship that she had encountered in the Green Park just such another Italian greyhound, who had made no secret of his admiration of Tina. Tina's coquetry had to be described; this led to an amusing account of the jealousy of Mr Rivenhall's spaniel, brought up by him from the country for a couple of nights; and in this way, by easy gradations, Lord Charlbury found himself discussing pheasant-shooting, fox-hunting, and various other sporting pursuits. These topics lasted until the Kennington turnpike had been passed, by which time his lordship's faculties, at first bewildered, were very much on the alert. He fancied that the mischief was back in Sophy's eye. At Lower Tooting, he politely allowed his gaze to be directed to the curious churchtower, with its circular form surmounted by a square wooden frame, with a low spire of shingles above it; but when Sophy leaned back again

in her corner of the chaise, he said, watching her face: 'Sophy, are
we by chance eloping together?'

Her rich chuckle broke from her. 'No, no, it is not as bad as
that! Must I tell you?'

'I know very well you have some abominable scheme afoot!
Tell me at once!'

She threw him a sidelong look, and he had now no doubt that
the mischief was back in her eye. 'Well, the truth is, Charlbury,
that I have kidnapped you.'

After a stunned moment, he began to laugh. In this she readily
joined him, but when he had recovered from the first absurdity of
the notion, he said: 'I might have known there was devilry afoot
when I saw that your faithful Potton was absent! But what is this,
Sophy? Why am I kidnapped? To what end?'

'So that I may be so compromised that you will be obliged to
marry me, of course,' replied Sophy matter-of-factly.

This cheerful explanation had the effect of making him start
bolt upright, exclaiming: '*Sophy!*'

She smiled. 'Oh, don't be alarmed! I have sent John Potton with
a letter to Sancia begging her to come to Lacy Manor at once.'

'Good God, do you place any dependence upon her doing so?'

'Oh, yes, certainly! She has a very kind heart, you know, and
would never fail me when I particularly desired her help.'

He relaxed against the squabs again, but said: 'I don't know what
you deserve! I am still quite in a puzzle: why have you done it?'

'Why, don't you see? I have left behind me a letter for Cecilia,
telling her that I am about to sacrifice myself –'

'Thank you!' interjected his lordship.

' – *and* you,' continued Sophy serenely, 'so that my uncle
may be silenced at last. You know, for I told you so, that I persuaded him to announce to poor Cecy his unalterable decision
that she was to wed you! If I know Cecy, the shock will bring

her post-haste to Ashtead, to rescue the pair of us. If, my dear Charlbury, you cannot help yourself in that eventuality, I wash my hands of you!'

'I can find it in me to wish you had done so long since!' was his ungrateful response. 'Outrageous, Sophy, *outrageous*! And what if neither she nor the Marquesa comes to Lacy Manor? Let me tell you that nothing will serve to induce me to compromise you!'

'No, indeed! I should dislike it excessively. If *that* happened, I fear you will be obliged to spend the night at Leatherhead. It is not very far from Lacy Manor, and I believe you may be tolerably comfortable at the Swan. Or you might hire a chaise to carry you back to London. But Sancia at least will not fail.'

'Have you told Cecilia that you have *kidnapped* me?' he demanded. She nodded, and he exclaimed: 'I could murder you! What a trick to play! And what a figure I must cut!'

'She won't think of that. Do you recall that I told you only the other day that she must be made to pity you instead of Augustus? Besides that, I am persuaded she will suffer perfect torments of jealousy. Only fancy! I was quite at a stand until I remembered what I had once heard pronounced by a most distinguished soldier! "Surprise is the essence of attack!" The most fortunate circumstance!'

'Was it not?' he said sarcastically. 'I have a very good mind to get down at the next pike!'

'You will ruin all if you do.'

'It is *abominable*, Sophy!'

'Yes, if the motive were not pure!'

He said nothing, and she too remained silent for several minutes. At last, having turned it over in his mind, he said: 'You had better tell me the whole. That I have only heard half I have no doubt at all! Where does Charles Rivenhall stand in all this?'

She folded her hands on Tina's back. 'Alas! I have quarrelled so dreadfully with Charles that I am obliged to seek refuge at Lacy Manor!' she said mournfully.

'And have doubtless left a note behind you to inform him of this!'

'Of course!'

'I foresee a happy meeting!' he commented bitterly.

'That,' she acknowledged, 'was the difficulty! But I think I can overcome it. I promise you, Charlbury, you shall come out of this with a whole skin – well, no, perhaps not quite that, but very nearly!'

'You do not know how much you relieve my mind! I daresay I may not be a match for Rivenhall, either with pistols or with my fists, but give me credit for not being quite so great a poltroon as to fear a meeting with him!'

'I do,' she assured him. 'But it can serve no good purpose for Charles to *mill you down* – have I that correctly?'

'Quite correctly!'

'– or to put a bullet through you,' she ended, her serenity unshaken.

He was obliged to laugh. 'I see that Rivenhall is more to be pitied than I am! Why did you quarrel with him?'

'I had to make an excuse for flying from Berkeley Square! You must perceive that! I could think of nothing else to do but to take out that young chestnut he has bought lately. A beautiful creature! Such grand, sloping shoulders! Such an action! But quite unbroke to London traffic, and by far too strong for any female to hold!'

'I have seen the horse. Do you tell me seriously, Sophy, that you took him out?'

'I did – shocking, was not it? I assure you, I suffered a real qualm in my conscience! No harm, however! He did not bolt with me, and Charles came to the rescue before I found myself in real difficulty. The things he said to me – ! I have never seen him in such a fury! If only I could remember the half of the insults he flung at my head! It is no matter, however: they gave me all the cause I needed to fly from his vicinity.'

He closed his eyes for an anguished moment. 'Informing him, no doubt, that you had sought *my* protection?'

'No, there was no need: Cecy will tell him that!'

'What a fortunate circumstance, to be sure! I hope you mean to contribute a handsome wreath to my obsequies?'

'Certainly! In the nature of things, it is likely that you will predecease me.'

'If I survive this adventure there can be no question of that. Your fate is writ clear: you will be murdered. I cannot conceive how it comes about that you were not murdered long since!'

'How odd! Charles himself once said that to me, or something like it!'

'There is nothing odd in it: any sensible man must say it!'

She laughed, but said: 'No, you are unjust! I have never yet done the least harm to anyone! It may be that with regard to Charles my stratagems may not succeed: in your case I am convinced they must! That may well content us. Poor Cecy! Only conceive how dreadful to be obliged to marry Augustus, and to spend the rest of one's life listening to his poems!'

This aspect of the situation struck Lord Charlbury so forcibly that he was smitten to silence. He said nothing of deserting Sophy when they stopped at the next pike, but appeared to be resigned to his fate.

Lacy Manor, which lay a little way off the turnpike road, was an Elizabethan house, considerably added to in succeeding generations, but still retaining much of its original beauty. It was reached by an avenue of noble trees, and had once been set amongst well-tended formal gardens. These, through the circumstance of Sir Horace's being not only an absentee but also a careless landlord, had become overgrown of late years, so that the shrubbery was

indistinguishable from the wilderness, and unpruned rose bushes
rioted at will in unweeded flower-beds. The sky had become
overcast all day, but a fitful ray of sunlight, penetrating the lowering clouds, showed the mullioned windows of the house much
in need of cleaning. A trail of smoke issued from one chimney,
the only observable sign that the house was still inhabited. Sophy,
alighting from the chaise, looked about her critically, while
Charlbury tugged at the iron bell-pull beside the front door.

'Everything seems to be in shocking disorder!' she observed. 'I
must tell Sir Horace that it will not do! He should not neglect the
house in this way. There is work here for an army of gardeners!
He never liked the place, you know. I have sometimes wondered
if it was because my mother died here.' Lord Charlbury made a
sympathetic sound in his throat, but Sophy continued cheerfully:
'But I daresay it is only because he is shockingly indolent! Ring
the bell again, Charlbury!'

After a prolonged interval, they heard the sound of footsteps
within the house, to be followed immediately by the scrape of
bolts being drawn back, and the clank of a chain removed from
the door.

'I am reconciled, Sophy!' announced Charlbury. 'Never did I
hope to find myself existing between the covers of a library novel!
Will there be cobwebs, and a skeleton under the stairs?'

'I fear not, but only think how delightful if there should be!' she
retorted. She added, as the door was opened, and a surprised face
appeared in the aperture: 'Good-day, Clavering! Yes, it is I indeed,
and I have come home to see how you and Mathilda go on!'

The retainer, a spare man with grizzled locks and a bent back,
peered at her for a moment before gasping: 'Miss Sophy! Lor', miss,
if we'd thought you was coming – ! Such a turn as it give me, to
hear the bell a-pealing! Here, Matty! Matty, I say! It's Miss Sophy!'

A female form, as stout as he was lean, appeared in the

background, uttering distressful sounds, and trying to untie the strings of a grimy apron. Much flustered, Mrs Clavering begged her young mistress to step into the house, and to excuse the disorder everywhere. They had had no warning of her advent; the master had said he would take order when he returned from foreign parts; she doubted whether there was as much as a pinch of tea in the house; if she had but known of Miss Sophy's intention to visit them she would have had the chimneys swept, and the best parlour cleaned and taken out of Holland covers.

Sophy soothed her agitation with the assurance that she had come prepared to find the house in disarray, and stepped into the hall. This was a large apartment, panelled and low-pitched, from which, at one end, a handsome staircase of oak rose in easy flights to the upper floors of the house. The chairs were all shrouded in Holland covers, and a film of dust lay over the gate-legged table in the centre of the room. The air struck unpleasantly dank, and a large patch of damp on one wall made this circumstance easily understandable.

'We must open all the windows, and light fires!' Sophy said briskly. 'Has the Marquesa – has a Spanish lady arrived yet?'

She was assured that no Spanish lady had been seen at the Manor, a circumstance in which the Claverings seemed to think they deserved to be congratulated.

'Good!' said Sophy. 'She will be here presently, and we must strive to make things a little more comfortable before we admit her. Bring some wood, and kindling for this fire, Clavering, and do you, Matty, pull off these covers! If there is no tea in the house, I am sure there is some ale! Bring some for Lord Charlbury, if you please! Charlbury, I beg your pardon for inviting you to so derelict a house! Wait, Clavering! Are the stables in decent order? I don't wish the chaise to drive away, and the horses must be baited, and rubbed down, and the post-boys refreshed!'

Lord Charlbury, abandoning his scruples to enjoyment of this situation, said: 'Will you permit me to attend to that matter for you? If Clavering will show me the way to your stables – ?'

'Yes, pray do so!' said Sophy gratefully. 'I must see which rooms are most fit to be used, and until we have a fire lit here it will be most uncomfortable for you.'

His lordship, correctly interpreting this to mean that he would be very much in the way if he stayed in the house, went off with Clavering to lead the post-boys to the stables – happily still water-tight, and under the charge of an aged pensioner, whose rheumy eye perceptibly brightened at the sight of even such cattle as job-horses. A stout cob, and a couple of farm-horses, were the only occupants of the commodious stables, but the pensioner assured him that there was both bedding and fodder enough, and further undertook to regale the post-boys in his own cottage, which adjoined the stables.

Lord Charlbury then strolled about the gardens until some heavy drops of rain drove him back to the house. There he found that the covers had been taken off the chairs in the hall, a duster employed, and a fire lit in the gigantic hearth.

'It is not really cold,' said Sophy, 'but it will make everything appear more cheerful!'

His lordship, dubiously eyeing the puffs of smoke issuing from the fireplace into the room, agreed to this meekly enough, and even made a show of warming his hands at the small blue flame showing amidst the coals. A more violent gust of smoke caused him to retreat, seized by a fit of coughing. Sophy knelt to thrust a poker under the black mass, raising it to let the draught through. 'It's my belief there may be a starling's nest in the chimney,' she observed dispassionately. 'Mathilda, however, says fires always smoke for a while when the chimneys are cold. We shall see! I found some tea in one of the cupboards in the pantry, and

Mathilda is bringing it to us directly. She had no notion it was there: I wonder how long it has lain hidden in the cupboard?'

'I wonder?' echoed his lordship, fascinated by the thought of this relic of forgotten days at Lacy Manor.

'Fortunately, tea does not turn bad with keeping,' said Sophy. 'At least – does it?'

'I have no idea, but that we shall also see,' returned Charlbury. He began to walk about the hall, inspecting the pictures and the ornaments. 'What a shame it is that this place should be left to go to ruin!' he remarked. 'That is a charming Dresden group, and I have quite lost my heart to that Harlequin over there. I wonder your father would not rather prefer to hire his house to some respectable people while he is employed abroad than let it rot!'

'Well, for a great many years he allowed my aunt Clara to live here,' exclaimed Sophy. 'She was most eccentric, and kept cats, and died two years ago.'

'I don't think she took very good care of the house,' said Charlbury, putting up his glass to inspect a landscape in a heavy gilded frame.

'No, I fear she cannot have. Never mind! Sir Horace will soon put it to rights. Meanwhile, Mathilda is to set the breakfast parlour in order, and we may sit there, and be cosy presently.' She frowned slightly. 'The only thing that troubles me a little is dinner,' she confided. 'It does not appear to me that Mathilda has the least notion of cookery, and I must confess that I have not either. You may say that this is a trifling circumstance, but –'

'No,' interrupted his lordship, with great firmness. 'I shall say nothing of the sort! Are we dining here? Must we?'

'Oh, yes, I am sure we must make up our minds to that!' she replied. 'I am not quite certain when we may expect to see Cecilia, but I hardly think she will reach us before seven o'clock, for she was gone to Richmond with my aunt, you know, and they will very likely spend the afternoon there. Are you interested in pictures? Shall I take you to show you the Long Gallery? The best ones are hung there, I think.'

'Thank you, I should like to see them. Are you expecting Rivenhall to accompany his sister?'

'Well, I *imagine* he will. After all, she will hardly set forth alone, and he must surely be the person she would turn to in such a predicament. There is no saying, of course, but you may depend upon it that if Charles does not come with Cecy he will follow her swiftly. Let us go up to the Gallery until tea is ready for us!'

She led the way to the staircase, pausing by a chair to pick up from it her large travelling-reticule. The Gallery, which ran along the north side of the house, was in sepulchral darkness, heavy curtains having been drawn across its several tall windows. Sophy began to fling these back, saying: 'There are two Vandykes, and something that is *said* to be a Holbein, though Sir Horace doubts it, and *that* is my mother's portrait, done by Hoppner. I don't remember her myself, but Sir Horace never cared for this likeness: he says it makes her simper, which she never did.'

'You are not very like her,' Charlbury remarked, looking up at the portrait.

'Oh, no! She was thought a great beauty!' Sophy said.

He smiled, but made no comment. They passed on to the next picture, and so the length of the Gallery, when Sophy supposed that Mathilda would have set the tea-tray for them. She thought the curtains should be drawn again, so Charlbury went to the windows to perform this duty for her. He had shut the light out from two of them, and had stretched out his hand to grasp one of the curtains of the third when Sophy, from behind him, said: 'Stay just as you are for an instant, Charlbury. Can you see the summer-house from where you stand?'

He stood still, his arm across the window, and had just begun

to say: 'I can see something through the trees which might be —'
when there was a loud report, and he sprang aside, clutching his
forearm, which felt as though a red-hot wire had seared it. For a
moment, his senses were entirely bewildered by the shock; then he
became aware that his sleeve was singed and rent, that blood was
welling up between his fingers, and that Sophy was laying down
an elegant little pistol.

She was looking a trifle pale, but she smiled reassuringly at him,
and said, as she came towards him: 'I *do* beg your pardon! An
infamous thing to have done, but I thought it would very likely
make it worse for you if I warned you!'

'Sophy, have you run mad?' he demanded furiously, beginning
to twist his handkerchief round his arm. 'What the devil do you
mean by it?'

'Come into one of the bedchambers, and let me bind it up! I
have everything ready. I was afraid you might be a little cross, for
I am sure it must have hurt you abominably. It took the greatest resolution to make me do it,' she said, gently propelling him
towards the door.

'But *why*? In God's name, what have I done that you must
needs put a bullet through me?'

'Oh, nothing in the world! That door, if you please, and take
off your coat. My dread was that my aim might falter, and I should
break your arm, but I am sure I have not, have I?'

'No, of course you have not! It is hardly more than a graze, but
I still don't perceive why —'

She helped him to take off his coat, and to roll up his sleeve.
'No, it is only a slight flesh wound: I am so thankful!'

'So am I!' said his lordship grimly. 'I may think myself fortunate
not to be dead, I suppose!'

She laughed. 'What nonsense! At that range? However, I do
think Sir Horace would have been proud of me, for my aim was

as steady as though I were shooting at a wafer, and it would not have been wonderful, you know, if my hand had trembled. Sit down, so that I may bathe it!'

He obeyed, holding his arm over the bowl of water she had so thoughtfully provided. He had a very lively sense of humour, and now that the first shock was over, he could not prevent his lip quivering. 'Yes, indeed!' he retorted. 'One can readily imagine a parent's pleasure at such an exploit! Resolution is scarcely the word for it, Sophy! Don't you even mean to fall into a swoon at the sight of the blood?'

She looked quickly up from her task of sponging the wound. 'Good God, no! I am not *missish*, you know!'

At that he flung back his head and broke into a shout of laughter. 'No, no, Sophy! You're not missish!' he gasped, when he could speak at all. 'The Grand Sophy!'

'I wish you will keep still!' she said severely, patting his arm with a soft cloth. 'See, it is scarcely bleeding now! I will dust it with basilicum powder, and bind it up for you, and you may be comfortable again.'

'I am not in the least comfortable, and shall very likely be in a high fever presently. Why did you do it, Sophy?'

'Well,' she said, quite seriously, 'Mr Wychbold said that Charles would either call you out for this escapade, or knock you down, and I don't at all wish anything of that nature to befall you.'

This effectually put a period to his amusement. Grasping her wrist with his sound hand, he exclaimed. 'Is this true? By God, I have a very good mind to box your ears! Do you imagine that I am afraid of Charles Rivenhall?'

'No, I daresay you are not, but only conceive how shocking it would be if Charles perhaps killed you, all through my fault!'

'Nonsense!' he said angrily. 'And if either of us were crazy enough to let it come to that, which, I assure you, we are not – !'

'No, I feel you are right, but also I think Mr Wychbold was right in thinking that Charles would – what does he call it? – *plant you a facer?*'

'Very likely, but although I may be no match for Rivenhall, I might still give quite a tolerable account of myself!'

She began to wind a length of lint round his forearm. 'It could not answer,' she said. 'If you were to floor Charles, Cecy would not like it above half; and if you imagine, my dear Charlbury, that a black eye and a bleeding nose will help your cause with her, you must be a great gaby!'

'I thought,' he said sarcastically, 'that she was to be made to pity me?'

'Exactly so! And that is the circumstance which decided me to shoot you!' said Sophy triumphantly.

Again, he was quite unable to help laughing. But the next moment he was testily pointing out to her that she had made so thick a bandage round his arm as to prevent his being able to drag the sleeve of his coat over it.

'Well, the sleeve is quite spoilt, so it is of no consequence,' said Sophy. 'You may button the coat across your chest, and I will fashion you a sling for your arm. To be sure, it is only a flesh wound, but it will very likely start to bleed again, if you do not hold your arm up. Let us go downstairs, and see whether Mathilda has yet made tea for us!'

Not only had the harassed Mrs Clavering done so, but she had sent the gardener's boy running off to the village to summon to her assistance a stout, red-cheeked damsel, whom she proudly presented to Sophy as her sister's eldest. The damsel, bobbing a curtsy, disclosed that her name was Clementina. Sophy, feeling that Lacy Manor might be required to house several persons that night, directed her to collect blankets and sheets, and to set them to air before the kitchen fire. Mrs Clavering, still toiling to make the breakfast-parlour habitable, had set the tea-tray in the hall, where the fire had begun to burn more steadily. Puffs of smoke still from time to time gushed into the room, but Lord Charlbury, pressed into a deep chair, and given a cushion for the support of his injured arm, felt that it would have been churlish to have animadverted upon this circumstance. The tea, which seemed to have lost a little of its fragrance through its long sojourn in the panty cupboard, was accompanied by some slices of bread-and-butter and a large, and rather heavy plum-cake, of which Sophy partook heartily. Outside, the rain fell heavily, and the sky became so leaden that very little light penetrated into the low-pitched rooms of the Manor. A stringent search failed to discover any other candles than tallow ones, but Mrs Clavering soon brought a lamp into the hall, which, as soon as she had drawn the curtains across the windows, made the apartment seem excessively cosy, Sophy informed Lord Charlbury.

It was not long before their ears were assailed by the sound of an arrival. Sophy jumped up at once. 'Sancia!' she said, and cast her guest a saucy smile. 'Now you may be easy!' She picked up the lamp from the table, and carried it to the door, which she set wide, standing on the threshold, with the lamp held high to cast its light as far as possible. Through the driving rain she perceived the Marquesa's barouche-landau drawn up by the porch, and, as she watched, Sir Vincent Talgarth sprang out of the carriage, and turned to hand down the Marquesa. In another instant, Mr Fawnhope had also alighted, and stood transfixed, gazing at the figure in the doorway, while the rain beat unheeded upon his uncovered head.

'Oh, *Sophie*, why?' wailed the Marquesa, gaining the shelter of the porch. 'This rain — ! My dinner! It is too bad of you!'

Sophy, paying no heed to her plaints, addressed herself fiercely to Sir Vincent. 'Now, what the deuce does this mean? Why have you accompanied Sancia, and why the *devil* have you brought Augustus Fawnhope?'

He was shaken by gentle laughter. 'My dear Juno, do let me come in out of the wet! Surely your own experience of Fawnhope must have taught you that one does not *bring* him: he comes! He was reading the first two acts of his tragedy to Sancia when your messenger arrived. Until the light failed, he continued to do so during the drive.' He raised his voice, calling: 'Come into the house, rapt poet! You will be soaked if you stand there any longer!'

Mr Fawnhope started, and moved forward.

'Oh, well!' said Sophy, making the best of things. 'I suppose he must come in, but it is the greatest mischance!'

'It is you!' announced Mr Fawnhope, staring at her. 'For a moment, as you stood there, the lamp held above your head, I thought I beheld a goddess! A goddess, or a vestal virgin!'

'Well, if I were you,' interposed Sir Vincent practically, 'I would come in out of the rain while you make up your mind.'

Seventeen

Lady Ombersley, and her daughters, driving soberly home from Richmond, in the late afternoon, reached Berkeley Square to find Miss Wraxton awaiting their return. After affectionately embracing Lady Ombersley, she explained that she had ventured to sit down to wait for her, since she was the bearer of a message from her mama. Lady Ombersley, feeling a little anxious about Amabel, who was looking tired and had complained of a slight head-ache on the way home, answered absently: 'Thank your Mama so much, my dear. Amabel, come up to my dressing-room, and I will bathe your forehead with vinegar! You will be better directly, my love!'

'Poor little dear!' said Miss Wraxton. 'She looks sadly peaked still! You know, ma'am, that we have put off our black gloves. Mama is desirous of holding a dress-party in honour of the approaching Event – quite a small affair, for so many people of consequence are out of town! – but she would not for the world fix upon a day that will not suit your arrangements. You behold in me her envoy!'

'So kind of her!' murmured her ladyship. 'We shall be most happy – any day that your mother likes to appoint: we have very few engagements at present! Excuse me, I must not stay! Amabel is not quite well yet, you know! Cecilia will arrange it with you. Say everything from me to your Mama which is proper! Come, dearest!'

She led her youngest daughter to the stairs as she spoke, quite failing to perceive that Cecilia, to whom Dassett had silently handed Sophy's note, was not attending to a word she said. Under the butler's interested gaze, Cecilia, reading the letter in the blankest amazement, had turned alarmingly pale. She looked up, as she reached the end, and started forward, her lips parted, as though she would have recalled her mother. She recollected herself in a moment, and tried to be calm. But the hands with which she folded Sophy's letter shook perceptibly, and her whole appearance was that of one who had sustained a severe shock. Miss Wraxton observed it, and moved towards her, saying solicitously: 'You are not quite well, I am afraid! You have not received bad news?'

Dassett, whose fingers had itched to break open the wafer that sealed Sophy's letter, coughed, and said disinterestedly: 'Will Miss Stanton-Lacy be returning to town this evening, miss? Her abigail is in quite a taking, not having had any notion that Miss was going into the country.'

Cecilia looked at him in rather a dazed way, but pulled herself together sufficiently to reply with tolerable composure: 'Yes, I think so. Oh, yes, certainly she will come back tonight!'

If this answer failed to gratify Dassett's thirst for knowledge, it at least made Miss Wraxton prick up her ears. Taking Cecilia's arm, she led her towards the library, saying in her well-modulated voice: 'The drive has fatigued you. Be so good, Dassett, as to bring a glass of water to the library, and some smelling-salts! Miss Rivenhall is feeling a trifle faint.'

Cecilia, whose constitution was not strong, was indeed feeling faint, and could only be grateful when obliged to lie down upon the sofa in the library. Miss Wraxton deftly removed her pretty bonnet, and began to chafe her hands, abstracting from one of them the note which Cecilia was feebly clutching. Dassett soon came in with the desired requirements, which Miss Wraxton took from him, with a calm word of thanks and of dismissal. The faintness, which had only been momentary, was already passing off, and Cecilia was able to sit up, to sip the water, and to refresh herself with a few sniffs at the smelling-bottle. Miss Wraxton, meanwhile, in the most assured manner possible, had picked up Sophy's letter, and was making herself mistress of its contents.

'*You wondered, dearest Cecy, why, at the last, I would not accompany you to Richmond. Let this note be my explanation! I have thought long over the unfortunate situation in which you are placed, and I see only one way to put an end to the distress you have been made to suffer through my uncle's implacable determination to see you married to C. I believe him to have been strengthened in this resolve by C. himself, but I will not pain you by writing more on this subject. Were C. removed, I cannot but believe that my uncle must soon relent towards F.*

'*Charles will tell you that we have quarrelled. While the original fault I must own to have been mine, his manner to me, the language he held — so violent, so uncontrolled! — makes it impossible for me to remain any longer under this roof. I am removing immediately to Lacy Manor, and have prevailed upon C. to be my escort. Trust me to make it impossible for him to leave Lacy Manor tonight! He is a gentleman, and although his heart can never be mine, his hand I am persuaded he must offer me, and you may be easy at last.*

'*Do not fear for me! You are aware of my wish to establish myself, and although my affections are no more engaged than C.'s and I must shrink from the means his indifference forces me to employ, I daresay we shall contrive to rub along tolerably together. If I can be of assistance to you in this way, my dearest cousin, I shall have my reward. Ever your devoted Sophy.*'

'Good God!' exclaimed Miss Wraxton, startled out of her calm. 'Is this possible? Bad though I have thought her conduct, I would not have believed that she could have gone to such lengths as this! Unhappy girl! There is not a word of contrition! No breath of shame! My poor Cecilia, I do not wonder that you should find yourself overcome! You have been wretchedly deceived!'

'Oh, what are you about?' Cecilia cried, starting up. 'Eugenia, you had no right to read my letter! Give it to me at once, if you please, and never dare to mention its contents to a living soul!'

Miss Wraxton handed it to her, but said: 'Rather than have me summon Lady Ombersley to you, I thought you would prefer that I should discover what had so much upset you. As for not mentioning the contents, I imagine this news must be all over London by tomorrow! I do not know when I have been so much shocked!'

'All over London! No, that it shall not be!' Cecilia said vehemently. 'Sophy – Charlbury! It cannot, *must* not be! I shall set out for Ashtead immediately. How could she do such a thing? How *could* she? It is all her goodness – her wish to help me, but how dare she go off with Charlbury?' She tried to read the letter again, but crumpled it in her hand, shuddering. 'A quarrel with Charles! Oh, but she must know he does not mean the things he says when he is in a rage! She *does* know it! He shall go with me to fetch her home! Where is he? Someone must go at once to White's!'

Miss Wraxton, who had been thinking, laid a detaining hand on her arm. 'Pray calm yourself, Cecilia! Consider a little! If your unfortunate cousin has quarrelled so bitterly with Charles, very likely his going could only do more harm than good. I believe you are right in this, however, that it will not do to let matters take their course. The scandal that must result would be such as none of us could contemplate without revulsion. I dread the effect it may have upon dear Lady Ombersley above everything. The wretched girl must be rescued from herself.'

'And Charlbury!' Cecilia interjected, wringing her hands. 'It is all my folly! I must set out at once!'

'You shall do so, and I will go with you,' said Miss Wraxton nobly. 'Only permit me sufficient time, while you order your Papa's chaise to be got ready, to write a note for my mother. I daresay one of the servants would carry it round to Brook Street for me. I shall inform her merely that I have been persuaded to pass the evening with you here, and she will not find it remarkable.'

'You!' exclaimed Cecilia, staring at her. 'Oh, no, no! I mean, it is excessively kind in you, dear Eugenia, but I had rather you did not come!'

'You will scarcely go alone,' Miss Wraxton reminded her.

'Sophy's maid shall accompany me. I beg of you, do not let a word of this pass your lips!'

'My dear Cecilia, surely you will not permit a servant into your confidence? As well tell the town-crier! If you will not accept my company, I must think myself obliged to divulge the whole to Lady Ombersley. I consider it my duty to go with you, and I am persuaded it is what Charles would desire me to do. *My* being at Lacy Manor must lend propriety to the whole; for an engaged woman, you know, stands upon a different footing from an unattached girl.'

'Oh, I do not know what to say! I wish to heaven you had never set eyes on Sophy's letter!'

'I think it may be as well for all of us that I did set eyes on it,' replied Miss Wraxton, with a smile. 'You are scarcely in a fit state, dear Cecilia, to conduct this delicate affair with any degree of composure, let me tell you. Which is it to be! Shall I go with you, or do you prefer me to lay the whole before your Mama?'

'Very well, come then!' Cecilia said, almost pettishly. 'Though why you should wish to, when I know very well that you dislike Sophy amazingly, I am at a loss to understand!'

'Whatever my sentiments towards your cousin may be,' pronounced Miss Wraxton, looking quite saintly, 'I trust that I may never forget my duty as a Christian.'

The ready colour flooded Cecilia's cheeks. She was a gentle girl, but this speech made her so cross that she said waspishly: 'Well, I daresay Sophy will contrive to make you look foolish, because she always does, and it will serve you right, Eugenia, for meddling in what does not concern you!'

But Miss Wraxton, knowing that her hour of triumph had arrived, merely smiled in an irritating way, and recommended her to think what would be best to say to her mama.

Cecilia replied with dignity that she knew just what she should say, and moved towards the door. Before she had reached it, it was opened, and Dassett came in again, this time to inform her that Lord Bromford had called, and desired the favour of a word with her.

'You should have denied me!' Cecilia said. 'I cannot see Lord Bromford now!'

'No, miss,' said Dassett. 'But his lordship seems quite set on seeing either you, or her ladyship, miss, and her ladyship is with Miss Amabel and does not wish to be disturbed.' He gave his deprecating cough. 'I should perhaps mention that his lordship, knowing that Miss Sophy has gone out of town, is extremely wishful to learn of her direction.'

'Who told him that Miss Sophy is gone out of town?' Cecilia said sharply.

'That I could not take it upon myself to say, miss. Not having received any orders to the contrary, I did not consider it my place to deny the fact, when his lordship condescended to enquire of me if it was true.'

Cecilia cast rather a helpless glance at Miss Wraxton, who at once took the conduct of affairs into her capable hands.

'Pray desire his lordship to step into this room!' she said.

Dassett bowed, and withdrew.

'Eugenia! Take care what you are about! What do you mean to say to him!'

Miss Wraxton replied gravely: 'That must depend upon circumstances. We do not know how much he is aware of, and we ought not to forget that *he* has as much interest in your cousin as any of us.'

'No such thing!' Cecilia said. 'Sophy would never marry him!'

'She has certainly shown herself unworthy of his devotion. I hope she may not have cause to be thankful to marry *any* respectable man who offers for her.'

Since Lord Bromford was ushered into the room at that moment, Cecilia was spared the necessity of answering her.

His lordship was looking extremely anxious, but no anxiety could suffice to make him abate the formality of his greetings. These were performed with great punctilio, nor did he forget to make civil enquiry after the state of Amabel's health. He then begged pardon for importuning Miss Rivenhall to grant him an audience, and, after only a little circumlocution, came to the point of his visit. He had seen Miss Stanton-Lacy driving along Piccadilly in a hack-chaise and four, Lord Charlbury beside her, and baggage tied on behind the chaise.

'My cousin has been called suddenly out of town,' said Cecilia, in a cool tone that might have been expected to have damped pretension.

'With only that fellow for her companion!' he exclaimed, very much shocked. 'Besides – and this is a circumstance which makes it appear the more extraordinary – I was engaged to drive out with her this afternoon!'

'She had forgotten,' Cecilia said. 'She will be so sorry! You must forgive her.'

He regarded her intently for a moment, and what he saw in her face caused him to turn towards her companion, and to say earnestly: 'Miss Wraxton, I appeal to you! It is useless to tell me that Miss Stanton-Lacy has not left London clandestinely! How should Rivenhall have permitted her to go off in such a fashion? Pardon me, but Charlbury's attentions – marked, you will agree, beyond the bounds of propriety! – have given rise to the most dreadful suspicions in my mind. It cannot be unknown to you that I have an interest there myself! I had flattered myself that upon Sir Horace Stanton-Lacy's return to England – But this sudden departure – baggage strapped on behind, too!' he stopped, apparently overcome.

Miss Wraxton said smoothly: 'Miss Stanton-Lacy is at all times impatient of convention. She has driven down to her home at Ashtead, but I am confident that the persuasions of Miss Rivenhall and myself must weigh with her, and she will return to London with us tonight. We are about to set forth for Ashtead immediately.'

He seemed to be much struck, and said at once: 'This is like you! I understand you, I believe! I have known that fellow for a libertine these many weeks! Depend upon it, he has quite taken her in! Does Rivenhall accompany you?'

'We go alone,' Miss Wraxton said. 'You have guessed the truth, and will readily appreciate that our endeavours now must be fixed on keeping this unhappy event from the ears of the world.'

'Yes, indeed!' he said eagerly. 'But it is not to be thought of that two delicately nurtured females should undertake such a mission, unsupported by the firmness of a man! I think I should escort you. I think it is what I should do. I shall call Charlbury to book. His conduct in this affair has shown me what he is. He has grossly deceived Miss Stanton-Lacy, and shall answer for it!'

An indignant protest rose to Cecilia's lips, but Miss Wraxton intervened swiftly, to say: 'Your sentiments do you honour, and, for my own part, I must say that I shall be grateful to you for the protection of your escort. Only the most stringent necessity could prevail upon me to undertake such a mission without the support of a responsible gentleman!'

'I will have my horse saddled at once!' he announced, in a voice of stern resolution. 'I can tell you, it will be wonderful if I do not call Charlbury out! I am not, in general, an advocate of the barbarous custom of duelling, but circumstances, you know, alter cases, and such conduct must not go unpunished! I will be off home on the instant, and shall be with you again in the least time possible!'

He barely stayed to grasp both their hands before hurrying from the room. Cecilia, fairly weeping with annoyance, began to upbraid Miss Wraxton, but this lady, losing not a jot of her self-possession, replied: 'It was unfortunate that he should have been aware of Miss Stanton-Lacy's elopement, perhaps, but it could do no good to leave *that* suspicion in his mind. I own, the presence of a man of sense will be a comfort to me, and if, my dear Cecilia, his chivalrous nature should prompt him to renew his offer for your cousin's hand, it would be a solution to all our difficulties, and, I must add, a great deal more than she deserves!'

'That prosy bore!' Cecilia exclaimed.

'I am aware that Lord Bromford's merits have consistently been undervalued in this house. For my part, I have found him a sensible man, feeling just as he ought upon serious subjects, and having a great deal of interesting information to impart to those who are not too frivolous to attend to him.'

Unable to control her swelling emotions, Cecilia ran out of the room, more than half inclined to take her mother fully into her confidence.

But Lady Ombersley, finding that Amabel's pulse was too rapid, was so wholly absorbed in the sufferer as to have little attention to spare for anyone else. Knowing the delicate state of her parent's nerves, Cecilia forbore to add to her anxieties. She told her merely that a message from Lacy Manor had taken Sophy post-haste into Surrey, but that since she felt it to be unfitting for her cousin to remain in a deserted house alone, she was setting out, either to bear her company or to persuade her to return to London. Upon Lady Ombersley's showing some astonishment, she divulged that Sophy had quarrelled with Charles. This distressed Lady Ombersley, but scarcely surprised her. Too well did she know her son's bitter tongue! She would not have had such a thing happen for the world, and must, she said, have gone after Sophy herself had not Amabel seemed so unwell. She did not like to think of her daughter's travelling alone, but upon hearing of Miss Wraxton's resolve to go with her was able to be tranquil again, and to give her permission for the journey.

Meanwhile, Miss Wraxton, busily writing in the library, was unable to resist the temptation of inscribing a note to her betrothed, as well as to her mama. Now, at last, Charles should be brought to acknowledge the moral turpitude of his cousin, and her own magnanimity! She gave both notes to Dassett, with instructions for their immediate delivery; and was presently able to climb into the Ombersley travelling-chaise in the happy consciousness of having punctiliously performed her duty. Not even Cecilia's pettishness had the power to allay her self-satisfaction. Never had Cecilia shown herself so out of temper! She replied to her companion's moralizings with the briefest of monosyllables, and was even so unfeeling, when the rain began to fall, as to refuse point-blank to have the third seat in the chaise pulled out to accommodate Lord Bromford, riding unhappily behind the vehicle, with his coat collar turned up, and an expression on his face of the most acute misery. Miss Wraxton represented to her the propriety of desiring one of the out-riders to lead his lordship's horse, while his lord-ship travelled in comfort within the chaise; but all Cecilia could find to say was that she hoped the odious man would contract an inflammation of the lungs, and die of it.

Scarcely an hour later, Dassett was as nearly put out of countenance as it was possible for a person of his dignity and experience to be by the arrival in Berkeley Square of a second post-chaise. This, also a hack-vehicle, was drawn by four sweating horses, and was caked in mud up to the axles. A number of trunks and portmanteaux were piled on the back, and on the roof. A soberly-dressed individual first jumped down, and ran up the steps of the Ombersley mansion to set the bell pealing. By the time the door had been opened by a footman, and Dassett stood ready to receive guests upon the threshold, a much larger figure had descended in a leisurely way from the chaise, and, after tossing a couple of guineas to the postilions, and exchanging a jovial word with them, trod unhurriedly up the steps to the door.

Dassett, who afterwards described his condition to the house-keeper, as fairly flummoxed, found himself unable to do more than stammer: 'Go-good-evening, sir! We – we were not expecting you, sir!'

'Wasn't expecting myself,' said Sir Horace, stripping off his gloves. 'Devilish good voyage! Not a day above two months at sea! Tell your people to see all that lumber of mine carried into the house! Her ladyship well?'

Dassett, helping him to struggle out of his caped greatcoat, said that her ladyship was as well as could be looked for.

'That's good,' said Sir Horace, walking over to a large mirror, and bestowing an expert touch or two upon his cravat. 'How's my daughter?'

'I – I believe Miss Sophy to be enjoying excellent health, sir!'

'Ay, she always does. Where is she?'

'I regret to inform you, sir, that Miss Sophy has gone out of town,' replied Dassett, who would have been pleased to have discussed the mystery of Sophy's disappearance with almost anyone else.

'Oh? Well, I'll see her ladyship,' said Sir Horace, displaying, in the butler's opinion, an unnatural want of interest in his only child's whereabouts.

Dassett took him up to the drawing-room, and left him there while he went in search of her ladyship's maid. Amabel having just dropped off to sleep, it was not many minutes before Lady Ombersley came hurrying into the drawing-room, and almost cast herself upon her brother's manly bosom. 'Oh, my dear Horace!' she exclaimed. 'How glad I am to see you! How sorry to think – But you are safely home!'

'Well, there's no need for you to ruin my necktie, just because of that, Lizzie!' said her undemonstrative relative, disengaging himself from her embrace. 'Never been in any danger that I knew of! You don't look very stout! In fact, you look quite knocked-up! What's amiss? If it's stomach trouble, I knew a fellow once, ten times worse than ever you were, who got himself cured by magnetism and warm ale. Fact!'

Lady Ombersley made haste to assure him that if she looked knocked-up it was only through anxiety, and began at once to tell him about Amabel's illness, dwelling fondly on Sophy's goodness through this trying period.

'Oh, Sophy's a capital nurse!' he said. 'How do you go on with her? Where is the girl?'

This question flustered Lady Ombersley quite as much as it had flustered Dassett. She faltered that Sophy would be so sorry! If only she had guessed that her Papa was on his way to London she would surely not have gone.

'Yes, Dassett said she was gone out of town,' responded Sir Horace, disposing his large limbs in an easy chair, and crossing one shapely leg over the other. 'Never expected to find any of you here at this season, but, of course, if one of the children is ill, that explains it. Where's Sophy gone to?'

'I think – I was busy with Amabel when Cecilia told me, but I think she said that dearest Sophy had gone down to Lacy Manor!'

He looked surprised. 'What the deuce should take her there? The place ain't fit to live in! Don't tell me Sophy's putting it to rights, because I'm by no means sure – However, never mind that!'

'No, no, I don't think she had any such idea! At least -- Oh, Horace, I don't know what you will say to me, but I very much fear that Sophy has run away from us because of something that happened today!'

'Shouldn't think so at all,' said Sir Horace coolly. 'Not like my little Sophy to enact you a Cheltenham tragedy. What did happen?'

'I do not properly understand it: I was not here! But Cecilia seemed to think that – that Sophy and Charles had fallen out! Of course, I know he has a dreadful temper, but I am persuaded he cannot have meant – And Sophy has never before taken the least notion when he – Because it is not the first time they have quarrelled!'

'Well, don't put yourself in a taking, Lizzie,' recommended Sir Horace, maintaining his placidity without effort. 'Fallen out with Charles, eh? Well, I thought she would. Daresay it will do him good. How's Ombersley?'

'Really, Horace!' said his sister indignantly. 'One would suppose you not to have a scrap of affection for dear Sophy!'

'You're out there, old lady, for I'm devilish fond of her,' he returned. 'That don't mean I'm going to make a cake of myself over her tricks, though. Daresay she wouldn't thank me. You may depend upon it she's up to some mischief!'

As Dassett came in at this moment, with suitable refreshment for the traveller, the conversation had to be suspended. When he had withdrawn, Lady Ombersley resumed it, saying: 'At least I am able to assure you that you will see Sophy tonight, for Cecilia has gone with Miss Wraxton to bring her back!'

'Who's Miss Wraxton?' enquired Sir Horace, pouring himself out a glass of Madeira.

'If you ever listened to a word anyone says to you, Horace, you would know that Miss Wraxton is the lady Charles is about to marry!'

'Well, why didn't you say so?' said Sir Horace, sipping his wine. 'Can't expect me to carry a lot of names in my head! I remember now, though: girl you said was a dead bore.'

'I never said any such thing!' retorted Lady Ombersley. 'To be sure, I cannot quite like – But it was you who said she sounded to you like a dead bore!'

'If I said it, you may depend upon it I was right. Quite a tolerable wine, this. Now I come to think of it, you told me Cecilia was in a way to be married too: Charlbury, ain't it?'

Lady Ombersley sighed. 'Alas, it went off! Cecilia could not be brought to accept him. And now Charles has ceased to object so very much to Augustus Fawnhope, and although Ombersley says he will never countenance it, I daresay he will. You may as well know, Horace, that Lord Charlbury has been showing Sophy a great deal of most distinguishing attention.'

'Has he, by Jupiter?'

They were interrupted by the sound of an impatient step on the stair, to be following an instant later by the hasty entrance into the room of Mr Rivenhall, who held an open sheet of letter-paper in one hand, and had not stayed even to divest himself of his driving-coat before dashing upstairs in search of his mother.

Mr Rivenhall was looking extremely forbidding, and also a little pale. After stabling the chestnut that afternoon, he had first gone off to Bond Street, to work off some of his fury in a sparring-bout with Gentleman Jackson, and had then repaired to

White's, where he had spent an hour playing billiards, and fighting an impulse to go back to Berkeley Square, to tell his provoking cousin that he had not meant a word of it. It was when he left the billiard-room that he encountered his friend Mr Wychbold. Mr Wychbold, obedient to his orders, asked him whither Miss Stanton-Lacy was bound; and upon his replying curtly: 'Nowhere, to my knowledge,' said, not without an inward qualm: 'Yes, she is, dear boy! Saw her driving off in a post-chaise and four. What's more, she had Charlbury with her.'

Mr Rivenhall stared at him. 'Driving off in a post-chaise and four? You are certainly mistaken!'

'Couldn't have been!' said Mr Wychbold, sustaining his rôle manfully.

'Foxed, then. My cousin is at home!' He added, as his friend seemed inclined to argue the matter: 'What's more, Cyprian, I'll thank you not to spread such a tale about the town!'

'No, no, shouldn't dream of doing so!' Mr Wychbold made haste to assure him.

Mr Rivenhall then went off to the subscription-room, with the intention of playing a rubber or two of whist. The tables were all made up, and it was while he stood watching the play of a hand, his eyes on the cars, and his mind dwelling obstinately and uneasily on Mr Wychbold's ridiculous delusion, that Miss Wraxton's note was brought to him. The perusal of it had the effect of instantly killing any desire to play whist, and of sending him off to Berkeley Square without one word of excuse to those who had invited him to take part in the next rubber. He let himself into the house, found Sophy's letter to him laid upon the table in the hall, read it, and straightway went up the stairs two at a time in search of Lady Ombersley.

'Perhaps, Mama, you may be able to explain to me –' he began to say, in a furious voice, and then broke off short, perceiving that she was not alone. 'I beg your pardon! I did not know –' Again he broke off, as Sir Horace raised his quizzing-glass, the better to observe him. 'Oh!' he said, a wealth of sinister meaning in his voice. 'So it's you, is it, sir? Famous! You could not have come at a better moment!'

Shocked at the most unrespectful tone he had adopted, Lady Ombersley ventured on a feeble protest. 'Charles! Pray – !'

He paid no heed to her, but strode forward into the room. 'You will no doubt like to know, sir, that your precious daughter has gone off with Everard Charlbury!' he announced.

'Has she?' said Sir Horace. 'What has she done that for, I wonder? *I've* no objection to her marrying Charlbury! Good family; handsome property!'

'She did it,' said Mr Rivenhall, 'to infuriate me! And as for her marrying Charlbury she will do no such thing!'

'Oh, won't she?' said Sir Horace, keeping his glass levelled on his nephew's face. 'Who says so?'

'*I* say so!' snapped Mr Rivenhall. 'What is more, she has not the smallest intention of such a thing! If you do not know your daughter, I do!'

Lady Ombersley, who had listened in speechless dismay to this interchange, now found enough voice to say faintly: 'No, no, she would not run away with Charlbury! You must be mistaken! Alas, Charles, I fear this is your doing! You must have been dreadfully unkind to poor Sophy!'

'Oh, dreadfully unkind, ma'am! I actually had the brutality to take exception to her stealing the young chestnut from my stables, and, without one word to me, driving him in the Park! That she is not lying with a broken neck at this moment is no fault of hers!'

'Now, that,' said Sir Horace fair-mindedly, 'was wrong of her! In fact, I'm surprised to hear of her behaving so improperly, for it is not at all like her. What should have got into her to make her do such a thing?'

'Merely her damnable desire to pick a quarrel with me!' said Mr Rivenhall bitterly. 'I see it all now, clearly enough, and if she is not careful she will find she has succeeded better than she bargained for!'

'I am afraid, my boy,' said his uncle, an irrepressible twinkle in his eyes, 'that you do not like my little Sophy!'

'Your *little* Sophy, sir, has not allowed me – us! – one moment's peace or comfort since she descended upon this house!' said Mr Rivenhall roundly.

'Charles, you shall not say so!' cried his mother, flushing. 'It is unjust! How can you – how *can* you, when you recall her good-ness, her devotion – !' Her voice failed; she groped blindly for her handkerchief.

The colour rose also to Mr Rivenhall's cheeks. 'I do not forget that, ma'am. But this exploit – !'

'I cannot think where you can have had such a notion! It is untrue! Sophy went away because of the intemperate language you used towards her, and as for imagining that Charlbury was with her –'

'I know he was with her!' he interrupted. 'If I needed proof, I have it in this note she was so obliging as to leave for me! She makes no secret of it!'

'In that case,' said Sir Horace, refilling his glass, 'she is certainly up to some mischief. Try this Madeira, my boy: I'll say this for your father, he's a capital judge of a wine!'

'But, Charles, this is terrible!' gasped Lady Ombersley. 'Thank heaven I did not forbid Cecilia to go after her! Only think what a scandal! Oh, Horace, pray believe I had no suspicion!'

'Lord, *I'm* not blaming you, Elizabeth! I told you not to let Sophy worry you! Well able to take care of herself: always was!'

'I declare, Horace, you pass all bounds! Is it *nothing* to you that your daughter is in a fair way to ruining herself?'

'Ruining herself!' said Mr Rivenhall contemptuously. 'Do you indeed believe in such a fairy-tale, ma'am? Have you lived with my cousin for six months without getting her measure? If that Spanish woman is not also at Lacy Manor at this moment I give you leave to call me a blockhead!'

'Oh, Charles, I pray you may be right!'

Sir Horace began to polish his eyeglass with considerable assiduity. 'Sancia, eh? I was meaning to speak to you about her, Lizzie. Is she still at Merton?'

'Pray, where else should she be, Horace?'

'I just wondered,' he said, studying the result of his labours. 'I daresay Sophy may have told you of my intentions in that direction.'

'Of course she did, and I paid her a visit, as I suppose you must have wished me to do! But I must say, my dear Horace, that I cannot conceive what should possess you to offer for her!'

'That's the trouble,' he replied. 'One gets carried away, Lizzie! And there's no denying she's a devilish fine woman. In fact, it wouldn't have surprised me to have heard she had someone else dangling after her. Pity I settled her out at Merton! But there it is! One does these things on the spur of the moment, and it is not until one has had leisure to reflect – However, I don't mean to complain!'

'Plenty of beauties in Brazil, sir?' enquired his nephew sardonically.

'I don't want any of your impudence, my boy!' said Sir Horace genially. 'Fact of the matter is, I doubt if I'm a marrying man!'

'Well, if it's any consolation to you,' said Mr Rivenhall, 'you may know that my cousin has being doing her possible to hold Talgarth off from the Marquesa!'

'Now, why the devil,' demanded Sir Horace, roused to irritability, 'must Sophy meddle? Talgarth, eh? Didn't know he was in

England! Well, well! He has a great deal of address, has Vincent, and, what's more, I'll wager he has an eye to Sancia's fortune!'

Lady Ombersley, quite affronted, broke in on this, exclaiming: 'I think you are quite shameless! And what has all this to do with poor Sophy's escapade? You sit there, as though you had no concern in her affairs, while all the time she is trying to ruin herself! And you may say what you choose, Charles, but if it is true that she has gone off with Charlbury, it is the most shocking thing imaginable, and she must be brought back at once!'

'She will be!' said Mr Rivenhall. 'Can you doubt it, when you have sent off Cecilia and Eugenia, in the highest style of romance, to rescue her, ma'am?'

'I did no such thing! I knew nothing of this, but naturally I would not let your sister go alone, so when she told me that Eugenia had been kind enough to offer to accompany her, what could I do but be grateful?' She paused, struck by an unexplained circumstance. 'But how do you know that they went to rescue her, Charles? If Dassett is so lost to all sense of his position as to gossip to you −'

'No such thing! I am indebted to Eugenia herself for my information! And I must take leave to say, ma'am, that if you and my sister had been so obliging as to have kept this news to yourselves, I might have been spared a damned impertinent letter from Eugenia! What can have possessed you to have confided such a tale to her is something I can never cease to marvel at! Good God, don't you know that she will spread it all over town that my cousin has behaved outrageously?'

'But I did not!' almost wailed his mother. 'Charles, I did *not!*'

'One of you must have done so!' he said impatiently. He turned to his uncle. 'Well, sir, do you mean to remain there, commending my father's taste in wine, or do you mean to accompany me to Ashtead?'

'Set out for Ashtead at this hour, when I have been travelling for two days?' said Sir Horace. 'Now, do, my boy, have a little common-sense! Why should I?'

'I imagine that your parental feeling, sir, must provide you with the answer! If it does not, so be it! *I* am leaving immediately!'

'What do you mean to do when you reach Lacy Manor?' asked Sir Horace, regarding him in some amusement.

'Wring Sophy's neck!' said Mr Rivenhall savagely.

'Well, you don't need my help for that, my dear boy!' said Sir Horace, settling himself more comfortably in his chair.

Eighteen

THE FIRST FEW MINUTES FOLLOWING THE ARRIVAL OF THE Marquesa's party from Merton were taken up with that lady's freely expressed complaints of the situation in which she found herself. The draught occasioned by the opening of the front door had caused the fire to belch forth clouds of acrid smoke into the hall, and not all Mrs Clavering's distracted efforts had sufficed to make this apartment look other than neglected. Mrs Clavering, much impressed by the richness of the Marquesa's attire, stood bobbing curtsies to her; and the Marquesa, quite unimpressed by Mrs Clavering, said: '*Madre de Dios!* If I had brought Gaston it might then have been supportable, and if my cook as well, better still! Why must I come to you in this house, Sophie? Why do you send for me so suddenly, and when it is raining, moreover? *Su conducta es perversa!*'

Sophy at once told her that she had been summoned to play a duenna's part, an explanation which made an instant appeal to one in whose veins ran the purest Castilian blood. So well-satisfied was the Marquesa that she forgot to enquire why Sophy had placed herself in a situation that required the attendance of any other duenna than her aunt, but said approvingly that Sophy had conducted herself with great propriety, and she grudged no fatigue in such a cause. After that, she became aware of Charlbury's presence, and with an effort of memory even recalled his name.

'Hallo, are you hurt?' Sir Vincent asked, nodding at his lordship's arm-sling. 'How came that about?'

'Never mind that!' said Sophy, relieving Charlbury of the necessity of answering. 'Why are *you* here, Sir Vincent?'

'That, my dear Juno,' he replied, his eyes glinting at her, 'is a long and delicate story. I might, you know, ask the same question. I shan't, of course, because explanations are apt to be tedious, and what is teasing me more at this present is the far more important subject of dinner. I fear you may not have been expecting so large a party?'

'No, I was not, and heaven knows what we shall find to eat!' Sophy admitted. 'I think, perhaps, I should go into the kitchen, and discover what there may be in the larder. For it is very likely, I must tell you, that my cousin Cecilia will arrive to dine here. And more than probably Charles also!'

'Oh, Miss Sophy, if only you'd have given us warning!' exclaimed Mrs Clavering distressfully. 'I'm sure I don't know how to contrive dinner, not for the likes of you, miss, for I am not accustomed, and there's nothing ready but a pig's cheek, which Clavering fancied for his supper!'

'It is evident,' said the Marquesa, removing the plumed hat from her luxuriant curls, and laying it down on a chair, 'that this *moza de cocina* knows nothing, so that I must exert myself a little. That is bad, but worse, *infinitamente*, that we should starve. And you will remember it, Sophie, and be grateful to me, so that you do not quarrel with me! For I must tell you, *de una vez*, that I think it will not suit me to be married to Sir Horace after all, for he is very restless, and Brazil I should not like, but, on the contrary I will remain in England, but an English cook I will not have! So

I have married Sir Vincent, and I am now not the Marquesa de Villacañas, but Lady Talgarth, which is a name I cannot pronounce *convenientemente*, but no matter! One must accustom oneself.'

This speech not unnaturally stunned her audience into silence for several moments. Sir Vincent drew out his snuff-box, and delicately inhaled a pinch of his favourite mixture. It was he who broke the silence. 'So the murder is out!' he remarked. 'Do not look so aghast, Sophy! Remember that our dear Sancia is to cook the dinner!'

'This,' suddenly announced Mr Fawnhope, who had not been attending to a word of the conversation, 'is a singularly beautiful house! I shall go all over it.'

He then picked up the lamp from the table, and bore it off towards one of the doors that opened on to the hall. Sir Vincent took it from him, and restored it to its place, saying kindly: 'You shall do so, my dear young friend, but take this candle, if you please!'

'Sir Vincent,' said Sophy, a martial light in her eye, 'if I were a man, you would suffer for this *treachery*!'

'Dear Sophy, you shoot better than nine out of ten men of my acquaintance, so if any one of us had the forethought to bring with him a pair of duelling-pistols – ?'

'No one,' said the Marquesa, with decision, 'shall shoot a pistol, because it is of all things what I most detest, and, besides, it is more important that we should prepare dinner!'

'I suppose,' said Sophy regretfully, 'that that is true. One must eat! But I now perceive how right my cousin Charles was to warn me to have nothing to do with you, Sir Vincent! I did not think you would have served Sir Horace such a back-handed turn!'

'All is fair, dear Sophy, in love and war!' he said sententiously.

She was obliged to bite back the retort that sprang to her lips. He smiled understandingly, and moved towards her, taking her hand, and saying in a lowered voice: 'Consider, Juno! *My* need is far greater than Sir Horace's! How could I resist?'

'"*Amor ch'a nullo amato amar perdona*,"' dreamily remarked Mr Fawnhope, whose peregrinations about the hall had brought within earshot.

'Exactly so, my poet!' said Sir Vincent cordially.

'I need Miss Wraxton to translate that for me,' said Sophy, 'but if it means what I think it does it is no such thing! However, there is nothing more foolish than to be making a great noise over what cannot be helped, so I shall say no more. Besides, I have more important things to think of!'

'Certainly that is so,' agreed the Marquesa. 'There is a way of preparing fresh-killed chickens, so Vincent shall at once kill me two chickens, for chickens this woman tells me there are in abundance, and I shall contrive.'

She then withdrew with Mrs Clavering to the kitchen-premises, her demi-train of mull-muslin sweeping regally behind her over the floor, and picking up a great deal of dust on the way. Sophy and Sir Vincent followed her; and as Mr Fawnhope had by this time discovered the library, and had gone in to inspect the books by the light of his tallow candle, Lord Charlbury was left alone. He was soon rejoined by Sir Vincent, who came back into the hall bearing a crusted bottle, and some glasses. 'Sherry,' he said, setting down the glasses. 'If the slaughter of chickens is my fate, I must be fortified. But I trust I shall prevail upon the retainer to commit the actual deed. How *did* you hurt your arm?'

'Sophy put a bullet through it,' replied his lordship.

'Did she indeed? What a redoubtable female she is, to be sure! I suppose she had her reasons?'

'They were not what you might be pardoned for imagining!' retorted Charlbury.

'I never indulge commonplace thoughts,' said Sir Vincent,

carefully wiping the neck of the bottle, and beginning to pour out the wine. 'Not, at all events, in relation to the Grand Sophy. Here, try this! God knows how long it has lain in the cellar! I collect I don't drink to your elopement?'

'Good God, no!' said Charlbury, almost blenching at the thought. 'I am devoted to Sophy – quite and unalterably devoted to her! – but heaven preserve me from marriage with her!'

'If heaven did not, I fancy Rivenhall would,' observed Sir Vincent. 'This wine is perfectly tolerable. Don't finish the bottle before I come back, and don't waste it on the poet!'

He strolled off again, presumably to oversee the execution in the hen-roost, and Lord Charlbury, rendering up silent thanks for his wounded arm, poured himself out a second glass of sherry. After a short interval, Mr Fawnhope emerged from the library, bearing a worm-eaten volume in his hand. This he reverently displayed to his lordship, saying simply: '*La Hermosura de Angélica!* One never knows where one may light upon a treasure. I must show it to the Marquesa. Whose is this enchanting house?'

'Sir Horace Stanton-Lacy's,' replied Charlbury, in some amusement.

'Providence must have led me to it. I could not imagine what brought me here, but it doesn't signify. When I saw Sophy standing in the open doorway, holding aloft the lamp, the scales fell from my eyes, and all doubts were resolved. I am engaged to dine somewhere or other, but I shan't regard it.'

'You don't feel that you should perhaps ride back to town to keep your engagement?' suggested his lordship.

'No,' replied Mr Fawnhope simply. 'I prefer to be here. There is also a *Galatea*, but not an original copy.' He then sat down at the table, and opened the book, poring over it until interrupted by Sophy, who came in with a bundle of candles tucked under one arm, and a shallow wooden box held carefully between her hands. Beside her, a mixture of curiosity and jealousy, pranced her little greyhound, from time to time springing up to reach the box.

Mr Fawnhope leaped to his feet, and held out his hands to take the box from her. 'Give it to me! An urn you might bear, but not a sordid box!'

She relinquished it, saying practically: 'Mrs Clavering will bring that presently, but it is not yet time for the tea-tray, you know. We have not dined! Careful! Poor little things, they have no mother!'

'Sophy, what in the *world* – ?' exclaimed Charlbury, perceiving that the box contained a brood of yellow ducklings. 'You do not mean to cook these for dinner, I do trust?'

'Good gracious, no! Only Mr Clavering has been rearing them in the warmth of the kitchen, and Sancia complains that they will run under her feet. Set the box down in this corner, Augustus: Tina will not harm them!'

He obeyed her, and the ducklings, all vigorously cheeping, at once struggled out of the box, one of them, more venturesome than the rest, setting forth on an exploratory expedition. Sophy caught it, and held it cupped in her hands, while Tina, quite disgusted, jumped on to a chair, and lay down with her head pointedly averted. Mr Fawnhope's smile swept across his face, and he quoted: "'*Lo, as a careful housewife runs to catch One of her feather'd creatures broke away!*'"

'Yes, but I think that if we were to spread something over the top of the box they will not break away,' said Sophy. 'Charlbury's driving-coat will answer famously! You do not object, Charlbury?'

'Yes, Sophy, I do object!' he said firmly, removing the garment from her hands.

'Very well, then –' She stopped, for Tina had lifted her head, her ears on the prick, and had uttered a sharp bark. The sound of horses and of carriage-wheels was heard. Sophy turned to Mr Fawnhope, saying quickly: 'Augustus, pray will you step into the kitchen – you

will find it at the end of the passage at the back there! – and desire
Mrs Clavering to give you a cloth, or a blanket, or some such thing?
You need not make haste to return, for I daresay Sancia would like
you to pluck a chicken.'

'Is the Marquesa in the kitchen?' said Mr Fawnhope. 'What
is she doing there? I wish her to see this book I have found in
the library!'

Sophy picked it up from the table and gave it to him. 'Yes,
pray show it to her! She will like it excessively! Pay no heed if you
should chance to hear the door-bell: I will open the door!'

She fairly thrust him towards the door at the back of the hall
and, having seen him safely through it, shut it and said in a con-
spiratorial voice: 'Cecilia! Take care of the ducklings!'

She was still holding the one she had picked up, when she set
the front door wide. The rain had stopped, and the moonlight
showed through a break in the clouds. Hardly had Sophy opened
the door than her cousin almost fell upon her neck. 'Sophy! Oh,
my dearest Sophy – No, it was too shocking of you! You must
have known I could not wish – Sophy, Sophy, how *could* you do
such a thing?'

'Cecy, pray take care! This poor little duckling! Oh, good God!
Miss Wraxton!'

'Yes, Miss Stanton-Lacy, *I*!' said Miss Wraxton, joining the
group in the porch. 'You did not, I fancy, expect to see me!'

'No, and you will be very much in the way!' replied Sophy
frankly. 'Go in, Cecy!'

She gave her cousin a gentle push across the threshold as she
spoke. Cecilia stood transfixed, as Charlbury, rising from his chair
by the fire, stepped forward, his left arm interestingly reposing in
its sling. Cecilia was carrying a reticule and a feather-muff, but
she let both fall to the ground in her consternation. 'Oh!' she
exclaimed faintly. 'You are hurt! Oh, Charlbury!'

She moved towards him with both hands held out, and his lordship, acting with great presence of mind, hurriedly disengaged his arm from the sling, and received her in a comprehensive embrace. 'No, no, dearest Cecilia! The merest scratch!' he assured her.

Such heroism caused Cecilia to shed tears. 'It is all my fault! My wretched folly! I can never cease to blame myself! Charlbury, only tell me you forgive me!'

'Never, for wearing a hat which prevents my kissing you!' he said, with a shaken laugh.

She raised her head at that, smiling through her tears, and he contrived to kiss her in spite of the hat. Sophy, effectually blocking the entrance, observed this passage with all the air of one well-satisfied with her labours.

'Will you be good enough to allow us to enter?' said Miss Wraxton, in frozen accents.

'Us?' said Sophy, quickly looking round. She perceived a stout figure behind Miss Wraxton, in a soaked coat and a sodden beaver, and, after peering incredulously for a moment, exclaimed: 'Good God! Lord Bromford? Now, what the deuce does this mean?'

Cecilia, who had cast off her hat to join her muff on the floor, raised her head from the broad shoulder that was supporting it, to say huskily: 'Oh Sophy, pray do not be cross with me! Indeed, it was not my doing! Charlbury, what happened? How do you come to be hurt?'

His lordship, still clasping her to his bosom, rolled an anguished eye at Sophy. She came promptly to this rescue. 'Only a flesh wound, dearest Cecy! Footpads – or do I mean highwaymen? – yes, highwaymen! Just a flurry of shots, you know, and poor Charlbury had the misfortune to be hit! But they were driven off, and we took no other hurt. Charlbury behaved with the greatest presence of mind imaginable – perfectly cool, and *more* than a match for such rascals!'

'Oh, *Charlbury*!' sighed Cecilia, overcome by the thought of such intrepid conduct.

His lordship, soothingly patting her shoulder, could not resist asking: 'How many of the desperate ruffians did I vanquish, Sophy?'

'That,' said Sophy, quelling him with a frown, 'we shall never know!'

Miss Wraxton's cool voice broke in on this. However glad she might be to see Cecilia's difference with Charlbury made up, her sense of propriety was really lacerated by the spectacle of Cecilia nestling within his lordship's arm. 'My dear Cecilia, pray recollect yourself!' she said, blushing, and averting her gaze.

'I do not know what I should do!' suddenly announced Lord Bromford, in lamentable accents. 'I came with the purpose of calling this fellow to book, but I have caught a cold!'

'If that is to my address,' said Charlbury, 'a cold may well be the least of the ills that will shortly befall you! Don't tread on the ducklings!'

'No, indeed!' said Sophy, swooping on one that had narrowly escaped death under Bromford's foot. 'What a clumsy creature you are! Do, pray, take heed where you are stepping!'

'I should not be amazed if already I have a fever,' said Bromford, uneasily eyeing the ducklings. 'Miss Wraxton, these birds! One does not keep birds in the house! I do not understand why they are running all over the floor. There is another! I do not like it. It is not what I have been used to.'

'I hope, dear Lord Bromford, that nothing that has occurred this day is what either you or I has been used to,' responded Miss Wraxton. 'Do let me beg of you to take off that greatcoat! Believe that it was no wish of mine that you were compelled to ride through such a downpour! If you have done your constitution any lasting injury I can never forgive myself for having accepted your escort! Your boots are wet through! Nothing can be more fatal than chilled feet! Miss Stanton-Lacy, *is* it too much to request that a servant – I presume there is a servant here? – should be sent for to remove Lord Bromford's boots?'

'Yes, because he has gone out to kill chickens,' replied Sophy. 'Cecy, help me to collect the ducklings, and put them back into the box! If we were to place your muff on top of them they will very likely believe it to be their mother, and settle down!'

Cecilia having no fault to find with this scheme, it was at once put into execution. Miss Wraxton, who had coaxed Lord Bromford into a deep chair by the fire, said: 'This levity will not serve, Miss Stanton-Lacy! Even you will allow that your conduct demands some explanation! Are you aware of the terrible consequences which must have followed on this – this escapade, had your cousin and I not come to rescue you from the disgrace you appear to regardso lightly!'

Lord Bromford sneezed.

'Oh, hush, Eugenia!' begged Cecilia. 'How can you talk so? All's well that ends well!'

'You must be lost to every scruple of female delicacy, Cecilia, if you can think it *well* for your cousin to show such a brazen face, when she has lost both character and reputation!'

The door at the back of the hall opened to admit the Marquesa, a sacking-apron tied round her waist, and a large ladle in her hand. 'Eggs I must instantly have!' she announced. 'And Lope de Vega I will not have, though in general a fine poet, but not in the kitchen! Someone must go to the chicken-house, and tell Vincent to bring me eggs. Who are these people?'

It might have been supposed that the appearance on the scene of the Marquesa would have filled Miss Wraxton's Christian soul with relief, but no such emotion was visible in her countenance, which, on the contrary, froze into an expression of such chagrin as to be almost ludicrous. She could find not a word to say, and was unable to command herself enough even to shake hands with the Marquesa.

Lord Bromford, always punctilious, rose from his chair and bowed. Sophy presented him, and he begged pardon for having contracted what he feared would prove to be a dangerous cold. The Marquesa held him off with the ladle, saying: 'If you have a cold, do not approach me! Now I see that it is Miss Rivenhall, whose beauty is entirely English; and that other one, also in the English *estilo*, but less beautiful. I do not think two chickens will be enough, so that man with the cold must eat the pig's cheek. But eggs I must have!'

Having delivered herself of this ultimatum, she withdrew, paying not the smallest heed to Lord Bromford's agitated protest that all forms of pork were poison to him, and that a bowl of thin gruel was all that he felt himself able to swallow. He seemed to feel that Miss Wraxton was the only person amongst those present who was likely to sympathize with him, for he looked piteously at her. She responded at once, assuring him that he should not be asked to eat the pig's cheek. 'If it were possible to remove you from this draughty hall!' she said, casting an angry glance at Sophy. 'Had I known that I was coming to an establishment which appears to be something between a fowl-yard and Bedlam, I would never have set forth from town!'

'Well, I must say I wish you had known it, then,' said Sophy candidly. 'We could have been comfortable enough, if only you and Lord Bromford had minded your own business, and now I suppose we must make gruel, and mustard foot-baths!'

'A mustard foot-bath,' said Lord Bromford eagerly, 'would be the very thing! I do not say that it will entirely arrest the chill: we must not raise our hopes too high! but if we can prevent its descending upon the lungs it will be a great thing! Thank you! I am very much obliged to you!'

'Good gracious, you absurd creature, I did not mean it!' Sophy cried, breaking into laughter.

'No!' said Miss Wraxton. 'We may readily believe you have not a grain of womanly compassion, Miss Stanton-Lacy! Do not be uneasy, Lord Bromford! If any efforts of *mine* can save you from illness they shall not be spared!'

He pressed her hand in a speaking way, and allowed her to press him gently down again into his chair.

'Meanwhile,' said Charlbury, 'let us not forget that eggs the Marquesa must have! I had better try to find Talgarth and the hen-house.'

Sophy, who was looking thoughtful, said slowly: 'Yes. And I *think* – Charlbury, bring a candle into the breakfast-parlour, and let us see if it is warm enough yet for Lord Bromford to sit in!'

He went with her into this apartment, and had no sooner passed the doorway than she clasped his wrist, and said in an urgent undervoice: 'Never mind the eggs! Go to the stables, and direct the Ombersley servants to pole up the horses again! You may change them at the inn in the village, or, if not there, at Epsom! Take Cecilia back to London! Only think how embarrassing for her to be obliged to meet Augustus now! She would dislike it excessively! Besides, it is quite ridiculous for so many people to be crowded into the house, and not at all what I bargained for!'

He grimaced, but said: 'If I do it, will you go with us?'

'What, to sit bodkin between you? No, I thank you!'

'But I cannot leave you here!'

'Nonsense! It would not suit me at all to be going to London yet!'

He set the candlestick down, and took her hands in his, and held them firmly. 'Sophy, I owe you a debt of gratitude: thank you, my dear! You may command me in anything: shall I remove Miss Wraxton?'

'No, for I have had a capital notion about her. She shall stay to nurse Bromford, and very likely they will make a match of it!'

His shoulders shook. 'Oh, Sophy, Sophy!'

'No, do not laugh! I do feel I ought to make some provision for her, poor girl! I cannot permit her to marry Charles, and make them all unhappy at Ombersley House, but I am persuaded she and Bromford would deal extremely. Do not make me any more pretty speeches, but go down to the stables at once! I'll tell Cecy!'

She then thrust him back into the hall, and, while he let himself out of the house, went back to the group about the fire, and said: 'It is tolerably cosy in the parlour, and if you choose to sit there for a little while, Lord Bromford, one of the bed-chambers shall be prepared for you, and I will send Clavering to pull off your boots. Do you take him in, Miss Wraxton, and see him comfortably bestowed!'

'I trust the chimney may not smoke as badly as this one!' said Miss Wraxton acidly. 'Nothing could be worse! Lord Bromford has coughed twice already!'

'How shocking! You should take him away at once.'

His lordship, who was sitting in a miserable huddle, shivering and sneezing, thanked her in a feeble voice, and rose from his chair with Miss Wraxton's kindly help. Hardly had they gone into the parlour, than Mr Fawnhope came into the hall, saying severely: 'The drawing of hens is revolting! No one should be called upon to witness such an operation! The Marquesa must have eggs.'

Cecilia, who had given a violent start, and perceptibly changed colour, exclaimed: 'Augustus!'

'Cecilia!' said Mr Fawnhope, staring at her in astonishment. 'You were not here before, were you?'

'No,' she said, blushing furiously. 'Oh, no! I – I came with Miss Wraxton!'

'Oh, was that how it was?' he said, rather relieved. 'I did not think I had seen you.'

She said resolutely, but in some little agitation: 'Augustus, I will not trifle with you! I must tell you I find I have made a great mistake. I cannot marry you!'

'Noble, noble girl!' Mr Fawnhope said, much moved. 'I honour you for this frankness, and must ever deem myself fortunate to have been permitted to adore you. The experience has purified and strengthened me: you have inspired me with a poetic fervour for which the world may yet thank you, as I do! But marriage is not for such as I am. I must put aside the thought. I *do* put it aside! You should marry Charlbury, but my play you must allow me to dedicate to you!'

'Th-thank you!' faltered Cecilia, a good deal taken aback.

'Well, she is going to marry Charlbury,' said Sophy bracingly. 'And now that that is settled, Augustus, pray will you go and find the eggs for Sancia?'

'I know nothing of eggs,' he said. 'I fetched Talgarth from the cellar, and he has gone in search of them. I am going to write a poem that has been taking shape in my brain this past hour. Should you object if I entitled it *To Sophia, Holding a Lamp*?'

'Not in the least,' said Sophy affably. 'Take this candle, and go into the library! Shall I tell Clavering to light a fire there for you?'

'It is of no consequence, thank you,' he replied absently, receiving the candlestick from her, and wandering off in the direction of the library.

No sooner had the door closed behind him than Cecilia said, in some confusion: 'Has he understood me? Why did you not tell me that he was here, Sophy? I do not know how to look him in the face!'

'No, and you shall not be called upon to do so, dearest Cecy!

Charlbury has gone to order the chaise: you must go back to Berkeley Square immediately! Only conceive of my aunt's anxiety!'

Cecilia, who had been about to demur, wavered perceptibly at this. She was still wavering when Lord Charlbury came back to the house, cheerfully announcing that the chaise would be at the door in five minutes' time. Sophy at once picked up her cousin's hat, and fitted it becomingly over her sunny locks. Between her efforts, and those of Lord Charlbury, she was presently escorted, resistless, out of the house, and handed up into the chaise. His lordship, pausing only to bestow upon his benefactress a hearty embrace, jumped up after her; the steps were let up, the door slammed upon the happy couple, and the equipage was driven away. Sophy, having waved a last farewell from the porch, turned back into the house, where she found Miss Wraxton awaiting her, in an alarming state of frigidity. Miss Wraxton apprehending (she said) that no assistance from the Marquesa need be expected, desired to be conducted to the kitchen, where she proposed to brew a posset, used in her family for generations as a cure for colds. Not only did Sophy lead her to the kitchen, but she also quelled the Marquesa's protests, and commanded that the Claverings set water on to boil for a mustard foot-bath. The unfortunate Claverings, labouring up the back-stairs with coals, blankets, and cans of hot water, were kept fully occupied for nearly half an hour, at the end of which time, Lord Bromford was tenderly escorted upstairs to the best spare-bedroom, divested of his boots, and his coat, coaxed into the dressing-gown Sir Vincent had had the forethought to pack into his valise, and installed in a winged chair by the fire. Sir Vincent's protests at having not only his dressing-gown, but also his nightshirt and cap wrested from him were silenced by Sophy's representations that she herself was relinquishing to Miss Wraxton her portmanteau, with all the night-gear which it contained. 'And considering how unhandsome your behaviour has been, Sir Vincent, I must say that I shall think it excessively shabby of you if you demur at rendering me this small service!' she declared roundly.

He cocked an eyebrow at her. 'And you, Sophy? Will you not be remaining here for the night?' he laughed, seeing her at a loss for an answer, and said: 'In a previous age you would have been burnt at the stake, and rightly so, Juno! Very well: I will play your game!'

Within half an hour of this passage, Sophy, seated at the table in the hall, which she had drawn into the ingle-nook by the fire, heard the sound for which she had been waiting. She was engaged in building card-houses, having found an aged and grimy pack in the breakfast-parlour, and she made no attempt to answer the imperative summons of the bell. Clavering came into the hall from the back premises, looking harassed, and opened the door. Mr Rivenhall's decisive accents pleasurably assailed Sophy's ears. 'Lacy Manor? Very well! Be good enough to direct my groom to the stables! I'll announce myself!'

Mr Rivenhall then shut the aged servitor out of the house, and stepped into the hall, shaking the raindrops from his curly-brimmed beaver. His eye alighted on Sophy, absorbed in architecture, and he said with the greatest amiability imaginable: 'Good evening, Sophy! I am afraid you must have quite given me up, but it has been raining, you know, the moonlight quite obscured by clouds!'

At this point, Tina, who had been leaping up at him in an ecstasy of delight, began to bark, so he was obliged to acknowledge her welcome before he could again make himself heard. Sophy, laying a card delicately upon her structure, said; 'Charles, this is too kind in you! Have you come to rescue me from the consequences of my indiscretion?'

'No, to wring your neck!'

She opened her eyes at him. 'Charles! Don't you know that I have ruined my reputation?'

He took off his driving-coat, shook it, and cast it over a chair-back. 'Indeed? In that event, I am quite out: I was ready to swear I should find the Marquesa with you!'

The ready laughter sprang to her eyes. 'How odious you are! How came you to guess that?'

'I know you too well. Where's my sister?'

Sophy resumed her house-building. 'Oh, she has driven back to London with Charlbury! I daresay their chaise may have met you on your way.'

'Very likely. I was in no case to be studying the panels of chance vehicles. Did Miss Wraxton accompany them?'

She looked up. 'Now, how do you know that Miss Wraxton came with Cecilia?' she asked.

'She was so obliging as to send a note round to White's inform-ing me of her intention,' he replied grimly. 'Is she here still?'

'Well, she is, but I fancy she is very much occupied,' said Sophy. She bent to pick up one of the ducklings, which, awaken-ing from a refreshing slumber under Cecilia's muff, had climbed out of the box again, and was trying to establish itself in the flounces of her gown. 'Take this, dear Charles, while I pour you out a glass of sherry!'

Mr Rivenhall, automatically extended his hand, found himself in possession of a ball of yellow down. It did not seem to be worth while to enquire why he was given a duckling to hold, so he sat down on the table's edge, stroking the creature with one finger, and watching his cousin.

'That, of course,' said Sophy serenely, 'explains why you have come.'

'It explains nothing of the sort, and well you know it!' said Mr Rivenhall.

'How wet your coat is!' remarked Sophy, spreading it out before the fire. 'I do trust you may not have caught a chill!'

'Of course I have not caught a chill!' he said impatiently. 'Besides, it has not been raining this last half hour!'

She handed him a glass of sherry. 'I am so much relieved! Poor Lord Bromford contracted the most shocking cold! He had meant to have called Charlbury out, you know, but when he reached us he could only sneeze.'

'*Bromford?*' he exclaimed. 'You do not mean to tell me he is here?'

'Yes, indeed: Miss Wraxton brought him. I *think* she hoped he might have offered for me, and so saved my reputation, but the poor man was quite prostrated by this horrid chill, which he fears may descend upon his lungs. It puts all else out of his mind, and one cannot be surprised at it.'

'Sophy, are you trying to humbug me?' demanded Mr Rivenhall suspiciously. 'Even Eugenia would not bring that blockhead down upon you!'

'Miss Wraxton does not consider him a blockhead. She says he is a man of sense, and one who –'

'Thank you! I have heard enough!' he interrupted. 'Here, take this creature! Where is Eugenia?'

She received the duckling from him, and restored it to its brethren in the box. 'Well, if she is not still brewing possets in the kitchen, I expect you may find her with Bromford in the best spare-bedroom,' she replied.

'*What?*'

'Persuading him to swallow a little thin gruel,' explained Sophy, looking the picture of innocence. 'The second door at the top of the stairs, dear Charles!'

Mr Rivenhall tossed off the glass of sherry, set it down, informed his cousin ominously that he would deal with her presently, and strode towards the stairs, accompanied by Tina, who frisked gaily at his heels, apparently convinced that he was about to provide sport for her of no common order. Sophy went down the passage to inform the harassed Marquesa that although two of the dinner-guests had departed, another had appeared in their stead.

Mr Rivenhall, meanwhile, had mounted the stairs, and had, without ceremony, flung open the door of the best spare-bedroom. A domestic scene met his affronted gaze. In a chair drawn up beside a clear fire sat Lord Bromford, a screen drawn to protect his person from the draught from the window; both his feet in a steaming bath of mustard-and-water; a blanket reinforcing Sir Vincent's dressing-gown over his shoulders; and in his hands a bowl of gruel and a spoon. Hovering solicitously about him was Miss Wraxton, ready either to add more hot water to the bath from the kettle on the hob, or to replace the bowl of gruel with the posset of her making.

'Upon my word!' said Mr Rivenhall explosively.

'The draught!' protested his lordship. 'Miss Wraxton! I can feel the air blowing about my head!'

'Pray close the door, Charles!' said Miss Wraxton sharply. 'Have you no consideration? Lord Bromford is extremely unwell!'

'So I perceive!' he retorted, advancing into the room. 'Perhaps, my dear Eugenia, you would like to explain to me what the devil you mean by this?'

She replied instantly, her colour heightened: 'Thanks to your sister's inhumanity − I can call it nothing else! − in refusing to permit me to offer a seat to Lord Bromford in the chaise, he has taken a shocking chill, which I only pray may not have a lasting effect upon his constitution!'

'I never credited Cecilia with so much good sense! If she had had enough to prevent her, and you, from setting forth upon an expedition which was as needless as it was meddlesome, I should be even more grateful! You have for once in your life been thoroughly at fault, Eugenia! Let it be a lesson to you to be a little less busy in future!'

Those best acquainted with Mr Rivenhall's powers of self-expression would have considered this speech a very mild reproof. Miss Wraxton, in whose presence he had hitherto most meticulously guarded his tongue, could scarcely believe her ears. 'Charles!' she uttered, outraged.

'Did you imagine that you would make me believe ill of Sophy with your foolish and spiteful letter!' he demanded. 'You have tried to set me against her from the outset, but you over-reached yourself today, my girl! How dared you write in such terms to me! How could you have been so crassly stupid as to suppose that Sophy could ever need *your* countenance to set her right in the eyes of the world, or that I would believe one word of slander against her?'

'Sir!' said Lord Bromford, with as much dignity as could be expected of a man with both feet in a mustard-bath. 'You shall answer to me for those words!'

'Certainly! When and where you please!' replied Mr Rivenhall, with alarming promptitude.

'I beg you will not heed him, Lord Bromford!' cried Miss Wraxton, much agitated. 'He is beside himself! If a meeting were to take place between you on *my* account I could never hold up my head again! Pray be calm! I am sure your pulse is tumultuous, and how shall I ever face dear Lady Bromford?'

He clasped her restraining hand, and held it, saying in a moved voice: 'Too good, too excellent creature! With all your attainments, your scholarship, still to retain those attributes peculiar to your womanhood – ! I cannot but think of the poet's lines –'

'Take care,' interpolated Mr Rivenhall disagreeably. 'You thought of them in connection with my cousin, and it won't do to repeat yourself!'

'Sir!' said Lord Bromford, glaring at him. 'I was about to say that Miss Wraxton has shown herself in very sooth –'

'A ministering angel! So I knew! Try for another poet!'

'I must request you, sir,' said Miss Wraxton icily, 'to leave this room immediately – and to take that horrid little dog of Miss Stanton-Lacy's with you! I can only be thankful that my eyes have been opened to your true character before it was too late! You will oblige me by sending an announcement to the Gazette that our engagement is at an end!'

'It shall be done at once,' said Mr Rivenhall, bowing. 'Pray accept my profound regrets, and my earnest wishes for your future happiness, ma'am!'

'Thank you! If I cannot felicitate you upon the contract you are no doubt about to enter into, at least I can pray that you may not be too sadly disappointed in the character of the lady you mean to marry!' said Miss Wraxton, a spot of colour burning in either cheek.

'No, I don't think I shall be disappointed,' said Mr Rivenhall, with a sudden and rueful grin. 'Shocked, maddened, and stunned perhaps, but not disappointed! Come, Tina!'

Descending again to the hall, he found Sophy seated on the floor beside the ducklings' box, preventing their attempts to escape. Without looking up, she said: 'Sir Vincent has found several bottles of excellent burgundy in the cellar, and Sancia says we shall not be obliged to eat the pig's cheek after all.'

'Talgarth?' exclaimed Mr Rivenhall, bristling with hostility. 'What the devil brings him here?'

'He came with Sancia. It is the most shocking thing, Charles, and how I am to face Sir Horace I don't know! He has *married* Sancia! I cannot think what is to be done!'

'Nothing at all: your father will be delighted! I forgot to inform you, my dear cousin, that he arrived in town sometime before I left, and is even now in Berkeley Square, awaiting your return. He appeared to feel no small degree of annoyance at learning of your efforts to save the Marquesa from Talgarth.'

'Sir Horace in London?' Sophy exclaimed, her face lighting up. 'Oh, Charles, and I not there to welcome him! Why did you not tell me at once?'

'I had other things to think of. Get up!'

She allowed him to pull her to her feet, but said: 'Charles, are you freed from your engagement?'

'I am,' he replied. 'Miss Wraxton has terminated our engagement.'

'And Cecy has terminated hers to Augustus, so now I can –'

'Sophy, I don't pretend to know why she should have done so, any more than I understand why you keep a brood of ducklings in the house, but neither of these problems interests me very particularly at this present! I have something more important to say to you!'

'Of course!' said Sophy. 'Your horse! Well, indeed, Charles, I am very sorry to have displeased you so much!'

'No!' said Mr Rivenhall, grasping her shoulders, and giving her a shake. 'You know – Sophy, you *know* I could not mean – You did not run away from London because of *that*?'

'But, Charles, naturally I did! I had to have some excuse! You must perceive that I had to!'

'Devil!' said Mr Rivenhall, and caught her into so crushing an embrace that she protested, and Tina danced round them, barking excitedly. 'Quiet!' commanded Mr Rivenhall. He took Sophy's throat between his hands, pushing up her chin. 'Will you marry me, vile and abominable girl that you are?'

'Yes, but, mind, it is only to save my neck from being wrung!' Sophy replied.

The opening of the library-door made him release her, and look quickly over his shoulder. Mr Fawnhope, wearing an expression of almost complete abstraction, came into the hall with a paper in his hand. 'There is no ink in there,' he complained, 'and I have broken the point of my pencil. I have abandoned the notion of hailing you as Vestal virgin: there is something awkward in those syllables. My opening line now reads, *Goddess, whose steady hands upheld* – but I must have ink!'

With these words, and without paying the least heed to Mr Rivenhall, he walked across to the door leading to the back-premises, and disappeared through it.

Mr Rivenhall turned a face of undisguised horror upon Sophy. 'Good God!' he said. 'You might have warned me that he was here! And what the deuce did he mean by that stuff?'

'Well, I *think*,' said Sophy confidentially, 'that he now means to be in love with me, Charles. He likes the way I hold a lamp, and he says he would like to see me with an urn.'

'Well, he is not going to see you with an urn!' said Mr Rivenhall, revolted. He cast a glance round the hall, saw a pelisse lying on one chair, and snatched it up. 'Put this on! Where is your hat?'

'But, Charles, we *cannot* leave poor Sancia with all these dread-ful people in the house! It is too base!'

'Yes, we can! You don't imagine I am going to sit down to dinner with Eugenia and that damned poet, do you? Is this your muff? *Must* we take these ducklings?'

'No, it is Cecilia's, and now they will be all over the floor again! Charles, how provoking of you!'

Sir Vincent, who had come into the hall with a couple of bottles, set them down in the hearth, saying: 'How do you do, Rivenhall? Sophy, is there any ink in the house? The poet is searching for some in the larder, and driving my poor Sancia distracted.'

'Talgarth,' said Mr Rivenhall, firmly grasping Sophy by one wrist, 'I beg you will take care of these infernal ducklings, and I wish you a very pleasant evening! Sir Horace has arrived in town, and I must instantly restore his daughter to him!'

'Rivenhall,' said Sir Vincent gravely, 'I perfectly understand you,

and I applaud your presence of mind. Allow me to offer you my
felicitations! I will convey your apologies to my wife. Let me advise
you to lose no time in taking your departure! The poet will all too
shortly return!'

'Sir Vincent!' cried Sophy, dragged irresistibly to the door.
'Give my portmanteau to Miss Wraxton, and beg her to make
what use she pleases of the contents! Charles, this is crazy! Did
you come in your curricle? What if it should begin to rain again?
I shall be drenched!'

'Then you will be well-served!' retorted her unchivalrous cousin.

'Charles!' uttered Sophy, shocked. 'You cannot love me!'

Mr Rivenhall pulled the door to behind them, and in a very
rough fashion jerked her into his arms, and kissed her. 'I don't: I
dislike you excessively!' he said savagely.

Entranced by these lover-like words, Miss Stanton-Lacy returned
his embrace with fervour, and meekly allowed herself to be led off
to the stables.

Afterword

by Jennifer Kloester,
Georgette Heyer's official biographer

A perennial favourite, *The Grand Sophy* is one of Georgette Heyer's funniest novels. A brilliant cast, a clever plot, and one of her superb imbroglio endings make *Sophy* an immensely satisfying read. First published in 1950, it was an instant bestseller and has been adored by readers ever since. (It was also a *New York Times* bestseller in 2011, only this time as an ebook.) Perhaps because her hero, Charles, was "not according to the accepted pattern," Heyer wasn't entirely sure about the novel while she was writing it, but her brother, Boris, assured her it was "most amusing." She hoped it would be a book to keep her readers "guessing throughout" and assured her publisher that it was definitely "one of her lighthearted Regency romances."

By now, Heyer was completely at home in the Regency period, and she was proud that *Sophy* contained "a wealth of accurate historical detail" deftly woven into the story. As one reviewer noted in the *Chicago Sunday Tribune*: "There is more to this than superb entertainment, for Miss Heyer's art is a facile and limber one. It is no small feat to make Regency London come to life, and to make its characters speak and act as did the people of that time and place, without too much quaintness or strangeness of manner." *The Grand Sophy* sits firmly in the middle of Heyer's "Golden Age" of Regency writing, and it is no surprise that Carmen Callil and Colm Tóibín included the novel in *The 200 Best Novels in English Since 1950*, for it is a story to be read and savoured again and again.

Glossary of Regency Slang

Excerpted from

Georgette Heyer's Regency World

by Jennifer Kloester

The definitive guide for all fans of Georgette Heyer, Jane Austen, and the glittering Regency period.

Glossary of Regency Slang

CANT

During the Regency it became the fashion for upper-class men to integrate into their everyday speech the language of certain of the lower classes. Mainly as a result of the rising interest in sport and the predominance of the horse in this period, many well-born males used boxing cant, racing cant, and the vocabulary of the stable hand and the coachman as part of their daily talk. In addition, forays by bored young men into the seedier parts of town saw the inclusion of phrases culled from the extraordinary and colourful slang used in London's underworld. The famous Regency writer and journalist, Pierce Egan, was undoubtedly one of the foremost exponents of sporting cant during the period, and Georgette Heyer enjoyed and made great use of the language in his lively tale of Jerry Hawthorn and his friend Corinthian Tom in Egan's book *Life in London*.

BOXING

a bit of the home-brewed: punching or hitting done by an untrained boxer

bone box: mouth

bottom: courage, guts, stability—in pugilism one who can endure a beating

a bruiser: a boxer

claret: blood

displays to advantage: boxes well, looks good in the ring or in a fight

to draw his cork: to make him bleed—particularly by punching him in the nose

fib him: to beat or hit someone

a mill: a fight, usually a boxing match or fist-fight

a milling cove: a pugilist or boxer

milling a canister: break someone's head

plant a facer: punch someone in the face

HORSES

beautiful stepper: a good horse with a fine easy gait

blood cattle: well-bred horses, thoroughbreds

bone-setters: ill-bred horses, inferior horses

bottom: a strong horse with good temperament and endurance

cattle: horses

hunt the squirrel: the often dangerous sport of following closely behind a carriage and then passing it so closely as to brush the wheel. Considered an amusing pastime by stagecoachmen and some sporting gentlemen, the practice often resulted in the victim's carriage being overturned.

neck-or-nothing: a rider who will try anything, a bold daring sportsman or sportswoman

part company: to fall off a horse

prime bits of blood: top quality horses

a screw: a very poor quality horse

a sweetgoer: a horse with an easy action

throwing out a splint: become lame as a result of swelling in the ligament next to the splint bone

DRINKING

a ball of fire: a glass of brandy

blood and thunder: a mixture of port wine and brandy

blue ruin: gin

boosey: drunk

boozing-ken: a tavern or alehouse

bosky: drunk

a bumper: a full glass

daffy: gin

dipping too deep: drinking too much

disguised: drunk

drunk as a wheelbarrow: inebriated

eaten Hull cheese: drunk

an elbow-crooker: a drinker

a flash of lightning: strong spirits, a glass of gin

foxed: intoxicated

fuddled: drunk

half-sprung: tipsy, mellow with drink

heavy wet: porter or stout, malt liquor

in his altitudes: drunk

in your cups: drunk

jug-bitten: tipsy
making indentures: drinking
on the cut: to go on a spree; to get drunk
shoot the cat: to vomit
to cast up one's accounts: to vomit
too ripe and ready: drunk
top-heavy: drunk

FEELINGS AND BEHAVIOUR

a bear-garden jaw: rude, vulgar language; a real talking to
be on the high ropes: to stand on one's dignity; to become very
  angry; to be excited
blue as megrim: depressed, sad, unhappy
break-teeth words: difficult words, hard to pronounce
buffle-headed: confused, stupid, foolish
corky: lively, merry, playful, restless
cry rope: to cry out a warning
cut one's eye teeth: to become knowing, to understand the
  world
dicked in the nob: silly, crazy
done to a cow's thumb: exhausted
fagged to death: exhausted
fit of the blue-devils: sad, miserable, depressed, in low spirits
fly up into the boughs: fly into a passion, lose one's temper
Friday-faced: a sad or miserable countenance—derived from the
  tradition of Friday abstinence which prohibited publicans from
  dressing dinners on Fridays
high in the instep: arrogant, haughty, proud
a honey-fall: good fortune
in a dudgeon: angry, in a bad mood

in high ropes: ecstatic, elated, in high spirits

kick over the traces: to go the pace; kick up larks; behave in a headstrong or disobedient manner

knocked-up: exhausted

make a mull of it: to mismanage a situation; to fail; to make a muddle of something

mawkish: falsely sentimental, insipid or nauseating

more than seven: to be knowing or wide-awake, experienced in the ways of the world

mutton-headed: stupid

napping her bib: to cry; to get one's way by weeping

ring a peal over one: to admonish or scold someone

set up one's bristles: to irritate or annoy; to offend or make someone angry

spleen: anger

to catch cold: advice to cease or desist; a suggestion that one should cease making threats

to pull caps with someone: to argue

to swallow one's spleen: to curb one's temper

within ames-ace: nearly, or very near

LYING

bag of moonshine: nonsense, a lot of nothing

bamboozle: to deceive, hoax or make a fool of a person; to humbug or impose on someone

Banbury stories: a long-winded nonsense tale, a cock-and-bull story

bouncer: a big lie

Canterbury Tales: a long, tedious story

a clanker: a huge lie

cut a sham: to deliberately trick, cheat or deceive

cut a wheedle: to deliberately lead astray or decoy by flattery and insinuation

doing it much too brown: to go over the top in telling a lie; to lie or cheat thoroughly

faradiddles: a petty lie; originally 'taradiddle'

flummery: false compliments

fudge: nonsense

fustian or fustian nonsense: pompous rubbish

gammon: nonsense, lies; to pretend, lie or deceive

gulled: duped, fooled, tricked

a hum: a falsehood, a deceit, a made-up story

pitching the gammon: to talk plausibly; to hoax someone; to flatter without restraint; to tell grand stories; to deceive merrily

plumper: an arrant lie—possibly from the false cheeks worn in previous centuries

shamming it: to pretend or make things up

slum: to speak cant or talk nonsense

to offer Spanish coin: to flatter with fair words and compliments

toad-eat: to pay compliments or to flatter in the hope of winning a person's favour or approval

whiskers: lies

MONEY

at a stand or a standstill: run out of money and in financial difficulty

blunt: money

brass: money

brought to point non plus: backed into a financial corner with few options for recovery

cheeseparing: miserly, niggardly, mean with money

dibs not in tune: not enough money; in a parlous financial state

dished: financially ruined

drawing the bustle: spending too much money

a dun: a persistent creditor

flush in the pocket or flush with funds: having plenty of ready money

full of juice: wealthy

gingerbread: money

grease someone in the fist: to put money into a person's hand; to bribe someone or give them a monetary incentive

gullgropers: a professional moneylender, especially one who does business with gamblers

hang on someone's sleeve: to rely on someone financially

haven't a sixpence to scratch with: flat broke

high water with him: wealthy; he has lots of money

in deep: in serious debt

in dun territory: in debt

in the basket: to be in financial difficulty—from the practice of putting those who could not pay their gambling debts at a cock-fight into a basket suspended above the pit. The term also relates to those purse-pinched stagecoach travellers who could only afford to travel in the boot—originally a large basket strapped to the back of the carriage.

low ebb or at ebb-water: a lack of money

low water: lack of money

nip-cheese or nip-farthing: a miser

not a feather to fly with: no money, dead broke

note of hand: an IOU

on the rocks: financially ruined, bankrupt

outrun the constable: to overspend; to live beyond one's means

plump in the pocket: to have plenty of ready cash

pockets to let: no money, penniless

purse-pinched: short of money

raise the wind: borrow money

the ready: money, particularly money in hand

recruits: money, often money that is expected

the rhino: money

the River Tick: standing debts

rolled-up: no money and in serious financial trouble

run off one's legs: to have spent all one's money

run on tick: to buy on credit

swallow a spider: to go bankrupt

swimming in lard: very wealthy

tip over the dibs: to lend or give money to someone

to bleed: to extort money either openly or in an underhand way

to fleece: to swindle

to frank someone: to pay their way

to stand huff: to pay the bill in a tavern; to pay for everyone

under the hatches: in debt

vowels: IOUs

well-breeched: having plenty of money in your pockets—a prime target for robbery

well-inlaid: plenty of money

NOT THE THING

a bridle cull: a highwayman

a cursed rum touch: a strange person; an odd or eccentric man who is also annoying

a flat: an honest man; a fool, one who is easily tricked; a greenhorn

fulhams: loaded dice

half flash and half foolish: having a small knowledge of cant and a limited experience of the world

an ivory-turner: one who cheats in dice games

a peep-o-day boy: an unsteady young man always involved in pranks or larks

a rattle: one who talks too much

a rum 'un: a strange person, an odd or eccentric man

a sharp: a cheat who lives by his skill at manipulating the cards or dice

smoky: suspicious, curious

uphills: loaded dice; false dice made to roll to the higher or upper numbers—as opposed to downhills which fall to the lower numbers

PEOPLE

all the crack: in the mode, the height of fashion

an ape leader: a woman beyond marriageable age; an old maid—so-called because of a proverb that says their failure to increase and multiply dooms them to lead apes in hell. Also used by Shakespeare in *Much Ado About Nothing* II.i.41 and *The Taming of the Shrew* II.i.34

awake on every suit: knowing what's going on, understanding the business

a bang-up cove: a dashing man who spends money easily; a good-natured splendid fellow

bang up to the knocker: first-rate; well dressed, turned out in prime style

bang up to the mark: first-rate

bird-witted: thoughtless, brainless, easily imposed upon, gullible, inconsiderate

a bit of muslin: a girl; an attractive female—though usually one who is ready to be seduced or taken as a mistress

bracket-faced: ugly, hard-featured

bran-faced: freckled

a chawbacon: a country bumpkin; a stupid man

a chit: a young girl

a cicisbeo: a married woman's lover or escort

clunch: a clownish person, awkward, foolish

complete to a shade: superbly dressed, dressed in the height of fashion

a diamond of the first water: a remarkably beautiful woman

a dowdy: a plain, ill-dressed female

a downy one: aware, a knowing intelligent person

a doxy: a whore

a green girl: a naive, inexperienced young woman

a hoyden: an active, tomboyish romp of a girl

a hussy: a forward, badly behaved female

a jade: a disreputable woman

a jilt: a woman who cries off from an engagement not long before the wedding

a Johnny raw: a novice, an inexperienced or untried youth

a loose fish: an unreliable person; a person of dissipated habits; a lecher or a drunk

a mort: a woman or wench; but could sometimes mean a harlot

an out and outer: one who is first-rate; a perfect person; excellent in every way

a prime article: a handsome woman, a beautiful female

a romp: a forward girl

a swell mort: an upper-class woman

a tabby: an old maid

a vixen: a shrewish woman

a vulgar mushroom: a pushing, pretentious member of the new rich—the reference being to mushrooms as a kind of fungus which comes up suddenly in the night

a wet goose: a simple or stupid person

Sex and Society

an abbess: a procuress of prostitutes, a female keeper of a brothel

barque of frailty: a woman of easy virtue

base-born child: an illegitimate child, a bastard

bird of paradise: a showy prostitute

by-blow: an illegitimate child, a bastard

carte-blanche: monetary support and protection offered to a man's mistress in place of marriage

chère-amie: a mistress—literally 'darling beloved'

crim. con.: short for criminal conversations—a euphemism for adultery

a game-pullet: a young prostitute or a girl likely to become a whore

Haymarket ware: a prostitute

an impure: a woman of easy virtue

incognitas: a masked or disguised prostitute

lady-bird: a lewd or light woman, a prostitute

light o' love: a mistress

lightskirt: a prostitute

loose in the haft: a man of easy virtue and few morals

on-dit: gossip—literally 'one says'

one of the muslin company: a prostitute; a female ready to be set up as a mistress

Paphian: a woman of easy virtue; relating to sexual love

a petticoat-pensioner: one who lives off a woman's ill-gotten earnings, a whoremonger

a rake: a man of great sexual appetite and few morals

side-slips: illegitimate children, bastards

a slip on the shoulder: to seduce a woman, seduction

trollop: a sluttish woman

MARRIAGE

become a tenant for life: get married off, get married

cry off: to change one's mind and call off the wedding

an eligible parti: a suitable marriage partner

leg-shackled: married

make an offer: propose marriage

on the shelf: unmarried and beyond the usual age of marrying

puff it off: announce one's engagement in the papers

riveted: married

set your cap at a man: to try to win a man's favour and a proposal of marriage

smelling of April and May: madly in love

Reading Group Guide

1. What did you think when Sophy first arrived at her aunt's house? Describe how you pictured her before she arrived. How accurate are you at guessing what people will be like before you meet them? Are you more often confirmed in your first impressions, or are you more often surprised?

2. Charles disapproves of Sophy from the moment she arrives. Do you agree with Charles's assessment of her? What would you have done in Charles's place?

3. What would have happened if Sophy's interference had back-fired? Describe how the Ombersley family might have turned out if Sophy had never interfered. Do you think they're better off for her manipulations?

4. Georgette Heyer is known for her historical research. What is your favorite time period to read about? Is there any historical time period you wish you could visit or live in? What attracts you to that time period? What are your favorite things about living in today's world?

5. What did you think of the gentlemen in the story? Did you find Charles a sympathetic hero or difficult to warm up to? Are there any qualities in Charles that you would like to see more of in people today?

6. Were there any scenes in the book that made you laugh out loud? Were there any that made you cringe? Describe your reactions.

7. What did you think of the animals and the way people interact with them in the book? Do you have or have you ever had horses, dogs, monkeys, ducklings, parrots, or any other exotic pets? What pets do you have now?

8. Describe the family dynamics of the Ombersleys. Do you have colorful characters in your family? What is the best thing about your own family dynamics?

9. Sophy goes on her own to a bad neighborhood to confront the villainous Goldhanger. Do you think this was courageous or foolish? Would you do the same, or would you ask someone to go with you for backup? Have you (alone or with someone else) ever vanquished a bully or enemy by standing up to them? Describe your experience.

10. Have you read any other books by Georgette Heyer? Which are your favorites? Which are your least favorite and why?

About the Author

Georgette Heyer is an international bestseller with over twenty million copies sold worldwide. A natural-born storyteller, she composed her first novel, *The Black Moth*, at the age of seventeen to amuse her brother while he was ill. She got her first publishing contract when she was eighteen. *The Black Moth* was published when she was nineteen and became an instant success.

Heyer was very close to her father, who supported her writing and encouraged her to pursue publication. His sudden death in 1925 when she was twenty-two was devastating. She missed him terribly—but she kept writing for the rest of her life.

She wrote country-house mysteries, historical novels, and the romances for which she became most famous. In her romances, Heyer skewers human nature with shrewd insight, razor-sharp wit, and a genius for sheer delightful romantic comedy. She brings to life a kaleidoscope of unforgettable characters: quirky, resourceful heroines, irresistible heroes, chilling foes, enchanting urchins, overbearing aunts, long-suffering husbands, rapscallion friends, and more.

Georgette Heyer was a very private woman and refused all media attempts to discuss her works or personal life. She was married to George Ronald Rougier, an engineer and later a barrister, with whom she had one son, Richard. Despite her reluctance to be a public figure during her lifetime, the brilliant Georgette Heyer is beloved by millions of readers and has inspired generations of authors. Her work lives on to inspire millions more.

Frederica

THE PRACTICAL FREDERICA HAS MET HER MATCH

Despite her youth, Frederica has been head of her family for years. Between introducing her beautiful sister to society and extricating her enterprising brothers from one scrape after another, she's far too busy to think about herself.

Frederica has brought her brood to London to elicit the patronage of their cousin, the Marquis of Alverstoke, but he is surprisingly aloof—until an accident throws the marquis and Frederica together and allows for the blossoming of the perfect partnership. And it might finally be Frederica's turn for love.

"Overflowing with fun and family."

—Library Journal

For more Georgette Heyer, visit:
sourcebooks.com

Arabella

One small lie will reveal a gem of a truth

Arabella Tallant, the daughter of a modest country clergyman, is on her way to London to be launched into the Season by her godmother. Her carriage breaks down outside the hunting lodge of the wealthy Mr. Robert Beaumaris. Overhearing her host's suspicions that she staged the breakdown in order to meet him, Arabella pretends to be an heiress, a pretense that deeply amuses the jaded Beau.

Amazing how complicated life can get after one little lie goes viral…

"Wickedly entertaining; a superb comedy of manners!"
—Love Romance Passion

Why Shoot a Butler?

A MOST PLOT-TWISTING MURDER STRIKES THE IDYLLIC COUNTRYSIDE

Barrister Frank Amberley is driving along a lonely road when he stops to help a young woman in distress—and discovers a corpse. Evidence soon makes it hard to believe the innocence of the witness, Shirley Brown, as much as Amberley tries…

Every clue complicates the puzzle, and it's up to amateur but brilliant sleuth Amberley to find the killer. But as the facts of the enigmatic murder unfold, Amberley's not so sure he wants to learn the truth…

"Miss Heyer has the delightful talent of blending humor with mystery."

—Boston Evening Transcript

For more Georgette Heyer, visit:
sourcebooks.com

The Unfinished Clue

A WEEKEND SERVED WITH A SIDE OF MYSTERY

It should have been a lovely English country-house weekend. But the unfortunate guest list is enough to exasperate a saint, and the host, Sir Arthur Billington-Smith, is an abusive wretch hated by everyone. When Sir Arthur is found stabbed to death, no one is particularly grieved—and no one has an alibi.

All of the unhappy guests come under the scrutiny of Scotland Yard. Young and talented Inspector Harding has solved tough cases before…but this time, he discovers much more than he's bargained for.

"[A] worthwhile and classy mystery read."
—Burton Review

Behold, Here's Poison

A RESOURCEFUL DETECTIVE MEETS HIS MATCH IN ONE FAMILY'S DASTARDLY SCANDAL...

It's no ordinary morning at the Poplars. The master of the estate is found dead in his bed, and it turns out that his high blood pressure was not the cause of death.

It was poison.

Every member of the quarrelsome Matthews family has a motive, and none can prove otherwise. It'll take the witty Superintendent Hannasyde to catch the murderer in time to save the next intended victim.

"Heyer is an author to read—this means you!"

—New York Herald Tribune

For more Georgette Heyer, visit:
sourcebooks.com